Q

2017

For my family

G. P. PUTNAM'S SONS
an imprint of Penguin Random House LLC
375 Hudson Street
New York, NY 10014

Copyright © 2017 by Julie Shepard.
Penguin supports copyright. Copyright fuels creativity, encourages diverse voices,
promotes free speech, and creates a vibrant culture. Thank you for buying an authorized edition
of this book and for complying with copyright laws by not reproducing, scanning,
or distributing any part of it in any form without permission.
You are supporting writers and allowing Penguin to continue to publish books for every reader.

G. P. Putnam's Sons is a registered trademark of Penguin Random House LLC.

Emoji copyright © Apple, Inc.

Library of Congress Cataloging-in-Publication Data is available upon request.
Printed in the United States of America.
ISBN 9780399548642
1 3 5 7 9 10 8 6 4 2

Design by Jaclyn Reyes.
Text set in Electra LT Std.

This is a work of fiction. Names, characters, places, and incidents either are the product
of the author's imagination or are used fictitiously, and any resemblance to actual persons,
living or dead, businesses, companies, events, or locales is entirely coincidental.

ROSIE GIRL

Julie Shepard

G. P. PUTNAM'S SONS

1

MY BEST FRIEND'S name is Mary, but don't be fooled. She's no virgin.

As a matter of fact, she's with Todd Ryser right now in the stairwell that separates the second and third floors of Del Vista High.

I'm waiting for her in the girls' bathroom down the hall. Both places smell like pee, but at least I have a mirror where I can check to make sure my hair is behaving. Mary's told me about these sessions before, and because she likes me to stay close (*Jesus, Rosie, it's the least you can do!*), I've often been tempted to listen in. Sounds weird, I know. I've been insanely curious, and since I'm superbored, I decide to do it.

The hall's empty. After four o'clock, the school dries up like a desert. No flow of students, only the stray cactus who remains at her desk to grade papers. Plus the head janitor who roams around with keys jangling in his pocket, but I haven't heard any jangling up here on the third floor, so I figure I'm safe.

Once I reach the stairwell, I put my ear to the door. Faint movements. Rustling.

Then, Todd's voice. "You're so hot."

Mary doesn't answer him. She knows better than to read anything into words mumbled during stuff like this. We both do. I did that once with Ray, my first real boyfriend (and it wasn't even during sex, just fooling around with fingers and tongues), then spent months searching for the part of my brain I lost while riding a one-way train called "First Love." In case you didn't know, it ends up in an overpopulated city called "Dumped & Stupid."

When I press my ear harder, I hear heavy, rapid breathing. His. It's almost over. At least that's how Mary says it goes. I imagine his hands on her sunburned shoulders. They're bare today, exposed by my heather-beige tank top Mary insists looks better on her than it does on me.

Does it feel good? I've asked, because best friends have no boundaries when it comes to sex or borrowing each other's clothes.

It doesn't feel like anything, she's said, *other than sweaty. It's more about the sounds—the grunting the guy makes, the short, quick gasps when he's about to come.*

I prefer to use the word *climax,* even though Mary thinks it sounds silly. Just because we're seventeen doesn't mean we have to be so crude.

Things have gone dead quiet. I almost turn away when I hear Todd again. "Ivan was right," he says. "You are sweet."

I feel sick because it doesn't sound like a compliment from this side of the door. But I'm sure Mary only adjusts her clothes and grins up at him with lips he never kissed. For some reason, she says, they never kiss. And I know it must be true. Whenever she's done, the first thing I notice is her raspberry gloss, shiny and untouched.

When I hear Mary say, "Thanks," I can't help myself. I place my bag, packed with textbooks, on the floor and stand on it so I can peek through the small glass pane. There they are, on the concrete landing. I'm glad I looked, because she wasn't thanking him for being a jerk—she was thanking him for the bills in her hand.

I step off my bag, and not ten seconds later the doorknob turns. I almost trip over my own feet to hide behind the nearest corner. Todd comes out first. His black hair is plastered at odd angles around a face shimmering with sweat. His shorts are wrinkled and both ends of a canvas belt hang free below his shirt. He's cute, and I hate myself for thinking it. I hate myself even more for this odd sensation I know is jealousy. Out comes Mary. Her straight hair falls in soft brown sheets around her shoulders. She adjusts a strap of my tank top, which also looks wrinkled, and two of three buttons remain unfastened.

They part without speaking. He doesn't even nod or wave goodbye. There are three possible directions they can take, and passing me would be one of those ways. I pray Todd picks one of the other two, and he does. Mary chooses my way.

When she reaches me, she barely slows down to say, "Let's go."

I search her face for signs of distress as we move at a hurried clip down the hall.

"Are you okay?" I ask, trying to keep up. Her legs are a mile longer than mine and stretch out like pale white sticks in front of her.

"Don't break the rules," she says, then purses those glossy lips. Rule number one: No questions after. I can tell by her mood not to bring up the fact that she broke rule number five by not getting paid first. So I force a smile and stay quiet as we hustle down another set of stairs. Unlike the stairway she and Todd were in, this set is at the end of the building and has a first-floor exit to outside. She pushes her way through the metal door.

The fresh air greets us, but so does the hot sun. Mary slips a rubber band off her wrist and pulls her hair into a ponytail. It falls into a silky chocolate waterfall. I reach out and fasten one of the buttons on her tank top, then linger on the next one. I always do this, trying to delay our separation by adjusting a piece of her clothing or making mindless conversation. It just feels weird leaving each other, but Mary doesn't share those feelings.

"Stop," she says. "I can do my own buttons. See you later, okay?" Then she takes off down the sidewalk toward the back of the school, her sneakers slapping against the concrete. Mary crosses the spongy orange track and cuts through the football field. I watch her break into a run, book bag swinging behind her. If you didn't know, you'd simply think she was a girl racing home from school. But I do know, so I'm thinking something else. That what she just did was horrible. And how lucky I am that she did it for me.

· · ·

Once Mary's out of sight, I pick up the pace in the other direction so I don't miss the 5:10 bus and have to wait another fifteen minutes. By the end of September, I had given up asking my mom to borrow the Saab (or, as I like to call it, the Slaab-mobile) since at the last minute she'd always renege, and I'd end up scrambling for a ride. The bus system is pretty reliable and gives me an excuse to hit her up for some extra cash.

I make it to the bus stop in front of Del Vista as the groaning metal beast pulls up, clipping the curb. The doors open with a whoosh, and a blast of cold air saves me from the May heat. Even after all these months, Archie still doesn't say hi, but I nod and smile anyway, hoping one day to crack him.

I search for an empty seat. It's packed, but I spot one next to an old lady clutching a bag in her lap. I've seen her before, always lodged in the back. She looks up at me when I approach, not realizing it's her lucky day. Unlike some of the criminals that frequent the Miami-Dade transit system, I'm one of the nonthreatening seat buddies who won't attempt to steal what she's trying so hard to keep safe.

I settle in next to her, pull the sketchbook out of my bag. The bus ride home from school is a great place to get down the designs I've been creating in my head all day. Teachers think I'm paying attention, but what I'm really doing is studying their outfits, the colors they've chosen, the styles they believe flatter their figures.

The old lady makes an exaggerated snorting sound, breaking my concentration on a jumpsuit. She crinkles her nose as if she's smelled something foul, then dramatically turns her face to look out the window, wet with condensation. I ignore her and sweep both hands over the top of my head, hoping to tame my mane. South Florida weather is no friend of mine.

The year-round humidity is constantly turning my waves into a frizzy mess that even a fashionable hat has trouble hiding, and with summer fast approaching, the worst is yet to come.

At least my face, by most people's standards, registers as pretty. Oval-shaped with skin that rarely gets zits. Eyes the color of dark blue marbles. Lips naturally the color of Mary's favorite gloss, Rockin' Raspberry. And a cleft chin that used to make me self-conscious until someone once said it gave me a unique "model" look. I appreciated the compliment but knew I could never be one. I'm not tall enough at barely five foot three. Plus, I'm nowhere near thin enough and not about to give up root beer, salt-and-vinegar potato chips, or anything with a cherry filling.

The old lady scoots over, jamming herself next to the wall of the bus so the fabric of her faded, flowery dress doesn't touch me. Have I somehow offended her? The energy between us is tense and threatens to darken my mood.

Stop one: Miami Medical Center. Two people get off, six people get on. I don't know where they're going to sit. Indeed, four people have to remain standing.

Normally, I get a semi-pleasant riding companion, but the old lady doesn't seem too friendly. She's pulled out a ball of yarn and moves her needle at a brisk pace. I pass the time by working on the jumpsuit and imagining creative ways to annoy her, none of which I have the courage to carry out. Some people are big talkers. I'm a big thinker.

Stop two: Hibiscus Mall. No one gets off, three more people

get on, faces instantly sagging at their pole-clutching fate. I hang my head, knowing thick bangs will fall and cover my eyes. I should probably offer my seat to the sixty-something nurse who took blood and gave sponge baths all day, but I'm tired, too. Schools are like mortuaries—they drain the life out of you.

Stop three: I gather my things, because stop three is mine.

"You should button that up," the old lady says, quick and sharp as if she wanted to make sure to tell me before I left.

"Excuse me?" Instantly, I glance down at my denim shirt she's spying. It's one of my favorites, darted in the back so it makes me look extra-slim. There are an appropriate number of buttons undone—two—and nothing is showing. No cleavage, no bra. I don't know what her problem is.

"Girls your age get into all sorts of trouble these days. And then you go blaming everyone else."

I can't believe this lady. Anger wells up inside me and I say loud enough for everyone around us to hear, "My buttons are none of your business. That crappy knitting in your lap—that's your business."

That ought to shut her up. And it does. She purses her wrinkled mouth, accentuating the crevasses filled with traces of her orange lipstick.

I follow a trail of people off the bus, totally peeved from our exchange. I don't like to get like that, but if somebody pushes me hard enough, I push back.

The humid air instantly clings to me like a damp sweater I can't shed. I gulp in a breath of thick afternoon air and trailing bus fumes. I'm dropped three blocks from home, on a corner with a gas station that carries the most delicious root beer with a tree etched right into the glass, its roots wrapped around the bottle. I resist the urge to push through the double doors and clomp my feet with renewed purpose the other way. I'd love a soda, but satisfying my thirst now would only hurt me in the long run. Every dime counts.

2

OUR HOUSE is painted a hideous green, the color of dying moss. It makes me shudder every time I walk up, knowing it's mine, and that in order to get to the safe haven of my bedroom, I must walk through an equally hideous front door that was painted black by the previous owner. For the past year, my mother's boyfriend, Judd, has been promising to paint it, but his blatant aversion to (and, let's face it, inability for) manual labor has won out, and the door beckons me like death from its rusty hinges.

No one's home. The air is thick with stale cigarette smoke and the lemony air freshener my mom thinks masks it. She refuses to quit, even though the only thing louder than her hacking is the doctor's warning that she'll die if she doesn't. I pick up a pack Mom's left on the bench of Dad's old piano, determined to throw it away. It's my small, but necessary, contribution to keeping her alive. But when I reach my bedroom, I end up tossing it on the floor with the rest of my things, then heading to the bathroom because I'm in the mood for a cool bath.

As hot as it is outside, I don't last long in the cold water and swiftly adjust the tap. The hot water smooths the edge, the one that old lady carved into me. After, I wrap up in a robe and lock myself in my bedroom. I open the middle drawer of the nightstand. My fingers crawl over a stack of sketchbooks until they reach their intended target. A fuzzy orange sock tucked inside a scarf inside a bandana I haven't worn since I was twelve, in an awful school production of *Hair*. I settle into bed, cozy in that worn-out-after-school way. Plus, the lavender beads I threw in the tub have actually done what the bottle promised and calmed me down.

I pull out the contents of the sock. The Fund. I separate the bills into denominations, then add my half of the sixty bucks Mary earned this afternoon. Three hundred and ten dollars. Finally, I have enough, so I make the call. He answers on the third ring.

"John Brooks," he says, cold and rushed like a busy professional.

I'm so nervous, I wish I had one of those old-fashioned telephone cords to twirl around my finger. "Hi, this is Rosie Velvitt. We, um, spoke a few months ago."

"I remember," he says, with enough hesitancy to make it seem like he wishes he hadn't picked up. Then, "How are you?"

"I'm good. I finally have—I mean, I have the money," I stammer. "I've saved up. Can we meet?"

Silence. Is he trying to find a way to blow me off? I only hope he senses my desperation through the phone and takes pity on me. "Well, sure," he says slowly, as if he's still thinking about it. "Next week, my schedule opens up—"

"No!" I blurt out. "No, I can't wait. I've already waited so long."

"Okay, when did you have in mind?"

"Tonight?"

"I really can't. Already have dinner plans—"

"Please—" I start, and instead of any more stammering, I firmly say, "I've held up my end of the bargain. Please meet me after your dinner."

Heavy sigh. He knows I'm right. "Lou's Deli," he says. "Around ten?"

"Thanks. I'll be there."

Excitement mixes with relief and I doze off in my robe, the sock clutched in my hand.

. . .

I wake up to Mary sitting on my bed with her back propped up by a pillow against the wall. "Jeez!" I cry. "You scared the crap out of me!" It's dark out, so she's switched on my desk lamp and is using the light to file her nails. "How did you get in here?"

"How the hell do you think if Judd the Dud's home?" She motions to the window above my desk. The screen has been pushed out and is resting against the wall. "Last month, you finally popped out those pins so I could get in if a car's out front. Don't you remember?"

Not really. My memory hasn't been so good lately. I've got plans brewing and they're using up most of my brain's free space. I force a chuckle at the lapse.

Mary returns to her nails, sawing back and forth, back and forth. "You worry me sometimes, Rosie girl. You really do." She looks at me like my mom does when I've disappointed her, which, thankfully, isn't often. Mom's not involved enough in my life to know when she should be disappointed in the first place. As long as I go to school and stay out of jail, she thinks she's doing a pretty good job of parenting.

I take a deep stretch, then roll over to face Mary. She looks tired, but it could just be the way her eyes are small and focused on a task in dim light. Or it could be my guilt. "You okay?"

"Don't."

"I'm not breaking any rules. It's been a few hours." I yawn, then wait that right amount of time before changing subjects. "Then tell me."

"About what?"

"What it's like."

"I've already told you."

I scoot across the bed to get closer to her. "Not really," I say. Mary has told me some stuff, but now I want more. Seeing her with Todd Ryser today intrigued me. I want to know how it felt to be with him, but I couldn't come right out and ask her that. He was a means to an end, and Mary would get upset if she suspected more behind my request. I playfully pat her bare knee. "Tell me more. We're in this together. I want to know."

"No, you don't."

"I do. Tell me something. Anything."

She sets down the nail file and swings her long, slim legs over mine.

"His breath smelled like fish sticks from the cafeteria. Happy?"

"Ecstatic. What else?"

Mary props herself up on one arm and all of her hair falls behind her shoulders. She's still wearing my tank top, but she's swapped the miniskirt for a pair of denim shorts. The outfit doesn't look nearly as fashionable as what she had on earlier.

"He threw his condom on the floor and it landed next to a dead roach in the corner."

"Gross."

"Times ten."

"More."

She pauses a long time, then says, "I always choose something to focus on. Today it was the EXIT sign. It was cracked, right through the X and the I. The bulb was burned out, too. The silver frame was full of rust. I wondered who installed it, when it was installed. It looked old and neglected. Who's going to fix it? The guy that put it in? Is there a warranty on those things? Would the school get sued if there was an emergency and some poor kid panicked in that stairwell and couldn't find his way out? Also, I realized that Exit spelled backward is Tixe, which could be a cool name for a ticket company."

Mary has never rattled on like this and it makes me shaky. "Hey, if you want to stop . . ."

"Come on, Rosie. This isn't a choice."

"Of course it is."

"Not with our records it isn't. Jeez. Take a few cans of spray paint and we're goddamned criminals."

She's right about that. Mary's dad let us do stock in his hardware store until we blew it. What Mary doesn't understand is that taking the stuff isn't necessarily what made us criminals—it's her dad's store, after all—it's what we did with that stuff. Painted some bad graffiti on the park wall—our names scrawled so poorly you couldn't even make them out (spray paint is harder to use than you think)—until a cop arrived and put an end to the fun. We ended up with a misdemeanor and a bunch of community service hours. Of course, this just gave Mom a reason to hate Mary, for getting me dangerously close to landing in said jail. At least I made enough money that summer to buy a laptop and a powder-blue case for it.

"So," Mary continues. "The Gap isn't going to hire us. We can forget about something like babysitting because parents want references. Remember when I tried during winter break? Got the third degree. Adults think it's so easy for young people to get a job. It's not. It's harder."

"Maybe we should go back to your dad and beg."

Mary recoils. "Bite your tongue. I'm not going to beg that man for anything. Screw him."

My face drops in frustration.

"Look. I'm not ragging on you. We've both made mistakes." She rubs my arm under the terry-cloth sleeve. "So I've got this. I don't mind. I already gave away my virginity to some douchebag, anyway. May as well charge for the privilege now and help my best friend at the same time. Plus, you're not a total charity case since I keep half."

"Speaking of cases . . . Oh my God." I throw off the covers and scour the sheets.

"You looking for this?" Mary pulls the sock from behind her back and dangles it in front of me.

"Holy crap." I grab it, then clutch the furry ball to my chest for dramatic effect. "I thought my mom had—"

"She's not home. Only the Dud. I've got your back, Rosie girl." She winks a chocolate-brown eye. "In more ways than one."

I swat her playfully on the arm. "Stop." Then I collapse onto the bed, squeezing the sock and all its hope. "You're making this whole thing possible."

"Yeah, I'm a real hero."

"No, not a hero," I say. "You're a . . ." I search her face for the answer. "Savior."

"Don't get all sappy on me. Desperate times, Rosie, and all that shit." Mary adjusts her legs and slides one between mine. "Now what were you going to say before you thought Mommy Dearest stole your stash?"

"Oh, yeah!" A surge of excitement races through me. "The guy who agreed to consider my case—"

"You mean the guy you spoke to on the phone a couple months ago. The one who was too busy for you."

"That was okay," I say, dismissing her attitude with a flick of my wrist. "I didn't have his three-hundred-dollar retainer fee back then, anyway. But today with Todd put us past the mark." I shake the sock at her. "Three hundred and ten. So we're meeting tonight."

"And when did you set up this little rendezvous?"

"Called him when I got home."

Mary squints at me. "Three hundred and ten, huh? That means I've got three hundred and ten, too, which also means we've got over six hundred bucks. Forget about this guy. Forget about everything. Let's blow it all on a trip to the mountains," Mary says wistfully, even though what she truly wants isn't a trip, but a move. She's always dreamed of leaving Miami and heading out west, working in one of those national parks where she can wear boots and a ranger hat.

"One day," I say, pretending to agree with her. But I'll never go anywhere. Remember, I'm the big thinker. Mary's the doer.

While in many ways we're like oil and water, a marinade still needs both to work. That's us. We work, despite our differences. We met in ninth grade, two days after my father had a heart attack at the kitchen table while I was enjoying a bowl of cinnamon-raisin oatmeal. When he clutched his chest, I thought he was joking, like he always did about Mom's terrible cooking. The eggs did look especially runny that morning. His eyes grew wide, his mouth fell open, and then he slumped over his plate, knocking yellow slime to the floor.

Stop it, Dad, I said, gently poking him in the arm with my spoon caked with oatmeal.

You're scaring her, Clint, and you've made a mess of my kitchen, Mom said. *You and your practical jokes. If you don't pick up your head, I'm spilling this hot coffee down the back of your shirt.* And she would, too. She could be mean like that when you didn't listen to her.

We buried him two days later, which was when I met Mary. Not at the funeral. After. We were at a family friend's house. Everyone had gone back there when the service was over. I knew the hostess—Rita Hale. She would go shopping with my mom on the weekends or pick her up for dinner sometimes. She had an older son who still lived with her at home. He was one of those hot college guys that made me blush.

His name was Eddy, and as we circled the dessert table in his dining room, he said he liked my dress. I'm embarrassed to admit it, but even on the day of my father's funeral, I had carefully chosen my outfit. It was sleeveless, charcoal gray, and made my body look curvier than it actually was with an empire waist and darts aimed at my boobs. Before the service, I had admired myself in the mirror, then felt like the worst daughter in the world for doing it.

So there was Eddy, touching my arm when I reached for the pie cutter, telling me I had really grown up. It had been a couple years since he'd seen me.

"Hey, want to get some air?" He guided my empty plate back to the table. I held on to the cutter, since I had been looking forward to a piece of cherry cobbler. "Let's go outside."

I did want to get some air. Although it was a chilly October day, the Hale house was stifling and hot. Too many people, too much food, too much noise. The cherry cobbler could wait. Besides, Eddy Hale said I looked grown-up, which is music to every fourteen-year-old girl's ears, even on the day of her father's funeral.

But we didn't make it outside. Halfway to the front door, he took my hand and said, "Maybe it's too cold out. Let's just hang in my room." I went without thinking twice. He showed me his baseball awards from Florida International University and a bong that looked like a kaleidoscope. He rattled on about his fraternity, graduating, maybe opening a club. I allowed myself to get lost in these stories, aware that for the first time in three days my cheeks were dry. I didn't notice when he went to show me his baseball jersey hanging on the back of his door that he'd closed it.

"Come here," Eddy said, sitting on his bed, patting the space next to him.

I did that, too.

"Sorry about your dad." He had superdark eyes and a wide, bumpy nose that had probably seen a few fights. His lips were nice, but his teeth had that fang thing going on.

"Thanks," I said, beginning to sense this might be that awkward moment right before a guy kisses you. But that wasn't possible. Eddy was so much older than me and we had just been at my father's funeral. There was no way . . .

And then, yes way. He leaned in and kissed me, and I kissed him back, thinking, *Oh my God, I'm kissing a college guy!* And then thinking, *Oh my God, college guys move fast,* because his hand was already grabbing at my chest.

I scooted away. "No."

But Eddy didn't want to hear that. He pushed me down, pulled up my charcoal dress, grabbed my panties, tugged at them. At the same time, he was working on his own clothes, unzipping his pants.

"Stop!" I said, which made him instantly cover my mouth.

"Scream, and I'll hurt you."

So I didn't scream, even though I was terrified and wanted to unleash a storm of sounds trapped in my throat. But I still fought with my hands, bit with my mouth. The pressure, the pain, the confusion at just having heard the story about how he made a home run that won the championship and now he's forcing himself inside me and my dad is probably still warm in that coffin and I want a piece of the cherry cobbler and I have to get away, I have to go. I'm going.

That's when I realized Eddy had closed his bedroom door but didn't lock it. A girl had opened it and cried, "What the fuck are you doing?"

The rest was a blur. I only remember sounds—his zipper, the stomp of feet leaving the room, the click of a closed door. Then her touch—fixing my dress, removing the hair stuck to my tearstained face, the pads of her fingers on my shoulder. And then her voice—"I'm Mary. Are you okay?"

• • •

I roll over, untangle my legs from hers.

"You know, you could always pawn that piece-of-shit ring that piece of shit gave you," Mary says, and I use that as an opportunity to leave her and disappear into the closet. I need to get dressed and be out of here by nine thirty.

"No," I say from behind the closed door. I choose a pair of skinny jeans and an old button-down shirt of Ray's I never returned, then grab a woven belt that matches my silver sandals.

"He screwed you over, Rosie. Dumped you the minute he got a taste of those Tallahassee hoses."

I can't help but chuckle as I button up his shirt. I slide open the door. "Not *hoses*, Mary. *Ho's*, short for *whores*. And they're called *Tally Ho's*."

"Oh," she says, slightly embarrassed, then goes at it again while I adjust my belt. "Why would you even want to keep that ring?"

"No one's ever bought me anything before." He gave it to me the day after Valentine's Day. We had met in December, during winter break of my junior year. It was one of those crisp, clear South Florida days, and Mary and I and three other girls from our Biology class were at the beach. Of course, you can't get in the water, it's way too cold in December, but we still wore bathing suits and lay on towels to get a tan. That's when I got hit in the head by someone's Frisbee. It was Ray Mangione's, one of the hottest seniors at our school, and his body blocked the sun as he asked for it back.

So why the day *after* Valentine's Day? I'd been heartbroken and confused that he hadn't even given me a single flower on the day of, but it was a good thing I didn't show my disappointment. He said it was a test. Was I one of those girls who expected things on holidays? He hated girls like that, he told me, and since I passed the test, he gave me the ring.

"Besides," I say, thinking of the sparkly blue sapphire, the delicate silver band, "I like it."

"But you don't wear it."

"So?"

"So you may as well sell it and make a few bucks."

"I'm not selling it."

"It's been sitting in your jewelry box for what? Like nine months? You should pawn it or something unless . . . unless you're hoping that piece of shit will come crawling back, and when he does, you want him to be able to put it back on your finger."

"Stop calling him that." This is the trouble with best friends—they know the score, even when you haven't admitted to playing the game. "I'm not selling the ring, but it has nothing to do with Ray. He's moved on, and so have I."

We both know I'm full of it, but Mary backs off. "So where's this big meeting taking place?"

"Lou's Deli."

"Nothing like pickles and private eyes on a warm summer night."

"Think I can get out of here before she comes home?"

"Nope." Mary suddenly cocks her head. She has an uncanny ability to detect the sound of Mom's rickety Saab from down the block. "T minus three minutes," she says, then crawls out the bedroom window. Mary has never liked my mom.

3

I WAIT A BIT before facing them. I've learned it's better to let Mom settle in with a drink and a smoke before pouring out a lie I need her to swallow.

I find her and Judd snuggling on the couch. Because the *Real Housewives Who Are No Longer Married* is on television, she barely acknowledges me hovering in the hallway.

"Oh, hey, Rosie." Her greeting is about as warm as an ice cube. She offers a dismissive wave, two fingers clutching a lit cigarette. Judd's nursing a beer, but looks up and winks at me in that creepy way he does that makes me lock my door at night. I've put a robe over my clothes and pull it tight across my chest. He's twenty-nine, my mom forty-three. While I try not to wonder what he sees in her—it will only lead to disturbing images of them having sex in weird positions—I can see why he finds her attractive: silky platinum hair she's never bleached or straightened, eyes the color of lime Jell-O, and a petite figure resistant to cellulite and weight gain. We're not exactly twins.

Mom found Judd Lister not long after Dad died. He was browsing through an aisle of the bookstore that has all the

A *Dummy's Guide to* . . . books, which should have been her first clue. He's an assistant shift manager at Itchin' for Chicken and comes home with a bucket of cold fried chicken for dinner even if it's eleven o'clock at night and I've already gone to bed without a decent meal.

Times like those I miss my father most. He was a grilling master and loved to wear an apron that stretched around his growing belly, clicking his tongs in the summer air. He'd shout, *Get it while it's hot!* and I would drop whatever I was doing to join him outside with an empty plate and a watering mouth. Mom would show up eventually and eat whatever was left, stubbing out a cigarette on the grass beneath her shoe.

"Hitting the sack," I say.

"So early?" No need to check a clock or anything, since Mom knows what time it is based on the show she's watching.

"I'm tired." I try to force a yawn, but it's hopeless. It is only nine fifteen. Plus, that nap recharged me.

"Well, you don't need any extra beauty sleep," Judd says. "That's for sure." He dips his head and winks again. Does my mom not see this? Completely oblivious.

She swings her head to the side to get a better look at me. "You feeling okay?" And I panic because if she looks over the arm of the couch she'll be able to see the jeans and silver sandals I stupidly left on poking out from under my robe. I force a cough and rub my nose for good measure.

"Yeah, just tired. Long day. Two tests and a mile run in gym." All lies.

"You sure?" She's not above a little motherly probing in front of her boyfriend. Makes her seem downright parental. "Because if you are sick, don't contaminate the rest of the house. Stay in your room." And there goes that.

"She's fine, Lucy. Leave the girl alone." Judd squeezes her shoulder, gives me a third wink. He's on my side, he wants me know, which is such a crock and makes me want to puke.

I smile, shift my weight, attempt that yawn again.

"All right," she says, satisfied. "See you in the morning."

Judd starts tickling her and she almost spills her wine and they both instantly forget I'm still standing there. Normally, I'd be annoyed, but tonight their distraction is an advantage. Back to my room I go, then shut and lock the door behind me. I instantly shed my robe. Since the screen is already out, I am through the window in two minutes flat.

. . .

I've learned the bus schedule pretty well and the time it takes me to reach the stop nearest my house. But it doesn't do me much good tonight when the nine thirty bus arrives ten minutes late. I've already listened to three songs on my phone.

I board to find myself one of three passengers. Slow night. I slide into a gray plastic seat and watch as my neighborhood gives way to an area lined with fading storefronts and half-empty office buildings. We're passing Del Vista High when my cell phone vibrates with a text from a number I don't recognize.

wanna meet at sky square?

whos this?

Joe. yes or no?

I don't know any Joe, and he hasn't messaged me with the right information.

what's the code?

That's right. We have a code. Mary and I created an account on letshookup.com. According to the website, users have been screened for "past sexual offenses," so I figured we were semi-safe. But semisafe isn't good enough, which is where rule number two comes in — Mary never meets anyone alone.

When this guy doesn't text back, I suspect someone's been talking. Maybe Todd. Maybe Mary gave him my number, which is the contact. I make a mental note to rip her a new one.

code? I text again.

hilarious — u got a real biz going — come on, lets meet at the square

I consider this guy's offer. If he is a friend of Todd's, he can't be all that bad. Maybe another guy from school, or even another school. But Sky Square Mall? I don't think so. There are boundaries that must be kept. No cars. No parks at night. No best buddies who want a special, like two for one. Mary's not a loaf of bread. And no out-of-the-way places that could threaten her safety. So this suggestion to meet at an abandoned strip mall is immediately shot down.

No

u got somethin against parking lots?

Only those that haven't had cars parked in them for over ten years.

Yeah they give me the creeps

Obviously, I pretend to be Mary. Why confuse things? Also,

if a guy thinks there's multiple people involved, he may get spooked.

It only takes ten seconds for his reply.

u got a better idea?

Before I think of a response, ten more seconds pass and he sends another text.

hey I asked you a question

I don't like this guy. He sounds like trouble. I ask him where he got my number because clearly he didn't find us online.

A friend

I dont hav any friends (Which isn't exactly true, because I've got Mary and Paula in World History and plenty of other girls who compliment my outfits on a regular basis.)

A customer

I dont hav those either

Dont fool urself honey. u charge to spread ur legz

Oh my God. He did not just say that. I feel a flash in my chest that sets my whole body on fire. I manage to lock the phone with my shaky thumb. And then I jump in my seat when it vibrates again. Another text, but not from Joe.

You on your way?

I need a minute to steady my nerves, then tap out a quick message.

Yes. T minus ten.

• • •

John William Brooks, PI, sits in a booth at Lou's Deli with a steaming mug between his hands. I know him by the bright yellow shirt he said he'd be wearing. He's older than I had imagined. For some reason, I panic when he flashes a crooked smile and waves me over. Do I really want to do this? It's finally showtime and I'm frozen, a petrified actor about to go onstage.

He waves again, this time with both hands in the air like he's flagging me down, and when someone enters the door behind me, I'm forced to move.

"Rosie?" He rises from the seat to stand tall and thick like a tree.

"That's me." I slip into the booth, fixing Ray's shirt so it doesn't bunch up behind me.

"John. Nice to meet you." He crinkles his sunburned nose, which deepens the lines in his face. "Would you like something to eat? They're famous for their pie, you know."

I do know, and my mouth waters from the offer alone, but I say, "No, thanks," afraid that satisfying my sweet tooth will send me into a sugar high. I need to stay grounded and focused.

We sit in awkward silence, the buzz from the overhead fluorescent bulbs filling the space like angry bees. Only a couple other booths are occupied. Near us, an old man sits at an otherwise empty counter eating cherry pie, my favorite. I glance over at him every time his spoon clanks against the plate.

"So." John raps all ten fingers on the table, which reminds me of my father's piano playing—the way his hands barely moved, while his fingers did all the work. But John isn't making music. He's making the table vibrate, so I drop my hands into my lap. "Why the rush to meet tonight?"

"Well, I'm in school during the day, so—"

He peers at me with his steely gray investigator eyes. "Haven't you graduated already? I thought you told me you were eighteen."

"Almost eighteen."

His entire expression changes, like I just unplugged the light from behind his eyes. "You're a minor, Rosie."

"So?"

"You can't enter into a legally binding contract with me."

"But I will be in three weeks. May twenty-ninth."

"Then call me May twenty-ninth," he says, beginning to dig behind him, probably for his wallet to pay the bill and scram.

"No!" I fling my hand across the table to make him stay put. "Please don't leave. I've already waited so long. Can't we work something out?"

He's got his wallet in his hands now but doesn't open it, which is a good sign. I can tell he's running the situation through his investigative filter, looking for a solution. Then he says, "It's unethical, but I guess I could postdate the contract."

I don't exactly know what that means. But I say that it sounds like a great idea and remind him it's only a few weeks he has to be unethical.

He chuckles, but only slightly, and says, "So you're seventeen, which means you're a senior in high school. Shouldn't you be at home studying or something?"

"I already have a parent," I snap. "Well, sort of. Honestly, I'm here now because this is the only time I could sneak out."

John crosses his hands in the air like he's surrendering. "I don't want to know." He takes a sip from his mug, and I suddenly want to drink something hot, too. My stomach is in knots. "Scratch that," he says. "I do want to know."

"What, you never snuck out of the house when you were young?" I challenge him.

"Sure, to go to a club or some party. Not to meet a private investigator."

"Look. I'm not in any trouble. I promise."

John squints at me and bides his time by taking a long sip of his drink. He's sizing me up, wondering if a seventeen-year-old girl who sneaks out of the house is more trouble than she's worth. "When we spoke a couple months ago, you said you were looking for someone."

"I am," I say, relieved he's decided to continue the conversation.

"Well?" He raises his bushy eyebrows. "I'm a private detective, not a mind reader. You need to tell me who you want to find."

"So you'll take my case?"

"Maybe."

"Before I unload my hopes in your lap, I need to know."

"So do I. Who is it you want to find?"

"You first. What if you get busy again and blow me off?"

"Let's not play chicken here, Rosie." John's face has grown stern, almost annoyed.

Across the way, the old man takes a final bite of cherry pie and drops the spoon onto his empty plate. He looks over at me and dips his bald head. "Damn good," he says.

I pull my eyes away from him and back to John, who's waiting for my response. Realizing I won't win, I dig into my bag.

"Here." I hand over my share of everything Mary's earned in the past couple months, less ten dollars. I wasn't about to give him a dime more than he asked for.

"What's this?" he asks, not touching the bills resting on the table.

"Three hundred dollars. Your retainer fee."

He frowns, making deeper lines around his mouth. "My retainer's five hundred, Rosie. I already cut you a deal at four."

"You said three."

"I never said three."

He did. I could've sworn he did, but it doesn't matter now. I riffle through my purse and pull out the remaining ten dollars from my wallet. "Before I was sort of broke. Now I'm completely broke." When I slide the bill across the table, his face sags and a weak smile rises to his lips.

"That's all you've got?"

"Yep."

More squinting. It seems like this guy believes only half of everything I say.

"I swear. If I had more, I'd give it to you."

"Keep it," he says, letting out a sigh of resignation. "I'm already postdating the contract. What's the harm in bending another rule?" He smacks the table with both enormous hands, making me jump in my seat. "Besides, I couldn't live with myself, knowing I'd taken your last ten bucks. But if I do take your case, I have to know you'll be able to pay me for my services. No one works for free, even nice guys like me."

I guess he is kind of nice, and the sheer size of this man

instills confidence. I imagine all he has to do is ask a question once to have it answered.

So I say, "Of course I can pay you. No one expects things for free, even nice girls like me."

He smiles at my joke, then pulls out a piece of paper from somewhere on the seat next to him. Probably a briefcase. "Then let's make it official." He asks me for my driver's license so he can verify my full name and birthdate, then scribbles down information from it.

John spins around the paper—which I now see is a contract—and slides it in front of me. Easily working upside down (seems he's done this before), he indicates the parties involved, the retainer I've given him (three hundred dollars), and his hourly rate (fifty dollars), which unhinges me but I will myself to hide the shock.

There's some other stuff I'm too lazy to read, and when I glance up, he says, "Just sign here," and points right below a line that already holds his signature and the date, May 29, 2017. He offers me his pen to use.

"Okay, then. We're in business." He clasps his hands in front of him, ready to listen for the long haul. "Now. Who is it you want to find?"

I reach into my purse, pull out a picture, and slide it across the table. "My birth mother."

KNOWING THIS probably comes as a relief to you. Lucy—
the excessive drinker, smoker, and Judd the Dud lover—is my
stepmom. She married Dad when I was five, two years after
what I thought was my mother's death.

On my first day of kindergarten I was preoccupied with
pairing striped shorts with a plaid shirt (even then I was serious about my fashion choices), when my father sat on my bed
and drew me in close. He made sure I was listening, then said,
"Mom's going to pick you up today, okay? I'll see you when I
get home from work." I must have looked confused because
he swept the curls out of my eyes and cupped my chin in both
hands. "She's your mother now, Rosie Posie." His face confused
me even more—he looked happy and sad at the same time. It
was too much for my five-year-old brain to comprehend, but I
trusted him, so I nodded, then dropped to the floor to put on
neon-pink socks that matched neither the shirt nor the shorts.

And that was that. I never called her Lucy or referred to her
as my stepmother when introducing her to friends. As young
as I was, I could still tell my father was trying to cement this
new bond, and not long after they had married, he gave me a

necklace with two silver hearts and a handwritten card that said, *Death has taken one mother, but Life has given you another.* Looking back, it was corny and morbid, but I was still crushed when I lost it during recess in second grade. I didn't want to lose any more things or people, yet looking back, I'd never really had Lucy. This started to become clear after his death.

Which brings me back to that chilly October day. After he fell face-first into his plate of eggs, Dad was rushed to the hospital, where they performed emergency bypass surgery. Mom and I sat in a nearby lounge drinking warm sodas from a broken vending machine. Around noon, a doctor emerged and pulled up a chair in front of us. All of his skin was paper white, cracked, and covered in moles, even his hands. Everything from the faded name tag to the bleach-stained white coat made it seem it had been a long time since he cared enough to find just the right words to break bad news.

"Mrs. Velvitt," he said. "The surgery went fine, but it's still too early to tell."

Tell what? If he's going to be okay? I wanted to blurt out a hundred questions, but I could tell he wasn't done talking.

"He's got quite the history, your husband. Years of heart disease. Both parents and an older brother deceased due to cardiovascular issues. We'll need to keep a close eye on his recovery."

Heart disease? Since when?

The doctor's face was grim, his hollowed cheeks sinking into a set of crusty, thin lips. "Plus, he's got arrhythmia, so that puts him at added risk."

Mom didn't look fazed by all this news. Her stony expression made it clear she already knew my dad had a fragile ticker. I felt betrayed in that lounge, sitting on a smelly, ratty couch. But more than that, I was terrified of losing another parent. First my real mother and now my dad? Could life really be that cruel?

Later, when Dad was moved to another room, I asked Mom why I hadn't been told about his bad heart. I would've helped somehow. Gone on walks with him, swapped his beloved pound cake for fruit.

"Because kids don't need to know stuff like that, Rosie." And then she left with a lighter and her pack of cigarettes. She left a lot that night, and because there was a NO SMOKING zone around the perimeter of the hospital, she had to cross the street to puff away. That was fine by me. It gave me more time alone with my father, which turned out to be a terrible thing.

Around midnight, Mom said she needed something sweet, maybe a cookie. She offered to bring me back one, which sounded good since I was hungry and tired and studying for a math test I wanted to do well on.

Maybe she pulled it closed. I don't know. But that time she left, the door made a loud bang when it shut behind her. From my chair, I saw Dad's eyes open. Then he cleared his throat and patted the blanket with trembling fingers. I shuffled over with my hands stuffed into the kangaroo pocket of a University of Florida sweatshirt.

He looked old, a blanket drawn up to his neck, oxygen tubes plugged into his nose. I sat on the edge of the bed, scared to get too close and accidentally yank out something that was attached to him.

The box, he said.

What box, Dad?

Brown box . . . at . . .

Where? Tell me. I'll bring it to you.

No. There was a slight movement of his head. *For you, Rosie. It's . . . for you.*

And what happened next is why being alone with my father was a terrible thing. His face seized. It literally froze. I started shaking him because now I didn't care about pulling anything out. I just wanted his face to move, twitch, anything. All the machines hooked up to him went berserk, and a team of nurses came scrambling in and shoved me aside. But it was too late. That thing called arrhythmia the old doctor had mentioned earlier? Caused a stroke.

My grief was dulled only by Dad's cryptic message. All I could think of was racing home to dig around and find the box, even though he never told me where it was. I didn't get the chance until the following day. I needed to do it when my mom wasn't around, since it seemed like it was meant for my eyes only. So when she went to the funeral home to make arrangements, I got busy snooping. In closets, drawers, even deep inside the garage where I was afraid of running into roaches. I was determined to find that brown box, but all the determination in the world didn't help me.

• • •

"Looks kind of young to be your mother," John says, waving the picture between us.

"It's an old photo." Duh. Taken years ago. My mother is cocooned in bulky ski clothes; even her hands are tucked into gloves. Only her face is exposed, beaming and pink on a cold winter day.

"I was joking. It's part of my job to inject humor whenever I can."

"I'm not hiring a comedian." My words come out sharper than I intend.

He examines it with one hand while holding his mug in the other. If he spills anything on the picture, that would be the end of that, so I snatch it back.

"Can you find her or not?" I ask.

"I once found a needle in a haystack." John fishes out a five-dollar bill from a weathered black wallet and slips it to the waitress when she drifts past our booth.

"If you don't think you can, let me know now."

"Why, so you can google her?" he asks, which of course I have. You'd be surprised how much you can't find when all you have is a name. "Everyone thinks they're Sherlock Holmes these days because of the Internet." He rolls his eyes like he's had this conversation a hundred times.

I suffer enough with adult attitudes from Mom, some teachers, and Archie the bus driver, who ignores me. I unzip my purse, place the photo in a separate compartment, and slide across the vinyl seat. Then I throw out my hand with an open palm. "I'll just take back my money and you can rip up that contract."

He stands to intercept me. "I'm not ripping up any contract. But if you want to find her, you have to be tough. And you have to put up with my jokes."

"Your bad jokes," I clarify.

"Those, too."

He puts a ginormous hand on my shoulder, the weight of it feeling firm and safe. "I'm good, Rosie, but not good enough to pull a calf out of a donkey's ass. An old picture isn't much to go on. I'll need more."

"I have more," I assure him, then sit back down in the booth and order a piece of that cherry pie.

5

OBVIOUSLY, I found the box. Otherwise, how did I have that picture of my birth mother to show John? I know you're curious, but I actually love this part of the story, so don't rush me.

My father might have made good money in the scrap metal business, but he wasn't so good at saving it. Mom and I were forced to move the following summer, from our three-bedroom house in a nice neighborhood called Hammock Lakes into a two-bedroom house in a not-so-nice neighborhood without a name. The first thing I noticed about the new house was that black front door. Even at fifteen, I knew it was a bad sign. But Mom said it was cheap and allowed me to stay in the same school.

Moving sucks. The packing, the planning, the tossing of childhood memories into a trash bag. It was all bad, the worst of which was my fear of never finding the box. It seemed the one thing my father had left me was destined to die with him. I had no idea what was in there, but it didn't matter. Someone tells you something on his deathbed, you listen.

And then, about six months ago, my mom roped me into watching one of her beloved reality shows. She pulled me down on the couch, slurring inside a glass of dark red wine. *Give it a chance*, she said, with a grip on my hand I knew I couldn't break. Not that I wanted to break it. We didn't do much to- gether, so even watching a trashy show was better than nothing.

Forgotten Rooms was a program where people allowed a decorator to come in and reorganize a wasted space, usually a den or something. But that week's episode was about attics. Now, I don't know why Mom was all excited, since most South Florida houses don't have those huge attics that can be trans- formed into bedrooms. At least I've never seen any, and none of my old friends ever had one growing up or I can assure you we would've had sleepovers in it.

Anyway, she loved the before-and-after pictures, and kept batting my arm, hacking, sloshing her drink, hacking some more, saying she wished we had an attic to transform. The host of the show was one of those glamorous women who just hap- pen to know construction and wore a tool belt to prove it. She's with her lucky couple who agreed to the project so they could be on television.

The host used a hook at the end of a pole to release the ceiling hatch. While she was doing that, and letting a small ladder unfold from inside, she was educating the couple about the history of attics. Sizes, shapes, and the purposes many people use them for—mostly storage. But then she paused for dramatic effect, turned around to the couple, who was following her up the ladder, and said, *Or to hide stuff.* She winked, and it was as if she had winked right at me. I literally had to turn away from my mom, fearing the lightbulb in my head somehow illuminated through my eyes.

Dad had said the brown box was at . . . ? And that was it. I thought it was somewhere, like *at the back of my closet* or *at the bottom of my drawer*. I didn't realize until then that *at* was actually part of another word: *attic*. The box was in the attic of my old house. It wasn't big enough to make into a spare bedroom, but it was definitely big enough to hide a box.

Of course, there was a small problem: How was I going to get in there? It had been around three years since my father died, and our house sold quickly once we put it on the market a few months later. But the new owners hadn't kept me away for long.

Close to my fifteenth birthday—only a few months after Dad died and as Mom's parental lenses were growing increasingly foggy with liquor—I had started taking the bus to my old neighborhood. I learned that if I took the 246 West, then I could switch to the 19 North, which would drop me fairly close, leaving only a short walk to Hammock Lakes. Once I got into the development, it was only another few blocks to Grove Street, 1100, the fourth house down on the left.

The first time I went, it was almost dark by the time I arrived. I walked up to the house as if I were simply heading home, *la-di-da*, then slowed my pace as I drew near. I studied the trees, the grass, the light fixtures—looking for signs of change, knowing there should be some since the family inside wasn't mine. But the only differences were the cars in the driveway and the numbers on the front of the house that were now silver instead of white.

I hid behind one of the palm trees that acted as a barrier to the house next door. And there, in my bedroom window, a soft yellow glow lit up sheer pink drapes. I couldn't breathe. Another girl was enjoying my bedroom with its own bathroom and window overlooking the lake, while I was relegated to a green house with a black door and no yard.

I was devastated but would return whenever something triggered a memory—finding Dad's grilling apron jammed under a stack of clothes, or Judd's fingers haphazardly running along the keys of Dad's piano. Back then, I just wanted to see my old house. But after watching that program with my mom six months ago, the visits took on a mission. I had to get *into* the house.

Finally, I got lucky two months ago. It was Sunday, the fifth of March, and it was one of those days that made you feel sad and lonely simply because the weather was crappy. A wet gray mist had hung around all day. I started reminiscing about making burned cookies with my dad and his homemade barbecue sauce with diced jalapeños. When my emotions were nice and raw, I repeatedly called and texted Ray, who wouldn't pick up. Then, when I tried talking to Mary about missing him, she shut me down. I was on the verge of something, and it wasn't good.

So I took the bus, aching for a glimpse of a life that had been buried deep in the ground with my father. It had been a while since I'd visited, walked along the sidewalk that still had my initials carved into one of the concrete squares. And there it was—a FOR SALE sign pounded into the overgrown lawn. No cars in the driveway, no mail spilling from the mailbox, and no sheer pink drapes on my old bedroom window.

I inched closer, put my hands against the glass window of the living room, where I would nestle into the sofa and read on rainy weekends. The house was empty, the front door locked. But I had once lived in this house, and I had once been locked out. I knew how to get in.

The rear sliding glass door released under my special touch. I promptly closed it behind me and surveyed the tile floor, still bright and white. My eyes were drawn immediately to the spot where Dad's piano had been, against the far right wall, where there was a window he said let in just the right amount of natural light. He didn't like any kind of lamp resting on the old Chickering upright Mom insisted was a magnet for termites. I had been surprised she brought it with us to the new house. She probably plans on hawking it at a garage sale one day when things get too tight. It's only a matter of time.

I walked directly into the kitchen, knowing I'd be hit hard, but still anxious to see the honey-colored cupboards and the oven I burned my first batch of sugar cookies in. The tears came swift and fierce. There was my father, slumped in his chair, runny eggs staining the cuff of his work shirt.

I ran to my old bedroom, curled myself into a ball on the carpet that had changed from forest green to berry pink, and howled like a sad, injured cat. I cried myself to sleep, and when I woke, Mary was there.

"What are you doing here?" Was I dreaming? No, she was sitting next to me, running her fingers through the thick carpet.

"I knew you needed me."

"How—"

"Because you hung up on me three hours ago after you told me you wanted to call Ray and I told you if you did I'd never speak to you again."

I wasn't about to tell her that I had called him. Texted him, too, like twenty times, but he never responded. I yawned and struggled to collect my thoughts.

"No." I rubbed at my swollen eyes. "I mean, how did you know I'd be here?"

"I came with you once before. Don't you remember?"

Vaguely.

"When you had your last major meltdown," she continued. "Jesus, Rosie, it was just a few weeks ago. You thought Lucy had stolen your sketchbooks, but then you found them the next day, stuffed in an old pillowcase."

It wasn't quite that way. Mary was the one who suggested Lucy had taken them, but I didn't want to get into it and changed the subject. "How did you get in?" My brain was fuzzy, but not too fuzzy to ask questions.

"You left the sliding back door open. Sloppy, Rosie, very sloppy. You'll never make it as a professional burglar." She let out a dry snort, trying to lighten the mood, but I was still groggy and confused. "Now come on," she said, glancing at the bare window. "It's getting dark. We should go."

We were both wearing cutoff denim shorts and snug pastel-colored tees—not exactly criminal attire, but sassy enough to be looked at twice if caught sneaking out of a house up for sale.

"Not yet. I came for something." I rose from the floor, shaking my leaden legs awake.

"Something other than torturing yourself with painful memories? You're a sadist."

Mary followed me out of my old bedroom and into the hallway that was once lined with family portraits and some of my bad elementary school art. I stopped in the middle of the hall, pointed to the attic hatch, and said, "I need to get up there."

"For what?"

"My dad left me a box."

"From the grave? That's some tricky shit." She frowned. "You never told me."

"I'm telling you now," I snapped. "Can you please help? I need a ladder or something."

"Well, empty houses don't usually have ladders just sitting around," Mary said, hands on hips, suspicious of this whole thing. "But I think I saw a folding chair near the front door. Sometimes Realtors keep them at properties when they're waiting all day during open houses."

Pays to have a best friend whose mom is a Realtor, but I've often wondered how good Mrs. Perkins is at selling houses. She's not that friendly, and her eyes are always darting all over the place when we talk. Mary says it's just nervous energy.

Anyway, she was right. I dragged the chair into the hall and asked Mary to hold it steady for me.

I opened the hatch carefully, so the interior ladder wouldn't drop on my head.

"Wow. Cool," Mary said, as the rickety wooden steps unfolded in front of me. "Why didn't we ever hide out up there?" I looked down to see her beaming at me mischievously.

"Because it's not that kind of attic. There's barely room to breathe up here. It's full of insulation stuff." I climbed the ladder and peeked inside the dark cavern, hoping I wouldn't have to go any farther. I'm kind of claustrophobic. "Of course, I wasn't smart enough to bring a flashlight." After fumbling around, all I had were fingertips coated in dust and dirt. I climbed down the ladder and off the chair, then plopped to the floor and angrily wiped my dirty hands on my shorts.

"Quitter," Mary said. "Let me have a shot." She stood on the chair and didn't even ask me to hold it for her. Then she climbed the ladder and stuck the top half of her body way into the attic. She was taller than me, with longer arms, and those two things alone gave me hope.

Mary grunted, shifted her body in different directions.

"Feel anything?"

"Nope." She sounded far away, like she was deep inside a cave.

Aggravated, I pulled my knees to my chest and dropped my head between them in defeat. Moments later, I heard her sneakers descending.

"Except for this," she said, presenting me with a dusty brown box.

6

THERE IS STILL the taste of Lou's cherry pie on my tongue
when I shed my clothes and slip into the robe I'd tossed on the
floor earlier. An old sleeping bag rests at the back of my closet,
wrapped up like a pink jelly roll. The box is inside it. I pull it out
and carry it with me into bed. The brown leather has peeled off
at the edges. Stains dot the top, random circles I imagine were
made by the rain. I hold it to my nose, hoping for a whiff of him.
But it doesn't smell like my dad. It just smells old.

The small silver clasp on the front releases at a flick of my
finger. My heart always races when I lift the lid. Carefully,
I extract each piece and lay them out on the comforter I've
smoothed over my lap. Everything is so old, I'm afraid one hasty
move will bend a picture or rip the brittle piece of paper that
holds my dad's handwritten words.

May 29, 2009

Dear Rosie Posie,

Today is your tenth birthday. I just tucked you into bed wearing
the polka-dot pajamas your best friend, Nicolette, gave you at

your party. You love them so much, I hope you don't insist on wearing them to school tomorrow, claiming a belt, socks, and shoes will mask their intended purpose.

So you've found the box, and in it this letter, which means I've passed away. I've lived with a secret that at first gave me peace, but has grown to torture me as you cleverly cheat at cards, never fail to burn cookies in the oven, and create strange, beautiful outfits from nothing. Just like her.

I've put off writing this for a long time. I chose today because while you and all your friends were outside playing in the pool, I was in the kitchen feeling another sharp pain in my chest. As I placed the candles on your birthday cake, I promised myself that today was the day. Tonight. No more waiting. One might say it was risky, taking a chance like that, and it was. Because I've been sick a long time. My heart is fragile and could stop beating at any moment.

I've been lying to you, Rosie, and not just about my health.

Sometimes a lie is told to protect people. Last month you lied to that new boy at school, telling him everyone was making fun of your outfit, when really they were laughing at his lisp. By the time you read this letter, you may have forgotten that story, but I hope you at least remember that I listened and understood. You had lied to spare him.

I want to spare you, but once I'm gone, it's only right that you know what I've kept from you, if not why. While this letter is meant to reveal the core of my secret, there are other layers that must die with me. I'm sorry, Rosie. You must think I'm a coward, and you'd be right.

Your mother—your real mother—is alive. She didn't die from an illness. You were a respectful child and never pushed me for more. As you've gotten older, I suspect you've become instinctive, too, and know that wanting details would only cause us both pain. I thank you for that.

Lucy knows the truth, knows why Justine and I had to part ways. She can tell you without the heartache that would've crushed me all over again if I were to try. She wants to be a good mother. I've seen her give you extra raisins in your oatmeal and rub your back when you couldn't fall asleep. But it's been challenging. She doesn't understand you like I do and struggles against your creative spirit. The incessant sketching, the multiple outfits that make loads of laundry. I think she feels separate from us. After all, you and I are blood.

Know that I loved your mother very much, especially for giving me you. The other items in this box are all I have left of her. They're yours now, so treasure them. If you're brave enough, they may even lead you to her.

I hope you can forgive me,
Dad

Forgive him? Possibly. I loved my dad, but those other "layers" he mentioned worry me. Like waiting for the other shoe to drop. Dad's parting words feel more like a warning than a confession, which is why I needed to hire a private detective to find my mother and get to the bottom of things. I don't want to wait my entire life for that other shoe.

My poor father. I'd like to think he was blind—not blinded by love. Those extra raisins? Dumped like a mound of sweet and chewy insects. And when I didn't want to finish them, her piercing glare was all I needed to know that every last one had better be eaten. She did rub my back. Once. While my father stood at the doorway and praised her affection. But what he didn't see was the deliberate, tight squeeze she gave my neck before leaving my bedside. Back then, I couldn't understand why she didn't love me like a mother should. But as I got older, it became clear. I wasn't hers. We weren't blood.

I carefully refold the letter and place it to the side.

Since I didn't feel comfortable leaving it with John, I add the photo of my mother to the rest of the stuff and take stock.

A picture from some sort of party, blurry people gathered behind them. Maybe not a party, more of a casual thing by the way my parents are dressed—Dad in jeans, a T-shirt, and a baseball cap; my mother in a pair of white capris and a red sweater, a yellow headband struggling to tame her wild dark hair. They're on a couch. She's on his lap, wrapped in his arms, one hand grabbing the brim of his cap. They're not just smiling, they're playing. I've peered at this photo of her until my eyes cross and I feel a headache coming on. I do resemble her—the big eyes and mouth, definitely the hair—but the overall shape of my face is more like my father's, the cleft chin designating me a true Velvitt.

The other picture is only of my mother—the one I showed John at the deli—looking pudgy, bundled up in a ski jacket, a pink pompom sprouting from her head. I imagine my father snapping the picture, giving her directions for a pose. Her arms are stretched out like a *V*, as if to say, "We're finally here!" Above her, a giant letter *C* on a rustic wood sign. Beneath it, two words mostly obstructed. Letters sprout around her—*C*, *M*, and *N*—but most are blocked by flyers and my mother's bulky figure. I turn it over. *Justine* is written with a heart over the *i*. I've always wondered if it was my father or my mother who wrote it that way.

A copy of my birth certificate. Nothing weird there.

And my favorite item in the box—a leather bracelet, about an inch wide, with two names embossed, separated by a flower: Justine and Leni. It's only my favorite because I imagine her wearing it, but I'm insanely curious about this Leni person. What kind of name is that, anyway? Was it a boyfriend? But that would be spelled Lenny, and why would my dad ever keep something from one of my mother's old boyfriends and then leave it for me?

I lean over to examine it under the light of my lamp. The way the leather is worn and scratched, and the flower has lost its color. Based on my research, it's the kind of bracelet kids were making during the '70s. I figure they each made one, and Leni has a faded leather strip of her own, kept with other mementos carrying equally faded memories.

It's kind of cool, I guess. Mary and I have done similar things. When we were fifteen, we found a dead lizard, took off its back legs and used them as charms on plastic anklets; at sixteen, we dyed blue a chunk of hair at the base of our necks (so our mothers couldn't see); and on my seventeenth birthday, we each used a match to make a tiny burn mark on the inside of a wrist. It didn't hurt that much, because we took a swig of vodka from my mom's stash first. The scars will bind us for life.

Like the letter, I put the bracelet to my nose and inhale, hoping to smell my mother, but it just smells old, too. It goes back in the box with the other things. I close the lid and snap the silver lock. I'm too tired to jam it back in the closet, so I shove it under my bed, making sure the dust ruffle is doing its job of hiding the mess under there.

It's almost midnight. I snap off the light, curl up in my bed. It's been a long day, but a good one because it's the beginning of my quest for answers. Sure, I want to know why my father lied to me. But even more than that, I want to know why my mother let him.

7

BACK TO THE NIGHT I found the box.

I couldn't grab it out of Mary's hands fast enough. We left my house the same way we went in, and as we walked through my old neighborhood, I struggled to read my father's letter in the fading light of day. Then I read it a second time, out loud, so Mary could hear. We held hands on the bus ride back but didn't speak. When I arrived home, my brain felt like pea soup. And I hate pea soup.

It was close to seven o'clock before I walked through the door. Any normal parent would have been all over me, wondering where I disappeared to, but all Mom could slur over her glass of wine was "Perfect timing!" when I found her in the kitchen. Wine made her happy and excited. She took a drag from her cigarette and coughed. "Judd's brought home a bucket of dark meat." I also hate dark meat. It's fatty and slips through my fingers.

I rubbed my eyes, still swollen from the crying episode in my old bedroom, and looked at her as my stepmother, my father's accomplice. For the past two and a half years I had put up with her drinking, her smoking, her nasty comments about my hair or makeup. Now I had to put up with her being a liar, too.

"Where is that damn thing?" She was busy scrounging through the utensil drawer with one hand, clinging for dear life to her glass. God forbid she put it down to search for the tongs. We could never simply dig in with our hands.

I had no intention of sticking around. I held the box near my back, prepared to dart off, when Judd came up from behind me and snatched it from my hands.

"What's this?" he asked, taunting me. He was still wearing his uniform that consisted of a chicken-cartoon tie and a badge pinned to a dingy white long-sleeved shirt. I could smell the oil and garlic on his clothes.

I thought fast. My mind had to be quicker than theirs, which were already dulled by alcohol. "It's a jewelry box."

"Kinda junky for a jewelry box," he said, taking a swig of wine.

"Give it back." I lunged at him.

He kept me at arm's length, but his fingertips still managed to reach my waist, where they twitched and rubbed against my shirt.

"Where did you get it?" Judd peered at it curiously, as if he, Itchin' for Chicken's assistant shift manager, had an eye for spotting antiques.

"A friend."

"Which one?"

"Mom, tell him to give it back."

"Give it back, babe," she mocked, without any real conviction, before launching into a coughing fit that had her gripping the countertop.

It was clear he was not going to give it up until I did. "Fine. It was Mary."

"Ah, the famous Mary," he said, handing it back to me. "Will I ever get to meet this best friend of yours?"

And subject her to your predatory eyes? Never.

"Don't even try," Mom said. "She keeps her under lock and key."

"That's totally not true," I said, because it wasn't like that. Mary wouldn't allow herself to be kept under lock and key by anyone. And if someone did try, she'd claw her way out until her nails were bloody, which says a lot because Mary likes her nails nice. "You saw her that one time at—"

"We're just bustin' your chops, Rosie," Judd interrupted.

I sniffled away the last of my runny nose, which made my mother spin around. "Have you been crying?" She clacked together the tongs she had finally found.

"Allergies," I said, thinking fast on my sneakered feet.

"Since when?" She put down her wineglass and inched closer.

"They can develop with age, you know. One day, boom, you're allergic to some crazy flower you passed on the way home."

I started to shuffle away when Mom said, "Wait," her flat eyes suddenly sparkling with interest. "Let me take a look at that." She was surprisingly quick for being sloshed. The box was almost in her clutches when I yanked it away and tucked it under my arm.

"It's private, Mom." I offered up one of those if-someone-sees-this-I'll-be-embarrassed looks. "Please." Parents usually fall for that, especially around other people, like boyfriends. It makes them appear fair instead of heartless.

She waited a beat. "Go wash up, then. But you'd better hurry, because I'm hungry and I've just spotted two breasts hiding at the bottom of that bucket with my name on them."

"And these two have my name on them," Judd said, playfully grabbing at Mom's chest, only partially hidden by a low V-neck sweater. She poked at him with the tongs, but then allowed him to maul her with his mustached mouth.

I left the room, wondering if she ever loved my father. If she ever loved me. Because no matter what she did, I had grown to love the lady with pretty gold hair who bought me my first set of colored pencils and a thick pad of seemingly endless white paper. Even now, knowing she'd kept a secret from me for years, I still do.

8

IT TOOK A LOT of willpower not to barge through that black door and confront her, but I knew it was best that I didn't. A strange thought had occurred to me on the bus ride home from my old house. While Mary held my hand and seemed to stare absently out the window, my mind was moving at warp speed, struggling to fit this odd new piece into the puzzle of my life.

Imagine if this piece had three prongs. Two prongs fit fine into the other pieces. One, my dad was obviously trying to protect me from something. Two, my stepmother went along with the charade. But the third prong didn't fit anywhere. Why, after my father died, hadn't she told me the truth? This was the part of the secret that bothered me most.

I couldn't come up with any logical answer by the time I got home, so I figured I'd keep the whole thing under wraps. I'm no actress, and have no dreams of becoming one, but the quality of my upcoming performance had to be Oscar-worthy. There was no other way. Until I understood why my stepmom had—for over three years—continued with this sham, I had to keep the secret to myself. And Mary, of course.

The only thing I did know was that I had to find my real mother. But after endless online searches yielded zilch, I realized I had to bite the bullet and hire a professional.

Did you know that private investigators prefer to get paid for their time? I thought if I told some nice guy my sob story, he'd do it out of the goodness of his detective heart. Thought maybe they work for free sometimes, like lawyers, if they can get behind a cause, and what better cause than a poor young girl searching for her long-lost mother?

When I started calling around, three men hung up on me, and one woman asked what kind of drugs I was on. So when I got to John William Brooks, PI, the only thing I told him was that I was really, really short on funds but really, really needed help finding someone. I faked a sniffle into the phone, then made some additional, unintelligible noises until he spoke.

John lowered his retainer fee but said his hourly fee was nonnegotiable. I agreed, even though I had no idea at the time how I'd be able to pay any of it. When he told me he wasn't able to see me for a while because he was involved in a "big case," I agreed to that, too. I needed time to start the Fund.

There was also no place to go digging for cash, like a savings account, or anything. I only started receiving an allowance when I turned thirteen, about a year before my father died, and often spent it at the Goodwill store—adding a funky designer piece to my wardrobe whenever I could. Mom's kept up with my allowance, but by half, since money's tight. And if I don't remind her, she'll skip a week, too. Stealing from her wallet wasn't an option because she, like me, knows how to blow through money once it falls into her hands. Besides, how much did she ever have in there—five, ten bucks? I was going to need a lot more than that.

I didn't know what to do until the idea was—excuse the expression—thrust upon me. I'm not trying to be funny. I'm only trying to find a way to explain how it all started, how Mary came to be in the stairwell with Todd Ryser. Don't judge her, admire her. Best friends say they'd do anything for you, but I dare you to test that theory. Most won't. But Mary's different. She'll not only take a bullet for me, but she'll also remove it with her bare hands and then stitch herself up with the needle I've threaded.

. . .

It was a Saturday afternoon, about a week after I found the box. A storm was coming. The clouds were thick and gray, heavy with rain. Judd and Mom were in the living room, lost in a *Guns Galore* marathon on TNT. I was slogging through *Moby-Dick* for English class, but every time a shot was fired on the television, I jumped out of my desk chair. My nerves were already on edge. I had to get out of the house.

I decided on a long white cotton tee, cinched at the waist with a belt, and a pair of dark red leggings. Gold ballet flats topped off the outfit and were comfortable enough to walk long distances. My hair wasn't cooperating that day, so I bunched it up as best as I could and stuffed it into a knot on top of my head.

I swiped a pair of Mom's fake gold hoop earrings and put them on after I left.

The bus stopped right at the entrance to the food court of the mall. I had just wanted to be alone, which is of course when you run into friends who want you to join them. Paula, from my World History class, and her two best friends (Rachel and Iris, who always dye their hair the same color orange) linked arms with me and dragged me to a table. They gorged themselves on milk shakes and burgers while I drank lemonade and tore through a bag of chips. The three of them giggled about guys I didn't know and almost snorted milk shakes through their noses when a song came blaring through someone's phone at the next table.

"Come shopping with us," Paula said. She wore frosty-blue eyeliner that matched her shirt. "Forever 21 has a humongous sale going on."

Rachel and Iris nodded at the same time, as if with one giant tangerine head. Rachel's prettier, with petite features and a great smile she always flashes. Iris has a flat, wide face and an overbite braces never fixed.

I thought fast because I still wanted to be alone, and even more now after spending fifteen minutes with them and not getting their inside jokes. "No, thanks. I'm meeting Mary."

"Who?" Rachel asked, crinkling her pinched nose.

"Mary," I said, then added, "Perkins," as if mentioning her last name would help them know who I was referring to. But they still shook their heads and the three of them exchanged a weird look that made me regret sitting with them in the first place.

"Well, we're on the hunt for graduation dresses, even though they're hidden under those hideous blue satin gowns." Paula shook her head, then tucked wisps of short blonde hair behind both ears. "Speaking of graduation, where are you headed after—Seminole land or Gator country?" she asked, because most people end up becoming one or the other. But then she made a sheepish grin and said, "Sorry. You probably don't want to be in Tallahassee with what's-his-name."

I waved her off as if the reference to Ray hadn't bothered me. "I didn't apply to either one. I want to go to design school, so I applied to the Fashion House in Miami Beach. Still waiting to hear on acceptance."

"Cool!" Iris said with such enthusiasm that when she followed with, "Where else?" I deflated a little.

"Um, that's it. For now. I mean, if I don't get in, I'm sure there are other places—"

"Risky," Paula interjected. "I applied to all the state schools. You should really get in some other apps, Rosie."

"Or I can just blow off college." I grabbed one of Rachel's napkins and cleaned my greasy fingers. "Maybe I'll jet off to Europe and sketch on cobblestone streets."

"Don't forget the tin can for donations!" Iris snickered at her own joke, but then we all fell into an awkward silence.

"Well, you're looking at two Gators," Rachel said brightly, wrapping an arm around Iris. "And one Seminole." She stuck out her tongue in Paula's direction and then the three of them broke into a cackling fit.

I was ready to go, so I drained the last of my lemonade and

emptied the remaining crushed chips into my mouth. Checked my phone, told them Mary was waiting for me.

"See you at school," Paula said as I gathered my things.

I felt their eyes on me as I walked away, so I picked up the pace and got lost in the crowd.

I checked out the shoes in Skechers. I tried on a pair of high-wedge-heeled pink sneakers and a pair of those flip-flops that claim to work out your butt. Next I wandered into Victoria's Secret and tried on at least a dozen bras I left in the dressing room, then stood in front of a full-length mirror wrapped in a fuzzy robe until a salesperson asked what size I needed. Shooting for the extra-small always gets me off the hook. There are never any extra-smalls. So when she said, *I think I have one in the back*, I ducked out and got lost in the crowd.

You'd think the mall was my heaven on earth. All those clothes, those fabrics, those mannequins sporting perfectly chosen outfits. And it is, to some extent, especially in the designer section of places like Bloomingdale's or Saks Fifth Avenue. I keep a small notebook tucked in my purse for when inspiration strikes. But it's also my nemesis, taunting me with dreams I may never be able to fulfill. What if I don't get into Fashion House? Paula was right. I should've applied to more schools and increased my odds of getting in somewhere.

Anyway, I ended up at the makeup counter at Macy's, which is kind of strange because I don't like to wear it. I hate the way it feels on my skin, like it's suffocating the pores. But through a large-pane window palm trees were getting battered by a driving rain and I knew hanging out at the mall was better than heading out into that mess. Especially with my hair waiting to be difficult.

So I let a woman with a jet-black bob—Anya, MAC sales associate—have a go at my face because she was rocking her lab coat–looking uniform with a hot-pink tank underneath and five-inch wedge heels. She did a surprisingly good job, applying a very light foundation, smoky eye shadow, and champagne-colored gloss. When she placed a mirror in front of me, I didn't want to scrape it all off with one of those wipes. Mary probably would have loved it since she likes makeup way more than I do, always testing new shades of everything but her lip gloss. Rockin' Raspberry will never be replaced by another color. She says it's the perfect complement to her skin, even though I'm sure just about any color goes with pale.

I held the mirror a beat too long. Anya knew I liked what I saw, but all I could do was thank her and promise to send my friends who were also in the mall and would definitely, positively buy something. My own pockets were empty. I don't think Anya was too pleased, but still she patted my shoulder and, in a thick Russian accent, told me to have a nice day. I can't help that the lemonade and chips ate up what was left of my measly ten-dollar allowance.

And speaking of the lemonade, I needed to pee. Since I didn't feel like backtracking to Macy's or walking all the way to one of the mall's restrooms, I went into the nearby Dead End Bookstore. A girl named Margarita works there. She's nice and lets me use theirs if I'm hanging around awhile when the store is slow. On opposite sides of the counter, we flip through the pages of the latest *Vogue* or *Elle* magazines, making fun of models and pretending to choke from the perfume insertions. But secretly I'm studying the fashions, making mental notes about color combinations and style trends. One day, my designs will be in those magazines.

After greeting Margarita with a quick wave, I made a beeline for the bathroom. When I came out, I almost bumped into a guy who appeared to be waiting his turn. Apparently, Margarita's nice to a lot of people who are too lazy to find a public restroom.

"Whoa," he said, bracing me with his hands. "Come here often?"

Our eyes locked. He wasn't hot but he did have this amazing gold hair and long matching eyelashes.

"Only on days ending in *y*," I said, trying to be cute, which worked because his face broke into a smile that instantly improved his looks.

"These places are a dying breed, you know." With arms wide, he cast his eyes around the bookstore. "It's a shame, too, don't you think?"

"I guess. So long as there are books to read, I don't care how I get them."

He fell in step behind me as I snaked my way through the Memoir aisle, then Study Aids. "But there's something about being surrounded by them," he said, allowing his fingers to trail along the spines of SAT prep books. I had a bookworm on my heels and needed to lose him. Not because he was a bookworm — that was cool — but because he was a bookworm who was following me, so I said something I hoped would turn him off.

"I come for the magazines."

"What kind? New age stuff? Travel and leisure?"

"No. I'm shallow. Fashion rags for me." I parked myself in front of a row of glossy covers, all showing tan bikini bods, ready for summer. It was only March, but the fashion industry is always months ahead of the actual calendar.

He stood next to me and picked up a *Car and Driver* magazine, which is when I noticed the smell of gas and Armor All. It's distinctive. Judd uses it on Mom's Slaabmobile when he's trying to spruce the old lady up. I figured this guy worked in some kind of garage. Then I zeroed in on his hands. When I spied dirty fingernails and calloused knuckles, I knew my hunch was right.

"Hey, where are you going after you read about bathing suits and makeup?"

I didn't like his condescending tone. Besides, he was a grease monkey, not exactly my type. Ray was my type—preppy and clean, and always smelling like something in these magazines. His nails were kept perfect. We even gave each other manicures one day when we were bored at my house and feeling silly. "Didn't you have to use the bathroom?" I pointed out.

"Nope." He smiled and blinked those long lashes.

"Uh, okay . . ." I shuffled away from him so he'd know I wasn't interested.

The chips I had an hour ago were already wearing off. When my stomach growled I didn't care. Maybe it would turn him off.

"So," he said, propping himself up against the magazine rack. "Want to go somewhere?"

"What?" I asked, thinking I might not have heard him right.

I'd been distracted by an article claiming crocheted sweaters were making a comeback.

"I know someplace we can go." He cocked his head, stuffed his hands in the pockets of his tattered jeans.

I jammed the magazine back in the rack. "For what?" I asked, snotty but with enough ignorance to invite an answer. Stupid me. I had no idea what this guy was talking about.

"Whatever you want."

"I gotta go," I said, brushing past him. Margarita was busy with a customer, or I would have stopped to chat and gotten rid of this guy. She didn't even look up as I walked out of the store. I could feel him behind me, so I pretended to fiddle in my purse, snug against my hip.

"I know you don't have any money in there," he said, keeping step with me.

"What makes you say that?"

"'Cause I've been watching you," he said.

"Really." It wasn't a question. It was an I-don't-believe-you challenge. We emerged into the main thoroughfare among a lot of shoppers. I'd be lying if I said I wasn't relieved to be back in the crowds.

"You need money. I need, well, I'll tell you what I don't need. A girlfriend. I just need to get laid," he said.

"I'm going to call security." I looked around for someone—anyone—in uniform.

"And why would you do that? I'm not a pervert."

"All perverts aren't old and disgusting, playing with themselves in front of elementary schools," I said, weaving my way through people, trying to lose him. "And how do you know I need money?"

"Because you've tried on a hundred things and bought nothing."

So he had been watching me. I quickened my pace. I was about to grab anyone who seemed like they could protect me from this creep. A burly father would do.

"Hey, stop." He grabbed my hand, which I yanked away. "At least allow me to introduce myself," he said, as if that would make any difference. "Aaron's the name."

I ignored him and headed straight for the nearest mall exit with a bus stop in front.

"What's yours?"

"Leave me alone," I said, clutching my purse.

"That's an interesting name. Is it hyphenated?"

I refused to crack a smile, even though I wanted to.

"I'll give you twenty bucks," he said.

I stopped in my tracks. "Are you serious? I'm not a hooker."

"Right. You only look like one."

Of all days I had to experiment with makeup. I silently cursed Anya while wiping the gloss off my lips, then tore the earrings from my lobes. "Less hookerish?"

"Yeah." He smiled, and his entire face softened into this cute teenage guy who was only looking to get lucky.

"Listen. I'd thank you for the offer, but I'm insulted and completely creeped out." I took a peek at my watch. "I gotta catch the next bus. See ya never."

"Hey, I went about this all wrong," Aaron said. "How about some lunch? Just lunch."

I was getting hungry, but I said, "No, thanks." I kept walking at a brisk pace.

"C'mon. Let me make it up to you. I've been an asshole."

"No amount of sushi can undo that."

"Sushi, huh?" he said, batting those long lashes again. "My favorite."

• • •

It was still pouring outside, so Aaron, working hard to paint himself as a gentleman, offered to pick me up out front of Macy's, the entrance closest to his car. *Sure,* I told him, all casual, maybe a little flirty, but the moment he was out of sight I called Mary in a panic.

"Why didn't you ask me to come?" she asked, annoyed. Why do best friends always think you can't go anywhere without them, especially the mall? Sometimes, when I'm feeling the pangs of creativity, all I want to do is settle on a bench and draw while staring into a storefront window. Chatting it up with Mary only distracts me.

"Last-minute decision," I said. "Besides, I know you're further behind on *Moby-Dick* than I am. I was doing you a favor."

"Doesn't sound like a favor to me. Best friends are supposed to offer up cool alternatives to bullshit homework."

"Sorry," I said, almost whining. "But please, Mary, you have to listen to me. I need your advice."

"Shoot."

"I met this guy—"

"Thank God. Now you can throw that prick Ray back down the drain where you found him."

"Not that kind of guy."

"I'm not following you," she said, and I imagined her scrunching her eyes together like she does when she's trying to understand "what the author meant" in English class.

"You know how I've been racking my brain, trying to figure out a way to pay this PI."

"Uh-huh," she said, kind of garbled. I figured she was eating.

"I know it sounds crazy, like totally crazy, but this guy I met. He offered to pay me."

"For what?"

"What do you think?"

"No way!" She broke into a forced chuckle that instantly irritated me.

"Stop laughing, and tell me what I should do."

She got silent, and all I could hear was her breathing. "Look, Rosie, I know you want to find your mother. It's all you've talked about since we found the box last Sunday. But come on. This is nuts."

"It's not just about finding her, Mary. If I find her, maybe I'll find out why my dad lied to me. Why my stepmom's been lying to me. I have to know. And I need money to do it."

She sighed, breathed, sighed some more. I was getting anxious. Aaron would be pulling up any minute and I needed Mary's blessing. I couldn't get in his car without it.

"You're a virgin. You can't. I mean it, Rosie girl, you can't."

"But—but—" I stammered.

"Remember Eddy?"

Hearing his name turns me ice-cold. "Why would you bring him up now?"

"Because I didn't save you from that guy so you could turn around and do something like this."

Then right there—at the entrance to Macy's in the men's section with suits and ties and stiff-looking shoes—I began to whimper into my phone.

"Are you crying?"

"No," I said, but she knew I was.

"You see how upset you're getting? Blow this guy off. We'll find another way."

"There is no other way, Mary."

"There's another way."

An idea springs inside, one I hope she's hinting at. "You'll reconsider asking your dad about working at the store?"

"Absofuckinglutely not. Sorry, Rosie girl, but I can't give him any reason to keep his boot on my neck. He may treat my mother like a punching bag, but not me."

"A what?" I asked.

"Never mind." She paused, and I heard a deep sigh. "I just can't ask him."

"Well, I don't know what to do," I said, the panic rising in my throat. "I need to start making money now."

"So you'll put off hiring that PI. Come over. We'll hash this out."

"No!" I snapped. "She may be waiting for me!"

"Rosie, come on . . . ," Mary chided, as if I'd just said the craziest thing ever. But I didn't care what she thought. I wasn't going to put off anything. I wiped my nose on my sleeve as a black Mustang pulled up with Aaron behind the wheel. His windshield wipers banged back and forth, full speed. With one hand, he motioned for me to come out.

"I gotta go. He's here."

"Don't hang up!"

"I have to go. He's waiting. And it's raining. And I have to go." I was rambling. Was I slurring? I felt a weird sensation in my eyes, my head, like I was maybe getting a migraine. "Mary?" I asked, because I thought the phone had gone dead. There was a weird silence between us, a shift in energy that had me clutching the door handle without opening it. I rested my head against the glass, the phone still to my ear.

"Rosie, I'm here. Listen to me. You can't do this," she said. "But I can."

"What?"

"I'll do it. The some other way I just mentioned. We'll earn the money together."

. . .

Turned out Aaron liked her better, anyway. He thought I seemed a little prissy, and Mary, with her gutter tongue and raspberry gloss, proved more worthy of his money.

She met us at Bagsburg Park. By the time we got there, it had not only stopped raining, but the sky had cleared to powder blue and the sun pierced boldly through cotton-ball clouds. It was the kind of afternoon that drove people to parks like this and had them eating lunch on blankets. But we weren't here for lunch.

Aaron gave me a towel from his trunk, which I used to sit on under a big shady tree. It was still hot, but a fairly good breeze blew off the lake and made it bearable. He stayed with Mary in the Mustang. I pulled out my little sketchbook, desperate for a distraction, and started working on a robe like the one I tried on in Victoria's Secret. But this one would have no lapel, no collar, maybe a single button closure at the neck.

I had never been so grateful for tinted windows, though I did find myself staring at the passenger door, ready to save Mary if she came fleeing out. But she never came fleeing out, and the whole thing was over in twelve minutes. I had timed it on my phone.

At my request, Aaron delivered us back to the mall after he made good on his sushi offer (even though it was a drive-thru joint and the fish smelled fishy). I wasn't about to have him drive us home, where Mom could ask me questions if she was in a rare give-a-crap mood. I've learned to keep the mode of transportation—both coming and going—the same. If you get in one friend's car to go somewhere, you'd better come back in that same car or it raises all sorts of questions. She knew I was taking the bus and saw me head down the sidewalk, so I knew she'd better find me walking back, too. Even having Aaron drop us off in the neighborhood would've been a risk. Who knows if Judd would have gone out for cigarettes or something, and seen me getting out of this strange guy's car? I didn't want to chance an inquisition.

So we waited for the bus in front of the food court, silent, until Mary said, "It was no big deal, so wipe that look off your face."

"What look?"

"That guilty bullshit one."

How could I not feel guilty? My best friend just had sex for money. For me.

Mary dug into her shorts pocket and pulled out a wad of cash. "Here," she said, placing three ten-dollar bills in my hand. "Your cut."

I must have flinched, because she said, "What? You didn't think I'd hand over all of it, did you? I mean, really, Rosie. I earned half, don't you think?"

"Of . . . of c-c-course." Why was I stuttering? This was totally fair, and I cursed myself for hesitating. Plus, I was surprised she had negotiated another twenty bucks on top of the extra twenty I had already insisted on after Aaron's insulting offer. But I also wasn't feeling well and suspected it was the sushi. My head hurt. I was heating up fast on the bus bench and starting to melt. Mary, too, was picking the hair from her neck, wet with sweat. Even in March, after a storm, the air was thick with moisture.

"We split it down the middle. You want to find your mom. I want to get the hell out of this fucking furnace. I want out, Rosie, out of Florida. Away from my dad. Because if the heat doesn't suffocate me, he will." She looked worse than I did, with her pale, freckled face already pink and flushed.

I felt bad for her. At least I had a shot at my goal. I wasn't so sure about Mary's. Her parents were kind of strict, religious, and had no intention of letting her take off after graduation in a few months. They weren't mean, although her father had a bit of a temper I'd seen a few times and her mom was a little strange. She wore way too much makeup and was always skittering around the house cleaning stuff that didn't look dirty. Anyway, they'd made it clear—she was going to a local college while working at her dad's hardware store, Perkins Paints. She was sick about her dismal future, and I couldn't blame her. Plus, I think there was some stuff going on between her parents that had Mary worried, but whenever I brought it up, she quickly changed the subject.

I grabbed her hand. "Are you okay? 'Cause I'm not."

"Don't get all sappy on me, Rosie. If we're going to do this, we need some rules."

We hadn't had time to discuss the possibility of continuing this craziness, but obviously she'd been thinking about it.

"Rules?"

"Yeah, like don't ask me how I'm doing after. That will be rule number one."

"Okay," I said, grateful she was taking the lead on this. She could have whatever rules she wanted. I turned to her so she'd know she had my full attention.

"Rule number two. I'm never meeting a guy by myself. If I get hacked up into a million pieces, we both lose."

"Mary!" I smacked her arm. "That should be rule number one."

"Rule number three. Whatever I do with the money is my business. Don't question me."

"But you want to leave, right? I would never question that."

I wouldn't want to mix paint all day, either, or help someone choose the right grade of sandpaper. But I suspect there's more going on at home. There has to be.

"Things could change, Rosie girl. Remember that. Even for you. So it goes both ways. Even if you decide not to find your mother, for whatever reason, I won't hassle you. It's—"

"My business." I paused to let this all sink in, and then thanked her.

"Don't thank me. Honestly, I don't like people indebted to me, and I don't like to be indebted to people. Boot on the neck. Remember that, too."

"Okay," I said, and backed off. Then, even in the heat, even with us both sweaty and uncomfortable on the metal bench, she took one of my hands and laced her fingers with mine.

"Okay." She nodded at me. We understood each other. The ground rules had been set. We'd be all right, maybe even find a way to both get what we want. "Finally," she said, lifting me from the bench. The bus was coming, and with it the promise of ice-cold air-conditioning. "Let's get you on this thing. You look like you're gonna drop."

SO THAT'S HOW it all started. Finding the box, my dad's letter, and the plan we hatched to earn money so I could find my long-lost mother. It's what movies are made of, right? Drama, secrets, a colorful cast of characters. But this is no movie—it's my life—and it better have a happy ending. Otherwise, how can I live with what Mary and I have done?

As tired as I am, the excitement of meeting John William Brooks, PI, earlier this evening has kept me up past midnight, lying on my bed and sketching. I'm feeling so peaceful that when there's a knock on my door, I instantly become irritated. I choose to ignore it, pretend I'm sleeping, but unfortunately I've left my light on.

Another knock, softer. I don't move. It can be one of only two people, neither of which promises a good visit.

"Hey, Rosie, I know you're in there." It's Judd. "Your light's on."

"No, it's Rosie's ghost who forgot to shut it off."

Judd chuckles at my joke. I can always count on him for faking it, always trying to get into my good graces. Or something else, which makes me shudder.

"Feeling better?" he asks. I had forgotten about the little white lie I told earlier so I could slip out of here to meet John.

"Yep," I say, trying not to encourage an extended stay with anything more than a one-word answer.

"You sure?"

"Yes, Judd. I'm fine." Four words. Oh, well.

"Just checking."

Oh my God. Is he going to leave or not? "Good night," I say, hoping he'll move on.

"Can I come in?" he asks.

"Why?"

"I want to show you something," he says.

Please, Lord. Don't let it be something in his pants.

"I'm studying," I say. Always a great excuse.

"It'll only take a minute. Two, tops."

I check myself. "Hold on." I'm fully covered by my night-shirt, but that's not enough armor, so I pull on a pair of sweat-pants and a robe. I crack open the door. He jams his face into the narrow space like Jack Nicholson in *The Shining*. I jerk backward, away from his stubbly beard and garlic-chicken breath. "What is it?"

"What do you think?" He forces his arm through the slim opening and when I look down there's an open jewelry box in the palm of his hand.

"For me?" I ask, hoping to mask the shock.

"No, it's for Lucy," he says, like I'm an idiot. You can't even joke with this guy, he's so thick.

A not-too-shabby diamond ring sits nestled in a black velvet pillow. My heart lurches, thinking of the ring Ray gave me. It wasn't a diamond, but it still sparkled and he said the blue sapphire stone matched my eyes. Before he'd given it to me, had Ray shown someone, too, hoping to impress them?

"Uh . . ." I'm not sure what to say, because I know what this means. Judd the Dud is going to pop the question. "It's pretty."

"Do you think she'll like it?"

"Why wouldn't she?" The question is rhetorical. We're not friends. We barely like each other, and yet here he is, asking for . . . what—my honest opinion?

"Come on, Rosie." He squints at me with his dead blue eyes.

"I said it's pretty." Pause. "She has to say yes first."

"I'm not worried," he says. "Hey, can I come in?"

I'm still clutching the door frame, ready to slam it shut if he makes one wrong move. Even though he's been with my mom for over three years, I still don't trust him. And the older I get, the more I sense him ogling my body. Something about Judd has always given me the willies.

"I told you—I'm studying." I grab my World History textbook from the dresser and wave the heavy tome between us. I really should be studying because I've got a sneaking feeling we've got a quiz tomorrow.

His face drops and he snaps the jewelry box shut. "Fine. Just wanted your blessing."

"You have it," I say flatly. Honestly, how much enthusiasm does this guy want? Why would this be any kind of good news for me? As her husband, he's only going to further push me to the edges of any relationship I have with my mom. Those few months before she found Judd were actually the best we had. Crying through movies we sought to escape in; banging out chopsticks on Dad's piano even though neither of us knew how to play; going through his clothes he hadn't fit into in years and chuckling about the weight he'd put on. This ring meant she was officially moving on—probably without me.

I'm about to close the door when he grabs it and says, "You would've had plenty of time to study if you hadn't snuck out."

I refuse to fess up. "I have no idea what you're talking about."

"Next time"—Judd motions with his head to my bedroom window—"you may want to put the screen back," he says, and slithers down the hall.

10

TODD IS GIVING ME dirty looks. At first, I think he's just aggravated that I got a B on today's World History quiz and he scraped by with a D. Everyone else did pretty well, especially Paula, who's basking in the glory of her first A. I turn away and return my attention to the two answers I got wrong. But when I look over at him again, he flicks out his tongue and swipes his upper lip with it. Shocked, I spin around in my seat, certain I'm blushing. Then a sickening thought pops into my muddled brain. Did he see me yesterday, hiding behind the corner when he and Mary parted ways?

When I mentioned that I thought he was cute (while he was with Mary), I failed to add that for the past few months we've been kind of flirting and using our grades as a springboard. Not that there's any real competition between us. Todd isn't the greatest student. I'm pretty good and can pull off a fairly decent grade without burying my head in a book to get it. But the way he's looking at me now doesn't feel flirty. It just feels . . . dirty.

For the remainder of class, I don't look at him. It's hard to concentrate (but let's face it, World History is always a challenge), and when the bell signals our freedom, I make a beeline for the door. He's quick. One giant leap and Todd's able to block my path.

"What's the rush?" he asks. He's wearing his school football jersey like a trophy, like he's some big shot, when in reality he's the team's third-string quarterback who's never seen a minute on the field.

"Lunch. Someone's waiting for me."

"Got a hot date?"

"Maybe." I can do coy. I've never really had a "hot date." Even dates with Ray were only lukewarm. You can ask him, and he'd tell you in a sarcastic tone that would paint me as a prudish girlfriend he was smart to get rid of. Maybe I was. Just because I was crazy about him didn't make me crazy enough to lose my virginity to him. Eddy had ruined that for me. There was no doubt I was going to wait until I was married, when vows had been made and I'd been chosen as a mate for life.

"You mean 'probably.'" Todd's devilish grin confuses me.

"Whatever." I try to blow past him. The whole tongue-flicking thing kind of turned me off. Innocent flirting is more my speed—a wink here, a longish gaze there. Besides, I know Mary's waiting at our spot near the faculty parking lot, beneath a gigantic tree that provides privacy and shade. Today's menu: Hot Pockets she swears will still be hot from microwaving them this morning. Says the foil keeps them warm. The thought makes my mouth water, another reason to get moving.

"Hey, what's your problem?" he asks.

"Nothing, Todd. What's yours? Are you angry that I got a B and you got a D? I asked if you wanted to study together."

He narrows his eyes. "No, you didn't."

I thought I did. I say a lot of things to Todd when we're flirting. "Well, maybe we should."

"Should what?"

"Start studying together."

"Studying?" he asks, as if I've proposed the wildest idea ever. He fist-bumps two guys as they pass us, says he'll meet them in the cafeteria. "You're kinda nuts, you know that?"

I think of his tongue flicking and say, "And you're kinda nasty."

He grabs my wrist, and when I look into his eyes, there's a familiar angry gloss to them. Why do guys get so mad when they don't like your response? A flash of Ray—shoving me aside when I'd stopped his hands from crawling into my panties—has me yanking free of his grasp, and I punch him near his right shoulder.

"Hey, that's my throwing arm!" he says, which of course I knew. He rubs it while trying to laugh, but I'm sure it hurts. I made sure to dig some fingernails in there.

Paula had been hovering near us and says, "Like it would make a difference, Ryser. You'd still suck."

I appreciate the backup and link arms with her to leave, giggling in that conspiratorial way that pisses guys off. But once we're out of class, I drop Paula's arm and start walking ahead of her.

"Hey!" she calls out after me. "Where are you going?"

I don't answer her. I don't even turn around to wave goodbye. My legs can't carry me fast enough, down the hall, the stairs, and outside where I can shake off whatever just happened.

• • •

Mary's already eating, camped on her backpack beneath the tree. A toasty May afternoon has driven everyone else inside, which is fine by me. Let them all eat frozen fish sticks at sticky cafeteria tables. I'd prefer to be outside any day. Mary indulges me since she hates the heat. She's already piled her long hair into a knot on top of her head.

"Those things really still hot?" I ask.

"See for yourself." She tosses one at me and I almost drop it. "They're not called Hot Pockets for nothing."

I take a bite, careful not to burn my tongue. "I don't think you should meet any more guys from school," I say, tossing my backpack on the ground and sitting down next to her.

"Why not?"

"'Cause Todd was all weird in World History."

"News flash—Todd Ryser is weird, period."

"No, he's not," I shoot back, the part of me that's attracted to him rearing up in defense. I don't think Mary would be too happy if she knew I had a thing for him, so I quickly add, "I think he saw me."

"What do you mean?" Mary hands me a cold water bottle, which I immediately uncap. The cool liquid feels great going down my throat.

"Yesterday. When I was hiding behind the wall."

"No way," she says dismissively, and takes a swig of her own water bottle. "You've gotten good, Rosie girl. You're fucking stealth."

As confident as Mary is, I'm not convinced. "There are plenty of guys outside of school. Ones who don't know us. Why did we set up that online account if we're just going to take risks like this?"

"I can't help it that these guys trolled the Internet for sex and stumbled across our page. It is set up to be 'geographically accommodating,'" Mary says, mocking one of the website's promises. "You're being paranoid. It's only been two guys from Del Vista—Todd and Ivan."

One more bite and the Hot Pocket is gone. "And that's all it will be." I grab both of her hands in mine and give her the death stare. "I mean it, Mary. No more guys from school."

"Wow, what happened between you two?"

"Nothing." I'm afraid to tell her more—that our flirting turned sour and may have aggravated him to the point of squealing to the cops. For all I know, he thinks we're running some grand prostitution ring. Who knows what crazy things hormonal guys do?

"Fine. No more Del Vista Devils." Mary pulls a napkin from the bag and wipes her chin. "Jesus, it's hot out here. The things I do for you . . ."

"You want to go sit in that disgusting cafeteria? Be my guest."

"Stop," she says, knowing I'm on the verge of a mood. The

swift turn with Todd from friendly to frosty has left me irritated. "Here. This ought to cheer you up, calm you down, or whatever." Mary hands over a pouch of chocolate-covered cherries. They're my favorite, even when they're melted, like now.

"Thanks." I pop two in my mouth.

Mary rests against the tree, fanning herself with a notebook. A group of teachers piles out of a single car, growling about returning to class. Seems students don't have the lock on dreading school.

"Adults are so fucking bitter," she says, and we take a moment to digest her truth. I eat two more cherries, then finish my water.

"Speaking of adults, how did it go last night with the PI extraordinaire?"

"He's pretty cool, I guess."

"Did he show you his badge?"

"Private detectives don't have badges. They're not the police."

"Then identification of some sort?"

Come to think of it, he had asked all sorts of questions about me, but I hadn't asked John one about him. Only if he could locate my mother. "Yeah, he showed me something that looked like a driver's license," I lie. "Anyway, he needs more than the picture I gave him."

"That makes sense."

"I'll have to give him the birth certificate, too."

"Make a copy first."

"Of course," I say, even though I hadn't planned to. Mary's always been savvier than me.

"I'd have him sign some sort of paper for everything."

"Like a receipt?"

"Yeah, to show that he's kept your stuff," she says, rolling her eyes.

I hadn't thought of any of this, but Mary's right. What's to say he wouldn't just keep everything, lose it in a closet somewhere, and then say he doesn't know anything about anything when I try to claim it?

"Okay," I say. "I'll get a receipt."

"Seems like you're putting a lot of faith in this guy."

I know this tone, the one suspicious of adults. Mary suspects her parents snoop through her bedroom when she's at school and go online to check every move she makes on her cell phone. I don't have that issue with Lucy—at least I don't think I do.

Mary wipes away strands of hair sticking to her neck and complains again about the heat.

"I have to have faith in this guy," I repeat. "He's my only hope."

"So you're going to hand him the box with a bright red bow on top?"

"No," I say, quick to tell her that I have no intention of giving him the box. "What's your problem?"

"I just want to make sure he's not taking you for a ride."

"Beggars can't be choosy," I say. "It's not like I had my pick of PIs eager to take my case. I'm also underage, so that's another strike against me. John was cool and postdated the contract to May twenty-ninth."

"Is that legit?" she asks, on the verge of totally annoying me when my cell vibrates in my backpack.

I race to get it from the side pocket. "It's him." I read John's text aloud.

Need to meet. Lou's @ 8?

Mary covers the screen with her hand, preventing me from responding right away. "Get your shit together, Rosie. I mean it. Faith can blind people sometimes."

"Or light the way," I say, while tapping out **Sure. C u where the pie flies.**

11

IT'S EIGHT FIFTEEN on a Thursday night, and Lou's is empty except for a guy wolfing down a giant hamburger at the counter. I feel his eyes on me as I make my way to the same booth John and I shared last night.

All day I've been nervous about this meeting. It's impossible that John would have any news in only twenty-four hours, especially since I hadn't given him any more pieces to the puzzle yet. So it's another kind of news—the bad kind.

When I reach him, there is no mug of steaming anything on the table. A sweating glass of water with a lemon floating on top holds his attention. The moment he rises, my fears are confirmed. He's wearing a heavy, tired look, not the friendly one he greeted me with last night.

I toss my backpack into the booth and slide in. "What's wrong?"

"What makes you think something's wrong?"

"You don't seem quite as cheery as you did last night."

"Really?" He pops a big smile and his crinkled nose forces his cheeks into large, ruddy circles. "Is that better?"

"No. Tell me what's going on."

The smile drops, leaving behind a set of sad gray eyes. He fiddles with the loose tie around his neck, then steeples his hands in front of him.

"Can I get you something, hon?" The waitress has appeared, ready to take my order.

With a hangdog expression, John asks me, "Piece of pie?" I shake my head, and he politely dismisses her, says, "Maybe later.

"Remember that big case I had been working on? The one I was into when you first contacted me a couple months ago."

I nod, bracing myself.

"Got split wide open again."

I drop my head and start picking at the chipped Formica along the table's edge. I'm pouting but don't care.

"You knew I was worried about this, but you reassured me."

He makes a fist and props up the right side of his face with it. "I know. I'm sorry. This happens sometimes. You think something's sealed up tight and then it—"

"Gets split wide open," I mock. "So now what? I assume you rip up the contract and give me my money back."

"Well, I could do that," he says, and rakes his hand through his sandy brown hair. "Or I could pass on your case to someone else."

"I want you." It just comes out, whiny and desperate. No one can beat this gentle giant.

"I'm sorry, Rosie. Really, I am. But I can still help you find your mother."

Totally resigned, knowing he's my only option, I ask, "How?"

John motions to the burger wolfer at the counter who's spun around on his stool, wiping his mouth with a napkin. He waves sheepishly at me with the other hand. "That's how."

. . .

"This is Mac," John says, scooting over to make room for him.

"Nice to meet you," he says, extending a hand across the table. I shake it, but weakly. The name rolls around like a marble, pinging with familiarity in my head. Let's see. There's the Big Mac at McDonald's. Mac computers. MAC makeup. He looks about my age, with wavy brown hair to his shoulders and not an ounce of stubble on his face. When he walked over to our table I was able to make a quick style assessment—stiff khakis with a belt, an equally stiff green polo shirt, and boat shoes with socks. Not exactly a fashion plate.

He's brought his soda with him and slurps it through a straw. I don't want to like him because he's replaced John, the first person who's given me hope in a long time. But I can like his eyes. And possibly the hair, even though it's a little long for my taste.

"Mac here goes to the University of Miami," John says.

"Congratulations," I say, nice and pissy.

John ignores my attitude and then surprises me by wrapping a long thick arm around this guy. "Yeah, I'm pretty proud of my nephew." He gives Mac's shoulder a squeeze when he follows up with, "Go, Canes!"

"Your nephew?" What kind of operation is this?

"Took him under my wing years ago, right, Mac?"

Mac nods. "Yes, sir."

Yikes. This guy is as stiff as his clothes. He probably wears a suit to mow the lawn.

"I've gotten Mac up to speed. He's ready to take over."

As certain as John seems, I'm still on the fence. Just because this guy has the best green eyes I've ever seen doesn't mean they're trained to find long-lost relatives.

John squeezes Mac's shoulder again, maybe too hard, because I catch Mac wince and then laugh it off. "You two good?" he asks.

"Yes, Uncle John. We'll be fine." He offers a confident smile meant for us both.

"Then I'm off," John declares, starting to nudge Mac aside.

"Wait!" There I go again, unable to hide my anxiety. "Do you really have to go?"

"Rosie," he says, reaching across the table for my hand. "You'll be fine. I promise. And you're not losing me altogether. Anything Mac needs, I'll do my best to assist, but I can't take the lead on this." He releases my hand. "Now I'm going to skedaddle so the two of you can get to know each other."

I watch John leave, his big, lumbering body growing smaller as he crosses the restaurant and pushes through both doors to exit. I feel like a child watching a parent who's getting on a train and never coming back. And then it's just me and this guy Mac.

"So, how often do you get your uncle's leftovers?" I ask.

"Not often," he says, draining his soda. "Only when he thinks I can handle a case with the investigative tools I've already acquired."

"You look like you're sixteen," I snap. "There's no way you could even have a toolbox yet."

"I'm twenty. A junior at UM, double majoring in criminology and psychology. Plus, I've already satisfied a minor in political science." He twirls a finger in a circular motion next to the side of his head. "I'm learning how the mind works, so it will make me the best kind of investigator."

He's no slouch; he wants me to know that. University of Miami is a premier private school in the heart of Coral Gables. The only people at my high school who have applied there are at the top of our class.

"Just because you're book-smart, doesn't mean you're street-smart," I challenge him.

"I guess that's true," he says, "but my mom, Uncle John's sister, used to be a cop."

"Your mom? Really?"

"Until she swapped her patrol car for an office in the detectives' bureau. So, as you can see, this business is in my blood. I've been hanging around my uncle's office since I was fifteen." He stretches his arm across the table, his fingers almost reaching the fabric of my shirt. "See these pores? I've absorbed everything like a sponge. He even let me take over his old partner's office when he left last year. Got it fixed up real nice, too."

Blood? Skin pores? I want John back. He instilled a confidence that had actually given me some hope. This guy Mac is only flapping his lips about himself. Nice lips, but flapping, nonetheless.

He calls over the waitress. "Hungry?"

"Didn't you just have a massive hamburger?"

"There's always room for dessert. Uncle John told me this place is famous for their pie." When the waitress arrives, he says to me, "You're a peach kind of girl, right?"

"Wrong."

"Wait. Let me guess."

The waitress rolls her eyes, in no mood for this little game, so I say, "Cherry."

"Of course," he says, and I wonder what he means by that. "Two." He holds up two fingers, nice and manicured.

"Whipped cream?" she asks.

He waits for me to answer. "None for me."

"For me," he says, trying to be cute, and when she walks away I tell him that whipped cream only ends up melting into a milky mess and ruining it.

"How many cases have you worked on with John? Specifically missing-persons cases."

"Well, according to my uncle, your mother isn't technically missing. You're just trying to find her. There's a difference."

"Answer the question." I tilt my head to the side when he remains silent a beat too long. "Am I your first?"

"Why do you say it like that?"

"Like it's a bad thing, you mean?"

He nods, staring at me with eyes the same color as his shirt—pale, faded green, like moss that clings to a tree.

"Because it is!" I can't hide my frustration and just want to leave.

"Not necessarily. Haven't you ever heard about the new broom?" Measured pause. "It sweeps clean."

I know what he's getting at, but refuse to play along.

"I'm not some old, burned-out PI who will drink away your money and lie about hitting dead ends. Not that my uncle is one of those, either," he quickly adds, although he didn't have to. I can tell John's a decent guy.

I remain silent, still skeptical.

"Give me a shot," he says earnestly. "Let me help."

The waitress delivers two plates of pie and we both dig in. He polishes off his first, then asks to see the box.

"I don't have the box, but I have the stuff that was in it." I clutch my backpack, ready to unzip it.

"That works."

"But only if you promise to treat this like a real case, not just some extracurricular school activity."

He draws an imaginary cross over his heart. "On my honor."

I pull out the Ziploc bag I'd transferred everything into before I came, keeping it close to my chest. "And only if you really believe you can help find her."

"I once found a needle in a haystack."

"Is that a family joke or something? It's not funny."

Mac hangs his shaggy head, twists his mouth into a half smile. The longer I sit here, the harder it is to deny my attraction to his boyish good looks. He's kind of the opposite of Ray, who's dark and was always fighting a losing battle with stubborn facial hair.

"You know what else isn't that funny? The business of the business," he says.

I find myself clutching the bag even tighter. "The what?"

"The business of the business. That's what my uncle calls the finance part of his company."

"And he wants you to do it? Let me guess. You're actually a triple major, getting a degree in accounting, too."

This has him breaking into a full smile, giving me a glimpse of two straight rows of nice white teeth. I imagine he's the kind of person who goes every six months to the dentist, whether he needs a cleaning or not. "No. No accounting for me. But if I want to become a partner one day, I need to learn all aspects of the job, and his fee is one of them."

"Well, he took everything I had last night."

"That's what he told me." Mac pauses, an idea seemingly stuck in his throat. "Which got me wondering how you were going to pay his subsequent bills."

I hope my face doesn't flush at the answer I have no intention of giving him. He probably wouldn't be too keen to learn how I made the money to pay his uncle's retainer fee and probably less keen to learn we're going to keep it up until my mother's found. I scrape up the last bits of crust to fill the silence.

"No, not wondering—considering," he clarifies. "Considering an alternative plan." He's got a solution. I see it dancing in those mossy-green eyes of his. But he's busy scraping up the last of his whipped cream and licking the fork clean. Finally, he says, "Don't worry. I'm here to help." He slides his plate to the side and clasps his hands in front of him, back to business. "We can work something out, I'm sure."

Did he just wink at me? I hadn't thought anything of it earlier, but was he trying to peek down my shirt—Ray's shirt—when he first sat down?

"Of course." I nod knowingly. "There's always the barter system, isn't there?" I shove the Ziploc bag in the knapsack again.

"What are you talking about?" Mac asks.

"Hooking up. I get it." Oh, the irony. If he only knew. But it hasn't been me doing the dirty deed, and no matter how not-terrible-looking he is, it never will be. "Thanks for the pie, but no thanks for the deal." I drop my fork so it clangs on the plate. Bits of cherry sauce fly up and land on Mac's shirt.

He either doesn't notice or doesn't care because he softly says, "Wait," before I take off. He slides out of the booth so we're both standing. "That's not what I was implying. How could you ever think that?"

Uh, because that's all guys ever want in exchange for favors, that's how. But he seems legitimately insulted.

"Let me ask you something, and be honest." When I hesitate, he continues. "I mean it, Rosie. I need honesty."

I nod begrudgingly.

"What can you afford to pay?"

I'm not prepared for this question. Honestly, I don't know. How long can Mary and I keep doing this? I feel sick, fearing I haven't thought things through. A retainer was one thing. How did I think I'd be able to continue to pay a private investigator for his work?

I must look weak and wobbly because Mac is guiding me back into the booth, saying, "Come on. Sit back down." He signals a waitress and asks for a glass of water. I know it's for me.

"Let me put it this way: If you can't afford to pay, then you won't. The agency has done pro bono work before."

I know what *pro bono* means, even though I can see he's studying my face to see if I do. It's what I was originally hoping for since I had no money, but none of the investigators I called made the offer. "Your uncle will never go for it. He—"

"Will be proud of me for volunteering my services to a young lady in need."

"Look. I don't mean to be ungrateful . . ." Mary's words are swimming in my ears—all that stuff about being indebted to people. As much as this seems like a gift, I'm not so sure. I push aside the straw and finish my water with a final gulp. "Can I let you know?"

"You can," he says, all proper, dipping his head like he understands.

We say our goodbyes, but I leave the booth first. I imagine him watching me walk through the diner and out the door that jingles as I pass through it.

12

I CALLED MARY the minute I left the deli, but she preferred
to hash this out face-to-face. Said this was way too much to
discuss over the phone, especially after I mentioned Mac's
eyes more than twice. So here we are at her house on a Friday
night, sharing a culinary feast of popcorn and gummy bears.

"Sounds too good to be true," Mary says, chewing on a kernel. I tell her to be careful, it could crack a tooth. So she spits
it back into the bowl and I tell her she's gross. The bowl sits
between us on her bed where we're both stretched out, stacks of
pillows behind our backs.

"Which part?" I ask.

"All of it. The hot guy. The free lunch."

"Lunch? We only had pie."

"It's a saying, Rosie. There ain't no such thing as a free
lunch. Want my two cents?"

"Obviously. I can't make this decision without you," I say,
because we're a package.

"Don't take him up on it. We can afford this guy. Besides, if he's half as good as he says he is—plus the help of
his uncle who, according to you, said he'd be available for

whatever—then he shouldn't need all that much time to find your mom."

I suck on a lime gummy bear until it dissolves in my mouth. "I guess so. I mean, I hope so."

Mary's hair is still damp from her shower, and it falls in a straight dark sheet over the shoulders of a blue cotton shirt. I could never leave my hair free like that. If it isn't blow-dried and tamed immediately, all hell breaks loose. My only saving grace when it's wet is to knot it into a bun, which minimizes the frizz and creates some decent waves.

"Do you really want to owe him? Remember what I said about being indebted to someone. Totally blows."

"I did remember, which is why I told him I wanted to think about it," I say, as a disturbing thought occurs to me. "But aren't I sort of indebted to you?"

"Absolutely not. I'm benefiting from this little arrangement, too." She scoops up a handful of popcorn. "We have a good thing going, don't you think? Screwing guys for cash, or . . ." Mary makes a wicked grin. "Screwing guys *out* of their cash. I kinda like it."

"You do?"

"I'm not digging ditches."

"Seriously, Mary. We can stop. We've been given an out here."

"You've forgotten an important thing, which is sort of selfish on your part, but I won't bust your chops." Mary moves so she's sitting up with her legs crossed. She means business. "If we stop, the money stops, and there goes my plan to blow this joint." She scans her bedroom, her gaze resting on the corkboard above her desk, plastered with things we've gathered these past couple years—ticket stubs, pictures, menus, and loads of junky bracelets held up by thumbtacks.

"You're going to miss me if you leave," I say.

"Yeah, but not this place. I'm literally suffocating here."

"Your parents aren't that terrible." I flick a dismissive hand near her face. "Have you peeked inside my house lately?"

Mary's face turns grim in two seconds flat. "Look, Rosie, there are things you don't know. Things I haven't told you. Just trust me. It's better if I go."

"What things? We've been best friends for over three years. And now you're telling me you've been keeping stuff from me? Serious stuff that has you wanting to run away?" I feel a sting of betrayal, since I've never kept anything from Mary. "I thought you just didn't want to stay and work in your dad's store."

"That part's true."

"But what else? Tell me."

"It doesn't matter, Rosie. Besides, you're getting off topic and killing my sugar buzz." She polishes off the remaining gummies, then says, "I want to continue. If you don't want to fork over your half to one of the Hardy Boys, be my guest. Rule number three—it's none of my business what you do with your share."

Maybe I am being selfish. As long she's okay with it, I should be okay with it, too. And the more I think about it, twirling lemon gummies with my tongue, I don't want to feel some sort of blind gratitude to a guy who wears boat shoes with socks and piles whipped cream on a perfectly good piece of cherry pie.

Mary plops back down, throws a piece of popcorn in the air, and actually manages to catch it in her open mouth.

I love our Friday-night sleepovers. When there isn't a party we feel like crashing, or a new teen club to check out, we kick back and stuff ourselves with junk food and watch slasher flicks. And we always do it at Mary's house because her parents belong to a church group that plays poker on Friday nights.

I'm feeling a little better about my decision not to take Mac up on his offer. I prepare two bowls of ice cream, then meet Mary on the living room couch for a movie. We've just settled in when my phone buzzes in my lap. It's a text from a number I don't recognize, and I shoot Mary a look; she's already checking out my screen.

Tod gave me ur nuber

Everyone's guilty of typos, but this guy's extra-sloppy. Or nervous. I wait for more, tell Mary to pause the movie. Then I scroll through my earlier texts to check this number against the one from last night, the one from the guy who wanted to meet in an abandoned strip mall. They're different, so I text back.

Okay

There's no reason to ask for the code, since clearly he's not going to have one. I just hope he's not another guy from school. I don't care what Mary says. Del Vista stairwells are too risky.

Wanna hook up?

Mary and I are reading the texts together, and she gives me a thumbs-up.

"Are you sure?" I ask.

"Tell him eighty bucks."

"Seriously?"

"Yeah, why not?"

So I text him back: **$80**

Tod tld me 60

I slide my phone off. "Put the movie back on."

"What are you doing?" Mary asks, trying to grab my phone.

"I'm not negotiating for you like a used car. The price is the price. Forget it. Besides, this is nice," I say, gazing around the dimly lit room and focusing on the two bowls of mint chocolate chip in front of us. Our feet are bare, entangled on the coffee table. Her mom would definitely pitch a fit about that.

Mary looks stunned. Or annoyed. I'm not sure. "You're going to get all sanctimonious now?"

"What?"

"We just agreed twenty minutes ago that we'd keep going. You started all this—"

"Uh, no. You started all this. You offered."

"Because you needed me. You were fucking hysterical when you called me from the mall."

"I was not!"

"Trust me, you were. Crying like a little baby because some guy wanted to pay you to get it on with him."

hey u there? Another text, and this time, Mary successfully grabs my phone and taps in a response.

She tosses it back in my lap, says, "Let's go."

I read the exchange.

Mary: **80.**

His reply: 👍

We share a tense, silent bus ride to this guy's house, which is in a decent neighborhood about fifteen minutes away. I use the time to process the information he provided to the rest of my screening questions. He is a friend of Todd's, but doesn't go to Del Vista. He's a jug head at some military school in Ocala. I imagine him with a buzz cut and lean muscles that have been on the receiving end of an instructor's baton.

Now, I've said it before: Location is key. No abandoned strip malls. No beaches. No warehouses. A girl could get into serious trouble in those kinds of places. But in the backyard of some guy's house? A scream across the lawn could reach the neighbors in a matter of seconds, plus I'd be crouching in a nearby bush with some bug spray, anyway. It's half the price of pepper spray, and if it can take down nuclear-disaster-surviving roaches, it can take down some guy who can't take no for an answer.

Once the bus drops us off, at a stop that should only be a few blocks from his house, Mary ends the silence. "Sorry."

"Me, too," I say, even though I don't know what I'm sorry for. I just wanted to eat ice cream and watch teenagers get stabbed to death in their own homes.

She dips her head and smiles at me. Her hair shines in the moonlight, silky and straight, oblivious to the humidity. People say I should be grateful for my thick hair, but it's hard to be grateful for something that causes you so much aggravation. I smooth back a set of stubborn curls that refuse to be part of my ponytail.

"Was I really crying like a baby?" I ask, trying to remember that day two months ago. The memory's blurry but still manages to sting.

"Yeah, but it's okay. You're soft like that. If Aaron had propositioned me, I would've been like, Let's go, dude."

I bat her arm. "You would not!"

"Maybe not with such gusto, but opportunities are rare in this world, Rosie girl, and when they come your way, you gotta grab 'em. By the goddamned throat, you know?"

I'm not sure if this whole thing is an opportunity or a disaster. As much as Mary's been on board, I've never lost the nagging feeling that this is somehow going to end badly. We seem to be playing with fire, and you know how that usually turns out. So now, as we're walking along the street at eleven o'clock at night, I'm afraid of getting burned. This causes a swift panic and has me reconsidering Mac's offer. I take Mary's hand, prepared to turn around, when she stops and says, "This is it. Not bad."

Not bad at all. The house is a big two-story with a wide circular driveway lined on either side by palm trees. A newish Cadillac sits near the front door, lit up by two sconces on a wall, its rocky surface etched with ivy.

Glad Mary stuck to her guns and got the eighty bucks. Clearly, this kid can afford it.

He told her to meet him around back, in the shed. Based on the house, I'm now imagining it more of a small guest house used for storage than a shack with tools. Mary tiptoes around the side of the house to scout the location. She signals to me that the shed is on her side, so I go to the other side of the house and jam myself between a hedge and a wall. The concrete is unfinished and scrapes against my soft cotton tank. I know I'll have to dump it after seeing the damage. Already I hate this guy for ruining one of my favorite shirts.

I move sticks and leaves out of my way. The hedge is dense, but if I keep my head just right, I have a pretty clear view.

Someone emerges from the shed before Mary reaches the door. He's been waiting for her. Under the moonlight, on a freshly mowed lawn, they exchange words I can't hear. They both enter the shed, Mary first. Something about the way he ushered her in there bothers me. Like a predator who'd been waiting for its prey, not just some guy waiting to get lucky. He watches her enter. I wonder if this is it—if this will be the time something goes terribly wrong. I don't understand why I'm so spooked. Maybe it's that rickety shed, how it looks like something out of a Chainsaw Massacre movie. I realize I can't hang back here, so I decide to risk it and move closer.

It looks nothing like a small guesthouse. I was wrong about that. It's one of those old-school sheds built out of wood. It rests on a concrete slab, but must not have been constructed too well, because the entire frame tilts to the side and a series of rusty nails poke out at odd angles. I walk around the back, hoping my sandals aren't crunching through the grass as loudly as I think they are. There's a window on the back side. I hoist myself up on the chain-link fence to see through it.

On the way up, I scrape my knee on the scratchy metal and squelch a whimper. Once I've settled onto the top rail, I find the glass is blurry and dirty. There's a hole in the bottom, probably the result of a wayward baseball. The view isn't great, but it'll do.

It's dark inside until he pulls on a piece of heavy string in front of him, and then the shed is full of a dull orange glow. I get a good look at him. No wonder he's paying eighty dollars for sex. This guy needs to pay. His face is covered in acne, bright and red with tiny white bumps. Above hooded eyes are brows so sparse they seem to have been shaven clean off. I was right about the buzz cut, but didn't imagine the lightning bolts carved into the sides of his head. In both earlobes, flat black discs serve as spacers for larger future discs. I didn't know a military school would allow stuff like that. A cross dangles at the bottom of a chain around his neck. He's wearing a white tank top and jeans hanging so low, half his boxer shorts show. Ready to play.

When he opens his mouth to speak, I'm surprised I can hear him. Many thanks to the hole in the window and the person who put it there. "Raphael, but everyone calls me Ralph," he says, and makes a lame attempt to shake Mary's hand. She brushes his fingers with hers.

"Hey," she says. No names for us. That's part of the deal. I mean, we've made some up if we're pushed: One of my favorite designers is Coco Chanel, so we split it up. I'm Coco and she's Chanel, but we've never used them.

"I don't get to know your name?" Ralph crinkles his pimply nose.

"What for?" She flips on a winning smile. It's one of her best assets, since her teeth are pearly white and straight, and when her lips curl wide the gloss stretches across them like a raspberry slide.

But the smile doesn't work. He appears confused and cocks his head. That's when I notice he kind of looks like a dog—a bloodhound, maybe, with those droopy red eyes. But an irritated bloodhound because the acne makes him look angry. He turns the bolt on the rickety door to lock it.

"You don't have to do that," Mary says, flipping the bolt the other way.

"You want someone walking in on us?"

"Who'd be coming into a shed now?" Mary snickers while making another attempt to unlock the bolt.

"Relax," he says, which is a command that always has the opposite effect on people. "I'll put this down." He pulls a scratchy-looking blue blanket from a broken shelf. Then he grabs a bag of mulch and places it at one end of the blanket. I guess that's supposed to act as a pillow. He appears proud of this makeshift bed and extends his arms. "After you."

"We can just do it here, like, standing up—" Nothing fancy for Mary. Stairwells, sheds, it makes no difference.

"Suit yourself." He stands back, crosses his spindly arms over his chest. "You gonna take that off?" he asks, pointing at the black cotton tank dress she threw on before we left.

Mary says this is the worst part, when she has to get crafty about keeping her clothes on. Getting naked would kill any possibility of a swift escape. Besides, she says the guys couldn't care less if she stays clothed. A grope here, a touch there—that's all they need.

"I can just lift it up," she offers, reaching down for the hem of her dress.

"Well, that's no fun," he says. He pulls the undershirt over his head, revealing a pale chest with dark, hairy nipples. I catch a glimpse of Mary's face and know she wants to leave. "Come here."

Mary inches closer, her ballet flats sliding with dread against the concrete floor.

"Payment first," she says, holding out a palm. Mary always asks for money up front so that if she ever decides to scrub the mission, we're at least compensated for my time and her suffering. It happened once, which is why it became rule number five.

"After." He leans in and tries to kiss her, but she turns away. "No kissing."

"What?" He backs up, insulted.

"No kissing," she repeats. "That's my rule."

"Then no standing. That's my rule." Ralph takes her hand and pulls her down onto the blue blanket. Now I have to crane my neck to see what's going on, and I lean closer to the shed wall. "Take off your underwear."

She does, then balls it up and jams it into her purse she's kept close by. He wipes the sweat from his forehead. It's hot out here—it must be like an oven in there. His hand disappears under her dress as he tucks his head into her neck.

"No." She bats his hand away, maybe a little too hard.

"For fuck's sake! What's with you?" Ralph has just crossed the line. I mean *the* line. It happened with Ray when I'd let his eager hands go only so far before pushing them back.

"Sex. That's it. No touching. You knew that."

"I didn't know shit."

Uh-oh. Once a guy gets mad, it's tough to make a U-turn.

Mary tilts her head, offers up another smile to placate him. She doesn't need some nut job losing his marbles in a toolshed. Any one of the items hanging along the wall could be used to bludgeon her to death.

She needs to calm him, and she does. "Come on." Her voice is soft and sugary. Mary reaches over and touches the bulge in his jeans. He responds immediately, pushing her over so that she's pinned beneath him. He tries to kiss her, but she turns away.

"Stop!"

"Kiss me," he says. "It gets me superhard."

Mary shoves him off, pushes down her dress.

"What are you doing?"

"Leaving," she says, and when Mary leans down to get her purse, I see what she doesn't. Ralph has already popped up and barricaded the door with his body.

"No, you're not."

"Move." Her back is to me, hands planted on hips. "I reserve the right to leave at any time."

"You're some professional," Ralph mocks. "With all your rules and shit."

"And you're some horny fisherman who's just lost his catch."

I don't know if I would've egged him on like that, but Mary's braver than I am.

He doesn't budge from the door. She inches forward, clutching her purse. Sensing the heat of a threat, I'm ready to move in if I have to. I don't know what I'd do, but at least we'd outnumber this guy. Plus, I've got a mean bite. I've used it before.

"Look, Ralph," Mary says, back to her warm-glazed-doughnut voice. "It's nothing personal. Sometimes this just doesn't work out."

Ralph's face remains stony, which is good. He's thinking about what she said, maybe even agreeing with her. She waits— the right thing to do. Give this guy a minute to come to terms with this sudden change of plans.

"No hard feelings, okay?" Mary actually touches his shoulder.

I think she's successfully put out the fire until he says, "I've got hard feelings all right," and forces her hand onto the zipper of his jeans. He grabs the thin shoulder strap of her dress and uses it to tug her close. "You're gonna kiss me."

"No, I'm not!" She wrenches out of his grasp and lunges for the rusty knob, but the door's locked. I want to go in there but force myself to follow rule number four—no barging in unless she calls out to me for help. One time I did that, and Mary became furious, claiming she had things under control. We blew the whole thing and the guy bolted without paying (another reason to follow rule number five and get payment first).

It doesn't look like Mary has things under control now, yet she does manage to flip the bolt. The door cracks open, but Ralph is quick and slams it shut before she can escape.

"You're a tease, you know that?" His face grows angrier. "Now get down on the floor and take off that stupid dress." He pushes her. She slides next to the blanket, but not onto it.

How is she going to get out of this? I free my sandals from where I've secured them in the fence, ready to save her and screw rule number four. Then I hear Mary say something surprising. "Fine. But you first."

When he pulls off the jeans, the boxer shorts come with them. My heart skips at the sight of his body. I've never seen a naked guy before. Ray got naked once, but it was pitch-black, and still I touched him with my eyes squeezed shut.

From the ground, Mary says, "You need to bag that thing."

Ralph's already prepared. He leans down and picks up the jeans to riffle through one of the pockets. Mary's fiddling with something on her dress.

"This ripped." Her attention is on the strap he pulled. "I have to knot it."

"Here." Ralph attempts to inspect the damage, like a hero who's going to fix what he broke. "I'll do it."

"No, no, I just need some light." She gets up as if needing the bulb's glow. I have no idea what she's doing. I can't believe she's going to go through with it. He lies back down, out of view. I start to carefully, quietly remove myself from the fence so I don't have to actually watch the rest. I guess I'm curious about certain things, but not everything. I'm about to lift myself off the rail when I spy Mary lunging for the door. It flies open and she races out. Ralph follows, yelling at her to come back.

I pass him, trying to catch up to Mary, but trip on something, a sprinkler head, maybe. Ralph stomps toward me. I turn back and our eyes meet. He lunges for me. Terrified, I force myself to get up and run—run as fast as I can, ignoring my bloody knee and the howls of a naked mad dog.

13

BACK AT MARY'S, we need something to calm our nerves and so break into her parents' stash of rum. Vendors from her father's hardware store always give it as their company's holiday gift. That's good for us. Since there are like twenty stuffed in the back of their kitchen pantry, they won't miss one.

We're three shots in when my phone vibrates. I fear it's Ralph, and so does Mary. She shoots me a look and knocks back another. I'm already slow and fuzzy from the rum, so when the name appears on the screen, I assume my eyes are playing tricks on me.

As fast as my clumsy fingers can, I answer the call and say, "Hi."

"Hey, it's me."

I haven't heard Ray's voice in nine months, aside from some saved voice mails I listen to when I feel like torturing myself. I also have a few videos we made together (fooling around in a Coconut Grove head shop, licking a shared ice cream cone at Dairy Queen), which are even tougher to watch because he's not just talking to me, but with me. Still, I concentrate on the unique sound of his voice—deep and strong with a slight lisp that always made my insides feel like jelly.

Mary wants to know who it is, so I mouth his name. She rolls her eyes and tells me to tell him to go fuck off.

"You there?" he asks.

"I'm here."

"It's like old times," he says, and I know what he means. He'd always call late, and I'd huddle beneath my covers so Mom wouldn't hear me on the phone. We'd talk until we were too tired to say another word, then hang up with the promise of meeting before the first school bell rang.

"What's going on?" I ask, because I'm equal parts confused and elated. Ray had been gone barely a month when he gave me the old heave-ho back in September. My friends had told me to expect it (not just Mary, but girls like Paula, as well as Rachel and Iris, who shook their tangerine heads more than once at our relationship) even though I had a ring. That had to count for something. But it didn't. He broke up with me in a text, three weeks after he got to Tallahassee. I wasn't just crushed. I was pulverized.

"Nothing," he says.

"How's FSU?"

"Hard. Enjoy high school while you have it easy."

"You remember Fitzpatrick, don't you? I've got her for Science this year. Guarantee you she gives those professors a run for their collegiate money."

Mary's annoyed I haven't hung up on him yet, and makes a show of throwing back another shot and scrolling through her phone like she's bored by *The Ray and Rosie Show*, which she stopped watching long ago.

He doesn't respond to my pathetic attempt to remind him of our old life, the one we quasi-shared while he was a senior and I was junior—cramming down Wendy's during lunch because we only had forty minutes, texting during class even with the threat of losing our phones, and studying in the library after school, our textbooks touching.

All I get is a deep inhale as I clutch the phone for dear life. "Ray?"

"Yeah." Deep exhale. "So how're you doing?"

"Good," I say, which is the furthest thing from the truth tonight. I'm getting drunk because my best friend was almost raped—because of me—and my whole body hurts from running so far, so fast. What I really want to say is, *Good, but I'd be better if we were still together.* The words are perched to slip off my lovesick tongue. "And you?"

"You know . . . college stuff . . ." His voice trails off, followed by another inhale. He's smoking something, which means our altered states create an even playing field. But I wonder what we're playing.

Mary settles into her bed and grabs Henrietta—a creepy, faded purple hippo that would give me nightmares if I woke to it. She nestles it into her freshly scrubbed face and kisses it with lips free of her beloved raspberry gloss. On the floor, her shot glass lies next to the black dress that doesn't actually have a broken strap. She faked the rip, used it as a distraction to get out of the Rape Shed.

Desperate to keep the conversation going, I say something lame. "I can't believe your freshman year is almost over." Tell me you're coming home for the summer. Tell me you realized you made the biggest mistake ever by breaking up with me. Please tell me.

He exhales. "Been thinking about me?"

"Of course." Oh my God. He wants me back.

"When?"

"When what?"

"When have you been thinking about me?"

I'm flustered, because I can't tell the truth—that I go to sleep thinking about him, and wake up with the same thoughts. "Uh . . . I don't know. At different times, I guess. Especially when I pass by Dairy Queen. Remember when—"

"I remember." He cuts me off. "When else?"

Is this a test? Is he looking for a particular answer? I go in for the kill. One of our most romantic nights happened at Crandon Park on Key Biscayne, near the spot where we'd met a month earlier. One blanket plus two wine coolers equaled a partial skinny-dip and kissing in the ocean. "Whenever I go to the beach."

"And when else?" he probes. "Are you thinking of me when you're screwing guys for money?"

So that's what this call is about. A flash of heat blasts whatever bit of hope had been brewing. "What are you talking about?"

"Did you think I wouldn't find out? I know about Todd. And Ivan. They're friends with my little brother."

I'd forgotten about Alex, who's in my grade, because I've tried to forget about Ray. Seeing his brother in the hall was a constant reminder of what I'd lost, so I learned patterns to avoid bumping into him.

"How many have there been, Rosie?"

"Zero, Ray!" My voice rises, and Mary warns me to keep it down, her parents came home. "They're just lumping me in with—"

"In with what? In with who?"

I don't answer, my tongue twisted and swollen with rage. I'm not about to throw my best friend under the bus. No way. Plus, my mind is muddled from the rum, all gray and foggy. Did I have three shots or four?

"Fucking answer me!" he screams, but I can't remember the question. "Listen. I don't give a shit who you fuck. I dumped your ass because you're a goddamned prude, but at least now I know why." Ray chuckles, making my skin crawl. "It's because you wanted me to pay for it! Rosie the Entrepreneur. Classic."

Mary gestures to hang up on him, but I shake my head.

"Ray. Please." This is the first part of our conversation that feels familiar. All those times he was angry with me for no reason, and I'd beg him to forgive me.

"Please what?"

"Please believe me," I slur, slow and steady.

"Have you been drinking?" he asks. "Wow. Getting sloshed and getting nailed. You've done quite the one-eighty, Rosie."

"Getting what?"

"Don't play dumb with me. It was only cute when we were together."

I hadn't played dumb. I'd just listen to him explain things like the difference between a clutch hitter and a cleanup hitter during a baseball game. Then he'd pop a kiss on my cheek and say, "Aw, I need to teach you things."

"I'm not playing dumb, Ray. I swear, I'm not doing those things."

As if she heard his accusation, Mary explodes and tosses Henrietta at me. I wave her off and throw the smelly hippo back.

"So all these guys are lying," Ray says.

"Yes! Of course they're lying!"

The only way to fix this is to condemn my savior, my very best friend. That's what's going on here—these guys must have figured out I'm behind our crackpot operation and thrown us both into the fire. Best friends are meant to pay for each other's sins.

"My boys don't lie," he continues. "Besides, I may be five hundred miles away, but shit like this travels."

His boys. I was once his girl. Clearly, this midnight phone call was never about testing the waters for reconciliation.

"That's right. You are five hundred miles away from Miami, from me, so why do you care?" I should hang up right now, but the cord that once linked us feels strong. At least for me.

"Who said I did? Skanks just need to be called out, that's all."

Tears spring to my eyes. Every bone in my body feels like it's being crushed. But I'd feel worse if I betrayed Mary and told him the truth.

"You were such a good, sweet girl. What happened to you?"

"What happened to me?" I repeat. "Plenty since you dumped me five minutes after you left." If we had stayed together, he would know about the box, my birth mother, the whole thing. We'd always confided in each other—about little things like bad grades or trouble at home, and big things like his dream of becoming an architect and mine to become a designer. At one point, he'd even suggested I switch my focus to interior design so we could be a professional team. "But you're not interested in anything that's happened in my life, right? Because now you're a big man on a big campus."

"And getting all the ass I want without having to slap a fucking ring on it."

So that's why he got me the ring? It hadn't changed anything, but I realize now he was hoping it would. And then, just like that, the cord snaps.

"You want to know what happened to me?" I ask again. "You happened to me, Ray," I say, and swipe my finger to end the call.

Mary claps, beaming. "It's about fucking time."

I grab the bottle of rum and pour myself a celebratory drink. "Screw Ray. And screw that psycho Ralph. First thing tomorrow, we find a pawnshop."

. . .

In the middle of the night, Mary nudges me awake. "Rosie, you up?"

"No."

She lifts the cover from my shoulder and gently scratches my skin. "I have to tell you something. Roll over."

Her bedroom is dark, but moonlight slips through the bottom of her window shade and casts a silver glow across her face.

Eyes wide and fearful. Her bottom lip quivers when she says, "I was scared tonight. Like really, really scared."

I curl up close and wait for more. I'm kind of afraid to say what I'm thinking, that I wanted no part of this thing tonight. She was the one who insisted we go.

"I think you should take Mac up on it," she says.

I know what she means but still have to ask. "And what about the money? How will you get out of here after we graduate?" My voice is hushed, not that her parents could hear us from across the hall, but you never know. I've often suspected Lucy of hanging around my door, hoping to hear a snippet of a late-night phone call. I've heard the pitter-patter of her feet. I know I have.

"I'll just have to find another way. If I wind up dead in an alley, I'm not getting out of anywhere."

"Don't say things like that."

"Then do it, Rosie. Tell Mac he can be that guy, riding in on a white horse."

I nod. We close our eyes. She lets out a heavy sigh, and I feel her entire body sink into the mattress beside me. I wonder if she's been up all night, wrestling with this. After her comment earlier, I suspect there's more behind Mary's goal to run away than a life free of Perkins Paints. There's more to it.

It may not be much, but whatever I make on Ray's ring goes in Mary's pocket.

14

"THANKS for coming with me," I say.

"Did you really think I'd turn down the chance to see you hawk that thing?" Mary takes the velvet pouch from my hands. I asked my mom if I could borrow the car. She shot me down because she and Judd were spending the day at the shooting range, but did I want a ride? No thanks. I didn't want to tell her what I was up to. Selling Ray's ring? I'd get the third degree and didn't want to explain how it came to this. She liked Ray, but I think it's only because he always tossed her a compliment and yakked it up with Judd.

Mary's parents were equally accommodating, so we caught the ten a.m. bus downtown in search of a pawnshop.

Mary opens the pouch, plucks out the ring, and puts it on her pinkie finger. "Cheap."

"It is not," I snap, louder than I'd planned. Some guy wearing headphones gives me an annoyed look. Like no one ever argues on a bus. Whatever.

"You deserve better. A diamond. Not this stupid blue stone."

"He said it matched my eyes."

"Sucker." She pulls the ring off her finger and sticks it back in the pouch, pulling the strings extra-tight.

The mention of a diamond reminds me of Judd popping the question. It makes me queasy, the thought of him being my stepfather, if you can even call him that since Lucy's already my stepmother. I'm not sure how that works.

"So now that you've decided to take him up on his offer, tell me more about this guy Mac." I know Mary's only trying to distract me. Her face is turned to the window, taking in the Miami skyline. She likes to look at the city passing her by.

"He's kinda hot," I confess.

"Really?" Mary's eyes widen into flat brown saucers.

"In a buttoned-up kind of way."

"Don't tell me he wears polo shirts."

"And boat shoes."

Mary puts a finger in her mouth and pretends to vomit.

I swat her hand, tell her to stop. The headphones guy turns around, and I'm ready to suggest he turn up his music if we're such a distraction. Is it against the law to have a little fun on a Saturday-morning bus ride? When Mary sticks out her tongue at him, I swat her hand again.

"Stop hitting me," she says, and tucks her hands under her thighs. "So I guess last night's phone call prompted this little excursion. I know you're not selling it for the money since we've closed shop."

"Do you really need me to admit it? You were right. All this time, I was hoping he'd miss me and drive down to Miami in the middle of the night and put it back on my finger. Like right out of a movie. I was stupid, okay?"

"Not stupid. Gullible." Mary pauses. Then her expression changes, like she had a lightbulb moment. "I'm proud of you for finally standing up to that douchebag."

"Surprised, too, I see."

"Well, you're not exactly the confrontational type," Mary says.

"Because that's your job." So many times she's come to my defense. A teacher who gave me a failing grade. A girl who gave me a nasty look at the movie theater. She even blasted Ray the time he got too aggressive with me at a party—pushing me to have sex in some girl's bedroom—and told him to zip it up or she'd cut it off.

No wonder she's beaming right now. The Ray train has finally been derailed.

. . .

I don't shop around. The ring feels like fire in my pocket, and the only way to put out the flame is to dump it. A guy named Horatio at Pawn Universe offers me twenty bucks. He sees that I'm stunned and offers me twenty-five. Mary pokes me in the ribs, tells me not to take it. I'm in no mood to negotiate, so Mary makes a counteroffer of thirty. He ignores her, but as I spin on my sandals to leave, he cuts it down the middle.

I get a whopping twenty-seven dollars and fifty cents for the ring.

Outside the pawnshop, I put the money in Mary's hand. "Take it."

"Why? No."

"Yes. You're going to need it." I curl her fingers around the bills, dropping the two quarters in the front pocket of her shorts.

"I don't want it, Rosie. Besides, twenty-seven dollars isn't going to make or break my escape. Just blow it on something, maybe a hat. You love hats." I do, because they're not only a great fashion accessory, they also hide my hair when it doesn't behave.

We walk around a bit, headed in no particular direction. Neither one of us is in any hurry to get home. There's not much bustle since it's the weekend, even though downtown is slowly becoming a residential hot spot. But it is still early, and the smell of sidewalk trash and lingering gas fumes drive us into the first restaurant that smells halfway decent. It's close to noon and I'm starved.

"Forget the hat," I say as we settle into a table at Pita Central. I use my windfall to treat us to a giant Greek salad, two bowls of lemon soup, and all the flat bread with hummus the waiter would bring. We wash it down with delicious peach iced tea garnished with sprigs of mint. It's a Saturday-afternoon feast, especially tasty on Ray's dime.

15

NO MORE MEETING at Lou's. Since we had a legally binding contract (even though, according to Mac, it had been transitioned into a pro bono agreement), he insisted I come to the office after school, see where the magic happens. It's at the Coastal Square mall, not that far from Del Vista, so I take Todd up on his offer to drive me there when he sees me sitting on the bus bench, melting under the sun. It's the least he can do for tattling to Ray or to whoever was responsible for lighting the fuse. Someone talked.

We've never been in a car together, but since the heat between us has cooled since last Wednesday, I pretend I'm just hitching a ride with a friend. The air-conditioning feels great, and I direct one of the vents at my forehead to dry my bangs that have sprung into a curly mess.

"You kind of have a big mouth," I say. "Usually, it's girls who like to blab, but whatever. The cat's out of the bag."

"What are you talking about?"

"Well, I didn't mind you spreading the word, but when it got to Ray . . . I mean, he was my boyfriend last year, so he wasn't too happy about it, me being mixed up in something like that. You saw me that day, didn't you?"

"Uh . . . where?"

"Behind the wall, right outside the stairwell." I dip my head. "You know. After."

"No . . . ?" His voice tilts up, like a question, like he's confused.

"Okay. Well, you probably want to know why."

He shrugs like he doesn't care, but he must. Who wouldn't want to understand something like that? Besides, he seems to want to listen. His eyes are glued to the road but I can tell he's listening. "My dad died a couple years ago," I say. "And he left me a box with a secret letter. I know—sounds like a novel, right? But it's true. I thought my real mom had died when I was little, but no. She's alive, and she's out there somewhere." I pause, about to hold back the next thought, but it comes out anyway. "Or at least I hope she is. Anyway, I needed to hire a private investigator to help me find her and—surprise, surprise!—no one would help me for free, so—"

"Rosie," he snaps. "Stop. I don't care. It's none of my business." Both hands remain gripped on the wheel, his eyes still on the road.

I feel shut down and shut up and I don't like it. He turns up the music, but I reach over and spin the dial off. "Well, here's something that is your business. That guy Ralph should be locked up for attempted rape."

It's hard to tell with guys like Todd, but I think he's genuinely shocked by my claim. He's quiet, then says, "We don't really hang together, if you know what I mean."

I don't know what he means, but he cranks up the music again, which I take as a sign he's done talking.

My phone buzzes with a text. Perfect timing.

its joe. wanna meet

no

still no?

i dont know u

i got $

dont care

u will

What's that supposed to mean? Was this creep threatening me now? I huff, annoyed and a little freaked out.

"Business?" he asks.

"Stop being an asshole." I can't believe I called him that. Mary's rubbing off on me.

"I'll stop being an asshole if you stop being a psycho." He looks at me for the first time. His eyes are dead serious, and they make me want out of his car, away from him.

At the next light, he asks me why I need a ride to Coastal Square.

"Now that's none of your business." I had been on the verge of confessing that he's actually taking me to said investigator before he got snarky.

"Need an abortion? There's a clinic on the second floor."

"And how would you know that?"

"Just like I know there's a Dollar Store and a Subway there, too. That's all."

"I should've taken the bus," I mumble, tired of him, wondering what I ever found appealing. His chin juts out too much and a trail of dark hair crawls up his neck. He suddenly looks thin and awkward behind the wheel, his shirt too tight, his jeans too short.

"Thanks for the ride," I say when we arrive.

"Yep." He wipes the hair out of his eyes with one hand and grips the steering wheel of his less-than-macho car with the other.

He barely waits for me to gather my things and close the door when he peels away—as much as one can in a Prius. I make sure he's out of sight before I take the stairs to the second floor, enter the third door on the right, and into the office of Brooks & Associates, PI.

• • •

It's not fancy. Not even very nice. It's average, bordering on dismal. If this office was on a fashion scale, it would be closer to Payless than Prada. White tile floor, blackout shades on both windows. No artwork on the walls, no comfortable furniture to welcome distraught clients. A short hallway shoots out from the room I've entered, fluorescent lights spilling from open doors on either side.

"Hello?" I toss my backpack onto an empty plastic chair, the only one in the room.

"Be there in a minute!" It's Mac, calling to me from one of the rooms.

Something inside me flashed when I heard his voice, like a match being struck. What was that? It used to happen when Ray would call, or when I'd see him approaching me in the school hallway. His voice isn't deep like Ray's, but it's strong and friendly, almost musical.

"Hi, nice to see you again." He looks even better than he did last week. He's got a tan and his hair has been brushed slick behind his ears. I awkwardly shake his outstretched hand. "John's out. I hope it's okay that you'll just be seeing me today."

"Sure," I say, because it's kind of better than okay.

"How was school?"

"Does it really matter? It's the end of my senior year. I'm checked out."

"Grab your stuff and come on back," he says, then heads down the hallway. "You never told me where you're going to college."

"You never asked." When I enter his office, it's like I've left a barren planet and entered a den of riches. There's soft brown carpet on the floor and huge framed abstract photographs on creamy beige walls. A potted plant is nestled in the corner, reaching its dark green leaves toward the spilling sun.

"Fancy," I say, my eyes sweeping the room. "How often are you here?"

"I've got a pretty full school schedule, but I try to arrange my classes in the morning so I can come in for a few hours in the afternoon." He shrugs his shoulders. "But it's not like I'm here every day."

"You've got some uncle. Your very own office at twenty. Impressive."

"Twenty-one in two months."

"Eighteen in two weeks."

"I know." He crinkles his nose, sort of like his uncle does, and says, "Didn't need to be a detective for that. I just asked John why he had postdated the contract to May twenty-ninth."

"That's right," I say. "Big day. If you're good, I'll invite you to my birthday party." There is no party, but I like the sound of having one.

"And if you promise we'll play duck, duck, goose, maybe I'll come."

Oh my God. Are we flirting? I need to stay focused and crush this butterfly in my chest. "So you two are close," I say, changing channels.

"My uncle never had any kids of his own. He's always treated me like a son. When I showed an interest in the work, he took me under his wing." I imagine John's long arms tucking Mac into his feathery fold. "By the way, I believe this belongs to you." He hands over a sealed envelope. I don't need to open it, knowing all of my money is in there, and slip it into the side pocket of my backpack. "Just between us, he would never have charged you, even if I hadn't suggested doing it pro bono. He told me that sometimes people come to you wanting to find someone who's lost. And sometimes, they're the one who's lost."

John thinks I'm lost? I don't know how I'm supposed to feel about that, so I change channels again. "What are those?" I ask, pointing at the pictures.

He's already resumed his seat behind a large desk peppered with picture frames facing away from me. Why am I secretly hoping they hold images of his family and not of him cozy with some girlfriend? I'm shaken out of the thought when he claps. "I'll answer your question if you answer mine."

I take a seat in one of the chairs across from him. "What question?"

"College?"

"Oh, that one. Well, I want to go to design school, but maybe not right away. Thought I'd tour Europe, visit some of the better fashion houses, maybe show my sketchbook to a lead designer or two."

Mac nods, impressed. "Wow, sounds great."

"It does, doesn't it?" I smooth out my favorite ruffled skirt, then lock my feet at the ankles. "Too bad I'm not actually doing that."

Mac's face drops. "Oh . . . I—"

"It was a joke."

"And the fashion thing? Was that a joke, too?" He's staring at me with those moss-green eyes that pop against his caramel skin.

"No. That's real. Want to see?" It's not exactly something I shove in people's faces, but he seems genuinely interested, and for some reason I want to impress him.

"Definitely."

"I applied to the Fashion House last November. It's a design school in Miami Beach," I say, reaching into my backpack for one of my sketchbooks. "They have an excellent program, one of the best in South Florida, but it's tough to get in. I'm still wait-ing to hear." I happen to open it to the page I'd been working on when I met that nasty old lady on the bus. The jumper, only half-done. I turn it around so the design is facing Mac.

"Where did you learn to sketch like this?"

"I've always chosen art as an elective in school. Half the time I was forced to make crappy papier-mâché projects, but the other half I got some decent drawing instruction. Maybe I was born with a little talent, too." I imagine my mother gave it to me since the extent of my dad's artistic skill was putting a fresh coat of paint on the house.

Mac's still studying the jumper when he says, "This is interesting."

"Interesting good or interesting weird?"

"No. Interesting good."

"Thanks." I'm beaming, for sure.

"What is it?" he asks. I'm about to swat him across the table when he laughs and says he's kidding. He flips through more pages, pausing on a gown I explain would have a sequin-encrusted neckline, maybe cuffs, too.

He stops on a page full of cargo shorts and coordinating vests with lots of zippers and pockets. "These are cool."

"Those are Mary's favorite, too," I say brightly. It's always good when more than one person likes the same thing.

"Who's Mary?"

"My best friend. She's kind of outdoorsy, even though she hates the heat."

He nods, still studying the shorts, clearly impressed. "They're good, Rosie. You've got some serious talent."

I haven't shared my designs with a lot of people, mostly just

Mary. So this is a new feeling, warm and tingly, and I don't think it's only because he likes my drawings.

"I wish I really could go," I say. "I'd love to grab every one of my sketchbooks and jet off to Italy, or maybe France! Become someone's apprentice, run my fingers across soft fabrics all day, stab my fingers with needles, cut my fingers with scissors, and have all the charcoal pencils I'll ever need tucked into a smock." I press Pause on my fantasy. "I need to go to school first. I know that. Sorry for rambling."

"No, don't apologize. I think that's great. You have a dream, Rosie." His warm smile fades before he says, "It's important to have one." He closes my notebook carefully, and slides it back to me. Then he pulls a pen and legal pad from the drawer. "I hope you get your wish, and that Italy or France or wherever is in your future." He pops the pen cap, poises the tip above the yellow-lined paper. "But for now, let's talk about your past."

• • •

Part of me feels like we're two kids playing Clue, but there's no denying Mac's earnestness and dedication to his job. I don't know where to begin, so he prompts me with a stern, professional voice meant to get things rolling.

"Let's start with the box. When and where did you find it?"

"A little over two months ago, in my old house."

I tell him that it's up for sale, so the house was empty. Then I describe how I gained access through the rear sliding glass door. He nods like he's impressed with my breaking-and-entering skills, too.

"We found the box in the attic."

"Who's we?"

"Mary and I."

"Did you bring the contents of the box with you?"

Sometimes his language is so stuffy. But it's kind of cute, too. He's like an old adult in a young man's body. I lean over the chair to get it from my backpack. As I'm digging around, moving books out of the way, I feel Mac's eyes on me when he sort of leans forward. Can he see down my shirt at this angle? I pull together the collar of my blouse just in case.

"Voilà," I say, presenting the Ziploc bag to him.

"What happened to the box?"

"Safekeeping." The truth is, I imagine the scent of Dad's fingertips still on it and don't want to risk losing that.

"May I?" he asks, waiting for permission to open the seal.

"Of course. That's why I'm here." But I am nervous to have someone else's hands touch my dad's letter, the pictures, my birth certificate, the bracelet.

He must sense my hesitation because he asks, "Would you prefer I wear gloves?"

"Should you? I mean, because of fingerprints and stuff?"

"This isn't a homicide case. Plus, I assume these items have been held by you many times. Lifting prints wouldn't yield any other than yours, anyway."

"Oh." Suddenly, I feel stupid. "Then don't worry about the gloves. Just dive in."

He splays out his hands and says, "They're clean."

"Go ahead . . ." I egg him on with a smile.

"Why don't you come around on this side?" he offers. My insides clench. "Don't worry, I won't bite. Unless, of course, you smell like cherry pie."

"Which reminds me," I say, sidestepping the flirty comment. "Why did you think peach? The night we met. You thought I'd prefer peach pie."

He points at my left cheek. "You've got a small patch of blond fuzz right near your ear. Your face is kind of round and you've got that cleft in your chin, like the dimple at the bottom of a peach and . . ." He pauses as his cheeks bloom raspberry pink. "Possibly sweet."

"Possibly?"

"Not sure yet," he teases.

Now I'm blushing, too, and growing warm inside. Whether he knows it or not, this guy is using a blowtorch on my heart Ray managed to freeze. "Well, there's no chance of smelling like any kind of pie. I probably reek of Del Vista, which is a combination of old textbooks and Lysol." I join him on his side of the desk. He tells me to sit in his chair while he stands.

"Okay. Let's go through each item, piece by piece."

"I've already done that a hundred times," I say, making no attempt to hide my frustration.

"Look into my eyes," he says. "These are what you call a fresh pair. I'll find something, Rosie. And like dominoes, one clue will knock into another clue and before we know it, we'll have found your mother."

I can already hear the clicking and clacking of small white tiles.

16

LUCY COMES HOME beaming like a platinum-haired sun shower. After spending an hour with Mac yesterday and the two of us constantly referring to the woman I'm trying to find as my mother, I woke up today with the title stuck in my throat and can no longer use it for my father's second wife. I wouldn't go so far as calling her by name to her face—she hasn't been that bad these past twelve years, though after my dad died the proverbial gloves came off. One day she's offering to buy me new bras, and the next she's screaming through the house that she knows I stole her cigarettes (which is usually true, but most times she's just misplaced them or has already smoked more than she realized). So she can be a little unpredictable toward me. I get it. After all, I'm not her real daughter, just baggage that came with a ring. As much as I haven't wanted to believe it, that's the truth.

So Lucy has floated through the front door as if on a cloud made especially for her. I'm warming up four-day-old Itchin' for Chicken in the microwave, watching it pop and splatter oil against the plastic window.

"Lookie, lookie!" she sings, then muffles a cough. It's not her typical work attire of jeans and a tight blouse with one too many buttons unbuttoned that she wants me to notice. She's thrown out her left hand so fiercely she almost hits me in the face. I back up against the counter to get a better look. On her finger is the diamond ring Judd showed me last week. I'm glad it finally happened. I'd been waiting for him to pop the question and get it over with.

"He surprised me today at work. Took me to lunch and—"

The microwave dings. "Congratulations," I say.

Lucy's face falls like a child who's been sent to bed. "You don't sound very happy."

I force a smile. "There. I'm happy."

"Happy as a one-eyed toad." Lucy's voice has the nasty razor's edge she gets when someone's response doesn't match her expectations. "What's your problem?"

"I don't have one."

"Sure you do. It's written all over your face, which, by the way, needs a good scrubbing. It's all oily. And must you wear your hair like that, so crazy? You should pull it back once in a while."

I bite my tongue, clench my teeth, whatever I have to do so that I don't explode. She knows my mother's alive. It says so in my father's letter. Like me, Mac was scratching his head after reading it.

Mac: *Why has she never told you the truth?*

Me (trying not to roll my eyes): *Exactly. That's what I've been racking my brain about since I found out months ago.*

Mac: *This is our first clue, Rosie. I have a feeling the reason behind Lucy's silence may be linked to the whereabouts of your mother.*

Whereabouts. Mac's all about the detective lingo.

So if Lucy knows I know, her own reason for hiding the truth will be blown. Mac and I agreed it was best to keep up the charade.

"Let me see it," I say, pretending to cave a little.

Begrudgingly, she extends her hand.

"It's pretty."

"Pretty? It's gorgeous! Almost a full carat! The ring your father gave me was barely—"

"Don't," I snap. "You will not trash him." I turn away and press the microwave door, which always sounds like it's breaking when it opens.

"You're being selfish," she says.

I pull out the plate of sizzling chicken. "How is that?"

"You don't want me to be happy." The ring catches her attention again. "Did you ever think for once about my loneliness since your father died?"

I grab a fork and knife from the utensil drawer. The late-afternoon sun slices through the kitchen, lighting up our shoes, darkening our faces. "Uh, you found Judd like ten minutes after Dad died. When did you have time to get lonely?" I walk right past her and take a seat at the table. Stabbing the chicken with the knife, I pull back the skin with my fingers. It's a thigh. Dark meat. If I wasn't so hungry, I'd toss it at her, or at the very least, in the garbage.

"I take it back," she says, but it's clear by her tone she's poised to throw another dagger. "You're not being selfish." Here it comes. "You're being a bitch." And there it is.

Am I? It's just that seeing her wearing the ring makes it official. Her commitment to my father is over. Done. For some reason, it hurts and makes me angry. I hear Mac in my head, telling me to keep my cool. I stick a piece of chicken in my mouth and force myself to chew. I forgot to get a drink, but don't dare get up from the table.

"I'm sorry," she mumbles.

"No, you're not."

"Fine! Don't accept my apology!" Lucy shouts, her face pinched like a raisin.

"What's going on in here?" Judd appears in the kitchen doorway. I didn't even know he was home. It's four thirty on a Tuesday afternoon. He should be flipping fries in grease right about now.

Lucy pouts, her bright red lipstick becoming an exaggerated clown frown. "Rosie doesn't like my ring," she declares. "And she's got a fresh mouth." She starts rummaging around in the drawer next to the stove. "Where did you hide them? I know you hid them." Her voice is growing frantic, but I refuse to tell her where I put her pack of cigarettes. I've done it for years, hiding or flat-out dumping them. Did I really need another parent dying on me?

Judd sweeps into the room wearing dirty gym shorts and an undershirt that allows a full view of clumpy brown armpit hair. His creased cheek and glassy eyes are clear giveaways that our argument has woken him from an afternoon nap.

"You need to show your mother some respect," he says, sitting in the chair next to me. Then he grabs the chicken thigh from my plate and takes a bite. "And now that I'll be your stepdaddy, you'll need to show me some, too." He licks his fingers, puts what's left of the chicken back on my plate. Under the table, he grabs my knee and squeezes it. "Apologize to your mother."

I mumble something unintelligible into my napkin, just to get them off my back.

"Well, if I can't have a cigarette, I'll have a drink," Lucy spits.

"I'll fix it for you, babe." Judd narrows his eyes at me before grabbing a bottle of something from the cabinet. I'm afraid if I look close enough, claws will have sprouted from his fingertips. He's sneering with the twisted desire a predator has for its prey. It's a look that finally confirms what I've always suspected. He's coming for me.

• • •

Mary and I are on the phone. Over at her house, she may simply have her bedroom door closed, but mine is locked and braced by a chair. I'm not taking any chances with Judd on the prowl.

"So did he get down on one knee and cluck out the proposal while holding a bucket of wings?"

I can always count on Mary to make me laugh when I want to scream. "I don't think so, but thanks for the visual."

"You're welcome."

"I'm beginning to think . . . I don't know. If I do find my mother, maybe I can stay with her. I don't think Lucy wants me around anymore."

"News flash. She hasn't wanted you around for a long time," Mary says.

"Why would you say that?"

"Come on, Rosie girl. Do you need me to make a laundry list for you? 'Cause I could start with the time she left you waiting for her after school one day in ninth grade. Remember how cold it was? Rainy, too. You ended up taking the bus, and when you got home she said she forgot. That was it. No apology, no nothing. She forgot about you."

That's not how I remembered it. Lucy did apologize, said she got held up at work. "But she made me mushroom soup when I got home," I added, somehow feeling the need to defend her.

"Mushroom soup?" Mary asks. "What are you talking about? Lucy's never given you a hot bowl of anything. She's been a witch your whole life and you know it."

"Sometimes, maybe," I hedge.

"Sometimes my ass. She's Cruella De Vil minus the Dalmatians."

That makes me laugh again, imagining Lucy's platinum hair streaked with black, a fur stole wrapped around her shoulders. "Well, maybe I can escape her evil clutches. Mac is hopeful he'll find Justine—"

"That's the first time you've said her name out loud," she says.

I think for a moment and agree. "It's a pretty name, isn't it?"

"Gorgeous," Mary says, mocking me.

"Anyway, Mac says the things I gave him are like dominoes that will knock into one another."

"Dominoes, huh?" I imagine her rolling her eyes, all skeptical.

"Yeah, those were his exact words. I'm feeling kind of confident."

Silence.

"Mary?"

"By the way," she says, as if she hasn't been listening. "I've been thinking. Where does all this leave me?"

"Where does all what leave you?"

"Without the cash flow." She doesn't wait for me to answer. "I'll tell you where. Out in the cold, that's where. And now I'm freezing, Rosie. Thanks very fucking much."

I make sure my tone is soft, not accusatory when I say, "You're the one who wanted to stop after the whole Ralph thing."

"Well maybe I don't want to stop anymore."

"We agreed, Mary. That night was seriously messed up."

"The last few days have given me a chance to think. Take stock. It's fast, easy money I still need."

I thought we had both agreed we were done. Charging for sex was only a means to an end, and now that I've got that end taken care of, I'm not about to put Mary into any more potential Ralph situations. Or worse. Why is she refusing to hang up her stilettos?

"How much more do you need?" I ask.

"A lot."

"Like how much?"

"I don't know, Rosie! A lot, okay? Do you really want me to spend the rest of my life hawking hammers and nails? And get this: Last weekend, my dad said he's going to put me in charge of key making. Key making! Maybe if I'm good, I'll land the dead-bolt section, too!"

She's hysterical. I imagine her pale complexion turning beet red.

"That's it," I say, nice and firm. "Working at your dad's store can't be the only reason you want out."

"It's not. I told you I'm dealing with some shit at home."

"What kind of . . . shit?" I ask, not used to cursing.

Mary huffs and puffs in irritation, then says, "I'm only going to tell you because I don't want you harassing me anymore."

I didn't think I was harassing her. Best friends don't harass each other. They only want to know when something seems really wrong. I have to prompt her three more times until she finally caves.

"It's my dad."

"What about him?"

"He hits my mom. Happy now?"

"Oh my God, Mary. I had no idea."

"You're not supposed to. Why do you think she wears all that makeup? Looks like a fucking clown half the time."

"I can't believe they haven't split up. Why doesn't she leave him?"

"Don't ask me. I've begged her. She says it's against our faith. I say that's crap. She's just weak. He could end up killing her one day. I've done the research. Abuse escalates."

I'm at a loss for words. I feel terrible that she's had to deal with this all on her own, that she hadn't chosen to confide in me. But I get it. There's a lot of private stuff that goes on behind closed doors, and it's not always other people's business to know it. Not even best friends'.

Now I understand and don't think twice before saying, "You can have my money, too. Mac returned it to me yesterday. Three hundred dollars. It's yours."

"Are you trying to get rid of me?" she asks.

"What are you talking about? I'm trying to help."

"You don't need me anymore, especially because you've got Mac. You're probably hoping I'll take off so you don't have to split your time between us."

Mary's never spoken like this before, cold and bitter. Maybe spilling her family secret whipped her into this frenzy. She's not making sense.

"Don't be ridiculous," I say. "I'll always need you. You're my—"

"Savior," she says. "I know."

And then there's silence, because she's hung up on me.

17

I COULDN'T SLEEP last night, plagued by visions of Mr. Perkins slapping his wife's face or pushing her against a wall or . . . worse. And the thought of Mary witnessing it has me hoping she takes all the money, even though I had planned to spend my share on a bike. I didn't want to take the bus any longer or hitch a mercy ride from Todd. And I definitely didn't want to ask Lucy anymore if I can borrow the Slaabmobile. But I have to scrap that plan, so I'm on the bus, heading to see Mac.

Mary was a no-show in school today. I wasn't all that surprised. Her mom will sometimes let her stay home if Mary puts on a convincing enough act of being sick—an act she probably started right after she cut our call short last night. This way, there would be no awkward hallway run-ins, and I could enjoy my tuna fish sandwich under our tree in peace. Paula came over (with Rachel and Iris in tow, of course), wondered why I eat alone, and I was like, *I don't, Mary's usually here, but she skipped today*. Paula elbowed Iris in the waist when she and Rachel looked at each other sideways, then asked if I wanted to eat with them in the gym while watching the guys shoot hoops. I appreciated the offer, but told her I needed to study for a

Science quiz and pulled out a notebook to prove it. But there is no Science quiz. I just wanted to be alone to mentally prepare for my meeting with Mac after school. I'm excited to discuss my case, but I'd be lying if I said it was the only reason I labored over my outfit this morning and settled on white skinny jeans and a red tee that hugs my curves in all the right places.

I'm also trying a new look. It has absolutely nothing to do with Lucy's hateful comments yesterday, but I'm not above hearing a message, regardless of the messenger. So I blew out my hair this morning and pulled what I could into a ponytail, though my bangs still hover like a blanket above my eyes. I put on a little makeup—powder foundation, light mascara, and clear lip gloss.

I'm busy with my sketchbook when the bus makes its first stop. During World History class, while I should have been thinking about Genghis Khan, I was thinking about gingham fabric. I had an idea for a wraparound skirt, ready to flow from the tip of my sharp HB pencil. I'm focusing on the waistband when someone sits down next to me. Instinctively, I move over to make more room, and when I look up, it's the old lady from last week. She's clutching the same quilted bag. Thinning white hair is combed neatly behind her ears, rimless glasses sit high on her nose. She smooths out the yellow cotton dress beneath her before sitting down. There are plenty of seats on the bus, so I can't imagine why she'd choose the one next to me.

"Hello," she says, surprising me. I give her a half nod. I can hold a grudge with the best of them and continue sketching without looking at her again. Then, so she gets the hint that I'm not about to engage in any polite conversation, I pull out a set of earbuds from my backpack, ready to plug them into my phone and ears so I can tune her out.

"I almost didn't recognize you." When she stuffs her bag between us, she must get a glimpse of my sketchbook because she says, "That's very good."

I don't want to thank her, but I do, because having anyone compliment my work feels pretty fantastic.

We ride in silence for a few blocks, the air between us charged. I can tell she wants to say more, but I'm not about to encourage her. The sting of her comments last week feels fresh with her sitting next to me. I keep drawing, working on the skirt pockets. Since I'm sketching the skirt in gingham, I decide to rotate the checked pattern and put the pockets on the outside. The look is fresh, and I like it.

During the next stop, while people bustle down the aisle, she turns to me and says, "You look nice today."

I thank her again, this time with a little more conviction.

"Such a pretty girl. How old are you?"

"I'll be eighteen in a couple weeks." I push the earbuds in deeper to let her know I'd rather listen to music (even though there is none) than chat. She puts a bony, wrinkled hand on my phone. A gold band, too big, rests scratched and old at the bottom of her finger. I imagine it once shiny and new, fitting more snugly when it was originally slipped on.

"Please. Would you mind?"

I remove the earbuds as the bus pulls back into traffic.

"I was hoping I'd see you again. I'm terribly sorry about last week. I was having a rotten day, and I took it out on you." She casts her gaze down, the lids of her eyes creped and folded.

"No, no. It's okay . . . ," I say, because that's what you're supposed to say, but it's not. That was the day Mary was with Todd, and I'm never okay after one of her meetings. I was already fragile when this lady unleashed on me.

"Something about you reminded me of my granddaughter." Her eyes brim with tears as she studies me. "The hair maybe . . ." She lets her voice disappear into space, then clears her throat and starts again. "She took a wrong turn about a year ago and never came back."

I'm not sure if she means literally, like the girl ran away, but I'm not about to ask. I've got enough crap in my life without wading through someone else's.

"She looked like you, even smelled like you. Teen spirit, I guess you could say."

"What's in the bag?" I ask, partly because I'm curious, partly because she's freaking me out and I want to change the subject.

She doesn't answer, just pulls out the most beautiful scarves I've ever seen.

"So you do knit—"

"No, I crochet," she corrects me. "There's a difference. For starters, this is a hook, not a needle, and you only use one." She wipes her eyes dry. They're the palest blue I've ever seen, almost gray, and they twinkle from a beam of sun breaking through the bus window.

"Now this," she says, plucking a scarf from the pile, "would look perfect with your outfit." She's right. It's got layers of pink, red, and white. "Allow me." The old lady wraps it around my neck, then twists it in an unusual way so it looks like a loose collar. I take out my compact to use the mirror.

"I love it," I say, admiring the delicate design and hard work that must have gone into making it. "But I can't accept it."

She hushes me.

"I can't pay you for it."

"There are currencies other than money," she says. I don't pull away when she rests her hand on mine. "I'm Elaine."

"Rosie."

18

HE COMPLIMENTS MY SCARF, then gets down to business.

"Let's talk about your mother," Mac says, then corrects himself. "I mean, Lucy."

"I think she's bipolar."

"Why do you say that?"

"Because we had this major blowup yesterday and then she knocked on my door late last night, trying to make nice."

"Make nice how?"

"Apologizing, saying she was just excited about the ring, blah blah blah . . ."

"Hold up. What ring?"

"Judd the Dud asked her to marry him."

"And that's a bad thing because . . ."

"The guy's a douchebag," I say, unleashing another one of Mary's words that's so right on, even if it's harsh. I have yet to hear a slang word out of him, let alone a curse word, and Mac winces at the sound of it.

"All right. The boyfriend is no good," he rephrases. He doesn't realize how no good, how he eyes me like a shark circling bloody bait. "Let's get back to her. Why was it strange that Lucy came in to 'make nice,' as you say?"

"Because she never has. Once, when I was nine, I vomited rice pudding all over a chair in the living room. She threw a towel at me, told me clean it up. I was a kid and kept apologizing for the stain she swore would never come out. She ignored me for two days." I pause, play with my new scarf. "Don't look at me like that."

"Like what?"

"Like you pity me. Poor Rosie. Lost her father. Lost her mother. Break out the Kleenex."

"I'm not," he says, and comes around from his side of the desk and sits in the chair next to me. "I'm not looking at you with pity. I'm looking at you with admiration."

"Why do you always talk like an old person?"

"I do?" When he scrunches up his face, it makes his straight nose fold in like an accordion between his eyes. Clearly, he's never been accused of that before.

"Yes. Very sophisticated," I mock.

"You haven't seen me slurp spaghetti and meatballs or curse at the television during college basketball."

"That's true."

"Or fling a slice of pizza at the screen during the Super Bowl."

"You did?"

"Horrible call by the referee." He waves his hands. "I don't want to talk about it. Terribly upsetting."

I snicker, and when he knocks his knee into mine, I get that lit-match sensation deep inside.

He gets all serious again. "I admire you because you've got guts to take this whole thing on, not knowing what you'll find."

He's right about that. "Thanks," I say. "Okay, so back to the bipolar evil stepmother."

"She's the key, Rosie." Mac adjusts in the seat, flips a leg over one knee. "I got to thinking. She still works at the scrap yard, right? Where she met your father?"

"Of course. She was there two years before him and will probably stay forever because she thinks she runs the place. It fuels her ego. I've seen her boss around everyone from temps to construction workers."

"A real gem," Mac says, and I love how he's totally on my page.

"Sparkles like a diamond." I pause. "Not like the one Judd gave her. Could be cubic zirconia, for all I know. It looked kind of pasty in the box."

"Does the timing of Judd's proposal seem odd in any way?"

"Well, they've been together a long time, like over three years. The only thing odd is that he waited so long."

"Had Lucy been pressuring him?"

I pause before answering. "I don't know. I don't think so."

"So why now?" Mac asks.

"I have no idea."

"I'm a guy," he says, as if I haven't noticed. "No way I'd pop the question without timing it perfectly." My heart lurches at the thought of him asking someone to marry him and before I have the good sense to stop my mouth, out it comes.

"Are you . . . ?" That's the problem with guys being engaged—they don't wear a ring to let the world know they're off the market.

"I'm only twenty!" he exclaims, rubbing his wrists. "I'm not ready for shackles just yet."

"Are you close?" I can't help myself. "Do you have a girlfriend? I'm sure UM is full of pretty girls looking for more than a college degree." I imagine the same at FSU and Ray trolling the campus for them.

He shakes his head and returns to his side of the desk. "We're getting way off topic here." Great, now I've aggravated him. I go on the offensive.

"I already feel like a third wheel. Maybe this is Judd's way of giving me one last kick so I fall off."

"Possibly," he says, considering my theory. "But there may be a stronger motive than that." He pauses, and I can see the gears slowing down in his head. "Let's get back to her job."

"What about it?"

"There may be something there."

"There where?"

"At the scrap yard. Look, Lucy's definitely hiding something, right?"

I nod.

"She's not going to hide it at your house."

"How do you know?"

"Years of investigative work," he says, buffing his nails on his lapel.

"Very funny." I go along with the joke, but I am hoping his uncle is bringing his experience to the table and not relying on Mac to carry the load.

"It's not that funny. Don't forget—I've been around this office for years," he says, sweeping his hands in the air. "Got bitten by the bug in sixth grade. I was running for vice president of my class and suspected ballot tampering during the election process."

"Because you didn't win?" I'm surprised, not figuring Mac as the sore-loser type.

"No, because I did."

"I don't get it."

"I was new to the school and figured I didn't have a shot of winning but ran anyway. Mothers make you do that kind of stuff." He flinches, knowing the subject of mothers is a testy one for me. "Anyway, my dad was a pilot, and someone started a rumor that he had his own plane and he would take my friends anywhere in the world they wanted to go. I know," he says, acknowledging my skepticism. "It's stupid. But kids are stupid in sixth grade. I guess all two hundred and seventy-nine of them thought if they were nice to me, I'd take them on my dad's plane." Mac pauses for dramatic effect. "Which of course we didn't have." He shakes his head and breaks into a grin, the memory of it still holding comic value. "So I did some digging. My first foray into investigative work yielded quick results. Just so you know, people talk for candy bars."

I'm smiling so wide he must think I find the whole thing silly, but it's the opposite. He tells a great story, and it's a welcome diversion from mine.

"I found out that the kid who started the rumor was on the ballot committee. I got ahold of the ballots, went through every single card, and, well, I didn't win. Not even close. On one of the ballots, someone had even scribbled *Who's Mac Brooks? Sounds like a suit.*"

I chuckle because it's true, and enjoy the image of a twelve-year-old Mac poring over those cards, searching for the truth.

"I don't get it. Why did that kid make sure you won, then?"

"Because people like winners who have stuff, like planes. I think he really believed my dad did have one, and if the school rallied around me, I'd take them all over the world. Crazy, right?"

"Totally," I say.

"Anyway," he says, "I've spent a lot of time with my uncle, picking his brain about cases. Of course, he's the strictest of professionals, so I never knew names—or even places, most times—but John was always dispensing nuggets of wisdom. And one of them was, if someone is hiding something important, it's never kept in the home."

"I did that already, by the way. After I found the box, I got to thinking there may have been other things my dad left behind, maybe with Lucy, but a search of her bedroom was a bust."

"See?" he says, all proud of himself. "There still may be something, but it won't be where you can find it. Maybe she's got a safe-deposit box, which of course wouldn't help you because you'd have to be on a list to access it. Perhaps a locker—"

"Or an office desk."

Mac shoots his finger like a gun just as John did that first night I met him. "Bingo. Do you have access to her office at the scrap yard?"

"I haven't been there in a long time . . ."

"But if you did go, could you get into her desk?"

"I broke into my old house. I can definitely break into a drawer."

19

I USED TO ENJOY late-night smoothies until the blender woke Lucy one too many times and she threatened to stick my hand in it the next time the whirring noise interrupted her sleep. But I've finished the assigned reading for English, tackled a Physics chapter, and actually managed to get eight out of ten Pre-Calculus problems correct without cheating online. I deserve a treat. Plus, my meeting with Mac this afternoon still has me riled up and plotting a way to visit Lucy's desk at the scrap yard without visiting Lucy. A cherry-yogurt smoothie will soothe my nerves and I'm prepared to risk a limb to make it.

It's almost eleven thirty. Lucy's been asleep for about an hour already. I should be safe, but to be extra-safe, I decide to pour everything into the blender but use it in the room farthest from her bedroom, which I call the den. It's not really a den. It doesn't have book-lined walls or comfy chairs for watching television. It's only got an old desk and a ratty sofa Judd sleeps on when he and Lucy are fighting.

We used to have a den in our old house. I liked to read on the thick carpet, my back propped up against the sleeper sofa. There was a long, sweeping floor lamp that stretched high above my head and lit up my book or magazine. Sometimes, when I'd wander in, I'd find my dad hunched over his desk, still working even though he had left the office hours before. Not wanting to disturb him, I'd turn to leave.

Stay, he'd say.

But you're working.

I can work with you in here. As a matter of fact, having you in here helps me think.

Really?

Really.

I'll be quiet, I promise.

Me, too, he'd say, because he was that kind of dad.

The room is dark when I enter, clutching the blender like a baby, my footsteps muffled by fluffy slippers with soft suede soles. I don't turn on the light, fearing it may cast its glow down the hallway and seep under Lucy's door. Besides, I know exactly where the outlet is, on the wall to my right. I've used it to charge my laptop a hundred times. The prongs slip in, and I press the button. The whirring sound doesn't sound so loud in here. I mentally pat myself on the back for a fine idea. And then—

"What the hell?!" Judd's voice is like unexpected thunder on a cloudless day. He lunges in the dark, flicks on the desk lamp with such force it slides across the laminate surface.

Instantly, I press a button—any button—to stop the noise. The thick pink liquid gurgles, then dies. "Sorry," I say sheepishly, because I obviously scared the crap out of him.

"What are you doing?" he asks, fiddling with his boxer shorts, making sure everything's tucked in.

I don't look anywhere near his hands, just straight into his eyes. "Making a smoothie."

"In here?" He runs both hands through his tangled hair, which looks oily, like it's been splattered by chicken grease at work.

"I didn't want to wake Mom."

"But it's okay to wake me?"

I unplug the blender and take it back in my arms. "How was I supposed to know you'd be in here? Why aren't you in the bedroom?"

"Why do you think." It's not a question. "Didn't you hear us arguing earlier?"

I hadn't. That's the beauty of headphones. I nod anyway.

"Sorry," I say again, and turn to leave, but Judd reaches across the small room and grabs my leg. I shake him off, thanking God for the sweatpants I had thrown on with my nightshirt.

"You don't have to run off." Judd's suddenly more awake than asleep. He pats the scratchy plaid sofa that always itches the backs of my thighs. It reminds me of the blanket Ralph threw down on the shed floor.

"Uh, yes I do." I lift the blender. "My cherry-yogurt-orange-juice smoothie awaits."

"Drink it in here," he offers.

"Straight out of the blender." I raise my eyebrows at his suggestion.

"Come here," he says. "Put that down."

"It's going to get yucky. Smoothies have to be consumed immediately."

"Put it down, Rosie. I want to talk to you."

By the sound of his voice—playful and flirty—he wants to do anything but. "We can talk tomorrow," I say, warning flags flapping in my chest.

"How many opportunities do we get to have a private conversation?" he asks.

I steel my eyes at him. This guy needs to hear a message and quick. "We shouldn't be having private conversations, Judd."

A sheet of cold shock spreads across his face. "Why are you getting so defensive?" On hairy legs he slithers over to me and stands barely a foot away. "I want to talk about your birthday, Rosie. That's all." He twists a corner of his mustache between two fingers.

The blender starts to feel heavy. "What about it?"

"I thought maybe we'd combine it with the wedding—"

"Why would you want to do that?" I interrupt.

"'Cause I'm a nice guy."

"Yeah, well, the older you get, the less birthdays mean," I say, hoping to slam the lid on any plan he's brewing.

He frowns a little, like I've hurt his feelings. "In any event," he says, which he loves to say, because he thinks it makes him sound smart. "I was thinking of a double celebration, like a half-coming-of-age, half-coming-together kind of thing."

I have no idea what any of that means, but the offer sounds strange, even for him. "That's nice of you, Judd, but—"

"But what?"

Here goes. "You're not my father. It's not your job to make birthday parties or dinner or anything else."

"But I will be," he says, his tone sharpening.

I shake my head, still clutching the blender, rocking with agitation on my fluffy slippered feet. "Look. I don't want anything for my birthday."

He inches closer. "But it's a big one," he says, rubbing up against me, grinning at his pun. I've known Judd since I was fourteen. From the moment I met him, my pedophile radar has been on varying degrees of alert. Right now, the needle's on high and ready to bust.

Both hands grip my waist, but because I'm holding the blender, I can't push him off. It's finally happening. He's making his move.

Oh my God. I need to call Mary. I need to get out of here right this minute and tell her.

I unsuccessfully attempt to wriggle out of his grasp.

He backs me against the wall, whispers in my ear, "Eighteen. You'll be legal."

"Yeah, to vote and buy lottery tickets. Now get off me." I force the blender against his ribs, hoping if I push hard enough it'll break them. "Or I'll scream."

"For who—your loving mother?" He purposely chokes on the word *loving*.

"I mean it, Judd. You're twice my age—"

"No, I'm not." He snorts, like I've offended him. "You obviously stink at math." Heavy breathing in my ear, the smell of grease and chicken swirling between our necks. "I've only got about ten years on you, and the older you get, the more you know how to satisfy a woman."

Desperate squirming. "You're marrying my mother."

"So?"

"Why would you—I mean, how could you—"

A flash of anger crosses Judd's face, making me flinch. I've seen this look before—on Todd last week after class, and on Ray when I refused to do things to him, sexual things. But Judd's face is darker, and he bites his own lip to keep the anger inside.

For a split second, I think he's going to hit me. I need to get out of here. But he grabs my waist again before I can get away. And then his mouth is on mine, forcing his tongue between my lips. The blender slips through my hands and crashes to the floor. I feel the smoothie pooling at my feet while I grunt and twist, trying to free break free.

"Shut up," he growls. "You don't want to wake your mother."

I pull away, but not before biting down nice and hard on his tongue, making him yelp like a dog. "Neither do you," I snap.

"Bitch!" A finger flies into his mouth, probably to check for blood, but there isn't any. "Clean up this mess."

"You do it." I turn for the door and there's Lucy.

"What the hell is going on here? I was dead asleep!" She's most annoyed at having been woken up. Imagine that. Her hair, usually pristine, is a shaggy mess, and remnants of mascara have created globs of black guck beneath her eyes.

Too bad about the "asleep" part. I push past her to my bedroom, but she's hot on my heels, screaming at me to come back.

"Talk to Judd!" I race down the hall, manage to shut my door and lock it.

"Come out of there!" She bangs on the door, making it rattle and shake.

"No!"

Then I hear Judd, having arrived at the scene, saying, "Babe, it's not what you think."

"You don't know what I think," she says. "If you did, you'd be gagging on this goddamned ring." I hear her light up a cigarette and take a drag that makes her cough. The smoke instantly finds its way under my door, so I pull some dirty clothes from my hamper and stuff them along the gap.

"He hit on me," I say through the door. "Your frickin fiancé hit on me."

"Judd, you'd better tell me what's going on."

"She came on to me," he says, at which point I kick aside the clothes and pull my door wide open.

"Liar!"

"You're half my age, Rosie, and . . . come on, you're like a daughter to me."

"Then why is your tongue swelling up?" I ask.

Lucy turns to him, sucks in a ton of smoke, and blows it out.

"He's talking funny, can't you tell?"

Lucy doesn't answer me, just stands there, staring at Judd, waiting for his story.

"Okay, look . . ." Judd backs up against the wall. The hallway is dim, but I can still see his pathetic expression, the complete opposite of the one I saw five minutes ago when he was acting like the big man in charge. He pushes back his greasy black hair. "First of all, it wasn't like that."

"Second of all, you're a pervert," I chime in.

"I had been drinking, all right?" He tries to take Lucy in his arms, but she backs away. "You know how I get when we've been fighting. I had too much, and I passed out, and then she—"

"What? What did I do? I was making a smoothie, Judd. That was it. Don't try pinning this on me."

"Well, you sent out signals, Rosie."

"Signals? Oh my God." I turn to Lucy. "Please don't believe him. I would never do that."

In that dim hallway, beside Judd's pathetic face, is Lucy's confused one. She's not sure who to believe, even though it should be me, her daughter. Maybe Mary's right, and I've just been fooling myself. I'll never really be hers.

I turn around and slam my door behind me. My heart beats wildly in my chest, being accused of something so disgusting. The next thing I hear better be the sound of his Ford truck peeling out of the driveway.

I call Mary and beg her to come over, but she's still frosty from our conversation yesterday and says, "Just spill, Rosie, but do it quick. If my mom hears me on the phone she's going to blow a gasket. Plus, I'm supposed to be sick."

"Judd attacked me."

"Are you okay? What happened? Did he hurt you?" She's wide awake now, firing off questions before I have a chance to answer even one.

"I'm fine, just totally freaked out. Thank God Lucy walked in on us—"

"And tossed that pervert's shit out on the lawn, right?"

"Not yet. They're arguing out in the hall, so there's still hope."

"Jesus. That's so messed up. I can't believe he finally tried something. He should be thrown in the slammer. Like that guy Eddy."

Why does she have to keep bringing him up? Hearing his name makes my head hurt, and everything starts to get cloudy. Suddenly, I'm so tired and I don't want to talk anymore.

"I'm beat. I'll see you tomorrow, okay?"

"Cheer up, Rosie girl," she says. "I'll bring Hot Pockets for lunch."

In the wake of our call is deafening silence. I don't hear them arguing or Judd's truck rumbling away as I'd hoped. From their bedroom, across the hall, travels a distorted melody of yelling and laughing. What could possibly be funny about what just went down?

I clench my teeth, squeeze my eyes shut, hating them both. Then I curl myself into a ball, hugging a pillow, jamming the sheets and blankets between my legs. She's never going to take my side. This kicks the waterworks into high gear and washes away whatever hope I'd held on to of Lucy loving me.

When the melody finally stops, I cry long and hard until I manage to fall asleep on a pillowcase soaked with tears.

20

THERE ARE NO Hot Pockets. I'm kind of bummed, but Mary said her parents were in a major fight this morning during breakfast and she didn't want to make any waves by going in the kitchen.

We have English together second period, but it's impossible to talk during class, so we pick up last night's conversation during lunch.

"I can't believe she let him off the hook," I say, because he never left the house last night, and I woke to their bedroom door closed and giggling whispers that had me on the verge of crying again. I take a bite of a fish stick, its center still frozen. The day is nasty, with clumpy gray clouds hanging over the school, threatening to ruin our picnic.

"Oh, of course you can. Did you really think she wouldn't?" Mary inspects the peanut butter and jelly sandwich she bought at the cafeteria, then takes a tentative bite.

"Moses parted the Red Sea. Miracles happen." I wipe my greasy fingers on a napkin, then hope to wash away the taste with the soda.

"I don't know how you ever slept last night."

"With a crowbar, that's how," I joke. I don't tell her I cried myself to sleep. She may think I'm weak, but now that I know she's been dealing with her own stuff at home, I want to seem strong like her. Maybe she's even been subjected to her father's wrath, too. I rack my brain. Have I ever seen bruises she wouldn't explain? Without realizing it, I'm scanning her body—her long legs, her forearms, her neck.

"What?" she asks, catching me sizing her up.

"Nothing." I shake the disturbing thought out of my head. "Could she be in denial? I think she—" I pretend to gag. "Loves him." I know the feeling, how it keeps you from seeing things right under your nose, like Ray staring at another girl. We went to the beach most weekends, so there were a lot of opportunities for his eyes to settle on another girl's butt. A couple times I even thought he'd been cheating on me—a string of flirty text messages, a girl who passed by us at a party one night and called him her *little architect*—but brushed aside the suspicions because he told me I was blowing things out of proportion. So I did, because I didn't want to lose him, my first official boyfriend.

"That explains it then. Lucy's wearing blinders the size of goddamned solar panels. How else could she not see that her fiancé hitting on her kid is a major red flag?" Mary waves her sandwich in the air, a gesture to ensure I don't interrupt her upcoming thought. I pick at the syrupy fruit cocktail and choose something orange. "Maybe that's it. You're not really hers, just some snot-nosed kid she helped raise. Why she kept doing it after your dad croaked is anyone's guess. So forget about last night, Rosie girl. You're not gonna win that battle." She puts a hand on either side of her face. "Solar panels."

"I guess," I say, trying to find a shred of solace in her theory, but still coming up empty. I don't know why I even care, but I do. We've still shared a life, me and Lucy, and as much as we've butted heads, I don't want her thinking I'd ever betray her like that.

She takes a final bite and her sandwich is gone. She rolls up the foil and tosses it in her bag. "But the war—now that's something else. That you have to win. So what's your plan?"

"Well, I overheard her calling in sick."

"Sick, huh?" Mary says, raising a skeptical eyebrow.

"Yeah, she always calls in sick when they have a fight. I think she does it so they can have makeup sex without me around." I pop a grape in my mouth and enjoy the sour-sweet explosion. "Anyway, it works to my advantage today. Going to skip last period and head over to the scrap yard."

"Good luck getting past Shoal," she warns, as if I need reminding of the legendary secretary who lives to thwart anyone's goal of leaving early.

"Maybe I'll bribe her with melon." I hold up my fruit cup.

She wags her finger. "Judging by Shoal's thunder thighs, you'd have a better chance with cake." Mary's flushed from the heat, but the glow makes her pretty. She wears more makeup than I do, especially foundation to cover the freckles she's grown to detest (thinks they make her look too young), and when she wipes away sweat from her nose, the foundation comes with it.

She's right about Shoal, and we share a chuckle before Mary gets serious again. "So what're you going to say once you get there? 'Don't mind me while I rummage through Lucy's shit'?"

"I'll figure something out," I say, hoping I do. Mary's usually the one with solutions.

"Aren't you worried she'll find out you went through her stuff?"

"Her car isn't called the Slaabmobile for nothing. I'm sure she keeps her desk like she keeps her car."

The gray clouds make good on their threat. A drop of water lands on the lone fish stick in my Styrofoam container.

"It's starting to rain," Mary says. "We'd better go." With both hands, she shovels up her stuff, then disappears across the field before I can catch her.

. . .

I've heard stories about the olden days, when schools were wide open and everyone came and went as they pleased. No gates, no security guards, no metal detectors. All you needed to skip school back then was a free hallway and enough guts and confidence to walk out.

It's not like that anymore. Now you need phone calls and passes and all sorts of proof that you have business outside of school. Del Vista is actually easier than most. It's public, so the entire faculty is overworked, underpaid, and eager to get you out of their face if you hang around long enough.

When I arrive between fifth and sixth periods, the office is quiet except for the clacking of keyboards hidden behind cubicle dividers. Every wall is covered in student artwork—none of it very good—but the overwhelming display makes for a good show when parents come calling.

Ever since Mary and I dodged the rain during lunch, it's been pouring. Outside, angry bullets of water pelt the single office window, creating a blurred view of the faculty parking lot.

The door closes behind me with a click that announces my presence. Mrs. Shoal greets me with an eye raise, meant to ask, *What do you want?*

I rest my elbows on the counter littered with graduation announcements and ticket forms. I've already got two for Lucy and the Dud, who will probably sit in the back of the Miami-Dade County Auditorium willing the time to pass quickly.

"I have a dental appointment." I point to my mouth as if she needs a visual to understand.

"Pass?" She extends her hand, palm up.

"I don't have one."

"Ms. Velvitt, you've been at this school for four years. You know the drill."

"My mom's sick," I say, which is sort of true. "That's why she didn't call or send me with a note."

The secretary dips her head, pulls down a pair of glasses that had been hidden in a tuft of frizzy dark hair, silver at the roots. I know that look—she thinks she's struck gold, caught me in a lie. "Then how are you getting to the dentist?"

"I have my license," I shoot back.

"But you don't have a car," she says, and holds up a small metal box at the front of her desk. "See this? Contains vehicle information for every pass issued to a car on the student parking lot. I know it by heart." Her frosty lavender lips curve into a grin. "Just the kind of girl I am."

"I didn't say I had a car *here*," I clarify, matching her attitude. I stroke the side of my jaw, up and down, then across. "My tooth is killing me. The appointment is in like thirty minutes and I have to catch the bus home. My mom said I could take her car." I do some fake grimacing, rub my temples to show I'm getting a headache.

Mrs. Shoal grabs the phone from the cradle on her desk. "Dentist's number?"

"Seriously?"

"Seriously." Mrs. Shoal's on the north side of sixty and icy about it. She probably hates young girls like me that don't need to color their hair or wrap their legs in cellophane to combat cellulite.

I struggle a bit, huff and puff, then say, "I don't have it. It's . . . you know, that dental office in the strip mall near . . . oh, what's that grocery store with the funny name?"

Mrs. Shoal's not playing. She's propped her head in her hands, enjoying the show.

"I really need to get going, Mrs. Shoal." Trying a little respect, even pulling out the sad-puppy-dog face that used to work on Ray when he was mad at me for no reason.

"Tell you what," she says. "I'm feeling generous today. Bring me a slip tomorrow from the dentist. How's that?"

Terrible, but I say, "Sure," then scramble out of the office so I don't miss the 2:15 bus.

21

I HAVEN'T MISSED coming here. Scrap Metal Mania is a filthy place, crowded with parts of things I can't identify, piles and piles of junk I can't imagine being good for anything. And yet it's been a Miami fixture for over twenty-seven years and has lined the Potillo brothers' pockets for just as long.

My father had already been working at Scrap Metal Mania for about a year when the owner, Roland Potillo, promoted him to machine operator helper. I was five and starting my first day of kindergarten when he dropped the bomb on me that his new wife—the pretty lady with shiny gold hair he had recently married—was my new mom and would be picking me up from school. Since he was starting a new position, he didn't know when he'd be home. He'd made me promise to remember every detail of my day, but when he finally came through the front door, it was dark outside, and he was too tired to prod for more after I'd told him *It was good.*

I remember wondering why he wasn't simply a machine operator, instead of a machine operator helper. I was a helper—at home, at school, even when we visited a strawberry patch in Homestead and I helped by carrying the bag. Surely my father was more than a helper. But I didn't have to wonder for long.

It seemed that with every new school year, my dad was being promoted to a new position. And for the last two years before he died, he was quality assurance manager, and we ate out twice a week and had a new car in the driveway.

Because I need to stay focused, I've shoved any memories of this place into the back pocket of my jeans as I approach the office—a squat, faded green building with a sign that has always had two letters missing. If you didn't know better, you'd think the name of the place was Scrap Metal Man, complete with the logo of a cartoon character whose body was made of kitchen appliance parts.

The rain has stopped, but the afternoon remains ugly and gray, and I have to avoid muddy puddles so as not to ruin my favorite wedge sandals, which I found for two bucks at Goodwill. Cars aren't lined up neatly in spaces, but parked haphazardly at odd angles. Half-dead palm trees do their best to provide a welcoming entrance on either side of a set of double doors, one of which is always locked. Even now, after a few years of not having visited, I know not to pull on the left one.

The right one opens how I remember, with a struggle at first, and then a quick release. Cold air and the smell of Lucy's cigarettes blast me when I walk through the door. For a scary second, I fear she's here, that she ended up coming into work, of all freaking days. But when my eyes dart to her desk—the largest one, near the back wall, littered with business licenses and community service awards the Potillo brothers won—a slim, athletic-looking black woman is sitting in Lucy's chair, inspecting her face in a silver compact.

She finally looks up when I make a humming noise and tap my banana-yellow fingernails on the counter. "Can I help you?"

"Hi, is Roland here?"

She gives me a blank stare, fusses with the collar of a sleeveless shirt that shows off well-toned shoulders. "Roland?"

"Mr. Potillo. The owner."

"Short, fat man? Wears a tie?"

I bring the side of my hand up to my chest. "About here?" She nods.

"That's him."

She scoots out from behind the desk to join me at the counter. She takes long, confident strides, and I imagine muscular legs under her snug slacks. "Sorry. I'm a temp," she says. "Just filling in for the secretary." Oh, how pissed Lucy would be to hear herself referred to as a simple secretary. She prefers administrative assistant, and then leans in close to whoever's listening and adds, *I totally run this place.*

"Rosie? Is that you?" Roland comes waddling out, looking older and fatter, but beaming like the sun. As usual, his tie is too short and ends halfway down his chest. It's bright and colorful, like him.

The temp strides back to Lucy's desk to answer a phone that started ringing. Without even giving me a chance to certify his claim, Roland wraps me in thick, hairy arms and hugs me tight. "I thought I heard your voice! Been a long time, but I'd never forget the sound of Clint's baby girl." He holds me at arm's length to inspect me. "Can't call you that anymore, though, can I?" Roland makes an exaggerated frown, as if he's sad that I've grown up and am no longer interested in the candy jar he keeps on his desk.

I force a smile because seeing him makes me sad, too. "I know it's been a long time," I say, struggling to push down the frog in my throat. Where did that come from? Stay on course, Rosie. Think of Mac. Your mission.

"So, big news!" Roland bellows, still clutching my hands. "Your mom and Judd. Those two are finally getting hitched!"

I now remember how everything out of Roland's mouth sounds exclamatory, like it should be on the front page of the newspaper. "Yep," I say dully, but what I want to say is, *Judd's a pervert, he attacked me last night. You're connected, Roland, can't you hire someone to break his legs or something?*

"Came over here like a real gentleman, took your mom out to lunch. Well, you know the rest." Roland's expression shifts again. His face is like a roller coaster, up and down, adjusting with the height of the conversation. "How long's your dad been gone, Rosie? Two years now?"

"Over three."

"Can't believe it's been that long. Seems like yesterday . . ." He's misty-eyed and his voice evaporates into the space between us.

"Judd's been living with you two a long time," he says, as if stating this fact helps the situation make more sense. "Nice fellow. A little young, if you ask me, but his heart's in the right place. I remember when he took you all camping to . . . what's that place up there?"

"Ocala," I say, instantly reminded of the marshmallows we burned and our tent that collapsed. Frustration led to laughter, and within an hour we were on our way to a hotel where we ordered room service after swimming in the pool. Recalling a good memory feels weird, and I shake it off.

"Ocala. Right. Maybe I should bring my own girls up there one day." He smooths the short tie while pushing out his barrel chest. "So, what brings you by, young lady?"

"Speaking of them . . . getting hitched," I repeat, reaching into the side pocket of my backpack. "I wanted to leave her something. It's a surprise."

Roland gazes at me skeptically, but not like Mrs. Shoal, who always stares you down with the assumption you're up to no good.

I pull out a sealed white envelope. "It's only a card," I say, hoping to take the big mystery out of it. There's nothing inside, only a blank piece of paper I won't be leaving, anyway.

He almost plucks it out of my hands. "I'll give it to her."

"No, no, it's . . . private."

"I can see that, honey. It's sealed."

"Would you mind if I left it on her desk?"

Roland hesitates, rocks back and forth on his stubby legs, cramped in a pair of snug khaki pants. "What's going on? Why wouldn't you just give her this at home?"

"Because it's—"

"Private," he repeats. "I got that."

I dip my head, muster up the puppy-dog face. Twice in one day. It's getting a little old, even for me. "I don't want Judd to see it. It's a . . . you know, mother-daughter thing." Slam dunk.

He's thinking again, weighing my words against his own, then says, "I know. Got three of my own, and Lord, how those girls love their mama." With an extended arm, Roland motions to the woman at Lucy's desk. "Ms. Cornish, would you come with me? Got a job for you in the storage room." He leans his chubby face into mine and whispers, "Give you a little privacy." Mental note to include him in my prayers tonight.

As they're leaving the main office, Roland turns back to me. "How's she feeling, anyway?"

I'm caught off guard, my heart already beating with antici-pation, my head focused on scouring Lucy's desk as fast as pos-sible. "Huh?"

"Your mom. She's sick, isn't she?"

"Getting better" are the first words that fall out of my mouth.

"Good. Don't know what we're going to do without her."

. . .

Without her? What? His parting comment has me spinning, but I can't dwell on it. I've got limited time before this office starts buzzing with activity. I remember late afternoon is when a lot of the workers come back from the field, and passing through here always seems to be a pit stop.

Nothing is locked. That's a good thing. All five drawers are open. Sift, sift, sift.

Nothing is here. That's a bad thing. Only stuff you'd expect to find in desk drawers—files, catalogs, service manuals.

Frustrated, I snort an angry breath through my nose. I rock back and forth in her chair, scanning the framed photos on her desk: zero of her and my dad, two of her and Judd, and one of us taken last year. It was a good day. We'd gone to the mall and bought matching outfits—white sundresses and sandals with rhinestones—then eaten lunch outside while birds pecked at our food. The waitress had taken the picture. I stare at the frozen moment trapped in a pitted gold frame and remember something else and think, no, it wasn't a good day. Mary came by after. She scowled at the dress, said Lucy was probably just drunk, and that she'd return everything when she sobered up. I was heartbroken, and even kept the tags on the dress, in case she was right. Had Lucy snuck a drink without me noticing? I just thought she was in a good mood.

I set down the frame when a phone stops mid-ring. The call must have been picked up somewhere else, but it's only a matter of minutes before Ms. Cornish returns to fulfill the only duty Lucy allows temps to do in her absence, which is answering phones.

Think, Rosie, think. There's got to be something here. I rock harder in Lucy's chair, part of me wanting to bust it, the other part of me knowing better. When I almost tip back into the wall, my foot knocks into something at the very bottom of the desk. I steady myself, then lean down to inspect. It's another drawer, but recessed and super-slim, which is why I must have missed it. Smack in the middle is a lock. I yank, but it won't budge.

I pull open all the other drawers again, looking for the key. My fingers shaking, I check inside folders, between catalog pages, even open up a stapler because that's where I'd hide it.

Then I scour the drawer right beneath her desk, the one that's usually full of office supplies and emergency makeup. Tons of paper clips fill the entire plastic valley of a full-length organizer. I pull it out farther. In the very back, behind a clump of tampons (genius!), I spy something shiny. A single silver key—small enough to fit that lock, big enough to give me the break I need.

· · ·

I text Mac on the bus ride home.

Found something

It takes him ten minutes to respond, which annoys me. Is he with another client who happens to be older and more beautiful and exactly his type and not an orphan who is on some crazy hunt for her long-lost mother?

What?

can i come by 2morow aft school?

Of course.

k

See you then.

Mr. By-the-Book. He can't even use text language. I force out a deep breath to calm myself. I'm still shaking from those last minutes at Lucy's desk. Crunched for time, I didn't question what I found. It was locked up—reason enough to take it. Then I quickly relocked the drawer and put the key back where I found it.

It wasn't a moment too soon. The clicking sound of Ms. Cornish's heels had me shoving the papers into my backpack. I thought Roland had seen, so I kicked the waterworks into high gear, blubbering about how hard it was to be there, missed my dad, blah blah blah. Roland bought it, wrapping a chunky arm around my shoulder and giving it a healthy squeeze. I think the temp was suspicious, though. I caught her staring at my backpack with curious eyes, then she asked in a clipped way if I wouldn't mind giving her chair back. Her chair. I did so gladly, then made Roland promise to keep my visit a secret until Lucy found the surprise envelope—which, of course, wasn't even there. It was already back in my bag.

I check my watch, make sure I'll be home right around the same time I'd return from school. A little after four o'clock. Close enough. Sometimes, Lucy actually pays attention to my schedule, especially if it's early enough that she hasn't had a chance to hit the sauce.

This afternoon's mission has worn me out. My brain is fried from combating Shoal and dodging Roland. I allow the bumpy rhythm of the bus to lull me into dreamy thoughts. Thoughts of kissing Mac. Better yet—Mac kissing me. It's the first time I've been attracted to someone since Ray. It feels different, too. Cleaner, softer. With Ray, from the moment we met at the beach, everything felt hard and rushed. It had only been a couple hours since his Frisbee had hit me in the head and we were out in the ocean where he tried to untie my bikini top. He was always trying to get down my pants and up my shirt. With Mac, it's nice that we can just sit and talk, maybe laugh a little. Not that there's been any official notice of interest on either of our parts. But it definitely feels like something is there, beginning to bubble beneath the surface.

22

I'M HAPPY to finally see John again when he opens the agency door for me. His craggy face lights up, making me feel welcome.

"How's my old friend Rosie?"

"Living the dream."

He reaches out with one of those half-shake, half-hug kind of things. Because he's so tall, my head grazes his shoulder. He's dressed nicer than both times I saw him at Lou's—gray slacks and a long-sleeved white shirt cinched at the neck with a dark red tie (positioned at the proper length, I might add).

"Is Mac here?" I ask, peering around him, concerned that he may not be. I've waited all day to show up in the outfit I labored over this morning. The beaded necklace and matching earrings, the snug capri pants, the soft yellow sweater I'm hoping he'll want to touch. I didn't check my hair fifteen times on the bus ride over here for nothing. I may have been suspicious at first when he offered to work for free, but Mac has proven to be professional and gentlemanly. I've not only become reassured by these qualities, I'm also oddly attracted to them. To him.

"What, you don't want to talk to me anymore?" John asks.

"No!" It comes out stronger than I intended. "Of course I

do." I smile wide, even touch the sleeve of his shirt, hoping to undo my rudeness.

The wrinkles in John's cheeks deepen when he smiles. "Good. I don't want you sore with me."

"Never," I say, and then Mac enters the room, his disheveled hair free from gel and resting just above his shoulders. He's wearing the same stiff khakis he wore the day I met him and a long-sleeved polo, but it's black and holds the creases of an expert ironing job. I look down, and there are the boat shoes, striped socks peeking out the top. Last week I found them geeky, today not so much.

"Hello there," Mac says, polite and perfect. Is his smile lingering? Is he staring at my fluffy sweater, wondering how it would feel to touch? I hope so. The three of us stand in a triangle, occupying the space between the lobby and the hallway.

"Well, I'm here if you need me," John says, flattening his tie, even though it's hanging fine. He turns to Mac before disappearing into his office. "You'll go over what we discussed," he says, his eyes darting at me. "Good to see you, Rosie."

"You, too," I say, really meaning it, but instantly distracted by his comment.

Mac extends his arm into the dark hallway. "After you," he says, and I can't go fast enough.

. . .

Before I hand over the document, I waste no time following up on John's cryptic remark. "What was your uncle talking about?"

"First things first. Let's see what you found yesterday." He wiggles his fingers in the air, palms up. An excited child awaiting a gift.

"That's second," I say, part cute, part serious. "Tell me."

"I will," he says, "but would you let me work in my own order, please?" He smirks, pulls out my Ziploc bag from a drawer, and places it in front of us. "I forgot to give you this," he says, and hands me a piece of paper. It's a list of everything in the bag, plus his signature at the bottom and a stamp of the office logo. "That's a receipt for your personal items. Just hold on to it."

I thank him and tuck it in my bag, making a mental note to tell Mary. I had totally forgotten about her suggestion and yet Mac still came through.

He proceeds to lay out the items, introducing each one as if I've never seen them.

"I've been studying each piece. We've got two pictures to work with. This one here, of your parents at some sort of social gathering. Let's call that the party picture. And this one, of your mother in the ski jacket. Let's call that the snow picture."

He's getting me excited, like there really may be a trail to follow.

"We've got the bracelet, which I'm not sure how it connects to anything, but it was hers, so that's fine." When Mac slides it to the side, I take it.

"Do you think I can have this back?"

"Of course," he says.

"It's a bracelet. I don't think it means anything. It's just something from her childhood I guess my dad wanted me to have."

"Cross it off the list, then, okay?"

I respect his professionalism too much not to do it right then and there, so I pull out the receipt and we both initial the eliminated item.

"Moving on," he says, getting back to work. "We have your birth certificate, which seems odd to me." When he looks up, there's genuine concern in his eyes.

"Why?"

"Because it's yours."

"Meaning?"

"These other items. They belonged to Justine. But the birth certificate belongs to you. So it got me thinking that there must be a clue in here." He scans the folded piece of paper I never gave much consideration. I figured Dad just wanted to leave me an extra copy.

"I think . . . I mean . . ." It's the first time Mac has stumbled through a thought. "I don't believe your father left these items randomly. I think they're clues."

A part of me thinks it's cool that my dad orchestrated this little mystery, but it's a really small part. The bigger part has always wondered why he didn't simply leave a single note in that box: *Your mother is alive. She is (fill in the blank with her location).* It's the why that's had me more nervous than anything. Maybe she's in jail. Maybe she took off with someone else. Or maybe she just took off. I've heard people do that sometimes, when they can't handle the pressure. Is that what happened? What if she couldn't handle me?

He folds up the birth certificate, picks up the pictures, and tucks them carefully back in the bag. "But clues to what? I'm still not sure."

"You can't leave me hanging!"

"I'm sorry. I don't mean to. I'm still doing some research, so I don't want to tell you anything until I know for sure. One of John's rules."

I pout, pick at an invisible tuft of yellow yarn from my sweater.

"Look, it may turn out to be nothing," he says, a weak attempt to pacify me. "Let's focus on what you found yesterday."

Something tells me there's no use arguing. Plus, he's not charging me, so I have to keep my demands to a minimum. I pull out the stapled stack of papers and slide it across the desk. Like a student waiting to get a test back, I sit and wait, my stomach in knots. But it does give me a chance to study Mac while he studies something else. The way his hair parts to the side and curls up at the ends. I bet it's soft. The caramel skin of his throat where it disappears into his shirt. The hair on his forearms, wispy and blond. I bet that's soft, too. I haven't wanted to touch another guy since Ray.

Immediately, I push the image of his face out of my head, wipe it away with a scouring pad until all I see is Mac again, his head hung over the stuff I brought. He's reading with fierce concentration, sort of like I do when I'm trying to figure out a pattern based on a magazine photo. I can see the design, but I'm not always sure how it got that way. I hope Mac has better analytical skills than I do.

He makes little grunting noises with the flip of every page.

I can barely keep the toes of my silver ballet flats from digging into the carpet.

"Well?"

Mac drops the document on his desk, shrugs his shoulders. "Looks like a standard will and testament." The flatness of his voice deflates me. "Nothing unusual jumps out at me—"

"Are you sure? I know I saw my name in that mess."

"It is, in several places. You were his daughter—of course there would be multiple references to you."

"You looked like you were skimming," I say. "Take your time."

His shoulders bristle in defense. "I could take all the time in the world and still not completely understand this document."

I don't believe him. He's like a Boy Wonder. Between his above-average intellect and weird-but-kinda-cute above-average maturity, I'm just waiting for his cape to slip out from under his shirttails. I wouldn't be surprised to learn that he flies around at night rescuing victims of random crimes. Aside from all that, he must be good if he's actually taking up space in this snazzy office. Family or no family—John William Brooks, PI, is not going to keep around someone who can't carry their weight. This much I can tell.

Mac rubs the back of his neck. "I've only taken a few legal classes so far to satisfy my criminology degree. John will need to take a look at this."

"Can he look at it now?" I ask, kicking myself for brushing him aside earlier.

"Follow me." Mac grabs the will, and I fall in step behind him.

"We need your help."

John slaps closed the file he had been reading and displays open palms to receive whatever we've got coming his way. "Figured as much. That's an awfully bright SOS sign illuminated above your heads." His lame jokes I don't miss.

Mac hands over the will. "Take a look at this." And then we settle into two cracked leather chairs opposite John's desk. He picks up a pair of reading glasses and gets busy while Mac and I sit like schoolchildren waiting for the teacher's instructions.

Since his office is at the end of the hallway, I've never seen it before. It's nowhere near as nice as Mac's, the extent of his decorating a sad hanging plant, its leaves drooping toward the tile floor. But it's more impressive in other ways, with a cluster of framed certificates on the wall and his diploma from the University of Miami in the center. Trophies and plaques with engraved footballs line two shelves on the wall to my right, bringing into focus what I had suspected at our first meeting. Behind him, a giant orange-and-green poster reads, IT'S ALL ABOUT THE U. John's one of those lifelong Canes fans.

My leg starts bobbing up and down like the needle on a sewing machine. I have a portable one in my room. Found it for five bucks at the Salvation Army. It can only do small jobs like hemming or appliqué work, but it's a workhorse and it's mine.

Mac places three fingers on my knee to stop the nervous shaking. I look into his eyes, which say everything I need to hear: *Relax. Trust me.* I nod. He pulls his hand back, but the damage is already done. I felt the heat of his fingertips burning right through my capris, making it official. I'm totally attracted to this guy.

For several more minutes, John flips through pages until a grin spreads across his face. "Well, here's some good news." Dreadful pause. "You've got money coming to you."

"Really?" I'm more surprised than excited, figuring it can't be much. After all, if there had been a lot of money left behind, I wouldn't have been forced to leave my old house. "How much?"

"Fifty percent," John says.

"Why do you say it like that? Fifty percent of what?"

"Well, at the time this will was drafted, in 2010, his estate was valued at close to a million."

"Please tell me you're talking dollars, not marbles," I say, my insides already beginning to crackle and pop at this unbelievable news.

"I am."

"So I get five hundred thousand dollars?"

"Give or take," he says. "It's been seven years. There's probably a bit more than that with interest, which is why money set aside in a trust is given as a percentage, instead of an exact figure."

"Wow. That's a lot of sketchbooks and designer shoes!"

John never lifts his eyes off the page, doesn't even crack a smile.

"Wait." My giddy excitement comes to a grinding halt. "If I get half, who gets the other half?" Like I even have to ask. John's expression confirms it. "So we each get five hundred grand." I let the number sink in and fill my mind with possibilities I'd never imagined. "It could be worse, I guess. He could've given her more."

"True."

"It still doesn't make sense, though. We're both getting money. Why keep my dad's will hidden from me? And why don't we already have the money? I don't get it."

Several minutes pass before John asks, "Is this the original?"

"What do you mean?"

"Is this a copy of what you found?"

"No," I say, afraid it's the wrong answer.

"Then you need to return it," he says, his eyes still glued to the pages.

"What?" I almost shoot out of my chair.

"You have to, Rosie, or she's going to know you took it."

"So? I have every right to see my father's will."

"Yes, but not by stealing her copy of it."

I snap my head to the side and bark at Mac. "You're the one who told me to go there!"

"Not with the intention of stealing anything, especially a legal document. I thought maybe you'd find—"

"What? Another secret box? Come on, Mac. This woman knows the truth about my mother—some giant secret my father obviously wanted her to keep, too. But even now, over three years after his death? It doesn't make sense."

I deflate in my seat.

"You should have made a copy," Mac grumbles, all irritated.

"When? In the two whole minutes I was alone?" I'm being snippy, but I can't help it.

"Please, you two." John removes his reading glasses to fix those steely-gray investigator eyes on us. "You want my help, you're going to have to pipe down." He continues to flip through the pages while I stew in my seat. The heat from Mac's fingertips has grown cold, but so have I, frustrated with the prospect of having to concoct another plan to return to Scrap Metal Mania.

"Well, well, well. What do we have here?" John's voice drops like a stone, but then he turns the page and says, "Wait a minute . . ."

Something in John's voice makes my belly do a somersault.

"Wait a minute . . . ," he says again.

"Tell us!" I blurt.

He uses his finger to trace line after line, hums, traces, then falls back in his seat once he's done reading.

"What did you find?" I ask, gripping the edge of his desk.

"The needle in a haystack."

I don't know what makes me more nervous—Mac, who's shot up out of his chair, or the bombshell John's about to drop. He's got that look in his eyes, the same one I saw at Lou's Deli when he told me he was passing off my case to someone else. Bad news is coming.

"There's a stipulation in the will. Regarding your stepmother."

"That can't be good," I say, knowing that a stipulation is just a big, fancy word for something—or someone—standing in the way of getting what you want. "If you tell me she can take my half for some stupid reason, I'm going to seriously lose it."

"No. It's not a stipulation for you, Rosie. It's a stipulation for her."

Okay, then. Go on, counselor.

"The will states, should your father predecease his spouse, Lucille Goss Velvitt—Lucy," he clarifies, "must continue to adequately take care of you until your eighteenth birthday, the age at which an individual is considered an adult."

I sense the stipulation slithering around the corner. "Or what?"

"Or she doesn't get her half."

My dad, even in death, protects me. My heart aches with a fresh wave of missing him. I'm all over the place. Ashamed of those times I cursed him for leaving us with nothing and having to move. Impressed that he hadn't squandered his money, after all. He had been saving it. For me. Well, for me and that duplicitous cougar.

"Lucy's half," John starts, perched to lay it on the line for me. "It's being held in trust until your eighteenth birthday. Like yours. She only receives it if she continued to raise you . . ." His voice trails off while he searches to repeat the exact words on the paper. "With proper parental guidance, which includes all basic needs of the minor Rose Annalise Velvitt, as well as reasonable care and support."

I almost choke at the last part. She definitely didn't support me the other night when I swore that her boyfriend stuck his tongue down my throat.

"So he was paying her off," I say, which is what it really means.

"In a manner of speaking. You can always contest it. Do your best to prove she was an unfit parent."

"To who?"

"The executor of the trust. Whoever that is." John pauses. "Has anyone ever visited since your father's death? You know, to check on you, see how you were doing?"

"No. Never."

"Then the lawyer"—John flips to the front of the will and reads from the letterhead—"Benedict Stephens or Russell Stephens is probably the executor. You could always plead your case to him."

The ungodly ring of John's cell phone—a cross between rodeo music and a holiday carol—breaks his concentration. He checks the screen, then says, "Sorry, kids. I have to take this," and hands the will back to Mac. "Don't worry. We'll pick up where we left off." We're dismissed with a signal to be quiet as he answers the call. Mac closes the door behind us, and I lead the way back to his office.

"This is so messed up," I say, plunking down into one of his seats. "Where do I go from here?"

"I'm not sure." It's the first time I've heard uncertainty in Mac's voice. I study the framed photos on the wall, trying to figure out what each one is. I can tell they're ordinary objects, zoomed in a thousand percent, but that's it. I grow frustrated and refocus my attention across the desk.

"I'm sorry, Rosie."

"What for?" I ask, because I'm legitimately curious. He hasn't done anything wrong.

"That you had to find out something like this. It can, you know, throw off someone's balance."

He's got that right. Ever since my father died—and that's been over three years—I've felt out of whack. Lost. Anxious. All I can say is, thank God for Mary. She's grounded me, been that soft place to land when I was perched to fall. Then finding the box a couple months ago only made things worse. After all these years, learning that my birth mother was alive? I think I'm entitled to be a little off balance.

I grab the will from his hands and toss it on the floor with as much care as Mary told me Todd used when he threw the condom into the corner. It lands with a soft thud near the far right leg of Mac's desk. He doesn't attempt to pick it up.

"So basically my dad paid Lucy to raise me."

He places a tentative hand on my shoulder, like he's trying to steady me. When I look up, his usually clear green eyes look murky. I feel it coming on—a loss of control moving in fast. Something's buzzing in my backpack. It must be Mary, texting or calling, but I can't get it now. I'm about to blow.

"All these years!" I scream. That's what comes out first. "It finally makes sense," I continue. "It's not that she's bipolar. She just can't stand me, but she's got to keep me around." More dots become connected. "If I take off, she doesn't hit the mother lode. What a conniving bitch!"

The buzzing continues, insistent, in my backpack. I know it's Mary, but I can't talk to her right now.

"Rosie—" he says, but that's it. Nothing else.

"I should've known," I say, trying to calm myself by focusing on one of his framed photographs.

"How? Unless one of those attorneys has tried to contact you, giving you a heads-up. But no one has, right?"

"No," I reply quickly, but do a mental scan, wondering if I've missed any calls recently or accidentally deleted any voice mails. No. I definitely haven't been contacted.

"They could've sent certified letters, but with you a minor, Lucy would've been able to sign for them," Mac says. "You would've needed some serious detective skills to have figured this one out. At least you were smart enough to hire us to use ours." Mac brushes an imaginary lapel and grins. I appreciate his attempt to lighten the mood, but I'm too angry and can't seem to unclench my fists.

"It's weird. I almost feel relieved to finally know the truth. But it's an ugly truth, and it kind of makes me feel ugly to be a part of it."

"Not possible." Mac puts a hand against my face. His touch calms me, actually makes the spinning in my head slow down. I also notice Mary has stopped calling.

I put my hand to his. "Thanks."

For a moment, I think he's going to lean in and kiss me, but instead he pulls away. The energy has shifted, leaving me feeling awkward and alone again. I glance around at each of the four large photos, framed in wide black wood.

"You never told me what these are."

"Do you like them?"

"Well, that depends," I say coyly. "Did you take them?"

"I did," he says.

"So what are they?"

"Two things actually. Simple impressions, but also puzzles."

"Puzzles? I don't get it."

He joins me in front of the one I'm staring at and strokes the glass, behind which is a photo of hundreds of tiny bumps. I can't tell if he's admiring his work or the subject matter, but his eyes appear glazed. "It's the problem solver in me. I like things I have to figure out."

"Or have other people figure out."

"Perhaps," he says with a smirk. Our little banter is just the diversion I need from wills, and inheritances, and evil step-mothers.

"Okay, I'll bite." I study the photo for a minute, then offer up an idea. "It's an orange."

"No," he says, and leans in. His forearm brushes against mine when he reaches out again to touch the glass. "See the dips, the shadows they make?"

I follow the lines he traces with a finger, and squint with fierce concentration at the image. I'm getting an idea, and when I take another look at the other three photos, I'm certain my hunch is correct. "It's a basketball."

"I'd give you a prize if I had one."

"And that's a football, a tennis ball, and a golf ball," I say, identifying each one as I point to it. "You think you're tricking everyone with the black and white."

"Everyone but you." He raises a single eyebrow and smiles, sending a bunch of electrical currents surging through me. I feel hot, suffocating in my sweater.

"I need to sit," I say, reaching out for the chair.

Mac spins around to grab it for me. We end up facing each other for that awkward extra second that gives me the courage, in my dizzying state, to kiss him. He jerks backward, like I've shot him with a stun gun or something.

"What are you doing?" He uses the back of his hand to wipe off the gloss I barely had a chance to leave on his lips.

"Uh . . ." My mind freezes. Had I misread his signs? I take the honest approach, slap my heart on my fluffy sweater sleeve. "I thought you liked me . . ." Lame, ridiculous. I want to crawl into a hole, embarrassed.

"It's got nothing to do with liking you, Rosie."

"Then what does it have to do with? You said I was sweet," I tease.

"You are."

"And that you like the little patch of fuzz on my cheek."

"I do." When Mac strokes the side of my face, I take it as a sign to try again. At first, resistance, but then his lips remain on mine. This time, he kisses me back. He tastes like oranges and mint gum. We instantly fall into a rhythm, our tongues darting in and out, our lips getting sucked in and released . . . until I raise my hands to clasp them around his neck and he breaks away.

"We can't," he says.

"Why not?" I'm more confused than ever.

"First of all, you're seventeen—"

"Only for ten more days. It's not like you're cradle-robbing or anything. You're only twenty yourself, big shot." I flirtatiously poke him in the chest.

"Second," Mac continues with even more firmness, "we're in a professional relationship."

"Oh. I see," I say, because what else is there to say? He's shut me down. Tears spring to my eyes. That happens sometimes when I'm not necessarily sad, just frustrated. I wipe away a tear before it has a chance to fall and take my mascara with it down my cheek.

"Don't," Mac says. "Please don't cry."

"I'm not," I say, trying to stay strong. I nuzzle into his chest, breathe in the detergent smell of his shirt. I'm waiting for something—a hug, anything—to give me some sort of hope, but instead he leaves me standing there, pathetic. I don't know what else to do but try again, lifting up my face and planting an urgent kiss he can't resist. And yet he does.

Mac backs up, holds me at a distance. "Rosie, stop." His voice is cold and hard, his eyes narrowed in confusion. I get it. I'm confused, too. I've never behaved like this, and yet a part of me is pushing against another part—deep inside—and it's desperate to take control. Plus, a dull pain has crawled up the back of my neck, promising a headache.

"Then why did you kiss me?"

"You kissed me. I only kissed you back." When he grins, I know it was meant as a joke, but I don't feel like laughing.

"You have a girlfriend, don't you," I say, more like a claim than a question. There's an anger bubbling just below the surface, and it's ready to burst. It won't be controlled.

"No, I don't have a girlfriend."

"Then what's the fucking problem?"

"What?" he asks, shock distorting his usually handsome face. "It's called 'professional ethics,' Rosie. It's called 'not taking advantage of someone when they're vulnerable.'" His anger is piercing.

I think I start to wobble because I feel his hands gripping my shoulders, steadying me. Calling my name over and over, asking me if I'm all right. I've closed my eyes, willing away the pain that's traveled to my head.

When I open my eyes—is it minutes later, or only seconds?— Mac is studying me like I'm a wounded animal. "Rosie, are you okay?"

Not really. But we're done here. I need to go. "Yeah," I say, "just getting a migraine."

"Don't forget this." He bends over and picks up the will from the floor. "If I were you, I'd put it back where I found it."

I hesitate to take the crumpled document. Between shoving it in my backpack and throwing it on the floor, Lucy will definitely know it's been taken. There's no use returning the will, but I take it from Mac's hand, anyway. Then I grab my backpack and head for the door, which he's already opened for me.

"I'll be in touch," he says, though somehow I doubt it.

23

"I BLEW IT."

"Blew it?" Irritated, Mary yanks the bedcovers from me, hogging them. It leaves my legs cold and bare. "You've got five hundred grand coming your way in two weeks, and you're worried about having blown it with some guy who probably has his boxers pressed?"

I playfully smack her arm and drop my head on the pillow, exhausted. "Maybe that's why I'm worried. Thanks to my dad, my future is taken care of. Getting into the Fashion House next fall—done. I don't need a scholarship anymore."

"You still have to get accepted," she points out.

"I know. But now I can afford to look at other schools, too, even ones that don't offer scholarships. And if things with Lucy really go south, I can afford to get my own place. So you see? I have the luxury of worrying about that sort of thing."

"Whatever," she says. I can tell she doesn't share my logic. "Don't take your eye off the prize. Because now we know there is one. Kind of worth it, if you ask me. All these years suffering through Lucy's moods. Mystery solved!"

"Mac could be the prize, you know. Have you ever seen *The Butcher's Wife?*" I yank the blanket, and Mary comes with it. She snuggles in close, strands of her chestnut-brown hair tickling my face. It's only nine o'clock, but I'm already in bed, taking advantage of the peace and quiet while Lucy's out shopping for a wedding dress and Judd's at work. I think she knew better than to ask if I wanted to join her. Since the other night, the three of us haven't spoken so much as grunted at each other. Fine by me. Besides, now I know the score. She's only kept me around these past few years so she can cash in.

"Are you sleeping?" I nudge Mary when she doesn't answer me.

"Well, I'm trying." She opens her eyes and, in a flat voice, asks, "What butcher's life?"

"The Butcher's Wife," I correct her. "It's a movie about a woman who meets the man of her dreams and moves to his home city, only to find there the real man she was meant to marry."

Mary lifts her drowsy head. "What's this got to do with your situation?"

"Maybe this whole mess with Lucy, my dad, the will—it was all meant to lead me to Mac."

"You're fucking kidding." Mary's suddenly wide awake, her brown eyes glowing from the light cast by my nightstand lamp.

"I mean, even if things didn't end so well this afternoon, our relationship can be salvaged. I can fix it."

"Relationship? You've only known this guy a week! Come on, Rosie girl, I think you're getting ahead of yourself here."

"He didn't kiss you, Mary. You don't understand. It felt . . . right. Not like Ray."

"You thought it was right with Ray, too. A week after meeting him at the beach, you were on this same road. Slow down." Mary rubs my arm.

We did move fast. Since we'd met during winter break, we had another ten days before school resumed. He'd pick me up every morning in his Jeep and we'd do stuff—movies, long walks through Coconut Grove along the bay, lunches at every fast-food restaurant we'd come across. (He always chose burgers; I always got chicken sandwiches.) We'd also go to the mall and try on fancy outfits we could never afford. That's when I told him about my dream to become a designer, and one Sunday, he spent an entire afternoon at my house, looking through my sketchbooks. He said I was crazy talented, and then we kissed until he tried putting his fingers between my legs and I said no for the first time.

Anyway, I don't want to slow down. Ever since I found the box, my life feels like it's picked up speed, even if it's not always going in the right direction. "So you don't think it's possible?" I ask. "That some people are meant to lead you to other people?"

She gets this look, the one she makes before unloading a theory I won't like. "Your entire life has been a lie, but you think it's okay because some college stud is at the end of this warped rainbow." Mary props herself up on an arm. She's wearing the nightshirt she keeps at my house for emergency sleepovers. "If I didn't know you so well, I'd think you're having delusions. But since I do, I'm going to chalk it up to your desperate attempt to make sense of all this shit."

Kissing Mac wasn't a delusion. I remember oranges and mint gum and his lower lip against my tongue. I'm right back there, in his office, when I hear this:

"Rosie, you awake?" It's Lucy, knocking on my door.

"Hide!" I whisper, pulling the comforter over Mary's head. It's a good thing she's skinny. All I have to do is pile a couple of pillows on top of her and she's all but hidden.

"Yes," I say through the door, holding the knob still.

"Can I come in? I want to show you something." I'm scared. Those were the exact same words Judd used when he paid me a visit with the engagement ring.

"I'm sleeping," I say, not ready to face her.

"You just said you were up. It's only nine fifteen."

"I don't feel well."

"It'll only take a minute."

Fake cough. "I don't want to reinfect you," I say, referring to her phony illness that got her out of work yesterday. We both know I know she wasn't sick. It's meant to be a jab.

She jiggles the knob, but the door's locked. "Open up."

I glance back at my bed, looking for signs of Mary, the faint rise and fall of the covers. There's nothing. She's gotten really good at hiding from Lucy. I open the door since it's no longer a request but a command.

She's all happy and shiny, her white-blond hair tucked into mini-barrettes on either side of her head. With pale blue eye shadow and bright red lips, she looks like a little girl who broke into her mother's makeup drawer.

"Here," she says, extending one of two shopping bags from the mall. "It's for you."

I don't want it. I don't even want to touch the handle of the bag she's gripping. "What is it?"

"Well, that isn't very nice." She muscles her way into my bedroom and plops down on the bed. Inside, I shriek. She will freak out if she finds Mary here. The truth is, she hasn't approved of our friendship since that first day we met, after my father's funeral, when I took off with her and didn't return home for hours. Then the whole spray-painting episode last summer sealed her disapproval.

Somehow, she misses crushing her. I hope she also misses the involuntary lurch my body made when she sat down. There's a gigantic mound of comforter at the far end of the bed. She must be under there. I sort of grab the bag and scoot Lucy off the bed at the same time, tell her to sit at my desk chair, which is more comfortable. Like I give a crap. I just need her off my bed.

"What is it?" I ask again, flipping on another light so I can get a better look.

"Open it," Lucy says, surveying the things on my desk. Of course, she finds my sketchbook lodged under a stack of textbooks and proceeds to open it.

"Don't." I lunge at her, grabbing the notebook before she has a chance to peer inside. She has no right to my dreams, especially now.

"Fine." She seems offended but doesn't challenge me. "Then open your gift, will you?"

From the bag, I pull out a dress the color of mint toothpaste from beneath a wad of white tissue paper. It's actually very pretty when I hold it up and inspect the silky fabric, impeccable stitching, and crystal-like buttons running down the back.

"It's my sorry gift," she says, almost knocking me off my feet. It's what my dad would say when offering a present after he'd gotten angry with me. He always felt guilty, even though I probably had it coming—not doing my chores around the house or breaking curfew. That kind of thing. I still have each one he ever gave me. They were usually small things, hair accessories or fake jewelry. A sorry gift was never anything extravagant like this dress.

While examining it against my body in the mirror, I nonchalantly ask, "What are you sorry for?" Is it possible she's going to come clean about my dad's will? Even though she called in sick today, she could've stopped by the office this afternoon and found it missing.

"The other night." She pulls a tissue from her shirt pocket and coughs into it.

Oh. I spin around to find her inspecting the tissue, which she swiftly tucks into her bra.

"Really?" I ask. Can she interpret the look in my eyes? It's saying, *Please have believed me. Please have believed me about Judd.* This could be a turning point. Even after everything I learned today, there's still a part of me that wants Lucy to take my side. It's the same part that wanted her to rub my back lovingly or add the perfect amount of raisins in my oatmeal to make it sweet. The part that wanted Lucy to care about me—not just because she had to because she married my dad. I rub the minty silk between my fingers as this hope resurfaces.

"He told me what happened. It was late, you were both—" She coughs again, mid-thought, and breaks into a full-out fit. Something mucousy and pink sprays from her mouth.

"What?" I toss the dress at the mound under which Mary is probably dying right now.

"Groggy," she says, patting her chest, trying to clear it.

"I wasn't groggy. I was making a smoothie in a blender."

Lucy closes the door and whispers, even though Judd's not home yet, "Men. They get nervous before getting hitched." Her face turns sad, contemplative. She believes her own warped theory. With her hands on my shoulders, she says, "I don't blame either one of you—"

"Uh, you kind of should. You should blame him—your fiancé—for attacking me."

"Really, Rosie? He attacked you?" She may as well have said, *Really, Rosie? You want to be a brain surgeon?* because my claim was that unbelievable.

Knowing this conversation is going to end up exactly how it did the other night, with me on one side and Lucy cozy next to Judd on the other, I say, "Forget it."

"Well, I had until you brought it up again."

"No. You brought it up again. I thought you said you were sorry."

"I am. I'm sorry Judd . . . did whatever he did. We had been fighting earlier, and, well . . . He promised nothing like that will ever happen again, and I believe him."

What a fool. I can't even respond. My teeth are clenched so hard, I'm afraid the two fillings I got when I was thirteen will crack.

"Let's move on, Rosie. Really, it's the only way."

She's right about that. I definitely want to move on and, like Mary, possibly away. With my inheritance, I can get my own place, a car, anything I need. The thought calms me and so does the silky fabric I've been mindlessly slipping through my fingers.

"Thank you for the dress. I hope it fits."

"It better. You need to wear it next weekend."

My head scrambles, thinking of the calendar. My birthday's a week from Monday. Did Judd get his way and talk my mom into throwing some big party for me? "For what?"

"Our wedding, of course!" Lucy's mood has risen and thankfully, so has she. Standing at the door, she says, "Next Saturday at La Rosa's. That little Italian place downtown."

Why do people always call Italian places little? La Rosa's is actually kind of big and fancy with a wraparound bar and local singing talent if you're there late enough. Not that I've ever been.

"How did you put things together so fast?" I ask.

"It'll be small, just a few friends, some of Judd's family. We're excited. And we want you to be excited, too. Let's put what happened the other night behind us, okay?"

"I said I would," I snap. At this point, I have no choice. But in another couple weeks, all bets are off. I've already done the research, and I can rent an apartment once I turn eighteen.

"I hope you like the dress." She shakes the other bag in her hand while opening the door. "Wait till you see mine!"

I can't usher her out fast enough. I even close the door too quickly behind her, nipping her ankle. But I need to check on Mary, and when I lift the covers, I find her sound asleep.

24

I DID NOTHING all weekend but sulk in my bedroom. Well, that's not true. Two bags of salt-and-vinegar potato chips occasionally brightened my mood, as did a *Hem for Your Life* marathon that had me cringing along with the judges as they tore apart wannabe designers' failed attempts at pagoda sleeves and made them cry. When I get my shot, I won't be weak like that. When it comes to the critiquing of my designs, my skin will be as tough as an alligator handbag with solid gold hardware. I can take it. I want to learn so I can get better.

By Sunday evening, the hum of Lucy's constant phone chatter about her upcoming nuptials had me seeking some peace and quiet. But not before I moved the Fund. Someone had been nosing through my nightstand because stuff had been moved around—and believe me, I know when my stuff has been moved around. Pleased with its new hiding place in my dresser, I walked to the corner market that sells my favorite root beer, bought two bottles, and finished them both on the way back.

Judd, on the other hand, had been rather quiet (could just have been due to his sore tongue, but whatever). Saturday afternoon, I overheard Lucy telling him to make his own damn tea—a chamomile-and-honey concoction with crushed ice—because he'd brought it on himself. I wouldn't exactly consider that taking my side, but still appreciated the nod in my direction.

I was glad to come to school today, forced to think about something other than what went down in Mac's office on Friday. The will, the kiss, the rejection. Not to mention the money, which could help me beyond design school and getting an apartment. Maybe I won't even stay in South Florida. There are great schools in New York, some of the best. Maybe, like Mary, the heat is getting to me. And if we do find my mother, I could always go to a school near her. Who knows? I could end up spending the rest of my life with her.

Third period, my phone buzzes during World History class. Paula, who sits next to me, shoots me a worried glance, knowing I'll get in trouble if Ms. Tuft hears it. Todd's ears have perked up, too, and he raises his eyebrows suspiciously. I give him a what-are-you-looking-at look because everyone's phones are always buzzing during class, even though teachers threaten to take them away if they hear them. Teachers do a lot of threatening, but very little follow-through. Unlike Mrs. Shoal in the office. When I failed to give her a note from the dentist, she swiftly handed down my sentence—an after-school detention. As pissed as I am, I have to give Mrs. Shoal credit. At least she's a woman of her word.

The phone vibrates again before I have a chance to pull it from my bag. I peer at the screen between my legs.

how bout tonite

It's a different number, but I know it's him. Joe. My fingers work stealthily in my lap.

stop texting me

but im horny

call someone else, biz closed

since when

STOP

u sure? cuz im not gonna give u another chance at bat

What does that mean? I don't even care, so I reply:

YES stop texting me

ok. 3 strks ur out

"Let me have that, Ms. Velvitt." The teacher is standing at the front of my row with her hand out. Ms. Tuft looks like an alien, with wide eyes that angle up high onto her forehead and a small, skinny body. Everyone refers to her room as Area 51.

I slide the phone shut and shove it in my bag. "Look. It's gone."

Todd's snickering behind his book. He's loving this.

"No, it's not. Now take it out of your book bag and hand it over."

"Please, Ms. Tuft, it'll never see the fluorescent lights of your classroom again. I swear."

"Swear all you want. Hand it over." She scans the room with her alien eyes. "You all need to learn that the rules are the rules."

I can't give her my phone. Might I suggest a different limb?

"I'll take detention," I offer. Mumbles around the room. Everyone enjoys a bit of drama at school—anything to break up the daily routine. Except for Paula. She seems kind of bummed for me and drops her eyes when I look her way.

Ms. Tuft smiles like she's won. "Deal."

Little does she know I'll be there anyway, at Mrs. Shoal's request.

Ms. Tuft strides victoriously down the aisle, back to the board. My brain has left the building, and I only catch a word here and there when she picks up her lecture about the Battle of Britain. I'm more concerned with the string of words Joe put together. Three strikes you're out. What's that supposed to mean?

Todd snickers again, then turns away. Could it be him? But he'd probably use some football reference instead, the stupid jock. Besides, now that I think about it, his hands have been holding his textbook the whole time. It's definitely not him. And I received the last text when I was with him in his car and his hands were definitely glued to the wheel. Or were they?

A strange sensation wriggles up my spine, settles in my neck. Fear.

I had refused to reach out to Mac over the weekend. Pride plus embarrassment equals silence. But I may need him for more than a missing-persons case. What if this guy Joe is nuts and wants to hurt me? Can you locate a person just by having their phone number? I'm getting scared. Mac could protect me. My private-investigator-slash-bodyguard. It has a ring.

Ms. Tuft taps the board with the end of her long, pointy stick. We're supposed to be paying attention, damn it, creating connections, forming opinions, making decisions.

Well, I've made one. I've decided to head over to Mac's office after school. Make that right after detention.

When I arrive at the library where after-school detentions are held, I realize I wasn't as clever as I thought. Both Mrs. Shoal and Ms. Tuft are waiting for me at the main desk. It's like a party.

"Thought you could pull a fast one, huh, Rosie?" Ms. Tuft has dropped the formalities. Four hours ago, I was Ms. Velvitt.

Mrs. Shoal looks up at the wall clock, a sad white plastic disc that's missing the seven. "It's three fifteen. Each detention lasts one hour. You'll be out of here at five fifteen," she says, as if I needed help with the calculation.

No, no, no. That will not do. I planned on heading straight to Mac's before his office closes. He'll be gone if I get there at five thirty, which I won't even make if I miss the bus.

"Can I do one detention today and one tomorrow?" I plead.

The two authoritarians peer at each other, communicating silently. You never know with Ms. Tuft. She really could be an alien and have telepathic powers. But they'd probably be lost on Mrs. Shoal, who's too average and boring to be anything but straight-up human.

In unison, they say, "No." Mrs. Shoal takes the lead. "You're to sit here." She pulls out a broken chair from underneath one of the tables. It makes a scraping sound against the floor that grabs everyone's attention. A cluster of guys at a nearby table looks up and snickers at my fate.

"Fine," I huff, then take out my phone. I hadn't wanted to give Mac a chance to turn me away, so I was going to show up unannounced. But now I'm going to have to text him, say that I really, really need to see . . .

"And I'll be taking that while you're here," Ms. Tuft says, plucking the cell from my hands. I lunge at her, trying to snatch it back. She knocks into Mrs. Shoal, whose wide body breaks her fall, but they both have that stunned, furious glare Lucy gets when I've irritated her.

The group of guys snickers louder and one of them says, "That's not good."

I am not victorious. Ms. Tuft still clutches my phone in her bony alien fingers.

I slink back into my chair while they bite their tongues nice and hard. What is said next must be measured. I will not get the best of them, no I won't.

So they take a moment to compose themselves. Mrs. Shoal checks her glasses, makes sure they weren't damaged, then stuffs them back in her bird's nest. Patting down her shapeless beige dress, Ms. Tuft bristles and wrings her hands.

"Two weeks until graduation, young lady. I suggest you keep it together." My History teacher wags the phone, then drops it into a front pocket of her tent dress. "This will be waiting for you in the main office. With the principal."

I'm supposed to be scared about visiting the Oz of Del Vista, but all I am is pissed. How am I going to reach Mac now?

• • •

My phone was waiting for me (with Principal Aguilar, who actually handed it back without a lecture), but it was dead. Do you know how hard it is to find a pay phone these days? Close to impossible, which is why I'm extremely lucky to find

Elaine on my bus again. I wonder where she's always going, since she's never gotten on or off the bus while I'm on it. Her face brightens when she sees me, but it's crowded and a man already sits in the seat beside her.

When I approach, she says to him, "Would you mind? This is my granddaughter." Elaine points up at me, and I smile dutifully.

"Thanks, Grandma," I say, and slide in when he relinquishes his seat.

We giggle as I settle in. "Would you by any chance have a cell phone?"

"Doesn't everyone these days?" She reaches into her crochet bag and pulls out a flip phone wrapped in a neon-pink case. "My daughter. Says the color makes it easier for me to find this way." Elaine studies the bright, shiny case. "I guess she's right," she says while handing it over. "Misplace yours?"

I hold up mine to show her a black screen. "Dead."

Elaine raises her thin gray eyebrows like she can't believe a seventeen-year-old could let that happen. I'm glad she's not like a lot of old ladies who pencil in bright orange arches.

"It got taken away in school today," I confess, "so I wasn't allowed to charge it anywhere, like during lunch."

"Don't tell me why."

"I'll be quick," I promise, then realize I don't know Mac's number by heart. "Um, can I call information first? I wouldn't ask if it weren't important."

She nods and I'm able to get the office number from the operator.

"John Brooks Investigations." I'm so glad Mac's answered, and just hearing his voice gets that match lit and burning in my chest.

"Hi, Mac, it's Rosie." I don't wait for him to say anything. "I need to see you." I sense Elaine's listening, but she's respectful and remains focused on turning lilac yarn into a flower.

He tells me he's about to leave the office, already late for a study group on campus. I allow for an awkward pause. He doesn't budge. "Please, Mac. I'm sorry for the way I acted. I've waited all weekend—"

"Why?"

"Why what?"

"Why did you wait to call me?" he asks.

I cup the phone with my mouth and whisper, "Because you gave me the bum's rush out of your office."

"Sorry." His clipped tone extinguishes the burning match.

"Honestly, I didn't think you wanted to hear from me." His silence isn't that encouraging, so I press on. "Can we meet? I really need to see you." My request sounds pathetic, but sometimes necessity trumps self-respect.

"Tomorrow."

"Okay," I reply, waiting for more.

"Goodbye, Rosie." And then he hangs up.

I flip Elaine's phone shut and hand it back to her.

"Men," she says, shaking her head, like we're two girls commiserating about boys.

"It's more than that," I say. "It's a business thing. Kind of complicated." Frustrated, I reach up to yank on the cable so the driver knows I want to get off at the next stop. But Elaine stops me by tugging on my shoulder.

"Are you hungry? It's almost five thirty. If we get to Lou's by six, I can buy us an Early Bird dinner."

I pause before answering. "Were you headed there, anyway?"

"No."

I love her honesty, so I sit. "Do you mind if I ask where you're always going . . . when you're on this bus, I mean."

That familiar twinkle resurfaces. "Oh, I don't go anywhere. I just ride. Something about the rhythm of the bus makes me crochet my best. Plus, it gets me out of the house. Not much does these days."

When she dips her head, I study the deep wrinkles in her cheek, the white fuzz around her forehead. This old lady is tough, but sad. I get that.

"I am sorta hungry," I say, then pull out my sketchbook and work beside Elaine for another twenty minutes until we reach our stop in front of the deli.

25

"SOMETHING TELLS ME you got a story," Elaine says, wagging an onion ring at me. A hot corned beef on rye sits smack in the center of her plate, two pickles on the side. She polishes off one and says, "Love these. You know they're cucumbers first, right? Before they're soaked in salty goodness and stuck in a jar."

"Uh-huh," I say weakly, since I didn't actually know that.

She eats her other pickle, then says, "I'm listening."

"You first."

"I'm old and boring. Haven't you noticed?"

"No. Tell me why you ride the bus all the time in a loop de loop."

"Already told you. Gets me out of the house. That's it."

"But why?" I ask, because if you want to get out of the house, it's usually to get away from the other people in it. Like for me, it's Lucy and the Dud. So I wonder if she lives with someone who makes her nuts, too.

"Eat your sandwich." She nods at my turkey-bacon club nestled on a mound of thick-cut potato chips.

"This looks great," I say, then take my first bite. Mayonnaise spills out the side, which I promptly wipe away with a napkin.

"It's always good here," Elaine says. "Have you ever had their pie?"

I nod vigorously, because my mouth is full.

"Then save room for dessert. Dinner comes with it," she says, and winks. The deli is packed with older people getting the Early Bird special like us. I glance at the counter, where I first spotted Mac, then at the booth where John first introduced himself. It's only been a couple weeks since we met, but I somehow feel close to them, or at least tied to them.

I try again. "Please tell me."

She grabs a napkin from a stack inside a metal container, then uses it to wipe her hands and mouth before speaking. "We had forty-seven terrific years," she says, and I know she means with her husband, the way her eyes fall to the gold band on her ring finger. "Number forty-eight? Not so terrific. Started forgetting things . . ."

"Like where he put the car keys?" I joke, because even Judd forgets and he's only twenty-nine.

"Like me," she says.

I'm such an idiot. My hand instinctively reaches across the table, but she makes no move to accept it.

"I ride to escape, Rosie. To see the world, as dismal as it may seem through a thick, smudgy bus window. To see something other than Alan, sunk into the sofa, staring at the television someone else turned on for him."

Elaine must read the concern in my face because she says, "Don't worry. He isn't left alone. Nurse Janna stays afternoons and evenings, when I'm too tired to do any more. Then I grab my crochet bag, walk to the corner, and get on the bus. He doesn't even know I'm gone."

No amount of crunching chips can fill the uncomfortable silence, though I do my best, give her some room to finish her story. I had only pushed her to deflect the telling of my own story, and now I wish I hadn't.

"I know what you're thinking," she says in between onion rings, her fingertips shiny from grease. "That I was rotten to you because I'm bitter. Because my husband's lost in his own head, so I take it out on the rest of the world."

"No, Elaine," I say, making another attempt to hold her frail, papery hand. "I wasn't thinking that." I give a little shrug. "Besides, you already told me it was because I had reminded you of your screwed-up granddaughter." I smile sheepishly. "Sorry."

"That was part of it," Elaine says, overlooking my remark. "The other part happened before you came on the bus. A kid with lightning bolts shaved into the side of his head and those discs in his earlobes. He looked like a troublemaker, and he was."

A sharp jolt cuts through me. I hope Elaine didn't catch the flash of recognition in my eyes. I inspect my sandwich, pull out a piece of bacon and crumble it between my fingers.

"The bus was crowded that day, but there was an empty seat next to me. He refuses to sit in it, though, saying that old people smell, and maybe I should clean my dentures once in a while." Elaine takes a sip of water, clears her throat. "I ignore him, keep my eyes on my crocheting, but he's getting others riled up. He starts pretending that I . . . well, passed gas," she says lightly, measuring her words, "and waves a hand in front of his face.

He's making a scene, this kid, and everyone is letting him. Not one decent person tells him to knock it off, so he keeps at it because he's got an audience, you see."

I see.

Elaine continues. "It got worse," she says, even though I can't imagine it could. Being humiliated like that on the bus? And no one stepping in? I was getting superheated. "Because I told him to sit down and behave himself. That got him riled up. He grabbed the ball of yarn I was using and started tossing it around to his friends in another row. It became tangled in their hands, and the scarf I was working on got yanked from my lap. Those heathens got their hands on that, too, and pulled it all apart. All that work. Ruined." Her eyes drop at the memory. "Finally, a man put a stop to it and returned the mess of yarn to me. I must've looked like I was going to cry, because the kid says, 'Old people shouldn't cry because death is coming soon and you're returning to Jesus.' He wanted me to make a big smile with my dentures."

I remember the gold cross around his neck and wish Mary would've yanked it off when she had the chance, rammed it between his eyes.

"But you want to know the worst part?" She leans in close. "I did want to cry, Rosie, because as hard as you may think your life is now, wait until you have trouble seeing, and your knees hurt, and the person you love most in the world doesn't even recognize your perfume anymore."

What can I say to that? I'm too busy choking on the giant reality pill Elaine has shoved down my throat.

"I studied him," she says. "While he clutched the rail above his head, I could see how skinny he was, how his body stretched out like a rubber band. I was hoping he'd snap in two. Instead, he got off at the next stop, which was just as fine by me. That's when you got on. I guess I'm the one who snapped."

"It's okay," I say. "We all do at some point."

"But it still doesn't excuse my behavior. I'm sorry, Rosie."

"You've already apologized." I wave her off with a chip.

"I can't help my husband anymore," she says, her eyes becoming glassy pale blue marbles. "She took off over a year ago, so I can't help my granddaughter, either. But whatever had you upset after your phone call . . . I can listen. Maybe I can even help."

26

I DIDN'T TELL Elaine every detail of my story, just the headlines—my father died, left me with a woman who's still keeping a secret he took to the grave, and now I'm searching for my birth mother. Elaine was so shocked, she ordered hot tea with a splash of brandy. Lou's is that kind of place.

While for the most part she was speechless and only nodded at me with wide eyes, Elaine did end our conversation with an offer to help—in an unexpected but awesome way. She offered to show my sketches to her daughter, who works at the Art Institute in Fort Lauderdale. I told her about my application to the Fashion House, but she said it can't hurt to apply to more than one school, echoing Paula's advice. Her daughter's not an instructor or anything. She works in administration, but has been there a long time and has connections with a lot of the staff. I honestly couldn't believe my luck, and leaned across the table to pop a grateful kiss on her cheek.

When our plates were empty and our conversation had run dry, Elaine paid the check and told me to meet her on Thursday's four o'clock bus with my portfolio.

I headed straight home after our dinner and created another portfolio with some recent stuff to highlight my range—the jumper, the robe, the gown I showed Mac, a trench coat that comes apart at multiple seams to become a long vest.

I place the sketches in a bright yellow folder with my name and phone number written in thick black marker on the front. She couldn't promise anything, especially since it was probably too late to apply for summer classes, but at least she'd stick my foot in her daughter's door. Much appreciated.

I hid the folder under my mattress to keep it safe, then plop back on my bed, exhausted. I want to snap off the light, escape into dreamy nothingness, but first I need to call Mary and tell her about Elaine and her run-in with Ralph. She's going to freak.

"That's a helluva coincidence," Mary says, grateful for the interruption of *Great Expectations*, which we have to read for English class.

"I know. I mean, I couldn't believe the coincidence part, but I could believe the way he treated her. He's a psycho."

"More than that. He is one bad dude. Messing with a nice old lady? He needs to be taken out. Does your Hardy Boy Wonder have any connections?"

I snicker, but Mary's silence has me thinking she's serious. "You're kidding."

"Of course," she says, "but, you know, there are other things we can do to take down that asshole."

"Meaning . . ."

She pauses, then says, "Never mind," which of course makes me mind. Mary never starts a thought she doesn't plan on finishing.

"Tell me," I say, suddenly feeling fearless. "I may just do it."

"Burn that shit down, Rosie girl."

"Burn what down?"

"The shed. Light that bitch up so he can't mess with another girl again. Who knows? He may get the message to not mess with old ladies, either."

"Come with me."

"I can't go back there. Plus, my dad's in a bad mood tonight. I'd be afraid if he caught me sneaking out. It's only a matter of time before his fists turn my way." The fear in Mary's voice makes me want to protect her, to be the doer instead of the thinker for once. "Look," she says, her voice brighter. "I really have to finish reading, so if you don't want to tell me what happens in chapters forty-seven through fifty-two, I gotta go."

So she goes, and I decide to go, too. Just like that.

I choose black sweats, a long-sleeved black shirt, and an old pair of black sneakers that went out of style two years ago. I should be fairly invisible. Now all I need to do is find a few things to complete the mission.

. . .

I've gotten pretty good at sneaking out of my house. I don't want a medal or anything, but if they were given out for such a category, I'd win the gold. A leaf is barely rustled as I crawl through the screenless window, the grass flattened into a quiet rug.

It's only a few minutes before the bus pulls up like an old friend, its doors cranking open with welcoming arms. I deposit my money into the slot. The driver smiles with tired eyes, tells me to take a seat up front. I do, but I'm afraid she's going to start talking. I know her kind. She's not like Archie, who's only interested in making his stops on time. She wants to make friends. She starts off all nice and easy, then goes in for the kill, telling me about her kid who's sick and her husband who can't find a job. Midnight rides tend to bring out the melancholy in people.

But I can't be someone's sounding board tonight. I've got to stay focused. So I slide over to the window seat and pretend to be deep in concentration while staring out at a starless sky. The driver gets the hint. She whistles and hums to fill the silence until I pull the cord fifteen minutes later, requesting a stop.

The bus drops me several blocks from Ralph's, but since I know my way, I walk fast and with purpose. Still, I took along the bug spray, just in case, and clutch it in my right hand.

When I arrive this time, the house doesn't seem so nice. The same Cadillac is in the driveway, but backed in near the garage. Without the front door lights beaming on it, it looks older and in desperate need of a wash. The lawn, too, is no longer freshly mowed, and weeds sprout through the brick pavers I cross on my way to the backyard.

I use my watch, not my cell, to check the time, since I don't want the screen lit up. Eleven fifty-five. Hopefully, everyone is tucked into bed, or at least thoroughly occupied by whatever people do at midnight.

I duck around the side Mary used, tiptoeing through the tall grass, confident in my sneakers and the protection they provide. There's my target, beckoning me to put it out of its pathetic misery. It should have been built better, nicer. Instead, it's become abandoned, occupied only by vermin, by which I mean Ralph.

Before I touch anything, I put on a pair of dishwashing gloves Lucy has never used. I found them under the kitchen sink, still sealed in their plastic packaging. They're bright yellow, and while I feel kind of silly wearing them, I know they're crucial. At a crime scene, fingerprints are the kiss of death.

I grab the handle, pretend I was the one being ushered inside. My stomach lurches when I open the door, the smell of fertilizer and mildew choking me. Immediately, I close the door behind me and see the lock that had kept Mary captive. Thanks to the back window, the moon casts enough light for me to work by. I study the cramped quarters, different now that I'm inside.

I'm instantly drawn to the wood walls. They somehow seem familiar. I pull off a glove and reach out, running a set of fingers up and down a plank, oblivious to the splinters lodging into my skin. I press my nose to it and breathe in the oaky, musty scent. It's unsettling, disturbing, but I don't know why. I'm struck by a memory of my very first best friend, a chubby little girl named Felicia who always wore her banana-colored hair in a fish-tail braid. I'd gotten stuck in one of those plastic cabins during recess in first grade. The door wouldn't open, no matter how hard I kicked. I became hysterical, screaming for help. She stuffed herself through a window and said, "Don't be scared. I'm here." I haven't thought of Felicia in years. It must be this shed, even though I can get out of here if I want.

When the memory of Felicia passes, a wave of terror creeps up on me. Maybe I'm channeling Mary's fear. A chill sets into my bones, sweat forms on my neck. My legs feel weak. I almost drop when a rattle outside breaks the spell. I rush to the window just in time to catch a glimpse of a cat jumping from the fence I had sat on almost two weeks ago.

I slip my hand back into the glove, pulling myself together, and rub away pinpricks between my eyes that promise a headache. Time is limited. For all I know, Ralph has another midnight date planned.

Near my feet rests the blue blanket he wanted Mary to lie down on. I pick it up. It is scratchy, and I begin to feel that same panic I felt when I touched the walls, so I toss it. Near a shovel lies a pile of rusty, discarded tools that I know—from the summer we spent working at Perkins Paints—can still do their job. I cringe, imagining what Ralph might have done to Mary with any one of those things if she hadn't managed to escape.

I ignore the potent smells and take in a deep breath to steel my nerves. I am doing a good deed, a necessary one. I'd like to think I'm saving some girl, maybe being someone's hero, even if she never knows. I thought he was a psycho then, but after hearing how he treated Elaine—one of the nicest, coolest old ladies I've ever met—Ralph and his Rape Shed need to be taken down.

I pull out a rag and two of Lucy's lighters from my canvas tote. Using both hands, I crack open the plastic cylinders and empty the fluid, which instantly disappears into the rag. I hope it's enough. I wasn't about to spend any money on this venture, but I'm rethinking my decision not to purchase a can of kerosene.

The bag of mulch Ralph had used as a pillow is still on the floor where he left it. Has he used it again? Has some poor girl been forced to lay her head on it and squirm beneath his stinky, skinny body?

I rip open the thick plastic bag, stuff the wet rag into the heap of rough brown chips. Looking around, I grab whatever else will catch quickly—a coil of rope, a wooden rake, and, of course, the blue blanket.

Out comes the third lighter I stole from Lucy's purse. I flick the wheel with an eager thumb. It's tossed onto the pile, which ignites immediately, ribbons of blue and yellow flame swarming through gaps in my makeshift bonfire. It doesn't take long for the flames to grow high, reaching their spastic orange fingers toward the roof. I want to watch, but the heat forces me out.

I pull the door shut and race across the lawn, much easier this time in sneakers. When I'm safely out of sight, at least a block away, I turn to see a thin trail of smoke billowing into the sky and wish that mad dog a good night.

27

YOU'D HAVE THOUGHT I wouldn't be able to sleep last night, between Elaine's offer and my first foray into arson. But I slept like a baby, especially after I'd told Mary I did it and she said she was proud of me. (Actually, she said she was very fucking proud, which made me happy.) And this morning I skipped off to school with a fully charged cell phone turned to silent, instead of vibrate.

So I'm in an extra-good mood today, especially because I'm about to enter the door to Brooks, PI, and make things right with Mac. I check my appearance in the mirrored door first to make sure a long day hasn't undone my schoolgirl chic—hair tamed behind a tortoiseshell headband, glossy lips, no mascara, and a snug tartan dress that had Todd sniffing around more than once today. It was kind of weird, because that ship has sailed, and we both know it.

"Are you coming in?" Mac pushes open the door from inside. I hope he didn't see me hesitating, checking myself out in the reflection. It seems he's mixed up his wardrobe a bit. He's wearing a beige sweater vest, but over a cool white tee that shows off his tanned forearms, and dark blue jeans instead of those stiff khakis. Let me just say it: Mac looks hot.

I answer by slipping into the dark room. It's depressing in here. The space needs flowers, lights, maybe a clown. I take the lead and head straight to Mac's office so we're in a friendlier environment. We take our usual seats at his desk.

"How are you feeling?" he asks.

"Better."

"I was worried about you," he says. "I probably should've called."

"It's okay, Mac. I was out of line. I don't know what got into me."

"Friday was crazy. Your dad's will answered a lot of questions. You were . . . overwhelmed."

Right. I guess so. But I was also feeling other things, like a loss of control. But I don't want to get into that now. I can sense a fresh start brewing here.

"So," he continues. "Did you have a chance to return the will to Lucy's desk?"

"No."

"Why not?"

"Because I can't pull off another secret visit."

Mac shrugs. "I guess it's not the end of the world. The lawyer will have a copy, anyway."

"Meaning?"

"Your birthday is in six days. The clock is ticking. She may be getting her ducks in a row."

"Preparing for payday," I say.

"In a matter of speaking. But John was telling me estate

matters could take some time to settle. It's not like she just shows up to the lawyer's office with you and the will and an empty duffel bag."

The image makes us both snicker, lightening the mood a thousand percent.

"Obviously, she knows she's got money coming to her. But she also knows something else—that your real mother is alive. We want to know why she hasn't disclosed this to you. That's the real mystery here." Mac pauses, and I can see his train of thought has shifted. "Whatever we find out, I'm glad your father left you money. You're going to be okay." He makes a silly grin. "Guess we could've held on to your three hundred bucks, after all."

"No, I gave it to Mary."

"What? Why would you do that?" He's not angry, just surprised. I could kick myself for letting that slip. But talking to Mac is easy. He always seems so understanding and ready to listen. Kind of like Elaine.

"Uh . . . well, she wants to take off after graduation, and—"

"I know she's your best friend, but remember what I told you. Settling your father's estate could take a while. Possibly months."

"It's okay, Mac. I wanted her to have it. She deserves the money more than I do, anyway."

"What do you mean?" he asks. "Why would she deserve it more?"

There's no turning back. I've dropped a hint about something straight into a detective's lap. Of course he wants to see where it leads.

"Because she's the one who earned it."

I can tell Mac is more confused than ever, and I make the commitment right then and there to come clean. I really like him and want to be honest. Hopefully, he'll understand.

"Have you ever had to make an extremely hard decision?"

When he nods sympathetically, I say, "No, not like which college to attend. I mean, a life-or-death decision."

"No."

"Well, when I found the box my father had left me—that was the kind of choice I faced. At least that's how it felt. The choice to find my real mother. The truth is, those first few days after reading the letter, I wasn't even sure if I wanted to. When I first met your uncle at Lou's, I almost didn't go inside."

"Really? Why not?"

"Because there's a reason my father lied to me. And when we find her, I'm going to know why."

Mac opens his mouth to say something, but then stops himself. I know what he's thinking. *If* we find her. She may not even be alive. The possibility has haunted me. While it's been easy to imagine some stuff—what she looks like, or another family she chose to become a part of—I haven't been able to deny the worst scenario. She may have passed away, too, like my father.

"So I made the choice," I continue, "and finding her was going to cost money, which I didn't have. I needed to figure out how to make some."

"Okaaay . . . ," he says, dragging out the word, wondering what the problem was.

"Look, Mac. I have a teensy-weensy record, okay?"

"How teensy?"

"Last summer, Mary and I were caught spray-painting a park wall. We got a misdemeanor for something called criminal mischief."

Mac nods like he would've already known the charge without me telling him.

"Plus community service hours," I add.

"But as a minor, your record would be sealed," he says, launching into criminology major mode. "A future employer wouldn't have been able to see it, or know about it, unless you disclosed it on your application."

"Once upon a time, that may have been true, Mac. But thanks to social media, we were tagged in an online news story about the incident. Someone looking to hire either one of us could've easily found the story if they googled our names."

"Fine. But even with a record, there are still ways to make money." Mac's face tightens with that weird look someone has before asking a question they're afraid to hear the answer to. "So how did you get that three hundred dollars?"

"I didn't steal it, if that's what you're thinking."

"Not thinking that," he says.

I hang my head. If I were a dog, I'd tuck my tail between my legs, too. "It wasn't even my idea." And then I blurt it out. "It was Mary's." A pressure valve releases in my chest.

"What idea, Rosie?"

I take in a deep breath before dropping the bomb. "To charge guys for sex. There. I said it."

I should've expected his stunned expression, but still—the hanging jaw, the wide, disbelieving eyes. They make me cringe, knowing the images that must have just raced through his mind. "You didn't," he says.

"I didn't. Mary did," I clarify, as if the distinction makes it any better.

He yanks his hand away to pace in circles, round and round, shaking his head.

"But how could she—" He stops and stares out the window.

I understand Mac's struggle to find a way to question this whole thing, so I jump in with the only answer I have. "You'd have to know Mary. She's . . . tough. She's always been there for me, Mac, especially when I've needed her most. It's complicated, but she's—"

"Some best friend," he says, finishing my thought. I read a million things into the way he's looking at me, as if Mary's the best kind of friend, and I'm the worst. For letting her prostitute herself while I sat on the sidelines with my bug spray.

"I wish we could've found another way." I stare right into his eyes so he knows I mean it.

"I think you could have, Rosie. I think you both could've come up with a better plan than that." His eyes flicker with a thought that causes him to back away from me. "Mary's not still . . . she knows the agency is working pro bono—"

"Of course not!" I snap. "The minute you offered to work for free, she fired her pimp." I dip my head. "Me." I hate lying to him, but does he really need to know we met Ralph that same night? Absolutely not. Besides, he doesn't seem amused, so I resume a serious tone. "But there is this one guy who keeps texting me. Kind of harassing me."

"I don't follow."

"That wasn't exactly a joke about the whole pimp thing. We used my number as a contact. I screened the calls for Mary, made sure the guy was okay. And I'd always go with her as backup. I've got the bug spray to prove it." I reach in my bag, but he stops me.

"I believe you," he says sharply. "Tell me about the texts."

"I don't know who he is. His name is Joe, or at least that's what he calls himself. Every time he's texted me, it's a different number, one I don't recognize."

"Every time? How many times has he contacted you?"

"Three. As a matter of fact, his last text yesterday said, 'Three strikes, you're out.' And the one before was threatening, too."

"Rosie, why didn't you tell me?"

"And explain it to you how?"

He pauses, understanding my dilemma.

"Okay, we'll deal with this Joe thing, I promise. But we've got bigger fish to fry first."

"What kind of fish?"

"Your birth certificate. It was forged."

· · ·

Again, Mac lays out the items from the box on the desk in front of us. A slice of afternoon sun lights up half of it, making the dark wood glossy and warm when I rest my forearms on it.

"The name listed as 'Mother' on your birth certificate is Justine R. Velvitt."

I tilt my head and give him a look like, *Obviously.*

"So we ran her name through TLO."

"What's that?"

"A super high-tech database. It uses something called data fusion that can help you find just about anyone."

"Wow. That's amazing."

"It can be," Mac says, "if you've got the right name."

"What's that supposed to mean?"

"I don't think that was her name. I mean, the Justine part, yes, because it's scribbled on the back of the snow picture." With a heart over the *i* but don't think I need to add that. "The rest I'm not so sure. Why else couldn't we locate her? The name has to be wrong."

"But it's on my birth certificate, right here." I pick up the worn piece of paper and point to the box in which her name is neatly typed.

"I know. That's why I believe it was forged."

"By who?"

"Your dad."

"Why?"

"Remember last Friday, when my uncle wanted me to tell you something? Before everything went haywire in here."

I remember. We were in the hallway, and John had given Mac a look, like they had a secret he wanted me in on.

"John took one look at this and was able to get the ball rolling." Mac picks up the party picture and points at the baseball cap my dad is wearing. It's white with a funky red logo, which he zeros in on with a fingertip. "See that? It's the letter F, the logo of Frontier Airlines, out of Denver."

"How would he have known that?"

"Before he accepted a football scholarship to UM, there had been scouts at his high school. One of them was from the University of Colorado. They give recruits all sorts of promotional stuff, even from airlines. He said he was given a cap just like this. Dumped it, of course, when he decided to go to the U."

"Mac, you're killing me with these stories going nowhere. Tell me how this helps us."

"Once John gave me some direction, I ran with it. Made a ton of phone calls until I hit pay dirt. I spoke to a human resources officer with Frontier who's been there for twenty-two years. I asked if a Clint or Justine Velvitt had ever worked there, because, let's face it—I'm sure your dad isn't wearing that cap because he was a college football recruit." He gives me another one of those goofy grins, but he's right. In this picture, my dad's thin and lanky—far from the heavier man he became as he got older. "The woman said no, but that the name Justine rang a bell and she'd look into some old records for me. Turns out, she was the one who worked for Frontier, but her full name was Justine Lenore Rickland. According to her employee records and pay stubs, she was always listed as single, even until she left in April of 2002."

"Why did she leave?"

"Woman said she had no idea, but it was abrupt. One day, Justine didn't show up for work, and no one ever saw her again."

"So what does all this mean?"

"I don't think they ever married, which isn't a big deal, but it is a big deal that your dad lied about it. Look, now that we know her real name, my uncle can run it through the database again for her social security number."

"Great," I say. "So that's what John wanted you to tell me?"

"Partly. There's more."

"About the birth certificate? Just because my dad altered her name doesn't really crack this whole thing open."

"It does when you combine it with the snow picture of your mother." He holds it between us, and I try to study it with new eyes. The partially covered sign she's standing in front of, the ski clothes that make her look like a pink marshmallow. Snow is at her feet, but I can still make out the tops of her furry boots.

"Did you happen to notice this?" He points to something stuck in the right post of the wooden sign. I had, and imagined the piece of paper flapping beside her in the winter breeze.

"It looks like a flyer or something."

"It's a *Sports Illustrated* cover."

"Oh." Squinting, I can make out the famous magazine logo.

"John may have been the professional athlete, but I'm still a sports nut. Kind of have one of those statistical memories that impress people at barbecues."

Everything about him impresses me, even the boat shoes with socks. Even his speech that constantly flips from casual to formal and keeps me on my toes.

"It's the February 8, 1999, issue. John Elway had brought

the Broncos to a Super Bowl win. Some fan must have tacked it up there."

"Which is where?"

"Copper Mountain, a ski resort in Colorado. She's standing in front of the sign."

"She and my dad were skiing. So what?"

"It was February 1999. I don't think your mother was racing down any hills then."

It takes me a minute to unroll the calendar in my brain, to understand the message in Mac's eyes. "Because she was pregnant with me at the time."

"Right. I don't know about you, but who would trek all the way out west and not ski at a ski resort? Couple that with the job at Frontier Airlines." He waits for me to catch on, but when I don't, he says, "I think they lived there, Rosie."

"And . . . ?" I ask, reading in his expression that there's more.

"I think you were born there, too."

28

"DO THESE THINGS make me look trashy?" Mary asks, studying herself in the mirror, a pair of dark brown hiking boots on her feet.

"Only when you wear them with those," I say, eyeing the supershort navy running shorts that she doesn't use for running but make her long legs look slim and athletic. I sigh, then drop my head to the side.

Mary turns, abandoning her reflection. "Cheer up, will you?"

I force a grin, then let it fade. She's dragged me to Outdoor Emporium, stoked at the idea of finally heading to the mountains and insisting she needs the right "gear." All I did was mention that my mother used to live in Colorado, but there's nothing to suggest she's still there. John's out of town for a few days, but when he returns, he'll run her accurate name through the database and get a social security number. Then we can pick up the trail after she left Frontier Airlines in 2002. But until that happens, I'm feeling agitated and in limbo.

"Don't you love all the shit in here?" Mary asks, meaning everything from bows and arrows to kayaks. I nod, but I'm interested in other things—like the fabric on shirts with built-in sunscreen and shoes that can be worn from land to sea. "I could see myself working in a park, you know? Like a big, important park. Yellowstone, maybe."

What's she rattling on about? The whole park ranger fantasy again? I guess everyone's entitled to their own dream. I keep nodding, even though I'm losing interest and drifting back to my meeting with Mac. And Mac's forearm hair that I want to stroke like a pet.

"I like them," she says, focusing on the boots, ignoring my bad mood. "Could you spot me the fifty bucks?" She sits on the plastic bench and starts untying the laces.

"Seriously? I gave it all to you—"

"I'm just messing with you, Rosie girl. Besides, we're going to need that money for our trip." She shoves the boots into the box. "These babies are going on my dad's credit card."

"Isn't that only for emergencies?" I follow her through a maze of fishing poles, surfboards, and archery equipment. When we reach the clothing section, I let my fingers touch all the different fabrics—soft cotton shirts, scratchy polyester Windbreakers, silky bathing suits.

"This is an emergency. We're going to brave the wilderness. I need the right shoes."

I grab Mary's shoulder, yanking her back before she reaches the cash register. "Hold up," I say. A woman with two kids shoots me a look. "Go ahead," I tell her, then pull Mary to the side. "Get them if you want, but don't get them for a trip that's probably not going to happen."

Mary frowns, whips her ponytail behind her. "And why wouldn't we be going?"

"Because I don't know if she's even there, that's why. And even if she is, Colorado's a big place. She could be anywhere. Let's just see what else Mac and John can find out."

"What's going on with you?" Her brown eyes grow dark and challenging, all the playfulness that was there moments ago gone.

"What do you mean?"

"You're acting weird."

"No, I'm not."

"Is it about the flight?" she asks, knowing I've got a fear of flying. It's not so much about plummeting to my death as it is about being stuck in that metal tube. I don't like being forced to stay in enclosed spaces. Remember the plastic cabin and Felicia with the fish-tail braid? Something about the way Mary is looking at me now—like she sees right through me—reminds me of her again and how she saved me.

The woman with the two kids is staring at me while she pays the cashier. "What's your problem?" I ask. This is what you get for shopping after school—irritated mothers with their offspring. She turns away, shuffles the boys to the other side of her, as if she's worried I'm going to snatch one of them.

"Jeez, Rosie girl. You're awfully snappy this afternoon."

"No, I'm not," I say, even though I am feeling on edge today.

"You've gotten cold feet. I can feel it."

Is she picking up on something I haven't had the courage to face? As exciting as it's been working with Mac, I can't deny the familiar fear is creeping back—the fear I had when I first read Dad's letter. Do I really want to know the truth?

I playfully kick out a foot and say, "Warm and toasty. Now come on, pay for those beauties and let's get out of here."

"Not until you tell me you're going to see this through."

I can't believe how she's pushing me, right here in the checkout line of Outdoor Emporium with a shelf of water guns poking into my calves. I must hesitate too long because Mary's face falls. "So we did all that for nothing."

"No, we made over six hundred dollars. That's not nothing. Besides, what about rule number three?" I challenge. "Whatever we decide to do with our own share of the money is no one else's business."

Mary firmly grips my arms. "Well, guess what? Rules are meant to be broken, and I'm officially breaking the shit out of number three with a goddamned hammer from Perkins Paints. I did a pretty fucked-up thing for you."

"Stop!" I snap, and everyone near me shrinks away in shock. You'd think I'd called her a dirty whore by the way they're staring.

"Next in line." The cashier leans over the conveyor belt, trying to get my attention. I don't respond fast enough, so she asks, "Can I help you?" more irritated this time.

"No," I say, not giving Mary a chance to swoop in and answer. "I'm sorry. Can you put these back?" I hand over the box of boots. "She doesn't want them, after all."

"She?" the cashier says, looking around me. I turn to find an empty space and Mary gone.

29

I'M WAITING FOR ELAINE on Thursday's four o'clock bus, the yellow folder clutched in my hand. She wasn't here when I got on at the stop in front of school. Was she having second thoughts about showing my work to her daughter? The portfolio is key to getting into design school—a good one should be able to stand on its own—but knowing it's been seen by the right people would definitely be an advantage.

The rainy afternoon fits my mood. I pick a spot on the window and analyze a snake of water as it travels down the glass. Why did Mary and I have to argue yesterday? She got all bent out of shape over nothing. Two arguments in two weeks. It's not like us. There's a shift happening, and I'm not sure why. With so much going on—the search for my mother, Lucy and Judd's upcoming wedding, my birthday—now is not the time to be on the outs with my best friend.

I need some good news. I need Elaine to come through for me.

Stop one: two people get on, four people get off.

Stop two: three people get on, no one gets off.

Stop three: I get off, because, as you know, stop three is

mine. Deflated, I exit the bus, shielding myself from the rain with my backpack, when I almost bump into her.

"Where do you think you're going?" Elaine asks, nudging me back up the steps. Archie doesn't ask for more money as Elaine slides her pass through the metal slot, just nods me through.

"I thought—"

"Faith, dear girl." She pulls off her poncho and slides into the first available row of two empty seats. I sit beside her, brush off the water from my hair before it has a chance to explode into a frizzy mess. "But I guess that's a lot to ask of someone in your position." She tucks the poncho near her feet. "Got sidetracked, that's all." The bus lurches, then eases into traffic. "You were getting off back there. That where you live?"

"Yeah," I say flatly, so she can see I'm not too happy about it. "I used to live in Hammock Lakes. Do you know where that is?"

"No, but it sounds pretty."

"It is. We had a pool and everything." I'm instantly transported back there, to summers spent grilling with my dad and lounging on a raft until the sun went down.

"Do you know the Singers?" she asks, interrupting my thought.

"Who? No." I shake my head.

"Well, they must be neighbors of yours if you live back there. Mrs. Singer has some of the most beautiful yarn." Elaine pulls out a multicolored ball, laced with threads of gold. "You can't find a skein like this anywhere. Worth walking in the rain to get it, too."

Elaine dries her hands on her polyester slacks, then holds them out. "Portfolio, please."

I pull it from my backpack and place it in her hands. She flips through the pages, pausing at some, blowing through others. I make a mental note that she liked the trench coat that can turn into a vest by unzipping the midsection and sleeves. "Very nice. You've got some clever ideas here." Then she closes the bright yellow folder and tucks it carefully into her crochet bag. "Don't worry. It's in good hands."

"I know."

Elaine turns to me. "I imagine it's tough for you, Rosie. You've been tested, but you've got to have faith in people. There are some decent ones out there." I immediately think of Mac and his uncle, knowing she's right. Even though Mary warned me at first, I chose to have faith in John, and it paid off.

She pulls out her hook and gets to work. "Perfect day for a long bus ride, don't you think?"

Most people would probably disagree with her. Sitting beside a cozy fire, bundled up in bed, watching a movie. Those are places you want to be on a rainy day like this. But as I look at Elaine, her head dipped toward a strip of yarn, I realize that this is her safe place, even after Ralph threatened to ruin it for her.

"How's your husband?" I ask, although it's a stupid question and one I immediately regret asking. Some people can't be healed, and by the way Elaine has described his condition, he could be like this for a long time.

But she's kind in the face of my stupidity. "He's fine. Actually watched the news with me the other night while sipping on a cup of his favorite tea. Decaf with a cinnamon stick."

"That's good." It comes out a little too bright, almost fake.

"Do you watch the news?" she asks. Something in her tone alarms me.

"No," I say, kind of embarrassed.

"Big fire was started in someone's backyard the other night."

I try to feign indifference, but my chest grows tight.

"Real big fire," she says, as if the size enhances her story. "Burned down a shed and then took out all the trees around it. Looked like a war zone."

"Wow."

"Young man who lived in the house. He was interviewed by one of the news people, that pretty one from channel six who has the short black hair and wears tight dresses up to her—" She catches herself, then continues. "Never mind. Anyway, she was interviewing this young man who looked mighty familiar."

I reach for my bag and riffle through it, in search of nothing.

"The lightning bolts shaved into the side of his head. It was him. That boy who gave me a hard time on the bus."

"Really?" I do my best to sound surprised.

"They say it was arson."

A flash of lightning pops in the sky. "How fitting," Elaine says, and then a clap of thunder follows. It's only a tad louder than the thumping of my chest. "This is what I've been talking about, though. Faith. Not just having it in people, but in the universe. I knew this kid would get what was coming to him, one way or another." She snaps an odd look at me.

Is it possible she suspects I'm behind this? There's no way. I'm being paranoid. She's already lifted the scarf she's working on—colored strips formed like a rainbow—to admire her progress.

I try to calm myself by sketching in one of my notepads, but it's no use. I'm still kind of rattled. I pop in my earbuds instead and listen to music until the stop comes that drops me a few blocks from Goodwill. I just feel like the roaming the aisles for a while. When I pull the cord, Elaine pats her crochet bag and says, "It's in good hands. I'll pass it on to my daughter when she comes to visit Sunday."

"Thank you," I say, because I don't think I had said it yet.

"Have a good weekend."

"I'll try." Thoughts of the dreaded wedding swiftly replace the ones I had been reliving in Ralph's backyard.

She grabs my hand before I leave. Her grip is surprisingly strong and warm. "Have a little faith, Rosie. It's good for the soul."

30

IT'S STILL DRIZZLING, but the worst of the weather has passed. And the dark gray sky has been replaced by sheets of dusty-rose-colored clouds. My mood has passed, too, thanks to Elaine, and it gives me the courage to approach Lucy with a request.

I find her in her bedroom, assessing herself in a strapless gown before a full-length mirror. She doesn't look half-bad for an old bride.

She spins around when I knock on the door frame, announcing my presence.

"Damn, it was supposed to be a surprise!"

Her expression is borderline irritated, so I say, "I would've seen it in forty-eight hours, anyway." Hoping to avoid an argument, I add, "It's pretty. The shoes are nice, too," I say, even though they're hideous. White satin pumps? I thought those had all been dyed to pastels for proms in the nineties.

"Thanks," she says begrudgingly, still checking herself out. "Crappy weather, huh?"

"Yeah."

Pause. Listen to the rain.

"Did you get a ride home?"

"No, took the bus."

"I would've offered to pick you up, but—"

"Don't worry about it," I say, still hovering near the door.

"Do my boobs look big in this?" She cups her hands around the lacy cream fabric.

I'm thinking this is a trick question, so I play it safe. "Not really."

"Darn." She reaches into the top of the dress and scoops up her breasts so they're jammed up high on her chest. "That's better."

I'm sensing a mood shift, so I go for it. "Can I bring a date?"

"To what?"

"The wedding."

"I didn't know you were seeing anyone."

"We just started . . . a few weeks ago . . . ," I lie. She has no right to know the truth about anything anymore.

Lucy grabs a cigarette from her dresser and lights up. I can't believe she's smoking in her wedding dress. "Where did you meet him, at school?" Hack, muffled cough.

"No, he's a little older."

"How much older?" Suddenly she's a concerned parent.

"Twenty. He's a junior at UM."

"A college boy," Lucy coos, the concerned parent vanishing into her cleavage as she studies it between drags. "And where did you manage to meet him?"

I'm not very good at thinking on my feet, but I am getting better. "Lou's Deli." This isn't exactly a lie. "A bunch of us were there after school. A group-study thing." But that part was. "Is it okay if I bring him?" I ask again, trying to stay on course, knowing I've taken a risk. But I didn't know which came first—inviting Mac or asking Lucy if I could. The whole "professional ethics" thing could stop me in my tracks. But I'm still going to try.

"Does this college boy have a name?"

"Mac." No last name necessary.

"Help me with the zipper, will you?" She lays the cigarette in an ashtray, then backs up, lifts away her soft platinum hair. To avoid touching her skin, I use one hand to hold down the fabric and the other hand to unzip.

"It fits you great," I offer, knowing the compliment will help my cause. "I love these beads going down the back."

"You can bring him, Rosie, okay? But don't think you're snowing me." She slips off the pumps and steps out of the dress, revealing a thin body, half my size. Then disappears into the bathroom and shuts the door. The tub faucet starts. "Make sure this date of yours wears something nice," she calls out. "Don't embarrass me."

My eyes dart to the cigarette smoldering in the ashtray, beckoning me.

"You still there?" she asks again. "Did you hear me?"

"I heard you," I say, then pick up the cigarette and burn a nice big hole in the toe of one of those pumps.

• • •

Mary has been avoiding me since our little spat in Outdoor Emporium yesterday. I hate when we fight. It feels like a part of me is missing. She was cold at school today and said she had to study during lunch, so I joined Paula and the tangerine heads in the gym and let a bunch of guys try to impress us with their jump shots. I asked Mary to come over after school, but she said she was busy. That was the final straw that forced me to do some uncharacteristic begging for the Slaabmobile. Lucy had taken a bottle of something red into the bath with her, so when I knocked gently on the bathroom door a half hour later, she slurred out the location of her keys.

It's been a while since I've been behind this ratty wheel. Besides the filth, the stench has me rolling down the windows and holding my breath at red lights. Cigarette ash floats like bits of gray confetti every time I step on the gas.

Mary's house isn't that far from mine, but it does require a bus transfer and six blocks of walking. I'm in no mood tonight and hope this rare opportunity to use Lucy's car was worth the sucking up I had to power through in order to get it.

I drive quickly through her neighborhood until I reach her street. As I approach her house, I expect to see light coming from her bedroom window, but it's dark. I idle in front of her house, debating. I try texting again.

u home? i'm outside

No answer.

A sick feeling starts to form in my belly. Has Mary dumped me? Think of Elaine. Have a little faith. Maybe she's not home. Simple as that. And yet the longer I sit here across the street, having cut the engine and the lights, I'm beginning to think she's done with me. Maybe our spat wasn't just a spat after all.

The light flicks on in her room. So she is home.

i know you're there—come outside

Still no reply. I can't hang out here all night. Lucy will sober up soon enough and wonder where her car is, forgetting she authorized my quick run to the drugstore for tampons.

Suddenly, the front door opens and the globe bolted to the wall next to it pops to life. A man steps out, but remains fairly shadowed in the dim light. It must be Mary's dad. I wave through the window I've got rolled down, but he doesn't wave back. Maybe it's not him, or maybe it is and Mary's told him to ignore me.

He keeps standing there and I'm beginning to feel uncomfortable. Surely he recognizes Lucy's car and yet he doesn't call out to me. He could be fighting with his wife. Maybe he hit her again, and that's why Mary's been so distant today. It's possible.

Mr. Perkins backs up and closes the door. A moment later, the globe sputters out.

So I restart the Slaabmobile and drive off, waving aside swirling ashes, wondering if today was the day his fists had turned Mary's way.

. . .

Fine. I'll have to take another leap of faith, and this one without Mary's support.

After a long, hot shower, I put on my most comfortable pajamas and climb into bed. I steady myself before dialing Mac's number so I'll sound calm and confident. He answers on the third ring.

"Hi, it's Rosie," I say, even though I assume he's got me in his contacts list by now. At least I hope he does.

"How are you?" It's been two days since our meeting when he unloaded the bulk of what he'd discovered—the forged birth certificate, my mother's job at Frontier, the fact that I was most likely born in Colorado. I had been kind of hoping to hear from him first, even if it wasn't about the case. Maybe just to say hi.

"I'm good," I say. "You?"

"Tired." He yawns loudly into the phone, then apologizes for it. "Had two finals today."

"How'd they go?" I ask, realizing we never talk about his life, school, or what makes him tired.

"Good, I think. Studied hard. Should pay off." He sighs. "Look, I haven't got any more news—"

"No," I cut him off. "That's not why I'm calling."

"Oh," he says, sounding kind of surprised. "What's up?"

It feels like he's rushing me, and it's sucking the faith right out of this call.

I forge ahead. "Are you free Saturday night? I know it's short notice."

"For what?"

Breathe. Don't sound too desperate. "Would you come with me to Lucy and Judd's wedding? It's nothing fancy. It's not in a church or anything. Have you ever been to La Rosa's? It's an Italian restaurant in Coral Gables. 'Do you, Judd, and you, Lucy, promise to make each other nuts for the rest of your lives? Yes? Terrific, let's have some pasta.' That's all it'll be."

"Slow down," Mac says, then waits a beat. "I don't think I should."

"Why not?"

"I already told you," he says, but in a nice way.

"I know. Professional ethics. I heard you." I pause, trying to come up with another angle. "So let's not look at it as a date, okay? It's not a date. It's a . . . favor. You're doing me a favor by not making me go alone."

"Why don't you ask your friend Mary to go with you?"

"Weddings require legitimate dates—scratch that. I didn't mean date. I just meant, you should go with someone other than your best friend. I can't exactly dance with her, you know?"

"I'm not sure . . ." His voice trails off. I imagine his eyes scrunching up, his lean fingers raking through the long mess of brown hair. He's trying to find the right words to blow me off.

There is the longest pause, so awkward. I toss the covers, suddenly feeling hot. "Tell me if you don't want to go. It's fine."

"I don't want to go."

"Really?" I can't believe he actually said so.

Deep sigh on his end. "It's just not a good idea. Tell him I'll be right there!"

"What?"

"Sorry, a friend arrived to pick me up for a game. That was my mom, letting me know he's here."

"What kind of game?" I ask, hoping to extend our conversation in any way possible.

"Basketball, down at the school gym. Just a pickup game." I don't know what a pickup game is, so I ask, and he goes on for like five minutes explaining what it is and that they do it every Thursday night.

"Sounds like fun," I say, even though it doesn't. I'm not much of a sports fan, but I do appreciate a good uniform and the odd color combinations that pop. "Well, I won't hold you up." I try to sound understanding, maybe even a tad pitiful.

It works. "You're not holding me up."

"Maybe I could come watch sometime. University of Miami isn't that far from my house. And you know I'm good at taking the bus."

"I know."

I think I hear him yawn for the third time since he answered the phone. "Wow, you really are tired. You could hang out on the phone with me instead of racing back and forth on some court."

"It would mean a lot less running," he jokes, which doesn't sound like a no to me. I curl up in the covers and put an extra pillow under my head.

"Talking on the phone isn't against your professional ethics, is it?"

"I don't believe so."

He hesitates, which makes me hope his mind is changing.

"Hold on," he says, and I wait for what seems like an eternity before he comes back on the line. "Okay. Let's hang out."

"Really?"

"I told my friend I was beat."

But he isn't too beat to talk to me for the next two hours. It turns into the longest conversation I've ever had with a guy, and definitely the best. Way better than midnight calls with Ray. Mac and I don't talk about sex or dirty things, but other things—important things, like my mother.

"When you think about her, what's the first thing that pops into your head?" he asks.

"The way she looks now. I imagine she still has big poufy hair like mine, only short, maybe streaked with gray, and the only lines in her face are there from years of laughing. I hope she's been happy all these years, even without me."

He talks about his family—his dad, the pilot who has their garage filled with model airplanes, and his mom, who finally got a promotion in the detectives' bureau. He's got two younger sisters, twins Maggie and Michelle, who pull pranks on him when he's sleeping. He tells me about his favorite professor, an old guy who knew his uncle way back when he played ball for UM. And I tell him about Ms. Tuft and Mrs. Shoal, and how they ganged up on me with a double detention. He says there's a place in the Keys called Islamorada Outpost that has cherry pie better than Lou's.

Then he asks me about life before my dad died. I launch into memories of my old house, struggling to keep the tears at bay. "I had the nicest bedroom with dark green carpet and lavender walls. Outside my window, a small lake lit up at sunset like an orange Popsicle."

"Sounds way better than my room," he says. "I've got tile floor, white walls, and a view into my neighbor's bathroom window."

"Is she at least hot?" I joke.

"No. It's a 'he,' and Mr. Hostetler is about eighty years old and sometimes forgets to close the blinds."

We both laugh, and then I say, "We had nice neighbors,"

because I want to add to the conversation even if it does make my stomach knot up. "Lots of families with kids who rode bikes and played dodgeball in the street. Sometimes Dad would put extra burgers on the grill and we'd invite half the neighborhood into our backyard. Life was good. You don't know how good when you're young."

"Tell me more. I like hearing about a time when you were happy."

It takes everything for me not to cry. As painful as the memories are, they're somehow even more painful to share. "Enough about me," I say, fearing if I round up any more, I'll definitely lose it. "I'd much rather hear about Mr. Hostetler."

"Uh, no you wouldn't. Trust me." Mac snorts, and I imagine him lying on his bed, holding the phone to his ear, imagining me, too. "Hey," he says, as if a strange thought just popped into his head. "Do you want to go out tomorrow night?"

"What?" I ask like an idiot, then ask like an even bigger idiot, "What about your professional ethics?"

"Hmm," he says, "I'm sure they're around here somewhere." I hear Mac making all sorts of noises, like moving books and papers around. "Nope. Can't find them."

I snicker, feeling all giddy. I can't believe Mac just asked me out on a date. Definitely beats me asking him, which I won't bring up again right now. The wedding is still two days away, giving me plenty of time to reissue the invitation.

"Text me your address and be ready at eight."

31

STILL NO WORD from Mary. The only thing more daunting than preparing for a date is doing it without your best friend. I can't believe she's acting this way. If I'm having second thoughts about trekking across the country, that's my business. She shouldn't judge me. After all, I'm not judging her whole park-ranger-fantasy thing.

Between outfit choices, I keep checking my phone, hoping to see the screen light up with a text from her. As I decide on a pair of faded jeans (torn in all the right places) and a heather-gray cap-sleeved top, the long-awaited glow catches my eye. I bounce on my bed to read the message.

we r gonna meet

Oh no. It's Joe. And what's with the future tense?

I text no with two angry taps.

yes

stop or im calling cops

c u soon

That's it. Officially freaked out, I waste no time going for the Fund. While Mary had agreed to accept the offer of my share, we also agreed that I'd keep it with me. Believe it or not, her mom's snoopier than Lucy. I shouldn't need much to buy a pocketknife. This way, at least I'll be able to defend myself if this lunatic follows through on his threat.

I pull open the bottom drawer of my dresser, clawing my way through old bras and panties. My heart races when my fingers keep missing their target. This is where I'd moved the Fund after I suspected someone had been snooping around in my nightstand. I didn't only move it—I transferred it, too. I'd found a new pack of Lucy's cigarettes and, just to be mean, pulled them all out, broke them in half, and sprinkled the tobacco around the house before dumping them in the trash. For days, Judd was checking the entire house for termites.

Mistake number one: I used that empty pack to hide the Fund.

Mistake number two: selecting this place, because it's not here. The empty pack or the cash. It's gone.

When there's a knock at my door, I almost jump out of my skinny jeans. "Go away!"

"Rosie. Open up." It's Lucy. These visits have to stop. Reason enough to get my own place.

"One minute!"

She jiggles the doorknob. "Why is this thing always locked?"

"So you can't come barging in whenever you feel like hassling me," I reply, kind of joking, kind of not.

I slam the drawer shut and yank open my door with enough force to cause a breeze to blow through Lucy's glossy white bangs. Immediately, her eyes fix on the dresser. I follow her gaze to the drawer, which had popped open a bit from my slam.

It's closed, but her eyes linger on the knob I have wrapped with a macramé chain I made at summer camp when I was eleven.

"What are you doing?" Her suspicious tone tells me she already knows.

"Just looking for something," I say, playing along, but there's no game here. She found the money. I'm not a hundred percent sure, though, so I need to keep cool.

"Going out?" She looks like she's going out herself, with crystal earrings dripping above her shoulders and a tight dress wrapped around her like black cellophane. The stitching is shoddy, and frayed threads pop around the plunging neckline.

May as well get it over with. "I'm seeing Mac."

"Your college stud?"

"The one and only."

"Is he picking you up, or are you meeting him somewhere? You should never do that, you know. Make him come get you. He'll respect you more."

"He is," I assure her.

Lucy eyes me dubiously as Judd calls from the other side of the house, asking where the hell she is. "Hold on!" she screams, then turns to me. "Pre-wedding shindig at Roland's house. I guess you could call it the rehearsal dinner, but I think it's only appetizers and cocktails. As long as they have wine, right?"

"I guess," I say, just telling her what she wants to hear.

She grips the door frame, then spins around. "Do you like the dress? It's new."

"Yeah, it's nice." Please go.

"The darnedest thing happened the other day. I was

scrounging around for a smoke. You know how I get when I'm out of cigarettes!" It's as if I can see it: a hammer being raised up, up, up. "And wouldn't you know, I found a pack in that drawer." Her nod at my dresser signals the hammer is ready to strike. "Such a sweetie, nagging me all these years to quit. Hiding my cigs, trying to keep me alive another day. Got a lot more than a fix, thank you kindly."

The hammer slams down on my head, blinding me.

"Where'd all that money come from?" she asks, no longer being cute. Her heavily made-up face means business.

"It was mine," I say bitterly.

"I figured as much. But how did you get it?"

"I didn't steal it, if that's what you're implying."

"I would never accuse you of such a thing," she says, raising an eyebrow. Uh-oh. Did she find out I stole the will from her desk? All this cat-and-mouse stuff is making me nervous.

Since I can't come up with a plausible explanation, I pull out this from my bag of tricks. "Actually, it wasn't mine. I was holding it for Mary." Which is kind of true.

"Were you now?" Lucy's eyes brim with disbelief, but she says, "In that case, you can tell your little friend that I'm sorry." She's as sincere as those televangelists who promise your donation is going straight to God and not their wallets. "I didn't spend it all . . ."

I perk up, hoping she's got some left, which she should since there is no way her dress cost anywhere near the six-hundred-something dollars she stole from me.

But then she clarifies, ". . . on the dress. I also needed a new pair of shoes for the wedding. Somehow my cigarette must have fallen yesterday and made this perfectly round hole in one of the toes."

Don't blow it by flinching, Rosie. She can't pin this on you without hard evidence. When my face doesn't betray me, Lucy continues. "Then I splurged on an expensive cabernet and two loaves of olive bread."

Everything we suffered through—letting strange, probing fingers touch Mary, allowing sweaty flesh to rub against hers, while I watched when I didn't want to, and listened when I couldn't bear to. All for a cheap dress and a bottle of wine. I wish there was a sinkhole beneath my feet that could swallow me up.

"Be home by midnight," she says, and shuts the door behind her.

32

SINCE THERE IS NO SINKHOLE, I collapse on the floor and call Mary, but she still won't answer. So I thrash around in a furious rage, kicking stuff and screaming at Lucy even though she's gone. By the time Mac arrives in a shiny white convertible, I've got a wicked headache. Still, I intercept him outside my crappy house with a smile and the warmest hello I can muster.

"I was going to knock," he says, already heading up the broken stone path that leads to the black door.

"That's okay. I saw you pull up."

"You look nice." He moves in for an awkward half hug. "Are they . . . here?" Mac asks, surveying the front set of windows, maybe thinking their noses would be pressed to the glass. The question makes sense, since both Judd's truck and Lucy's car are in the driveway.

"No. They were picked up by one of Lucy's co-workers about a half hour ago."

When Mac opens the car door for me, I slide into the soft leather seat and drop my purse near my feet. My whole body sags in comfort, and I let out a sigh that grabs his attention.

"Rough night?" He hops into the driver's seat and starts the engine. The car is immaculate and smells like clean laundry.

"Let's just say it's a good thing you weren't charging me to work on my case," I say.

"What happened?"

"All the money is gone," I say, turning away. "Everything I did—"

"You did?"

"What?" I ask, my head pounding so loud I couldn't make out what he said.

"You said everything *you* did." I hear him this time, but I'm still distracted by the pain settling between my eyes. "Are you okay?" he asks, probably because I've taken to kneading my forehead with my knuckles.

"Headache."

"Do you get them a lot?" His eyes carry that concerned look people get when you tell them something that sets off warning bells.

I'm quick to say no, but the truth is, I have been getting more. I've just chalked it up to all the stress.

"Well, I did play a role," I say, returning to our conversation. I don't want to discuss my headaches or my memory lapses or anything else Mary harps on me about. "It was wrong. I know. But we weren't hurting anyone . . ." Aside from me and Mary. Because as much as we tried to play it cool, you can't do stuff like that without it leaving scars.

Out of nowhere, Mac downshifts, pulls off the road, and into a Dunkin' Donuts parking lot. Part of me wants to buy a dozen and call it a night. He presses a button overhead and a tiny light illuminates the armrest between us.

"What's wrong?"

"Let's deal with this right now." With his most serious expression, he asks, "Have you ever done drugs?"

"What?"

"Just answer the question."

"No."

"Alcohol?"

"No. Well, last year, when Mary and I were about to do something courageous—or stupid, if you consider friendship bonding rituals silly—we took a swig of vodka first."

He doesn't notice me glance at my wrist because his gaze has shifted to the rearview mirror. Checking, always checking to make sure he's doing the right thing, not blocking anyone, not doing anything illegal. Which is why I don't tell him about the rum shots I did with Mary two weeks ago after the incident with Ralph. Why get into all that?

His focus is back on me and now his eyes are narrowed in suspicion.

"I swear," I say.

"Have you murdered, maimed, or kidnapped someone, committed tax fraud, violated your parole, or stolen even one dime from a hardworking individual?"

"Are you joking?" I can't help but giggle and it feels so good. It's like my face is opening up.

"No," Mac says, trying to stay serious, but I see his beautiful mouth curling up at the ends. "Answer the question."

"No to all of the above."

"Then I have news for you, Rosie Velvitt. You haven't committed the worst sin in the world—although it is illegal in forty-nine states. Even if you weren't the one perpetrating the act, you were still promoting prostitution. It's a third-degree felony, you know."

No, I didn't know.

"What you did was wrong, but it's behind you now, and it has to be behind us, too."

He just said us. I haven't been an us since Ray, when I was crushed into some pathetic, whiny dust. I can only hope it means something different this time.

"Okay," I say, grateful his impromptu interrogation has cleared the air we didn't go near on the phone. "Last week, in your office, I left feeling superconfused, and I don't want to feel that again. So I'm just going to come right out and ask first." I lean in closer, search for a smell I can recall in the future as smelling like Mac. But he just smells clean. "If I kiss you, are you going to pull away?"

"Why don't you try and find out?"

So I do. It's a kiss that lasts at least five minutes, his hands cupping my face so I stay close. He playfully tugs on my lower lip with his teeth and lets me do the same to him. My hands wrap behind his neck, letting his soft hair slip through my fingers. When we finally separate, our noses inches apart, he smiles and says, "You taste like raspberries."

He takes my hand and uses it to shift gears, onto the moonlit highway.

Part of me wishes Mac had taken us to some dark, cozy restaurant where we could do some serious talking and hand-holding. Candlelight, soft music, a waiter who brings us an appetizer on the house because we look like a young, hip couple who will spread the word about the restaurant's gracious ways.

The other part thinks the Sports Club is probably a better spot for a first date—bustling and busy, with plenty of distractions if conversation runs dry. Not that Mac and I have ever had trouble communicating, but you never know. I've never been here, but I can understand why Mac wanted to come. Behind a Plexiglas wall, a group of guys battle it out on the basketball court, slamming against each other, offering diners an unusual form of entertainment. Televisions show various sporting events while an old Eagles song blares through the sound system.

I grip Mac's hand as he leads us through a labyrinth of crowded tables to end up at a booth in the back. It's so stuffy in here, I'm regretting my decision to wear tight jeans and a shirt made of fabric that doesn't breathe.

He leans into me and softly says, "Did I already tell you how nice you look?"

Scratch that regret. "Yes, but a girl likes hearing it twice. So do you." He really does, looking spiffy as always in a button-down checkered Polo shirt and those dark jeans I love. I noted the shoes, too. The usual boat shoes have been replaced by honey-colored loafers with a brushed-satin buckle.

We slide into opposite sides of the booth and pick up the

menus already resting on a place mat filled with football team logos. A waiter wearing a referee uniform appears with a pen and pad, says, "Welcome to the Sports Club. Don't get teed off because there's no foul here."

"Excuse me?" Mac rubs his chin.

"It's what I have to say." A whistle and plastic badge bearing the name Jacques hang from the waiter's neck. He doesn't sound or look like a Jacques—more like a Rob or a Dean. He's got long, stringy hair and a set of probing brown eyes that flick back and forth between Mac and me. "Get it? We've got like ten slogans I can pick from. Want to hear another one?"

"Uh . . ." Mac stumbles.

"Do you have root beer?" I ask, hoping to cut this waiter's weak comedy routine.

"We do," he says. "And for you?"

"Iced tea for me." Mac holds the menu in both hands while scanning it. "We'll need a few minutes to decide."

"Okay," Jacques says. "Soup of the day is clam chowder." Then he leans down with a hand slightly cupped over one side of his mouth. "But I wouldn't recommend it. Kinda fishy." Pops back up and blows his whistle. "Drinks on the way, no time to play."

We share a dubious look and chuckle into our menus. Then Mac props his elbows up on the table and clasps his hands. Serious-conversation body language. "So how are things at home?"

"Same." I grab a paper napkin and proceed to tear it into

tiny pieces. "Well, not exactly the same. The happy couple is extra-happy because of their impending nuptials." A flurry of white paper floats onto the table in front of me. "Wish I didn't have to go."

"If the invitation still stands, I could take you."

"Really?" I'm excited and relieved I didn't have to ask him again.

"You did say I didn't have to wear a suit, though, right?"

I nod vigorously, but when he snorts I understand it was a joke. "Just kidding. I'll be presentable."

"Like I'd ever worry about someone who considers khaki pants and polos casual wear."

"You don't approve of that style?"

"Well, I'm not the fashion police, only a fashion snob."

"So I've noticed," he says. "I could tell you weren't impressed the night we met at Lou's. You were checking me out, especially my shoes."

"It wasn't so much the shoes as the socks you wore with them."

"What was wrong with the socks?"

"Nothing. You're just not supposed to wear them with boat shoes."

"Says who?"

"Says the girl who's going to be a world-famous designer one day."

"Root beer for the lady," Jacques says, returning with our drinks. He hands Mac his tea and tells him it's already sweetened when he reaches for a sugar packet. "Ready to order?"

Mac asks me what I want, then orders the same thing for both of us: burgers, hold the cheese, with football fries (whatever those are).

"The team thanks you for your order." Jacques snaps the menus out of our hands.

Once the waiter's gone, Mac asks, "What are you thinking?"

"It's that obvious there's a hundred things running through my head?"

"At least," he says. "And I assume most of them have to do with Lucy."

"I don't see how I can keep her from getting the money. My father left it to her. End of story."

Mac takes a gulp of his drink. "Contingent on raising you with adequate care and provisions," he says, repeating the will almost verbatim.

"Which she hasn't done. But how do I prove that? It's not like she beat me or anything."

"It doesn't have to be egregious behavior to prevent her from receiving the inheritance."

"I still find it hard to believe that I could keep her from getting the money because she was nasty to me whenever the wind blew the wrong way." I give it some more thought while taking my first sip of the root beer, which is almost as good as the stuff in that pretty etched bottle sold at the gas station near my house. "What about the whole 'of sound mind and body' thing? Or is that only in the movies?"

"You mean when your father had the will drawn up?"

I nod, still sipping.

"John already thought of that. He actually wanted me to discuss it with you."

"Glad I brought it up," I say coyly.

He smirks, says, "There are two possible problems with that angle. Let's start with the first one." Mac plays with the straw in his tea. "The will was dated November of 2010, which means—"

"I was eleven."

"Right. Was he sick then?"

"I don't think so." I think hard, trying to remember if there was a time when he wasn't feeling good, if I ever had suspicions about some mysterious illness that he and Lucy were trying to keep under wraps. But nothing comes to mind. "No," I say with confidence. "He was never sick. At least not that I saw. Now I know he had all sorts of trouble with his heart."

I can see his wheels spinning, processing it all. "That kind of illness wouldn't have affected his decision-making. 'Of sound mind and body' often pertains to the mental state of a person on their deathbed anyway—if the will was drafted at that time, near the end." This conjures up the image of my dad at the end—weak, pale, breathing through a tube.

"The second problem is this: Let's just say, for whatever reason, he was not of sound mind and body when he had the will drafted. That means everything else in the document can be brought into question. Disputed, even."

"Like the money he left me."

"Correct."

"So what can I do to keep Lucy from getting her share?"

"I'm not sure there's anything you can do, short of running away."

"We could run away together," I tease.

"Could you wait a few years? I've got another year at UM, and then grad school for my master's in criminology."

"Hmm . . . that might be a problem."

Mac always manages to make me smile in the middle of the most serious conversations.

"Where would you go?" He asks this like he wants a real answer, not a playful one.

"I've always wanted to go to New York."

"Really?"

"Doesn't everyone?" I ask.

"Not me," he says. "I'm a Florida boy."

"Well, if I want any sort of career in fashion, it's where I have to be."

"But first Paris, and then maybe Italy, right?" I love how he remembers the comment I made when we first met.

"Right," I say, not really joking. Because of my inheritance, anything is possible. Even a trip to Europe. "But first, a proper education."

"Any word from that school you applied to?" His question makes my heart sink, like it does with each passing day I don't hear from the Fashion House. The website says they have a rolling admissions process, so I could technically be notified anytime, but still. Paula was right when she said I should've put in multiple applications. Not great planning on my part.

"Not yet, but I may have another opportunity," I confess. "I met the nicest lady on the bus. Her name is Elaine. We've gotten kind of friendly. Her daughter works at a design school in Fort Lauderdale, so she offered to pass on my portfolio to her."

Mac's face lights up. "Wow, that's great, Rosie. Somehow the right people find a way into our lives."

Isn't that the truth.

Our burgers arrive and Mac dives right in. It reminds me of the first time I saw him at Lou's, with his head buried in his plate. I play with mine, decide on one of those football fries first. They're thick-cut and loaded with coarse pepper.

"Part of me says, let her have the money. Whatever. Maybe she was good to my dad in ways I never saw. Who am I to stand in the way of his wishes?" I devour three fries at once, they're so crispy and delicious. So far, this place is great, but the guys playing basketball at the other end of the restaurant are distracting, especially to my date, who I notice keeps checking out the game over my shoulder.

Mac almost chokes on his burger. "Now there's a switch. Where did this come from?"

"You know why I was so upset when you picked me up?"

"You started to tell me before I went into interrogation mode at Dunkin' Donuts. About the money you'd saved, that it was gone."

"It's not gone, like missing. It was stolen. By Lucy." I shudder, recounting the tragic turn of events. "She spent it on a cheap satin dress with shoddy stitching and a couple loaves of bread."

Mac crinkles his nose in confusion, but keeps eating.

"Plus a bottle of wine," I add, which makes Mac nod, as if it now makes sense. I let out a deep breath, then take a bite of my burger. It's good, but I've let it get cold. I swallow before continuing. "Here's a forty-three-year-old woman who is so hard up for money, she steals from her own . . . you know, daughter, or whatever. It's kind of pathetic."

"I'm sorry, Rosie." Deflated, Mac sinks into the booth. "She's done a lot of things, but this—this is low, even for her."

I straighten up in my seat. "Would you look at us? We're supposed to be having fun, but instead we're moping in our football fries."

"You want to have fun?" Mac pushes his plate away. "Follow me."

. . .

Mac deposits me on a stool before sealing himself behind the Plexiglas wall. By the time he's got the basketball in his hands, I've settled in with a great view of the court. Maybe this is considered one of those pickup games he was telling me about last night. At first, I'm totally turned on by Mac trying to impress me, and ready for the show. Until the other starring players appear onstage.

I push my face into the glass. It can't be him. Them. But it is. Mac is playing basketball with Todd, Ivan, and even—God help me—Ralph. That day Todd drove me to the Coastal Square mall, he said he and Ralph don't really hang together. What a liar.

With both fists, I pound against the Plexiglas, trying to get Mac's attention, but the glass is thick and his back is to me. His loafers are planted on the court while he shifts the ball between hands. No traveling for him. The other guys are circling like vultures. I should leave. That's what I should do. Bow out now before they see me, before it gets . . . ugly.

Smack! Two palms brace against the glass and puckered lips blow a kiss between them, but they're not Mac's lips. They're Todd's.

"Go away," I say, even though I know he can't hear me. It's basically soundproof in there. Todd makes an obscene gesture with his right hand, but common decency gets the better of him when he spies a little girl crawling up onto the stool next to me.

Behind him, under the fluorescent lights, the other guys— Mac included—are calling him back to the game. The cross still hanging around Ralph's neck shines like a menacing gold spear. The sight of it makes me recoil.

"Go," I plead, but he doesn't budge, his eyes boring into me with a mix of lust and hate. The longer he stands there, the more suspicious Mac is bound to be. Todd shakes his head with a devious grin, mocking me. He's going to make trouble for me. What's he planning on telling Mac? Lies, that's all. But maybe more. I feel like there's more. Tiny pricks between my eyes signal the return of a headache.

Todd winks, then shuffles backward.

It's like waiting for a tornado to hit. You see it coming, its cone of angry clouds whipping in an unpredictable pattern but still headed straight for you.

I can barely keep myself sitting upright, feeling wobbly and unsure, fearing the ground that was growing steady with Mac is about to crumble. All those guys with their stories, their lies. Gossiping about me and Mary. I can hear it now.

I can't wait. "Let's go!" I yell into the glass, banging against it with my hands. I've scared the little girl next to me. She crawls down off the stool and back into the arms of her mother who's at a table nearby.

Mac throws his hands up in the air, playfully refusing to leave the game.

My forehead is plastered to the Plexiglas, my hands now slipping against it, wet with sweat. And then it happens. Mid-bounce, Todd says something and Mac's face drops. It morphs into an expression I've never seen. He looks . . . what's that funny-sounding word? Bamboozled, that's it. Like he was clubbed over the head.

I hop off the stool and make my way for the large set of doors that lead into the court. I'm blocked by a heavyset waiter.

"Can't go in there."

"But I need to get my boyfriend. It's an emergency."

He peers down at my feet. "You're not wearing proper shoes."

"Neither is he," I say, even though there's no way this guy is going to check out Mac's footwear to make sure.

"Sorry. No one interrupts a game in progress. Court policy."

"It's a restaurant," I snap. "Not Madison Square Garden."

The waiter surrenders. "Which one is he? I'll get him."

But it's too late. Over the waiter's shoulder, I watch Mac shove Todd in the chest and within seconds it's an all-out brawl.

The waiter and I almost run each other over trying to get through the door.

"Stop!" I scream when I see Mac pinned beneath Todd's knees. The waiter was right about the shoes. I slip, then slide along the glossy court and end up a few feet from the fight. I crawl toward them, intercepting Todd's fist before it lands on Mac's face. In a circle, Ivan and two other guys are egging things on. But not Ralph. He's leaned down beside me, flicking his tongue in and out, in and out. I am this close to his pock-marked cheeks.

All the fear, the fury makes me grab the dangling cross and jam it into his chest.

He falls back, lets out a yelp. "That bitch just stabbed me!"

Everyone laughs, except for Todd who's still trying to get in another shot at Mac. I'm not about to let that happen. The three of us are a tangle of bodies squirming around on the court, but I make sure to snag the correct arm—his throwing arm—and sink my teeth into his flesh.

Todd scrambles away, shouting, "She bit me! God-damned animal!" He wipes the sweaty hair out of his eyes to inspect the wound. Unfortunately, it doesn't look like I drew any blood, though by the red blossom on Ralph's shirt, I was successful there.

I return my attention to Mac, whose lip is bloody, but so is Todd's.

The waiter, in a referee uniform like Jacques, finally decides to step in and tell everyone to go cool off.

Mac and I remain on the court in a protective huddle. His hair is a mess. It's in his eyes, his mouth. Dark red splotches cover his neck and jaw. I use the bottom of my shirt to wipe the blood off his mouth, but he pulls away. From pain or aggravation, I'm not sure.

"Your new boyfriend can't take a joke," Todd says, rearranging his clothes.

I don't even want to know what he's talking about. It can't be good, and it can't be funny. I grab Mac's forearm, trying to lift him up, but he shrugs me off. Mortified, all I can think about is reaching Mary, hoping she'll be there for me when I need her later. And I will be needing her big-time.

"Let's go," the waiter says, rounding everyone up and off the court.

Mac is ahead of all of us, stomping away in his honey-colored loafers. I lag behind, but ultimately push my way through the Plexiglas door and around gawkers eating burgers and football fries.

• • •

I spot Mac's convertible idling at the side of the restaurant.

I thought for sure he would've bolted, driven away at warp speed. But there he is, clutching the steering wheel, waiting for me. My heart pumps wildly as I yank open the car door and slip inside.

I catch my breath while fastening my seat belt before asking, "What did he say to you?"

"I can't repeat it." He shifts into reverse and peels out.

"Tell me."

"No."

At a light, I put my hand on his knee, which is nervously bobbing up and down. "You said you could put the past behind us." Even as I say it, part of me wonders what I'm actually asking him to forgive and forget.

"That was before some punk put his fist in my face."

"Of all the guys to be playing on that stupid court . . ." I couldn't believe my crappy luck. And looking at Mac's swollen lip, his luck wasn't so great tonight, either. "Tell me what he said."

He hesitates, but then says, "Ring around the Rosie, a pocket full of posies, ashes, ashes, we all fall into Rosie's . . ."

My body recoils, even without hearing the crude ending. Mac steps on the gas, racing through the green light, headed for the highway that will lead him back to my house. Where he can dump me off.

"Why would he say that?"

"I have no idea, Mac!" I shake my head, but this whole conversation feels like déjà vu. Didn't Ray accuse me of the same thing? My brain swims with muddling waves, which isn't helping the headache. Why has Todd spread this lie? I could kill him.

Mac asks who those guys were, especially the one who hit him.

"His name is Todd. We were kind of flirting for a while before—"

"Before what?"

"He was one of the guys who was with Mary." I dip my head. "Who paid her."

There's a shift in his expression, from anger to confusion. "So then why would he have said that about you?"

"Because I blew him off. Things got weird after that—you know, because Mary and I are best friends—and I basically let him know I wasn't interested anymore. But maybe he still is. Which is why I think he's the one sending me harassing texts." I pause, gathering my theory. Even though it couldn't have been him in class or in his car, he could've had one of those other guys do it. Like in that movie *Scream*, where more than one guy was the killer. "I got another one earlier, Mac. I'm getting scared that he's going to do something."

"Really?" he asks disbelievingly. A trail of sweat trickles down his neck and gets lost beneath his collar. "That seems kind of crazy."

The question itself isn't strange, just the way he asks it, like he thinks I'm lying.

"Here's a news flash: All guys aren't like you. As a matter of fact, most of them aren't. They do mean, hateful things when they don't get their way."

His eyes are back on the road, his hand gripping the stick shift with angry white knuckles. I want the ride home to last an eternity, or at least long enough for us to get past this. Move on. Get back to the place where we were in the booth an hour ago. But Mac's not budging, and every traffic light, every turn, takes me closer to my house and farther away from him.

"You don't believe me. You think I slept with those guys. That it was me, not Mary."

"I didn't say that."

"You didn't have to."

We drive the rest of the way in silence until the black door of the green house welcomes me home.

33

IT MAY NOT have been an epic tragedy like the *Titanic*, but I still could've used a lifeboat last night. Apparently, Mary is still peeved by our argument at Outdoor Emporium, but at least she responded to my barrage of texts with a happy or sad face, based on the message.

Todd punched Mac!

I bit him!

This was a good sign that she was warming back up to me, and I definitely needed it on this Saturday morning, the day of Lucy and Judd's wedding. I would've preferred a face-to-face, or at least a phone call. She was more like a dinghy after my spectacular sinking, but it was better than nothing.

And then, something. While forcing down a piece of cold chicken for lunch from Judd's fast-food filth house, there is a knock on our black front door. Lucy pops up from the kitchen table, taking a wing with her. Judd smacks her butt when she passes him, and it makes her giggle and me vomit a little in my mouth.

I crane my neck to see who the rare visitor might be. Lucy's blocking him, but it's a delivery of some sort because the guy asks, "Rosie Velvitt?"

"Uh, no," she says. I imagine the complete and utter deflation of her white powdery face. "But I'll see that she gets them," and she all but closes the door in this guy's face. Even I know you're supposed to give delivery guys a tip. I've already raced to her side to see what's come my way. Honestly, I have no idea who would send me anything.

Lucy pushes a clear cellophane cone of flowers into my chest. "They're for you."

I study the explosion of pink and purple flowers sprinkled with baby's breath. No one's ever bought me flowers before. Unless you count the time Ray accepted a dozen wilting roses from a street vendor and then turned to me after he dug into an empty wallet and asked if I had ten bucks to pay the guy. A card tucked inside says, *I believe you. Mac.*

I want to head straight to my room but know they need water and a vase, so I'm forced to return to the kitchen.

"Well, well, well," Judd says, all creepy. "What did you do to earn those?"

"Shut up."

"Rosie!" Lucy blurts. "Watch your mouth."

"I don't like what he's insinuating," I say.

"Maybe I'd like to know, too," she says, getting back to her bowl of wings. She uses her small Chiclets teeth to pull scraps of chicken from the bone.

"He likes me, okay? This guy Mac really likes me. That's it."

"Ray really liked you, too," Lucy says, "but you blew that. Maybe you can manage to hang on to this one."

If she only knew why he ultimately ended things—because I wouldn't have sex with him—a real, caring mother would applaud me, not condemn me. I had tried talking to her once about it, to tell her that Ray wasn't exactly the nice guy who calls her ma'am and compliments her tight sweaters. But Lucy didn't seem all that interested and wandered off into her bedroom with a glass of wine.

I ignore her and help myself to the only vase I can find in the cupboard—a tall glass one she tells me to be careful with, like I'm twelve. I fill it with water, cut the stem bottoms, and arrange the flowers so the purple ones ring the outside with the pink ones in the center, then intersperse the white baby's breath. So pretty. I won't let Lucy and Judd ruin this moment.

Back in my room, I set them on the nightstand. They do an excellent job of brightening things up, but the rush of receiving them is already wearing off. My mind and body are zapped from last night's Sports Club debacle. So I hop into bed and call Mac, but it goes straight to voice mail. Before I can tap out a text, he beats me to it.

Studying in the library.

They're beautiful.

Then another text because that wasn't enough. Thank you. (Followed by something I forced myself to do, knowing it was a risk.)

You're welcome.

I would let it end there, on a good note, but the wedding is looming and I just want to know now if I'm on my own.

R we still on for tonite?

I'm getting sleepy lying here, waiting for him to respond. And then:

The top hat makes me chuckle, and I write back: Great. Can't wait.

C u tonite

Did Mac actually use text language? I smile at the thought of somehow rubbing off on him. I curl up under the covers and slip into a nap.

When I wake, my bedroom is filled with the glow of a late-afternoon sun. I stretch and grin like a lovesick puppy when I turn and see the explosion of flowers beside me.

I'm feeling rested and kind of loved, a good emotional place to do some drawing. I grab my sketchbook from under the bed and start on a vest. Seeing Mac wear one the other day got my wheels spinning. Vests have been out for a while, which means it's only a matter of time before they make a comeback. I'm thinking oversized, no buttons, large pockets. I pull out the pencil lodged in the spiral wire and get busy.

Twenty minutes into a full-on suit, two knocks on my bedroom door. I don't want to stop sketching, so I ignore it. Drawing is my escape, especially when I allow myself the fantasy of a design that'll hop off the page and onto the runway. I'm there, in the first row, watching models of all sizes sport this suit—with a vest, without it, in tweed, in suede . . .

Knock, knock, knock. Three raps this time, followed by a jiggle of the knob. Someone's impatient.

"Rosie, you in there?" It's Judd.

"Nope, it's Rosie's ghost again who always locks the door."

"Can I come in?"

"No, you cannot come in."

"Please." Normal voice, and then, "I want to clear things up before the ceremony," in a whisper.

"I'm busy."

"With what?"

Forget it. He's totally broken my concentration. So I crawl out of bed, pull on a sweatshirt over my shirt, and socks on my feet. I clutch the doorknob without opening it. "There's a church about a mile away if you want to make confession."

"Don't be like that."

"Well, I'm not a priest and not about to absolve you of your sins."

"Look," he says, his breathing heavy against the door. "I'm sorry about what happened."

"No, you're not. You're only sorry you got caught."

"That's not true."

"Is so. Now go away."

"Please open the door so we can talk like adults."

"I am an adult. Well, not technically. But in two days I will be. You'll always be a cheating degenerate, no matter how old you are."

He doesn't respond. I believe Judd's gone, when he starts up again, all whiny. "I had too much to drink after your mom and I fought, and when you woke me up I was out of it—"

"Apologize without excuses."

"Fine. I'm sorry, okay? That's it. You need to forgive me before the wedding. I don't want to marry Lucy without having your forgiveness."

Is this guy for real? I just want him to go away so I can put on my new dress and make myself beautiful for Mac. "Well, if you promise to never, ever—"

"I promise, Rosie. Never, ever again." Pause. "Can I come in now?"

"No. I'm getting dressed." That was probably the wrong thing to say. I may have kicked on his pervert radar. "I'm mean, I'm dressed, but I'm putting on my makeup."

"I only need a minute."

"Go ahead."

"Not like this. Open the door."

So I do, because I need to see his face, show him I'm not scared or intimidated. At first, a crack, which he doesn't push through. This earns a wider gap, and I'm so shocked by what I see, I fling the whole door open to get a better look. No mustache. Hair slicked back and tucked behind the ears. Habitually pale skin slightly tan, as if he spent the day at the beach. An ice-blue tie is knotted perfectly at the neck of a crisp white shirt, and over that, a well-fitted black suit. Judd the Dud actually looks respectable on his wedding day. I wish Mary were here to witness the miracle.

"Your mother's getting ready," he whispers, sizing me up in my three layers of knock-around clothes. "You're not dressed."

"I know. I lied. Now what do you want?"

"I'm planning a surprise for her and I need your help."

"Go ahead," I say, tapping my watch. "You've got thirty seconds."

"I don't know if she told you, but Lucy's leaving her job."

So that's what Roland's parting comment was about. Lucy's quitting. Of course she is. Why would she keep pushing papers at a scrap metal yard with half a million dollars coming her way? I back away from the sliver of space I had given him when I opened the door, and try to act surprised when I say, "No, she didn't."

"She's had enough, says working around all the scrap metal is bad for her lungs."

"But smoking a pack a day isn't."

Judd tilts his head, knowing I've got a point. He stuffs his hands in his pants pockets and rocks back and forth on his newly polished leather shoes. "Irregardless," he says, which makes me cringe right along with *supposably*, his other favorite "word." "I'm taking her away from all that."

"You're a real knight in shining armor."

He bristles in his rented suit. "All I need is the shield and dagger."

"So where are you taking her? A table for two at Itchin' for Chicken?"

His lips curl into a forced smile. I'm pushing him, and he's trying his best not to push back. Got to give the guy credit for keeping his cool. "No," he says simply. "First, I'm taking her on a surprise honeymoon. Then we'll focus on finding her another job. Something less . . . harmful."

"So what do you need from me?"

"I want to take her on a cruise."

"Have a great time."

"On Monday."

"That's my birthday," I snap, because for some reason the thought of them taking off on it bugs me. Not that I want to celebrate with these two jokers—it's just the point. Toss me a gift, light a candle or two, pretend to give a shit.

"I know, which is why I want you to cut out of class early so we can have a birthday-slash-bon-voyage lunch. The ship doesn't leave until five o'clock."

I smell something rotten, but it could just be him. You can't work for years around garlic and grease without it seeping into your bloodstream. He makes a big, fake smile, and says "pretty please" like a little boy.

So I shrug, figuring, hey, it's a free meal. "I'll go, but it doesn't mean I forgive you for what you did. And it doesn't mean I'll forget, either."

He drops his eyes, the first gesture that appears to have a shred of authenticity. "Okay."

"I'll need a note excusing me." I can't be in Shoal's cross-hairs again.

"Nice. My first parental duty." He wiggles his eyebrows up and down, having slipped right back into creep mode. "I'll send you with one, signed by your new stepfather."

"Forget it," I say, about to slam the door on him.

"I was only kidding." He reaches out to poke me in the waist, but thinks better of it and swiftly pulls back his lecherous hand. "Promise you'll come."

The wet desperation in his eyes triggers an internal alert system. Something's up. But he's worn out his welcome, and unless I want to shower again, Judd's got to go.

"Fine. I promise. And now I'm getting dressed," I say, pushing him back in the chest with a stiff plastic hanger. I turn the dead bolt extra-hard so he hears it click.

34

THE HAPPY COUPLE took off twenty minutes ago, looking like they escaped from the top of a wedding cake. I watched from my room as Judd helped Lucy into the Slaabmobile, the hem of her wedding dress getting stuck in the passenger door without her noticing. It was poetic justice, seeing the white fabric trail like a wayward flag against the driveway and onto the street. She'll be furious when she gets to the restaurant. Though she'll think, *Perfect excuse to have a drink.*

The ceremony is scheduled for eight o'clock in the "chic basement" of La Rosa's, with a cocktail hour first to get their guests nice and liquored up. It's six thirty, and I'm waiting for Mac, who should be here soon. The dining room table gives me a clear view of the street, so I can see the moment he pulls up.

But I'm getting anxious and can't sit here any longer. I head to the full-length mirror hanging behind the hallway door for one final assessment to make sure I still look fresh. It took serious effort, but I blow-dried and tugged mercilessly at my hair until it lay flat. Then I used a straightener to seal in my work. I chose sparkly copper eye shadow and matching lip gloss, capturing a bit of that '70s feel. A silver pendant hangs from a delicate silver chain and settles right above my chest. Fake diamond studs are small enough to look real, and I envision Mac nibbling at them, playfully threatening to pull one out with his teeth.

When there's a noise outside, my head snaps in that direction. It's him. I shuffle into the living room, careful not to trip in my strappy satin heels. I pull aside the curtain, but no one's out front. A cat scurries across the street, two birds abandon the tree near our driveway and settle on the sputtering globe of a lamppost. Then that noise again, a scraping sound, but I can't tell where it's coming from. The front yard is still empty.

I let the curtain fall, then pull out the cell from my bag and dial Mac's number. He doesn't answer, so I send a text that I'm ready and can't wait to see him, in case he got sidetracked— which I find hard to believe. He's never been late for one of our meetings, and when he said he'd pick me up last night at eight, he was actually five minutes early. He'll be here.

Hanging around a quiet house is weird. No voices, no shuffling of feet. You take those everyday sounds for granted when there are none. Just you and the walls. And when you hear another noise that sounds like it's coming from inside the house— not outside—your mind goes in a dozen directions, none of them any good. Was it in the kitchen? The den? I wait for another sound to guide me, but there's only silence.

I decide to watch TV to keep my mind occupied. I don't want to wrinkle or dirty my dress by sitting on the couch, which has its share of stains, so I stand in front of the television, pointing the remote control at the screen. Lucy's favorite show, *The Real Housewives of Some Boring County*, is on, and two women are fighting—surprise, surprise—and screaming at each other. One even throws a vase that shatters against a wall. It's so loud, I don't hear him come up behind me.

35

"THREE STRIKES you're out," he says.

His voice sets off an explosion in my ears. I can't respond, because he's holding my mouth with his hand. But the smell of his fingers gripped under my nose—before he even spoke, I knew it was him. How had I not remembered Ray's love of baseball and the endless games he'd forced me to watch on the weekends?

"Told you we were gonna meet. In fact, we already know each other pretty well."

He drags me from the living room, twisting my ankle in the process.

"I can't believe you're Joe," I whimper, and he tells me to shut up. He puts one hand against my mouth while the other arm wraps around my neck, ripping off my pendant necklace.

"Let's have a little fun," he says, shoving me through my bedroom door and into the nightstand. The vase holding Mac's flowers tumbles and shatters on the floor. The water spills near my feet. He pushes me onto the bed. I hear a seam rip in my new dress, somewhere near the shoulder. He pats the back of his pants. "Seems I forgot my wallet. But you wouldn't charge me now, would you?"

I scramble to sit up, but he forces me back down. It's been a long time since I've seen him, and he looks different. I've been blocked from his social media accounts, though I got lucky a few times when he was tagged in someone else's photo. He's shaved his black hair into a crew cut, which makes his bushy eyebrows seem unnaturally thick. Dark stubble sweeps across the bottom of his face, and a tiny gold hoop dangles from one of his ears. He wears a cutoff fraternity shirt and gray sweats—not exactly the preppy high schooler who left me for Tallahassee nine months ago.

"Ray, please."

"Don't beg, Rosie. It's a turnoff."

"I mean, please don't."

Ignoring me, he pulls the shirt over his head, then climbs on top of me.

Lips quivering, voice shaking, I ask him why he kept texting me, pretending to be someone else.

"To see if the rumors were true. It was a test."

"I told you. It wasn't me! It was Todd—"

"Todd was fucking for cash." He chuckles at his joke, and when he does, I get a whiff of marijuana on his breath. That night he called me—he was smoking pot. But he's all riled up, too, which means he's probably on something else, something more.

"No. I mean, Todd spread those rumors. I didn't do that, Ray. You have to believe me. Besides, I never agreed to meet Joe, or you, or whoever, so I passed your test."

"It doesn't matter," he says, his fingers starting to explore my body. "You've turned into a little slut since I left."

"No, I haven't." I'm trying to get him to look into my eyes, to see me, remember me. I manage to put my hand along the side of his face. Maybe my touch will bring him back. But he's wild with anger and not thinking straight. "Listen to me, Ray. A lot has happened since you left."

I had wanted to tell him the truth about Lucy. But by March, when I'd found the box, it had been months since we'd spoken.

"Yeah, you started turning tricks."

One of his hands disappears into his sweatpants. He pulls out a condom and smacks the small silver square against my cheek. "Who knows what you've picked up. Don't want to catch anything now, do I?"

For months, I had dreamed of lying beneath Ray again, feeling his thumping chest, smelling the sharp odor of his favorite body wash. Feeling the slope of his lower back with my hands. But not like this. He's crushing me, and his breath—reeking of pot and alcohol—has me squirming to turn away.

He grabs my face. "I can't breathe, Ray. Please get off of me."

"Shut up already, will you?" He's got both my arms pinned to my sides. When I feel him hard between my legs, it unleashes a flood of panic. I can't lose my virginity like this. I can't lose it to him.

"Ray," I say, boring my eyes into his. "Stop. I mean it."

"I'll stop when I'm done." He manages to slide my underwear down to my knees.

"Stop!"

There's banging at my window. I turn my head, and there's Mary, pounding with her fists against the glass pane.

"Ray! Get off me. Mary is right there! She's gonna call the cops, I swear."

He bites my breast through the dress. "Let the stupid bitch call the cops. I'll be long gone by then, anyway."

She keeps pounding, pounding, while my head grows foggy with the smell of Ray.

"That's it," he says. "You know you want it. You always did. It's probably a good thing you started hooking. Maybe you'll know what you're doing now." He grabs the condom and rips it open with his teeth.

"No, Ray. Please. You have to stop."

"No, you stop," he says. "Stop fighting me." He bites the other breast and I scream out. He tugs down his boxers to put on the rubber.

There's a blinding pain in my head, and then Mary's pounding stops. Now there is only an eerie silence and a dusky purple glow lighting up my room. But she must still be outside, because she just said, "I'm here, Rosie. I'm here." And I imagine those words spilling softly from her raspberry-glossed lips.

Now there's more banging. It sounds hollow and far away. The scraping of footsteps nearby.

"Rosie!"

And then Ray is gone, as if a giant crane has lifted him off me.

I shuffle backward, onto the far side of the bed, and watch in horror and relief as Mac, in a fine navy suit, pummels Ray with both hands.

He lands some good blows to the face, but when Mac misses a shot, Ray drops to the floor and slithers out into the hallway. He kicks at Mac's shins while pulling up his sweatpants. He looks like a beetle, trying to right himself.

"Get off me, you lunatic!" Ray screams, his back against the wall.

"Get the hell out of here," Mac says, before dealing him a final blow in the gut. "Or you can hang around while I call the cops."

He checks Mac's posture before attempting to stand, then wipes the sweat from his forehead. "I want the ring back."

Mac shoots me a look. "You know this guy?"

I don't answer him. I answer Ray. "I pawned it," I say, feeling courageous now that Mac's here. He lunges at me, but Mac shoves him back.

"You'll sell anything, won't you?" The disgust in Ray's voice makes me wince, even though he's wrong.

"Yep. Got a whopping twenty-five bucks for it, too. Mary and I were able to split a salad for lunch. Thanks."

Ray puts a hand on Mac's shoulder and gives it a congratulatory pat, like they're friends. "She's all yours, bro." He grabs his shirt off the floor, mumbling, "Couple of losers." And then he disappears into the same hallway he snuck down a dozen times when Lucy and Judd were passed out in their bedroom.

I hear the front door open, then slam against the outside wall. As I fall on my side, letting the tears come, I imagine him walking the dark streets of my neighborhood, hoping to find a stray cat he can kick around. I'm disgusted with myself, knowing I was once that cat.

Mac returns to my bedroom after locking the front door. He scoops me up and lets me cry against the soft blue fabric of his suit. I cry even harder because he doesn't seem to care that I'm sure to leave dark wet stains on it.

"Are you okay?" he asks, stroking my hair I blow-dried just for him.

Exhausted, I nod into his chest, but then move to break free. "Where's my phone? I need to call Mary."

"Wait," he says. "Who the hell was that?"

I don't answer fast enough. He holds me at arm's length and says, "Oh, God, Rosie—was that—that guy 'Joe' who was sending you those harassing texts?"

I dip my head in silent agreement. Technically, it's the truth.

"You said you thought it was that guy Todd." Mac bolts from my bed and slams his fists on my dresser.

"I know. Obviously I was wrong!" I snap. Grabbing the sheet, I dry my face and wipe off what's left of my makeup. Copper eye shadow and kohl mascara smear across the white cotton fabric. What a mess I've made, and not just on the sheet. Remnants of last night's scuffle are all over his face—the slightly swollen upper lip and the scrape near his chin. I'm drowning in guilt and can only place a reassuring hand on his back.

Swiftly, he reaches into his pants pocket and pulls out his cell. "I'm calling the cops."

"No!" I yank the phone from his hands.

Mac's head jerks back. "That scumbag attacked you. Now he's on the streets, angry and bloody, and probably looking to take out his frustration on someone else."

"He won't. Trust me." I grasp his forearm, tense beneath his sleeve. "I don't want Ray getting picked up by the cops. That would only piss him off more."

"But he tried to rape you, Rosie, which is attempted sexual assault. Not to mention breaking and entering, trespassing . . . did he have a weapon?"

"No." I shake my head, fairly certain. I didn't feel anything on him, but even if he did have something, he never used it to threaten me. Probably figured his strength would be enough.

"Because if he did, that would be aggravated assault—"

"Mac, there was no weapon."

He almost looks disappointed. "You could still press charges."

"I don't want to. Why kick the hornet's nest?" That's how I'd always handled Ray—avoiding the hornet's nest because I didn't want him to stop loving me. But now I know that wasn't possible because he'd never started loving me in the first place.

"Because he broke the law—numerous laws—and he needs to be held accountable for that, and . . . he hurt you, Rosie. You can't let him get away with this."

Seeing Mac's determination makes me understand that forcing Ray to pay is right on so many levels, but I'm tapped out. The thought of dealing with cops right now will only put me over the edge. I just want this whole Joe thing behind me, so I use a strong, unwavering voice to convince him. "I'll think about it, okay? I'm shaken up, but I'm fine. Nothing happened."

"You're sure?"

I nod, furiously wiping what's left of the tears on my cheeks.

He takes a deep breath and checks his watch. "It's almost seven thirty."

"I don't feel like going."

"Then we won't," he says. "We can order takeout from Lou's and watch ESPN until you fall asleep from boredom."

"As appealing as that sounds, I don't think my absence is going to fly." I check myself in the mirror, raking both hands through my hair that was so pretty and smooth before Ray got ahold of it. "We have to go. Let me take a quick shower first."

"Are you sure you're okay?" he asks again. "He didn't—"

"Yes, I'm okay, and no, he didn't," I say. "And you? You've already had to defend me twice in two days."

"This isn't going to become a regular occurrence, is it?" His smile makes me want to burrow into his arms again.

"Nope. That ought to do it," I say, because nothing else should come crawling out from a dirty corner to make him think twice about me.

"In that case, we have a wedding to attend."

We both look down at the puddle of water and smashed petals. "Maybe we should clean this up first," he says.

"No, I'll take care of it."

He doesn't press me, shoves the cell back in his pocket. "I'll wait in the living room."

"Hey, Mac?"

He stops at the threshold of my door. His golden-brown hair is disheveled, a single gelled clump falling over one eye. His tie has pulled loose from the collar and exposes his neck, red and flushed.

"How did you know I was in trouble? Did you see Mary? Did you hear her banging on my window?"

"What? No. I didn't see her. She was here?"

"Yes. She must've taken off when you pulled up."

Mac lowers his head, squinting at me. "Why would she do that?"

"I don't know . . ." My head starts to grow foggy again.

"Well, the minute I approached the door, I heard screaming, so I ran in."

"It was open?" I ask, confused because I thought for sure it had been locked. After all these months, Ray must have still had a key.

"Criminals don't usually make a habit of locking the door behind them. Now go take a shower," he says, beginning to close the door. "Take your time. I'll be waiting for you."

I remain on my bed, unable to move. I take stock of what hurts. Ankle throbs, neck burns from where the chain was ripped off, and wrists are raw from Ray twisting them.

Then I think of Mary. Why did she show up and then leave? What did she see? Or worse—what did she *think* she saw?

36

"I HOPE LUCY won't be able to tell," I say, carefully strapping myself into the passenger seat of Mac's convertible. The dress had ripped near one of the armpits, but I managed to get creative with two safety pins and a crystal hoop earring.

"Don't worry," he says, pulling out of my driveway. "You did a good job patching it together. If you don't make it as a designer, you can definitely be one of those sewing people."

"You mean a seamstress."

"Right." Mac flashes me an award-winning smile.

I pull out my phone and text Mary. I want to let her know I'm okay, but I also want to know why she took off like that.

"Can we put the top down?"

"You'll get blown to bits," he warns.

"I don't care. This is a want-to-feel-the-wind-in-my-hair kinda night." I can't have anything pinning me down or holding me tight. I pull off the rubber band and shake out my hair so it's wild and free.

At the stop sign, he pushes a button on the dash. When nothing happens, he says it sticks sometimes. After a few more tries, the canvas top releases, then folds into the back of the car.

The dark blue summer sky becomes our roof. I pull down the visor to get one last look at myself in the mirror before supposed bits get blown.

"You don't need to check," he says, reaching over and flipping it back up. "You look fine."

"Fine, huh?" I tease.

"Spectacularly fine." He puts a hand on my knee, and I wonder if he can feel it trembling under the mint-colored silk.

"You, too," I say, "but I was looking forward to seeing you in that top hat."

We both snicker, and that ends the conversation for a while. Sounds of the city swirl around us in the way only a convertible can offer. I don't feel much like talking, anyway. But I am curious about something and turn to him with a question. "What made you believe me? On your card, it said you believe me."

"Remember the story I told you about running for sixth-grade vice president?"

"Yes."

"What I didn't tell you was that more than one kid got in trouble when I uncovered the truth. Another boy got suspended, too."

"Okay." I don't know where he's going with this, but I've learned the Brooks logic isn't always dispensed in a straight line.

"They both got in trouble because they were always lumped together." He turns to me. "Like you and Mary."

Lumped together. That was the exact phrase I'd used on the phone with Ray. Mac understands. But his expression has turned somber, and I can't bear to see those green eyes of his so sad.

At a stoplight, when he hasn't said anything in like five minutes, I say, "I wouldn't blame you if you just want to drop me off at the restaurant."

"And waste this good suit?"

"Seriously, Mac. This has all gotten way too—"

"Complicated?"

"I was going to say messy."

"Maybe I like messy."

I glance around his immaculate car and say, "I doubt that."

We travel a few more blocks before he replies. "I'm not dropping you off. I'm staying with you. Besides, I may have just saved your life," he says. "You're eternally indebted."

"I don't have any money," I say, knowing we'll both get the joke.

"Good thing I've got a job." He takes his hand off the gearshift and gives my knee a quick squeeze.

"So how late do you think we'll be?" I ask, when he checks his watch.

"You think I can fight? Wait till you see how I drive." He picks up the expressway, zooming through traffic with supreme skill. My body sinks into the seat, exhausted. "Close your eyes, Rosie. I'll let you know when we get there."

• • •

Roland Potillo is the first person I spot as Mac and I descend the stairs of La Rosa's and enter the basement. The room is lit by wall sconces and candles in the center of four large tables. Small vases of swimming yellow roses accompany place cards on white linen tablecloths. The place looks decent, even wedding-worthy. Everyone's dressed up, including Roland, whose tight black suit is doing its best to stay buttoned.

"Well, don't you look lovely," Roland says, grabbing both of my hands and pulling me in for a kiss on the cheek. "And who's the lucky fellow?"

"This is Mac," I say, presenting him like a prize. Well, I do feel like I've won something—an amazing guy who can forget my past, even when it keeps literally slamming him in the face.

"Nice to meet you, sir." They shake hands vigorously, up and down like a saw.

"Roland Potillo, Scrap Metal Mania," he says, a verbal business card that has me expecting phone number and e-mail address to follow.

Mac's mouth twitches, as if a bee just buzzed near it. He recognized the company name. "It's a pleasure," he says, then puts his hand on the small of my back. I love the feel of his fingers pressing against me.

I scan the crowd, looking for signs of the happy couple. "No one's seen them yet," Roland says. "But I suppose that's the way it should be. The bride and groom need to make a grand entrance." Roland wipes his forehead with a hankie he pulls from his suit pocket. I don't know why he's sweating—it's like fifty degrees down here.

He stuffs the cotton square back in its home, then leans into me. "Your little surprise gift made quite an impression."

"What?" I say, my attention snapping back like a boomerang.

"Whatever you left for Lucy in her desk last week."

Mac's light touch on my back goes into full-grasp mode.

"Why?" I ask. "What did she do?"

"Became sort of frantic, come to think of it . . ." Roland scrunches up his face, as if only now realizing her behavior was strange. "You'd think you had taken something, rather than left something." He's the only one who chuckles at his theory.

So that's that. She knows I took the will. Mac and I squeeze each other's hands at the exact same moment. A waiter approaches us with a tray of bite-sized garlic bread knots. Mac takes two and pops them both in his mouth at the same time. Roland takes one but only studies it, says he hopes there's no cheese inside.

I can't stand here anymore while he inspects his appetizer and my heart hammers in my chest. So I excuse us with the usual claim of having to use the restroom, and hope he can't detect the shaking in my voice.

· · ·

We tried not to look like we were racing, but Mac and I high-tailed it up the stairs, through the main dining room, and out to the balcony. It overlooks an alley, still slick and wet from yesterday's rain.

"I think the temp sold me out," I say. "She was eyeing my bag when I left."

I rest my weight against the railing, circling my ankle, testing to see if it feels any better. It doesn't. And my neck's still sore and my wrists still hurt and now Lucy knows I took the will. For some reason, that makes me nervous.

"Okay, so let's assume she knows. What's the difference? Last night you were resigned to letting her have her share of the money, anyway," Mac says.

"She's obviously got something up her sleeve. Why else wouldn't she call me out?"

"I don't know. Maybe it's as simple as avoiding a confrontation."

"Lucy? Avoiding a confrontation? I don't think so." I focus on a large puddle below, rippling from the vibration of nearby traffic. "Seriously, Mac. Why hasn't she said anything?"

"Why haven't you?" he challenges.

"What was I supposed to do? Charge into the house after our meeting last week and tell her I know she's a big fat liar?"

Mac crosses his arms. He's got something to say.

"Well?" I ask.

"I would have."

"Well, I'm not you, Mac, and you're not me. You've got parents that love you and an uncle who's given you office space. Sisters that pull pranks on you. I have none of that."

Mac's face falls, as if having those things is a curse, not a blessing.

"I've always wanted that. I've always wanted Lucy's love. Especially after my dad died, I thought maybe . . . maybe she'd want to be closer to me, too, since I was a part of him. But that didn't happen, and then she met Judd—"

"So you blame him? I mean, for the demise of your relationship."

"Maybe" is all I say, because my feelings about Judd are

complicated—almost as complicated as my feelings about Lucy.

"I didn't know you felt that way about her," Mac says, kind of surprised.

"Because I'm embarrassed, if you must know the truth. Imagine being desperate for your mother's love and never getting it."

"I'm sorry," Mac says. "But you still have more than most. Or you will. Five hundred grand. Plus a little something else." He tilts up my chin so he can kiss me. It's soft, but short, and I settle my head against his chest to take a breath. "And who knows? You may have your real mother at some point, too."

I pull away. "You really think so?"

"I think we've got a solid direction. Based on the facts we have so far, she's somewhere in Colorado. Always has been. Which is why, I believe, your dad forged a Florida birth certificate by changing the name of the hospital, the county, all that stuff. It was the first thing John checked. Your father didn't want anything to lead you back there."

That scares me. What else has my dad been hiding all these years?

"John should be home tomorrow," he says, "and then he'll run her name again—her real name. We'll have more answers soon. I promise."

Even outside, the whiny sound of violins reaches us from downstairs.

"I think I hear wedding bells," Mac says.

"Either that, or the death march."

So what do I say? That the ceremony was marvelous, and the bride and groom made a splendid appearance, and their vows were magnificent, and all that phony stuff?

Hardly. All I'm going to say is that I got through it. But I did notice one thing that everyone had to notice. Lucy loves Judd. I was seated in the first row of chairs with a clear view of her face. There were tears. But him? No tears, which made me suspicious. Never mind the fact that ten days ago he was trying to get into my pants. He must know about the inheritance. Is that why he's held on to her? A sliver of me actually felt sorry for Lucy, wondering how many more seventeen-year-old girls he'll go after.

Back at the table, I focus on the swimming yellow roses and nibble buttery garlic bread while Mac nurses a light beer. Or two. I haven't been keeping tabs on him. I could tell he was pleasantly surprised when the bartender set up in the corner didn't card him. He nudged me to get something, so I asked for a glass of wine and got a red one that tastes like feet.

During the first course, Lucy and Judd visit our table. He's got his arm around her waist; she's spilling out of her dress.

"So this must be Mac, the one who sent you flowers," Lucy says, eyeballing him. I'm surprised she remembered his name.

"Yep." My tone must be a little too clipped for her. She nestles her face in my hair, whispers in my ear.

"You're not still upset with me about the money, are you?"

In the same hushed voice, I sarcastically reply, "Yes, but don't worry. I won't ruin your wedding night."

"Like I'd let you . . . ," she says with a snake's tongue, then returns her attention to Mac.

"Nice to meet you," he says. "Congratulations to you both."

Judd reaches in, and he and Mac manage an awkward handshake over a basket of bread.

"You taking good care of my little girl?" she asks, but doesn't wait for his answer. She tips my chin up with two fingers. "You don't look so good. And what's this?" Her eyes dip below my shoulder.

"Nothing," I say, lurching away from her.

"You ripped your new dress already? Too tight? I told you to watch it."

Judd snickers at her dig, making me furious.

"All those chips and root beer sodas." Lucy tsks, and if I could, I'd yank off the silly flower headpiece and shove it down her cleavage. That sliver of pity I felt during the ceremony? It's now with the rest of the trash in the alley.

Mac swallows hard. "Yes, I'm taking good care of her." Under the table, he squeezes my thigh, which has been doing this uncontrollable-shaking thing. A couple hours hasn't done much to ease the trauma of Ray's attack. My insides remain twisted in knots that refuse to untie.

"She's a handful," Lucy says, pinching my cheek harder than necessary. "But worth it. A little rough around the edges, but—"

"Rosie's a lovely girl," he interrupts, which also shuts down Judd's snickering.

"What's that you're drinking?" she asks, even though the empty Bud Light bottle is sitting on the table right in front of him.

Mac picks it up as if to check for himself. "Just a light beer—"

"Hmm . . . by the way you're talking, I'd think you've been knocking back something a little stronger."

Oh my God. How could I have ever wanted someone like her to love me? She thinks this small tear in the armpit is bad? Wait till she sees the enormous red wine stain I'll be sure to have before the evening's over.

"Why not get him something, babe?" Judd asks. "Roland gave us an awesome bottle of Jack. Break it out. Rosie's got herself a nice guy here. Even more reason to celebrate."

I'm not sure what's going on here, but before I can decline on his behalf, Lucy drifts away and leaves Judd hovering over us. He doesn't look as crisp as he did a couple hours ago. The tie and jacket are gone, the white dress shirt bunched up around the waistband of his pants. "She'll be back in a minute," he says. "How 'bout a little game of whiskey pong, Matt?"

"It's Mac," I correct him.

"Whiskey pong?" Mac asks.

"You're in college, right? Same thing as beer pong, only with—"

"I get it," Mac says.

Judd grabs his shoulders like they're old friends and gives them a shake. "Then let's put that wedding gift to good use."

Mac, still in his grip, shoots me a nervous glance. I don't think he's a big drinker.

Judd takes off, visiting other tables to round up more players. I think he's already had enough. Not that I blame him, since he's become shackled to Lucy for life—or death. You never know. Lucy barely got through her vows without hacking. At one point, she even pulled out a tissue from the top of her dress and wiped her mouth with it. Before she tucked it back in, I thought I saw a spot of red but couldn't be sure.

37

TURNS OUT, Mac isn't so good at whiskey pong. It took Roland and another guy to carry and unload him into the passenger seat of his car. Lucky for him I know how to drive stick shift, thanks to Judd forcing me to learn one day in his truck.

When I cut the engine in my driveway, he snaps awake. Well, kind of.

"Where are we?" he asks groggily. It's cute seeing Mac drunk—so unlike his uptight, responsible self.

"My house." I jingle the car keys in his ears. Lucy and Judd are spending the night in a honeymoon suite at some hotel downtown.

"What time is it?" he asks.

"Almost midnight."

I grab my purse from the back, get out of the car, then open his door. His leg falls out.

"Come on, Mac. No sleeping in the car." I tuck my head under one arm, then hoist him up so I'm carrying him like he's a soldier injured in battle. It's never taken me so long to walk the path to my house. I have to fumble with my keys while trying to hold him up. I finally push open the black door and we all but fall into the house. Mac's shoe hits my bad ankle as we tumble onto the tile floor.

"Ow!"

He rubs my arm. "You're soft," he slurs, his breath thick with beer and whiskey.

Memories of Ray stir instantly, and I push him aside. He lands near the bench of my father's piano and stays there.

"You need a cold shower," I say, getting to my feet.

He grabs my good ankle. "No, come back down here."

I gently shake him loose, like a puppy. "Forget the shower. But at least crawl over to that couch so you can pass out properly."

And so he does. Poor guy probably had more to drink tonight than he's had the past three years in college. I find myself snickering as he slides along the tile floor, pulling himself up and onto the couch like a bag of bones. I place an afghan over him and his mouth falls slack.

The ringing of Mac's phone startles me. It vibrates toward the edge of the table where he threw it, but I grab it before it falls. It's John. Mac said he was still out of town, plus it's after midnight on a Saturday. Something's up.

"Hello?"

"Uh . . . is Mac there?"

"John, it's Rosie."

"Rosie? Why are you answering Mac's phone?" Not accusatory, more surprised. I wait a beat before answering.

"The wedding was tonight," I say, ready to launch into explanation mode. "Lucy and Judd. They got married."

"Oh."

"Mac took me. I hope that's okay. I really didn't want to go alone."

"It's okay, Rosie. It's fine. But can I talk to him?"

Uh-oh.

"Please don't be mad. Mac had a little too much to drink. He's fine, sleeping on the couch." I pause, waiting for John to reply, but he stays silent. "Do you want me to give him a message?" More silence. "John? Is everything okay?"

"Maybe it's better this way, anyway." No, he's not angry.

"What's better?" I ask.

"Telling you directly." He sounds really weird.

"Telling me what? Are you back in town?"

"Got in late tonight and passed by the office. Mac had left me your case folder on my desk, so I went through all of his notes. That nephew of mine did some good work."

I calmly agree with him, but I'm anxious and want to reach through the phone and yank words out of John's mouth.

"The impatient side got the best of me," he says. "I couldn't wait to run her name."

I don't know what he's going to say next, yet my whole body clenches with anticipation. "I'm listening," I say, so nervous I have to take a seat on my father's piano bench.

"I found her, Rosie. I found your mother."

38

I DO SOMETHING CRAZY. After repeatedly trying to wake Mac from his stupor, I slap him hard across the face. Well, not that hard, but hard enough for his head to pop off the couch and for him to cry, "What? What's happened?"

"Mac, sit up. John's on the phone." I'm holding it in front of his half-open eyes so he can see his uncle's name. He peers at the screen.

"Tell him I'll call him tomorrow." Then he says to the phone, "Hey, Uncle John! I'll call you tomorrow!"

I put the phone back to my ear. "No, he won't. We're calling you back in a few minutes once I've gotten some coffee into him."

I hang up and take Mac's face in my hands, forcing his droopy eyes to look at me. "He found her."

. . .

Sitting across from each other at the kitchen table, we've got steaming mugs of sludge and Mac's cell on speaker between us.

"She's in a sanatorium." John dumps it like a boulder in our laps.

"What? No way." It's the first thing that comes out of my mouth.

Mac reaches out and pats my hand. "Where did you find her, John?"

"Colorado, as we suspected, in a very small town called Burlington. I don't have much more information than that. Psychiatric institutions have several layers of confidentiality. They're not just going to disclose information about a patient because I ask. Mind you, I did my best to shake them down, but all I got was the sense she's been there a long time."

"So that's it?" I ask.

"It is. The rest is up to you if you want to pursue it."

The three of us remain silent. Mac sips his coffee, makes an exaggerated frown.

"Look," John says. "Why don't we all get together on Monday. It's late, and I'm beat. Been traveling all day. Can you come by the office after school, Rosie?"

"Of course." I'll go right after Lucy's surprise send-off lunch, which would probably be around the same time, anyway.

We hang up, and I'm literally shaking from the news. The coffee isn't helping. I need food, something in my stomach. I reach behind me, pull out a cookie from the ceramic jar, and offer one to Mac.

Inspecting it in the dim kitchen light, he asks, "Oatmeal raisin?"

"Yep."

He takes a bite, then says, "They're burned."

"I know. That's how I like them."

He puts his down while I nibble on mine and sip the hot coffee, which tastes good going down.

"So she's still there."

"Probably never left," he says. "At some point, your father took you and moved to Florida."

"I wonder what happened." My mind races with possibilities, but I rattle off the most obvious one. "Do you think . . . ?"

"Do I think what?"

"That my father put her in there? According to his letter, he loved her. Something must have happened."

"Or is still happening," Mac says.

"What do you mean?"

"She's in a mental hospital, Rosie. She's ill."

"I get it," I say, a kernel of sadness popping in my chest. But ill how? Or how ill? It makes a difference, the order of the words. Is she like Elaine's husband, Alan, staring at a television in some cold white room because she stopped recognizing my father? Or me?

I've read my father's letter so many times, I remember it word for word, have even recited it silently when I had trouble sleeping. *Justine and I had to part ways.* Had to, as if it was necessary. He didn't want to.

"So you think that's why he left her?" I've got a serious hunch that's the case, but I pose the question anyway.

Mac shrugs, takes another bite of the cookie. "I don't know."

"I can't believe it."

"Which part?"

"All of it. That John found her with your help. She's alive, but she's . . . you know."

I've painted a dozen scenarios about her, including ones where she's gone, too. Like my dad. Joined together in heaven. But most of them have been snapshots of her leading a normal life with another husband and a kid or two she wanted to keep. My dad said she was into fashion like me, too. I've imagined her as a famous designer who goes by an exotic name she made up.

But of the dozen scenarios, not even one involved her wrapped in a straitjacket or shackled to a bed for her own good.

Mac peers into his cup.

"More?" I offer.

"No. One cup of mud is my limit."

"Sobered you up, though, didn't it?"

"Not as much as this news."

"I know. I think I'm in shock." I return to the coffee machine, even though I don't want any more. I just don't know what to do with myself. My body is exhausted, but my mind is on overdrive.

"You can't possibly want more of that muck." Mac has come up behind me and wrapped his arms around my waist. I grip them, basking in the comfort. He kisses my neck.

"Are you still drunk?" I ask, spinning around in his embrace.

"Not after that coffee I'm not."

There's no use suppressing a smile, but still my hands keep his chest inches away. "I'm serious, Mac."

"Me, too. About you."

"Why?"

He places a finger on the cleft in my chin. "Because of this." Then trails up the side of my face and strokes the patch of fuzz on my cheek. "And this."

"That's not enough."

"I wasn't done," he says, then backs away. "You're honest and talented and you make me laugh."

"Hmm."

"You also wear fluffy yellow sweaters, always smell like fruity shampoo, and know how to drive a mean stick shift." His breath smells like cinnamon and burned coffee.

"Okay," I say. "You've convinced me." Then I sink into his arms he's wrapped around me and smell something else—hope.

39

I'M DREAMING OF MAC. We're in the woods, walking along muddy trails, yet I hear tapping, like nails on glass. I don't want to leave the trail and beg my brain to stay put.

Mac is leading. "This way, not much farther," he says, and then my foot plunges into something thick and wet, and I'm sinking, screaming for him to pull me out, and then I'm pleading to that same part of my brain to wake up, because I know I can.

"Hey, birthday girl!" It's a loud whisper that yanks me from the quicksand, out of the forest, away from Mac.

My alarm clock shows 5:57 a.m. I look to my door, expecting to see Lucy standing there, pretending to be excited about my birthday, but she's not. I notice a folded piece of paper on the floor, a note slipped under my door during the night.

"Rosie, open up!" Same loud whisper. I follow it to the window, where the tapping starts again. It's Mary, and she's holding a cupcake with a lit candle in the center. I scramble out of bed, pick up the note, then swiftly unlock the window for her and remove the screen. Don't want to wake the newlyweds who have yet to fully recover from the weekend. Yesterday, they holed themselves up in their bedroom all day, emerging only twice for food and drink. I was able to watch four episodes of *Hem for Your Life* in the living room, eating salty crackers and cream of broccoli soup for dinner.

"I thought you'd forgotten . . . ," I say, glancing at the paper while Mary contorts herself through the window.

"Forgotten about the day you turn legal?" She's rather sprightly for this time of day.

I accept the cupcake, my mouth watering at the thick spread of chocolate frosting.

"Forgotten about me altogether." I close my eyes, make a wish, and blow out the candle. When I hand it to her, she licks the frosting from the edges.

"Well, that's not possible, and we both know it."

"I've missed you," I say.

"Me, too. I'm sorry I've been such a wicked brat."

The bed creaks when we plop onto it at the same time, so I put a finger to my lips. "Mr. and Mrs. Lister are still sleeping it off." I divide the cupcake with my hands so we can share.

"Speaking of them, how did it go?" she asks. "Wait. Hold off on that. I want to know what happened with Ray. Your one-line text wasn't enough. I mean, I can see you're okay, but what the hell happened in here?" She surveys my bedroom looking for clues, but there are none. The flowers have been swept away, the sheets washed in extra-hot water.

"He broke in, tried to . . . you know."

"That prick. Like after all this time of saving yourself, you were going to lose it like that? To him? No fucking way, which is why I was ready to step in."

"What?" I ask, the chocolate on my tongue suddenly tasting like plastic. I peer at her, noticing she looks like a ghost, backlit by the sun struggling to rise in the east.

"Didn't you hear me? Through the glass." She nods to the window. "I said that I was here. I knew you needed me," she says, sucking the last of the chocolate off her thumb.

She's said that before. Like the time I was at my old house, searching for the box, and when I woke up after crying myself to sleep, there she was.

"So why did you leave?" I ask.

"Had to take off. My mom was calling from the hospital. He broke her nose, Rosie."

"No!" I grab her hand. Poor Mary. Now that I'm getting a better look, her eyes do look puffy. She's probably been crying all weekend.

"Want to know the worst part? She accepted his apology and a pitiful bunch of street-corner flowers. So I don't want to talk about my parents' dysfunctional relationship anymore. I'm done. I want to know what happened when Mac got in here."

"You saw him?"

"Cool-looking dude in a suit? Yeah, I saw him."

"I don't understand why you couldn't have stayed and made sure I was okay."

"Because you only need one savior, Rosie girl." A moment ago, Mary's face was shiny with excitement. Now it's dull and flat.

"Why can't I have two?"

"It doesn't work that way." She leaves my bed and settles into the desk chair, wearing the same plaid miniskirt she wore that day with Todd. But this morning, Mary's replaced my cream-colored tank with a large black shirt. She pulls it over her knees and tucks them into her chest. Her face, tipped to the side, still shows signs of an extra-early-morning rise. "You said you were okay. I sent you a dozen texts but never heard back. Figured you were busy at that sham of a wedding."

"We were," I say, then smack my lips with the last bite of cupcake. "Now that's what I call a birthday breakfast. Thank you."

Her face brightens from the compliment, but she's still sulking. "We, huh?"

"Listen to me. No one will ever replace you."

"I know," she says. "He just better treat you right. Otherwise, I may have to step in." She grabs a brush from my desk and pulls it effortlessly through her hair. It falls in caramel sheets around her shoulders, making me jealous. I'm certain my hair is a dark puffy mess that needs to be tamed by a headband, rubber band, or both.

"He will. He is."

"But if he ever stops, I'll be here." She scrunches up her face. "Or maybe not. I still plan on getting the hell out of here after graduation. One broken nose is about my limit. I can't watch it anymore."

"I'm just glad you're here now. I have to tell you something."

"Go."

"They found her."

Mary drops the brush, hops back on my bed, and playfully shoves me in the chest. "Get out!"

I topple backward into a mound of pillows. "She's still in Colorado."

"Oh my God, Rosie. I can't believe it." Her flat brown eyes turn electric. "When do we leave?"

"Well, she's not exactly living in a gated community doing carpool."

"What do you mean?"

"Let's put it this way—it's a good thing you're sitting down."

"Don't tell me." Mary puts up a hand. "She's on death row for killing her cheating husband."

"No."

"More glamorous?" She casts her eyes up at the ceiling, imagining another scenario. "Please don't tell me she's home-less . . . Oh no." Mary's face drops. "She's not . . ."

"No, she's not dead. She's alive but not well."

"Okay. I give up. Tell me." Mary takes in a deep breath and holds it.

"She's in a mental hospital."

Enormous exhale fueled by shock. "Your mother's a nut?"

"Don't say that!"

"It must be true. Why else would she be there?"

"I don't know."

"We'll find out." She rubs my arm, but stops mid-stroke, raising an eyebrow. "We are going, right?"

"Don't start that again," I say, reminded of our spat in the sporting-goods store.

"I will start that again." She laces her fingers with mine.

"It's about getting on a plane, right? 'Cause I can give you some potent shit to knock you out."

"Well, that's part of it."

"Forget about flying. We can even drive there." Her face lights up with the idea, and she says, "Road trip!"

"Stop," I say seriously.

"Think about everything we did, Rosie girl. All for the sole purpose of finding her. Well, she's been found, and now you're having second thoughts."

She's right. Even after Mac and I talked until two o'clock in the morning, I settled into bed (he took the sleeping bag on the floor) and launched into a panic. Now that I know she hasn't been gallivanting around Europe as a famous designer—or at bare minimum, become an average housewife with a minivan she's filled with other kids—I'm terrified of seeing my mother drastically different from those pictures in the box. Young, happy, beautiful. She could remain like that forever if I don't go.

Mary doesn't wait for me to respond, only grips my hands tighter and says, "Let's go right now. Forget about school."

"Can't. I promised Judd I'd let them take me out for a birthday lunch before they leave on their honeymoon." I wave the paper in front of her face. "He wrote me a note so I can get out early."

Mary leans over and parts my hair, like my third-grade teacher did when our school was on lice lockdown. I wrench away from her prying fingers. "What are you doing?"

"Looking for the incision."

"Excuse me?"

"Where they did the lobotomy."

I smack her arm. "It's just a farewell lunch, Mary."

"Oh, really? Are you sure it doesn't take place in some lawyer's office?"

"No, I'm not sure," I say, having already thought that when Judd made the offer.

"It would take some big, hairy balls to do something like that."

We both giggle at her crudeness. "Let 'em try," I say. "They know they'd have to drag me kicking and screaming. I'm sure it'll all come out after the cruise. In the meantime, I've got the house to myself for a week. It'll be a honeymoon for all of us."

"Party time!"

House parties are such a joke. A bunch of people come over, raid your kitchen for alcohol, and then take off to go somewhere else.

"We'll see," I say, even though I have no intention of throwing any kind of party. I need to get through today first—lunch with the newlyweds and my meeting with John.

"That's better than no," she says brightly. "By the way, make sure to wish them bon fucking voyage for me."

40

WHAT IS IT about vindication that tastes as sweet as cherry pie? After fourth period, I go to the main office and triumphantly hand the slip of paper to Mrs. Shoal. Through tortoiseshell magnifiers, she inspects Judd's note. I assume she's searching for some clue that would indicate a man didn't write the letter, maybe studying the handwriting, looking for dotted *i*'s and crossed *t*'s uncharacteristic of a masculine hand. I don't know. But she keeps me standing there for at least five minutes while she reads the simple paragraph over and over again.

"Can I go?" I ask, noting the time is pushing twelve o'clock. Judd said he'd be outside the front entrance at noon, waiting for me in the Slaabmobile because his truck is in the shop.

"There's no phone number on here," she said. "Need a number to authenticate it."

Really? I want to say. Authenticate? It's not a piece of art. It's a frickin pass. I rattle off his cell number and watch with pleasure as her face sinks in surrender.

She rips off a yellow sheet of paper from a cube on her desk and scribbles a message with a black Sharpie. It's the official one she has to write, in case I get stopped by one of the security guards who are on an equally pathetic power trip.

"Happy birthday," she says, still eyeing me skeptically over the tops of her glasses. I spin on my wedges, out the office door, and into the hallway warmed by the sun.

. . .

"So where are we going?" I ask, settling into the backseat. This bucket of bolts doesn't even have seat belts for rear passengers, so I fold my hands over my lap and say a silent prayer.

Lucy's wearing a bright yellow sundress I've never seen before and a straw hat with a ridiculously wide brim. She edges forward because it keeps hitting the headrest. Behind the wheel, Judd's sporting a Hawaiian shirt and silly black sunglasses too big for his face. It's clear his honeymoon surprise is a surprise no longer. A couple of crazy cruisers, that's what they are.

"Itchin' for Chicken, of course!" Judd says, then checks the rearview mirror for my response.

Lucy jabs him from her seat. "He's joking, Rosie. It's your birthday. We can't celebrate over fried chicken!"

Do I detect a slur in her voice? Maybe not. I'm just conditioned to search for the uneven rhythm of her speech. If she has been drinking, though, I hope she was knocking it back alone. Judd better be sober if he's carting me around.

"We thought we'd go to Hullabaloo's," she says, then reaches over and lets her hand linger on Judd's shoulder.

Hullabaloo's is one of my favorite restaurants. My dad used

to take us on special occasions. Hearing the name conjures up a mix of longing and dread that churns in my empty stomach. Splitting the bacon-wrapped crab cakes won't be the same without him, even after all these years. "But that's like an hour away," I say.

"Who cares?" she snaps. "We're celebrating. You're eighteen!" She pauses, stares out the window for an extra beat. "Where did the time go?"

"Behind us," I say, maybe a little sharp because Lucy turns around and shoots me a look.

"Don't be depressing." She adjusts her hat, plays with the metal hoops hanging from her ears. "Happy talk only."

"Fine. Hullabaloo's it is," I say, making a valiant effort to be a player on this dysfunctional team, but also remembering those awesome crab cakes with fried potatoes.

While the newlyweds bet on the number of onboard bars, I entertain myself like everyone does when they're not a part of the conversation—with my head down, fingers sliding across my phone at a feverish pace to multitask the time away. I text Mac and Mary, play a game, listen to a song, and text some more. Mac cuts our texts short, though, says he's about to leave campus, will call me later. Is it too much to hope for a birthday dinner? Better not get ahead of myself. I don't want to feel disappointed today. Sort of like Lucy just said, but different. Happy thoughts only.

She's right. Today is my eighteenth birthday. Maybe there's some news waiting that would make me extra-happy. I've been checking my application status online with the Fashion House, and every time it says *Pending*. I decide to try again, my heart beating fast like it always does, and it feels like it takes twice the time to load the page. Is this a good sign? I bob my legs, crack my knuckles, take a deep breath. Then there it is, the dreaded word at the beginning of a long letter I don't need to read: *Unfortunately*. I didn't get in. I can't believe it.

I keep the news to myself, not that Lucy even knows I had applied. I roll down the dirty window and let all of the Fashion House dreams get caught in the breeze and blow away. Judd says something about letting the cold air out, so I roll it back up. All I can hope now is that Elaine comes through for me. Now is the time to have faith, when things don't look so good. I may have a lot of money coming my way, but it won't buy admission into design school. I have to earn it.

Lucy starts humming along to a song on the radio, something old I've never heard. She's not half-bad, manages to hit all the high notes. It lulls me in the backseat, reminds me of a time I was carsick as a kid and her buzzing lips took my mind off the nausea. She knew it, too, and even reached into the backseat of my father's car to reassuringly pat my knee. She'd done some things like that. Not many, but some. I peer at her. She looks tired. Even all the makeup can't hide the dark bags under her eyes and a deepening set of frown lines around her mouth.

Lucy's humming relaxes me, even manages to dull the shock of the crappy news I just learned, until she breaks into a coughing fit.

"You okay, babe?" Judd asks, removing a hand from the steering wheel to place on her shoulder.

She reaches into the straw tote that matches her straw hat, and pulls out something. A stack of white napkins, like a gigantic wad you'd steal from a fast-food restaurant. She peels one away and covers her mouth until the coughing stops. I crane my neck to get a look and this time I'm sure. There's blood on it.

She stuffs the soiled napkin back in the tote, tells Judd she's "fine and dandy," then turns to look out her window. For the next ten minutes, no one speaks. My mind races with thoughts of what it could mean. Nothing good, that's for sure.

But Lucy doesn't seem so worried, and another song gets her humming again. So I let myself relax a little, forget about the Fashion House, and sink into the cracked vinyl seat. Even through the Slaabmobile's dingy windows, a bright afternoon sky still promises a pretty great birthday. I'm out of school and off to a special place for lunch. I'm on the verge of having a real boyfriend. Best of all—I'm going to have the house to myself for a week, so I can come and go as I please. Maybe check out some apartments. Maybe look for a car! I know, I know. I have to get the money first, and Mac said it could take a while, but still. Good times are coming.

I almost feel myself smiling when Judd pulls off at an exit I don't recognize.

"Isn't Hullabaloo's on Sunrise Boulevard? Why are you getting off here?" I sit up to get my bearings. We're exiting onto Stirling Road in Hollywood, at least five exits before Sunrise, which is in Fort Lauderdale.

"Just need to make a quick stop," Judd says after Lucy shoots him a warning look.

"Can't we go after? I'm starving."

"It won't take long," Lucy says.

Judd follows the ramp, then merges the Slaabmobile into a long line of cars stopped at a red light. I don't think I've ever gotten off here. Dunkin' Donuts, a Toyota dealership, a chiropractor, a Jamaican restaurant—seems harmless enough.

"Where are we going?" I ask again, clutching my backpack. Something gurgles inside me, and it's not hunger pangs.

They both ignore me this time, and Judd takes the next left into a strip mall with a Dollar Store, an auto repair shop, and a Mattress Giant. He parks, says, "Let's go." I guess he means all of us. My eyes scan the storefronts, while my brain tries to connect the names to a reason for this errand.

And then, two steps out of the car, I see it. Neurons fire. In the corner, where the strip mall makes an L, a white plastic sign stretches across to reach both sides of the building. In red capital letters it reads, STEPHENS & STEPHENS, ATTORNEYS AT LAW. On the door, a neon-green sign says, OPEN 7 DAYS A WEEK, like a Laundromat.

The blazing sun beats down on my head. I'm reaching into the backpack to grab a pair of sunglasses when Lucy takes my arm. "You don't need those," she says. "We're going in right over there." She points to Stephens & Stephens.

"Why?"

"Come on, Rosie." Lucy presses a hand against my back to push me forward. Judd pulls up his cargo shorts and huffs like he's tired of waiting.

"No," I say, planting my feet on the ground. Cars swerve

around us since we're standing in the middle of the parking lot. "What's going on?" I ask, even though I know damn well what's going on. But I want her to admit it.

"We can discuss it inside. Where it's nice and cool. I'm sure they've got some cold water in there for you." Now Judd's hand is also on my back.

"Don't touch me," I say, pulling away from them both.

"Rosie, it's boiling out here. Let's go inside." She cups both hands over her mouth to stifle another cough, but it's no use, and a spray of blood escapes through her fingers.

"Holy shit," Judd says, scrambling through his pockets, looking for something to give her. But she's got the napkins and is already riffling through her tote. There's a spot on her dress. And one on the top strap of her right sandal.

For a minute, we're all just standing there while Lucy pulls herself together. But it's hot and she's sick and I suspect things are going to get even worse really fast once I say, "You tricked me."

I'm embarrassed to admit that a microscopic part of me— think the head of a pin—was hoping I was wrong, but it's clear by the desperation spreading across Lucy's face that picking me up early from school had nothing to do with crab cakes and everything to do with a certain pot of gold left by Dad.

"Did you think I was just going to hand over five hundred thousand dollars to you two?" Little did she know that a mere three days ago I was actually considering it, but after this stunt—after realizing there isn't a shred of decency under that platinum bob—my tune has changed, and it's not one she's going to want to hum along to.

Lucy's eyes pop. "What are you talking about?"

"I know about the will."

"How did you—?" The shock behind the question is genuine.

"You didn't know I took it?" I don't believe her.

"No—no—" she stammers. "I—I—"

"Roland said you went ballistic last week, searching for something in your desk."

"Unbelievable." Lucy snorts, shaking her small nugget head. "I thought that temp had stolen my secret stash of cigarettes."

"So you didn't even think to bring it with you today?" I ask dubiously. All that worrying, wasted on this dope.

"Of course I did," she snaps. "But when I couldn't find it, I figured it had been misplaced, not that it had been stolen." She jabs the last word at me as if I'm a criminal who should be prosecuted for theft. When she's done something far worse for years—kept the truth from me. That should be a crime, too.

"He's got a copy," Judd pipes up confidently, motioning to the office and the lawyer inside who will not be billing for his services today.

"It doesn't matter who has what," I say. "I'm not going in there, Luuccyy." I draw out her name so it sounds like a dirty word. Her body caves in, as if I've shoved her in the chest.

"I know everything," I continue. Sweat drips down my face, probably taking mascara with it. But I don't care. Let me look ugly, even menacing. "My father may have left you money, but he left me a box, and in it clues I needed to uncover the truth about my real mother. A truth you obviously had no intention of telling me."

"Can we just go inside?" Lucy asks again. Her patience is wearing thin. If I poke her a couple more times, she should snap.

"I'm not going to make it easy for you two clowns to cash in on my father's death—"

"He left it for me, Rosie. In the will."

I have to hand it to her. She's doing her best to stay calm in the face of the hellfire I've unleashed right in the parking lot of some crappy strip mall. "I know. I read it."

There's the snap. "Your father's wishes will be honored, so we are going into that law office." She grabs my arm, her shiny red nails digging into my flesh. "Now move. I didn't wipe your snot and clean your ass for nothing."

I wrench out of her grip and almost back into a car that was driving around us.

"Hey, move it!" the guy yells, making an exaggerated turn of his steering wheel. Lucy flips him off, while Judd curses at him.

The driver throws his car into park. A big, muscular guy pours out. "You got a problem, buddy?" He's younger and taller than Judd, with a red buzz cut and arms laden with colorful tattoos. Judd cowers behind Lucy.

"Hiding behind your old lady," he says, then spits on the ground to show his disgust.

Even with her face partially covered by the straw hat, I can see Lucy flinch at the comment. If she grips the napkin any harder, she'll be sure to squeeze the blood out of it.

"You had some nasty words for me, tough guy. Now you can say them to my face." He cracks his knuckles, right out of a movie. I'd love nothing more than for this guy to take Judd down, but I have a feeling he's a lot of talk, too. Something in his face looks soft.

"We don't want any trouble," Lucy says, waving her hands apologetically. She's petite, but still manages to shrink like a piece of withered fruit. "Tell him you're sorry, babe."

This guy and I stand as a team, opposite Lucy and Judd.

"Didn't mean anything by it. I lost my temper," Judd says. "Just having a little family squabble."

I turn to the guy. "Don't believe him," I whisper, to which he snickers.

"Rosie!" Lucy snaps.

"And while you're at it, don't believe her, either."

The guy snorts. "You got a messed-up family." Then whispers, "But who doesn't?"

If he only knew.

Now that I've softened him up with some humor, he says, "Get out of the middle of this goddamned parking lot, or someone's gonna get hurt."

"Okay, okay," Lucy and Judd say, almost too gratefully, like they've avoided the guillotine. "Come on, honey, let's go." Lucy extends her hand to me as if I'm a little girl who needs help crossing the street.

The guy has returned to his car and unnecessarily revs the engine. I tap on the window. He cranks it down, because it's a junky old Camaro.

"Hey, can you give me a ride?" I ask. He hesitates, shaking his head in that I-don't-want-to-get-involved way.

"What do you think you're doing?" Judd asks, reaching me

before Lucy does. Two rabid dogs fighting over a bone. "She doesn't need a ride," he says to him, a hand clasped around my sweaty neck.

"Yes, I do," I plead, then silently mouth, "Save me."

Lucy yanks on my shoulder with her nails, then spins me around so I'm facing her when she delivers this warning: "Don't you dare get in that car."

She's desperate, dreams of the money disintegrating right before her catlike eyes. A coughing fit grips her, has her folding in on herself at the waist.

I gather up all the broken pieces of my shattered ego—the pieces that always hoped for Lucy's love—and hurl them at her in a single dagger. "Why don't you just die already?"

The suggestion earns me a slap across the face. Instinctively, I shove Lucy in the chest, which sends her tripping backward into Judd's stunned arms. Her tote falls to the ground and out tumble at least a dozen tissues soiled in blood she and Judd race to scoop up.

Cars have backed up behind the Camaro. People are laying on their horns, cursing through windows they've rolled down for that purpose.

Finally, the guy says, "Get in," and unlocks the door.

I'm barely in the car before Lucy charges us like a blonde bullet. She lunges for the door. I almost smash her hand in it when I slam it closed.

"Buckle up," he says.

Lucy grabs for my seat belt through the open window.

ROSIE GIRL

Her face is slick with sweat, red lipstick smudged into the skin around her mouth. Or is it blood?

"Don't think for one second that I won't tell the whole god-damned world your father's secret."

"You mean about my mother? I already know, Lucy. Go tell whoever you want."

The guy revs his engine, but Lucy maintains her grip. "More, Rosie girl. I know more."

41

MY RESCUER'S NAME is Tom Van Epp, but he told me to call him Van. He's not much of a talker, prefers banging his hands against the steering wheel to the thumping sounds of Megadeth. So I stare out the window, hoping to safely reach my destination, and, thanks to Lucy's parting shot, working to bury the worm gnawing its way through a dark, murky corner of my brain.

I want to tell Mary everything that just went down, but I'm not about to ask Van to shut his music off so I can call my best friend and yak for the next twenty minutes. So I text her.

U were right. No crab cakes.

Toldja

We text a few more times, but I tell her I'll call her later. Besides, I keep getting interrupted with calls from Lucy that I ignore. When my phone buzzes for the twentieth time, I'm ready to shut it off, but it's not her. The number isn't familiar, so I ask him to turn the music down so I can answer it.

"Rosie? It's Elaine."

"Hi!" I say excitedly, somehow trusting she wouldn't call me unless it was good news.

"You have a minute?"

I turn to Van. "Is it okay if I take this?"

He nods like he understands, so I say, "Sure, what's up?"

"My daughter thought your portfolio was excellent."

Thank God. I actually feel that part of my chest—tightened after I got denied by the Fashion House—begin to loosen. "Really, Elaine? That's awesome."

"She wants to set up an appointment for you to meet with an admissions counselor next week. Does that work for you?"

"Yes! Oh, Elaine, that's incredible. I can't thank you enough."

"I've passed on your phone number and e-mail address. Hope that was okay."

"Of course," I say, and thank her ten more times before hanging up and telling Van this awesome news, as if he cares.

So much has happened this afternoon. It's been like a seesaw—riding high with good news one minute, then hitting the ground in despair the next. I need to get my head straight and get off that seesaw. I use the rest of the car ride to focus, and by the time we reach the Coastal Square mall, I've got a plan.

"I saved you so you could go shopping?" Van asks as we slowly rumble through the parking lot.

"My friend works here." I had already texted Mac with an alert that I'd be coming by.

Van pulls into the first empty spot he finds, lets the car idle. "You gonna be okay? Your parents are a couple of whacks."

"They're not my parents." I yank on the door handle to let myself out.

"Take it easy," he says.

Out of the car I hesitate, then lean back inside. "Today's my birthday."

His pale face stretches into a toothy smile. "Well, happy birthday."

"Thanks for the gift."

"Anytime," he says, then reverses and rumbles off into the distance.

I blast up the stairs, through the front door, and into John's office first. He's not there, but the light's on and his laptop is open, so I figure he'll be back soon. A few steps back, and I'm in Mac's office.

"What happened?" he asks, closing a file when I appear. If I wasn't so angry, I'd take a moment to appreciate the worry in his voice, the concern on his face.

"Birthday lunch, my ass!" I toss my backpack on the floor. "They were dragging me to some lawyer so she could offer me up as proof. 'Lookie! I raised the little brat until she turned eighteen! Check the date on your desk calendar! Today's payday!'"

Mac strokes his chin, leans back in his leather chair. "The minute you told me about Judd's invitation, I knew something was up."

That's weird. I don't remember telling him, yet I must have. So much has happened these past few weeks, I can't even keep my social life straight.

"You did, too," he says, another thing I don't recall.

I pretend to remember and add, "So did Mary. Now I feel like such a fool, falling for it."

He sits next to me, still absorbing the news. "I can't believe it. I never thought she'd—"

"What, actually be the gold digger we knew she was?"

"No. That we knew." He smirks, giving my shoulder a soft squeeze. "I just thought since she knew you'd taken the will, it would've gone differently, that's all."

"She didn't know."

"But I thought her boss said—"

"He didn't actually say anything at the wedding, did he? We assumed her freak-out was because she discovered the will missing. Turns out, Lucy was only searching for a pack of cigarettes she suspected the temp had stolen."

"Unbelievable."

He hands me a cold bottle of water from the small fridge near his desk. I sip it before launching into the new theory I developed on my ride here with Van.

"She's sick, Mac. I mean like *really* sick."

"Lucy?" Mac joins me with his own water bottle, then offers me an open bag of pretzels.

"She's spitting up blood," I say. "Can't smoke for twenty years and not pay for it."

"So the timing of the wedding may have meant something after all," Mac says. "As her surviving spouse, Judd would inherit her share of the money."

"Oh my God. You think she's going to die?" The thought

of it—even after everything she's done, even after I wished that very fate on her an hour ago—still gives me a jolt of sadness.

"I don't know, Rosie, but last I checked, healthy people don't cough up blood."

I'm not heartless. The thought of Lucy dying is terrible, but the thought of Judd inheriting Dad's money is almost as bad. I hold a pretzel, unable to eat it. "No way. My father didn't save all that money for a twenty-nine-year-old scumbag who hit on his seventeen-year-old daughter."

The news shocks Mac. He beats on his chest to prevent an all-out choking fit.

"I'm fine, Mac. It happened a couple weeks ago. I set him straight. Don't worry."

"I certainly hope so," he says, in a way that makes me think he'd straighten him out properly if I hadn't. "How did you get away from them?"

"I took off with . . . ," I begin, but I'm not sure I want to tell him I hitched a ride with a complete stranger whose most redeeming feature was a fist aimed at Judd's face.

"On, I mean, on a bus."

"It doesn't matter. As long as you got out of there unscathed." He laces his fingers through mine. "So what's your next move?"

"I'm not going back to the house, that's for sure." I hold up my cell to show him a string of unanswered calls and texts. "They've been blowing up my phone. Like I'd answer either one of them."

"At least everything's out in the open, though, right? Everyone's cards are on the table." I slump in my chair, tapped. But then Mac pops up and says, "Oh, I got you something."

My heart picks up pace. A gift! For me! From Mac! I play it cool. "What for?"

"Lucy's not the only one who remembered your birthday. Hold on," he says, and disappears down the hall. When he returns, he's carrying a big white box with a pink ribbon on top. It feels cold when he places it in my hands.

"Was this in the refrigerator?" I ask. "Guess it's not a shirt."

"Just open it." He hands me scissors from his desk to cut the ribbon, and under the bow I find a sticker that says Islamorada Outpost. Inside is, of course, a cherry pie—an entire cherry pie with a perfect golden lattice crust and dark red fruit oozing through the holes.

"Don't tell me you drove all the way down to the Keys for this."

"I did," he says. "But I made it worth the trip and bought one for my family, too." He winks, and I can't help but lean across the cold box and kiss him. The last time I tried kissing him in this office, he pulled away. Now he's all in, returning my kiss, holding me around the waist. Even with a cherry pie between us.

"Why are you crying?" he asks.

I didn't know I was, but when I put a finger to the corner of my eye, it's wet.

"You wanted to try the peach, right?" His smirk makes me laugh and blubber at the same time.

"No," I say, placing the box down on his desk. "It's perfect. You know it's my favorite. This just happens to be one of those rare moments I'm not in the mood for cherry pie."

Mac drops his eyes.

"But I have to admit, I'm glad it happened. It shut the door on any hopes I'd had about Lucy. I'm free now." With our hands clasped, I fix my eyes on him and say, "You asked me about my next move."

Mac nods with brows knitted in concentration.

"I have to go."

He doesn't ask me where. He knows. We start poking around online, getting a better sense of where she is and how I'd get there.

"I'm afraid to fly," I confess.

"There are charter buses, things like that."

The thought of sitting with a bunch of strangers for a hundred hours makes me twitch.

"I thought you liked buses," he says playfully.

"No one likes buses. They're only transportation for people without cars."

Mac pauses, and I can see his wheels spinning. "I have a car," he says.

"No, Mac." I shake my head. "I'm not taking your baby."

There's a loud knock, and when we look up, there's John, his hulking frame filling the entire doorway. I wonder how long he's been standing there.

"You can't just waltz in there, you know," he says. He's wearing a bright floral shirt and jeans, a University of Miami baseball cap clutched in his hand.

"Oakridge is a mental institution, which means it's a secured facility. You have to be on a list," John says, helping himself to a pretzel from the open bag.

"What kind of list?" I ask.

"One that allows only certain visitors to see a patient."

My balloon pops. A minute ago, my body was fueled with adrenaline as Mac and I charted my course to Burlington, Colorado.

"How do you get on the list?" Mac asks before I do.

"A therapist, a counselor—someone like that has to approve you. Or . . ."

"Or what?"

"Or a family member, perhaps the individual that had your mother admitted."

"Like a hundred years ago," I say, defeat settling into my bones.

John raises an eyebrow. "It was a little less than that. More like fifteen." He pauses, takes a seat on the edge of Mac's desk. "Call Oakridge. You've got nothing to lose. Identify yourself, tell them your relationship to the patient. You never know. Someone may have placed you on the list." His face creases with that familiar smile, the same one I saw when we first met at Lou's. When he told me he once found a needle in a haystack.

Mac finds the website, and I punch in their number on my cell. If I get blown off, at least I won't have wasted my time making the trip. I'm connected with one person, then another, and then another who asks me a ton of questions. Mac pleads with his eyes for me to tell him what's going on, and I keep signaling him to hold on, relax. I'm nervous enough for all three of us.

And then, success. I thank her with a shaky voice, say I'll be there in a couple days. She makes sure I know that visiting hours are between ten and two. That's it.

"You were on the list?" Mac asks, no more surprised than I am.

"Yep."

"How? Who could have possibly put you on it?"

Something in John's expression tells me he knows, but I had to find out for myself.

"Clinton Velvitt. My dad."

42

SINCE I NEVER HAD LUNCH, and the pretzels didn't quite cut it, Mac takes me to Lou's. It's busy, but the same spot where we were first introduced is empty.

"What are you in the mood for?" he asks, as we slide into opposite sides of the booth.

I tell him about the amazing turkey-bacon club I had with Elaine.

"Then that's what the birthday girl shall have."

He grabs my hands across the table and gets playful, interlacing our fingers and flipping them over, back and forth. "What happened there?" He's peering at the insides of my wrists.

"Remember when I told you Mary and I took a swig of vodka before we did that friendship-bonding thing?"

Mac nods, but continues to stare at the small, whitish spots.

"We used a match to burn friendship scars. I know it's stupid."

"But why do you have two?" he asks.

"So what'll it be?" The waitress suddenly appears, snappy and ready to take our order. She pops her gum and taps her shoe, wants us to know she's in a rush. Mac orders the club sandwich for me and a hamburger for him, no cheese.

"I'm coming with you," he says, out of the blue.

"Is it about your car? Because I'll take care of it. I promise. Didn't I get us home from the wedding the other night without a scratch?"

"Yes, but no, it's not about the car."

"Then please let me go with Mary."

"Why?"

"Because she's my best friend."

"I know," he says, dipping a straw into his glass of water the waitress dropped off. "But I'm worried about the two of you making that kind of trip alone. It's almost two thousand miles one way, Rosie."

I put my hand on his. "I'll—we'll be fine. We always have been. Besides, she's always wanted to escape to the mountains. This is her chance. She may never come back."

Mac narrows his eyes, confused.

"She's dealing with stuff at home, too," I say, not comfortable telling him any more. It's not my secret to share. "She'd never forgive me if I didn't take her with me."

"I don't think Burlington is in the mountains. It's really far east."

"Yeah, but it's close enough. Plus, I owe her, don't you think?"

"Fair enough, but what about school? This trip will take at least two days up and two back."

"I'm sure you remember the last week of senior year is a joke. Teachers are strictly babysitters. Plus, even if they did try reaching one of my 'parents,' they'd be unsuccessful since those two are on the high seas."

"Perfect timing, I'd say." He takes a long sip of his water. "I have to go to the restroom real quick. Be back in one minute."

It wasn't one minute. It was five. And he returns with the waitress who's got one of those small chocolate cakes with a lit candle in the center. She winks at me, tells me I've got a keeper. Like I don't already know.

"Happy birthday," he says.

"Bathroom break, huh?"

"Make a wish."

I repeat the one I made this morning over the cupcake Mary gave me, then blow the candle out in a single breath. I'm about to take a spoon to the cake when he says, "Lunch first. You need to eat." Then he digs into his jeans under the table. "Here." He hands me some cash. Two one-hundred-dollar bills.

"No, Mac. I can't take it."

"How are you going to pay for things? Lucy took the only money you had." This is true. All of today's drama made me forget.

"But it's too much. I can't—"

"Then let me come," he suggests again. Of course, when he offered me the car keys in his office, it was with the intention that he'd be driving.

"No!" It comes out stronger than I intended.

"Fine," he says. "Then take the money. It'll pay for a couple cheap hotel rooms, some food." He pulls out his wallet and hands me a credit card. "And use this for gas. About the only places that don't check ID are gas stations."

"I would say that I'll never be able to repay you, but we know that's not true." I break into a smile, so happy I've got Mac, so happy that I'll have plenty of money one day to buy him lunch. "When I return, I'm going back to that law office, only I'll do it on my terms."

"I'll come with you then, if you want."

"I want."

"It's a long trip, Rosie," he says, getting serious again. "Promise me you'll take care of yourself."

"And your car."

"And my car," he repeats, grinning. "Don't forget. The top sticks."

43

"SWEET RIDE," Mary says, tossing a duffel bag into the backseat of Mac's convertible. "Can we put the top down?"

"No. This isn't a joyride," I tell her. "We're going, and then we're coming back. At least I am." Now that we're actually going, I wonder if Mary's got the courage to stay there, to really ditch her parents and never return. Her bag is kind of heavy and twice the size of mine.

I peel out of my driveway, knowing I took a chance even coming back here to get some things for the trip. For all I knew, Lucy and Judd canceled their cruise to come home and mope. But the promise of endless buffets, bars, and slot machines must have won out, because they weren't home to prevent our escape.

Mary buckles her seat belt over a white tank top that accentuates her scrawny shoulders. "Maybe later," she says.

"Later what?"

"We can put the top down."

"I promised Mac that I wouldn't. He says it sticks."

The bottom half of her face twists in disappointment, so I

say, "On the way back, okay?" Maybe this small incentive will keep her on track to come home with me.

"Okay." She turns to me, her freckled face shiny and excited. "Now, let's get this road trip started!"

There's no tempering her enthusiasm, so I let her play with the radio for a while until I tell her it's giving me a headache. I need to keep a level head, especially while driving. Mac told me to be careful with his car, never to stretch the gears, and not to let Mary drive. I agreed to everything, then kissed him until he broke free and made me promise not to put the top down because the mechanism is finicky.

I feel close to him, seated in his seat, my hands wrapped around his steering wheel as Mary and I drive the endless stretch of highway through the state of Florida. My plan is to make it to Valdosta, Georgia, before packing it in for the night, then get a super-early start in the morning.

Mary's at peace. Finally, she's on her way to the mountains. Well, sort of, since there aren't any mountains in Burlington, but I told her maybe we'll see some in the distance. Her bare feet are braced against the dash while she bobs her head to music only she can hear. She grows restless and rolls down the window to stick her feet out. Cars pass, and they don't even look twice at the pretty girl with her toenails painted red.

. . .

Three hours in, around Orlando, the sun begins to set. A warm yellow sky is giving way to a dusty orange, and the headlights of oncoming traffic grow brighter in my eyes. We've been driving in silence for a while. I think Mary's tired. She hasn't spoken much since we left.

But then she turns to me, the side of her pale face bathed in that yellow-orange glow, and asks, "So what are you going to do about Lucy and everything?"

"Before today, I was actually going to let her have the money. But now? I'm going to give her a fight." I haven't told her that Lucy's coughing fits now come with blood and that what I'm really fighting for is to keep the money out of Judd's dirty mitts.

Mary has curled up on her side, staring at me through tired, droopy eyes. "Good for you, Rosie girl."

"When we get back, I'm grabbing my things and slamming that black door behind me. And then I'm marching into Stephens & Stephens and setting those lawyers straight."

"I think we should both just stay in Colorado."

I shake my head. "I can't, Mary. Elaine called this afternoon."

"Ah, the fairy godmother," she says, a little snarky.

"I guess she sort of is," I agree, realizing it's true. "I should be contacted by one of the admissions counselors at the Art Institute of Fort Lauderdale for an interview next week. Her daughter said my portfolio was excellent."

"What happened to the Fashion House?"

"I didn't get in."

"Oh, Rosie," she says, matching my disappointment. "I'm sorry. That sucks."

"Well, it doesn't suck as bad now that I've at least got a shot somewhere else."

"So staying has nothing to do with Mac."

"No," I semi-lie. "I want to give design school in South Florida a chance. There's always time to make a move later if things don't work out."

Mary gets all pouty, but I keep my eyes on the road and my words decisive. "With the money my dad left me, I can rent an apartment this summer and begin school in the fall."

"Sounds like you've got it all figured out." The sadness in her voice is unexpected. I thought she'd be proud of me, taking charge of my life. With each passing mile, the inside of the car turns more gray, as does Mary's mood.

Suddenly, "What about me?" Her voice is small and cracks on the last word.

"What about you? You've got your own plans, right?" I ask.

"Who knows? Thanks to your evil stepmother, I don't even have our six hundred bucks."

"But once my father's estate is settled, I'm going to have tons," I say.

"How'd he get all that money, anyway?"

"John said he probably had shares in the company. He was with Roland a long time, you know."

"Uh-huh," Mary says absently.

"If you decide to stay in Colorado, I'll send you money. Whatever you need." As hard as it is to support her, I'll have to. My best friend deserves to be happy, too. Yet as the miles increase, so does my fear of losing her. Could she really stay behind out there? The thought of driving home without her fills me with dread.

ROSIE GIRL

I take my eyes off the road to get a good look at her and what I see gives me hope. I think she may be having second thoughts. She looks . . . I don't know. Scared, maybe. I rest my hand on her thigh, warm and snug in her jeans. Her head lolls to the side, and she faces the window until the sky grows dark.

44

AS PLANNED, we arrive in Valdosta around midnight and pull into the first halfway decent place we find off the highway. My butt hurts from sitting so long, and my feet are tired from using the clutch. Duane's Digs, a one-story U-shaped motel, boasts a fifty-nine-dollar-a-night rate on an illuminated sign, which fits my budget. I can't wait to take a hot bath and hit the sack. We never stopped to eat, so now I'm starving and hope to find a vending machine that might have little sandwiches and bottles of juice. But one look at this place tells me I've set the bar too high.

When we enter the lobby to find a nasty-looking guy behind the counter, I know we haven't made a great choice. He's leaning back in a chair, boots propped up on a small table where a television showing *Family Feud* captures his attention.

"Sixty-three bucks," he says, without looking over at us.

"But the sign says fifty-nine." I tap the car keys on the counter to get his attention.

"State likes their tax, little lady. It's actually sixty-three dollars and thirteen cents, but I'm cuttin' you a break." He spins around on the rolling chair. "You want it or not?"

Mary nods.

"We'll take it."

He screws up his pockmarked face, like I told him a riddle.

"Two double beds, please."

"Whatever strikes your fancy," he says, rolling his eyes while accepting my cash. He hands me a key card with instructions to the room. Then he leans across the counter, beer on his breath, and says, "By the way, there's free porn on channel twelve," as if it's a perk, like complimentary breakfast or a morning newspaper.

I snort before responding. "Uh, we're not a couple. Just friends."

Mary puts her arms around me, plants a giant kiss on my cheek. "Don't be embarrassed, baby. The world's changing."

I giggle, but the desk clerk doesn't find it funny. He stares at me with heavy-lidded, bloodshot eyes and says, "Checkout's at noon." Then plops back in his chair and turns up the television with the toe of his boot.

. . .

Sketchy. That's the best way to describe Duane's Digs, so I make sure to use the dead bolt and leave on all the lights. The carpet smells like vomit and the tub is broken, forcing me to settle on a lukewarm shower. From my bed, I've got one eye on a roach in the far corner and one eye on the doorknob. If it even slightly moves, I'm grabbing Mary and crawling out the back window.

To my left, Mary's curled up in her bed, a sheet of hair hiding her face. She clutches a pillow near her stomach, a low, almost inaudible snore coming from her nose. Her parents think she's on the Senior Sunrise—an overnight trip to Key Biscayne where the graduating class spends all night on the beach and then rolls into the water before the sleep is even out of their eyes. I have no idea what she's going to do when tomorrow comes and goes.

I'm having trouble falling asleep. I feel like I'm about to do something dreadful, like run a marathon or go off to jail. I should be excited. After all these months of wondering and searching, I'm going to meet my birth mother.

But I've got plenty of time to mentally prepare with another fourteen hundred miles to go. The plan: Get up at five a.m., drive until five p.m. Find a place to crash for a few hours in St. Louis, then hit the road again at midnight. The final ten-hour leg of the trip will get us to Burlington by about ten a.m. on Wednesday. As Mary said, "It's a shitload of driving," but we'll take turns, even though Mac said he didn't want her to. Drink Red Bull. Blast music. We'll get there.

I've been gripping my phone like it's a stone with magic powers, so when it buzzes, I jump under the scratchy sheets. It's a text from Mac.

Just checking on you. (Typical Mac—proper punctuation, no text language. My heart warms.)

We r fine—snug in a motel

Get some sleep.

i will

Good night.

nite nite

There's no way I'm getting any sleep. The roach in the corner will doze off before I do. My body may be tired but my brain is still running at full speed. I pull images of my mother into focus, then age them, hoping I'll be able to recognize her. I imagine her wearing thin cotton pants and a long-sleeved shirt, then a soft denim dress, and then wonder if she even has a choice of clothes. Maybe she has to wear a robe all day, or something ugly like sweatpants and a sweatshirt. Although I'm sure that's not the worst thing. Does she hear people screaming and crying all night? Is she one of them?

I force myself to stop thinking of her and that place.

My lids grow heavy and the long day wins around one a.m. I drift off, imagining my mother saying, "You finally found me." And making the wish I've made twice today come true.

45

WE STUCK TO MY PLAN and stayed on schedule: left Valdosta, stayed in St. Louis, then drove through the night. Mary slept most of the way, and only once asked me to stop so she could pee. I purposely kept my liquid intake to a minimum but did treat myself to a root beer around 3:30 a.m. which gave me a welcome shot of caffeine.

Around nine thirty Wednesday morning, we arrive in Burlington, Colorado, and within a few miles start seeing signs for the hospital. I should be exhausted. Instead, I'm ready to jump out of my skin and keep flipping down the rearview mirror to see if I look okay.

"Stop doing that or we're going to miss the exit." Mary stretches and says, "I have to get out of this goddamned car. But don't worry, Rosie girl. You look great."

So I resist the urge to check any more and ten long minutes later, we're there.

The entrance to Oakridge makes it look more like a country club than a hospital. I pass between two stone pillars, bushes exploding with red berries at each base. One says, OAKRIDGE, the other, MENTAL HEALTH CARE FACILITY, and beneath that,

ROSIE GIRL

EST. 1911. The grounds are wide and expansive, dotted by trees bursting with peach flowers. The morning sun breaks through a canopy of ficus trees lining a long road leading up to the building. I imagine if I roll down the windows, I'll hear birds chirping, maybe a harp playing. It's so beautiful out here, and I can tell by Mary's serene expression that she feels the same way. Her gaze hasn't left the window since we crossed the Colorado state line.

Large iron gates stop me at a small building. An old man with glasses perched on his bald head slides a window to the side, asks to see my identification. He studies my driver's license when I hand it over, makes a phone call, then tells me to continue going straight until a parking lot appears on my left.

I choose the first available spot. We grab our things and cross the lot until we reach a brick walkway. I'm wearing my favorite black pants with a yellow tank/cardigan combo, and the scarf Elaine gave me wrapped loosely around my neck. I don't care that the pink and red doesn't match. I actually hope it triggers something in my mother that will show we both love to pair mismatched items. Mary's dressed less fancy, in jeans and a sweatshirt, the same clothes she slept in. I wasn't about to argue. She's not here to impress anyone.

I had been holding Mary's hand, but let it go as we enter through the main door. It's pretty inside, too, with beige carpeting and soft aqua walls. Pictures of flowers and streams and ducks hang in white plastic frames. Potted plants bookend three sets of sofas, their glossy leaves reaching toward the sunlight flooding through wide panes of glass.

A woman rises from behind a sprawling counter. She could be a cashier, a librarian, a postal worker. She's got that kind of look, sort of haggard, all business, like she's been here awhile, does her job in her sleep. Around her neck, a plastic badge falls into the groove of her blue uniform shirt, the same one the guard wore at the gate.

Mary takes a seat on one of the couches while I approach the desk.

"Can I help you?" she asks.

"I'm here to visit a patient." My voice cracks between words.

"No need to be nervous. This facility isn't like those you've seen in movies." Her smile does its job and shaves off some of the edge.

"First-timers think they're walking into a scene right out of *One Flew Over the Cuckoo's Nest*." She slides over a clipboard with a pen attached, then points to a series of empty boxes. "Put your name here and the patient's name here. I'll also need to make a copy of your driver's license."

With my identification clutched in her hand, she disappears into a back office. I put a hand over my chest. Can she see my heart pumping through my sweater? I'm about to crack. I didn't think I'd be this anxious, but sweat is forming in my armpits. My breath is growing ragged. All this way, and I'm going to drop right here in the lobby.

"Here you go." She returns my license, says, "You can have a seat. Someone will be out shortly to accompany you to the community room. In the meantime, I'll need to check your bag."

"Check it for what?" I ask.

"I mean, put it in a storage locker. You're not allowed to visit with food, drinks, or any personal belongings like purses." She nods at mine, slung around my shoulder.

"Okay," I say, secretly stuffing something in my pocket, then handing it over. She hands me a small white card, says it's my claim check, like for a coat at a fancy restaurant.

I barely have a chance to settle in next to Mary when a tall, hard-looking woman emerges through a set of swing doors and instructs us to come with her. Obediently, we follow her down a cold white hallway, a stark contrast to the lobby. No carpeting, no plants, no pictures of ducks. The squeaking of her sneakers on the linoleum floor, the jangle of keys hanging off her belt loop are the only sounds I hear. That's actually a good thing. The woman at the desk wasn't far off with her movie reference. I was scared to death I'd hear crying, howling, even screams of terror penetrating the walls.

We're ushered through a set of double doors, then left at the threshold of a big room filled with tables and chairs, a soda and snack machine against the back wall. I am hungry, but don't want to meet my mother with onion breath while slurping a root beer.

A few tables are occupied by regularly dressed people. No straitjackets, no shackles. So far, so good. I look closer at the pairs. Unlike an ordinary hospital, it's hard to identify who's the visitor and who's the patient. There are no casts or bandages, only tears and laughter on both sides of the tables. One side is no more sad or happy than the other.

I choose a table where I can see the door, but when Mary

pulls out a chair, I say, "I think you should sit over there," and motion to the next table. "I don't want to, you know, overload her or anything."

"I get it," she says, and thrills me by not giving me a hard time.

I sit and wait. Fiddle with the buttons on my cardigan. Wiggle my toes feeling cramped in my shoes. Watch the door. After a few minutes, I figure out that visitors enter through the door I used, while patients enter through another door, near the soda machine. So I spin my chair around and wait some more. Ten minutes later, a woman steps through, wearing a blouse the color of cigarette ashes and loose beige pants. She's not alone. A black man in a white uniform is with her, smiles as he talks to her, even laughs at one point when the door makes a swooshing sound as it closes behind them.

From the two photos—now dubbed the party picture and the snow picture—I know that it's her. She's rail thin, with a full head of frizzy gray hair held back by a piece of red ribbon. A bow settles above one ear. Her lips are painted pink.

I sit up in my chair, and when I offer a little wave, he guides her by the elbow over to my table.

The man says, "You've got about an hour," while patting my mother's shoulder.

"Thanks, Al," she says, her voice soft and milky. He bows like a stage actor, then leaves through the same door they entered.

She turns her attention to me. "Well, aren't you a beauty?"

I can't take my eyes off her, memorizing the wrinkles near

her mouth, the mole on her jaw. Mary sniffles to get my attention. She wants me to speak, so I say the first thing that pops into my head.

"Do you know who I am?"

"Of course."

But does she? I don't know what I'm dealing with here and time is limited.

I'm about to say my name when she says, "You're my baby girl. My Rosemary."

I cock my head. "What? No. It's just Rose. Or Rosie. Everyone calls me Rosie."

"Okay," she says, like she's agreeing to something she knows isn't right. "I guess you already know I'm Justine. Everyone calls me Justine, so you can, too." She spends five minutes staring down at the shiny table, making me wonder if she's lost in her own blurred image. "He's sent me pictures. It's been a few years, though, so I wasn't sure."

"You mean my father?"

"I guess he got tired of sending them."

"No, that's not it. Dad, um . . . he passed away. Three and a half years ago. He had a heart attack."

Her tired face makes a micro-jolt, one eyebrow hitches. "Imagine that. I outlived him."

"They didn't tell you?"

"They could have," Justine says, then taps the side of her head. "My memory's not so good." She puts her hands on the table, clasps them together. We both stare at her frail fingers, interlaced like bony sticks. There's nothing to distract us. Flowers on the table, maybe a magazine, something to act as a conversation-starter. There's only white walls and some bad abstract art.

"So your father told you about me." Her eyes sweep the room. "This place. Before he died."

"No. He never got the chance." I understand now what Dad was saying in his letter. There's kindness in a half-truth, in a lie. He lied to spare me. That's what I'm doing now. She doesn't need to know about Lucy or the box or what I've been through without her as my mother.

"Then how did you find me?" she asks.

I'm secretly thrilled with this normal conversation.

"I hired someone to find you. A private investigator."

She squints at me. "Why would you do that?"

"Because I wanted to meet you." For the first time, I reach out to touch her fingertips with mine, but she pulls away, puts her hands in her lap. I want to run. Mary sniffles again to get my attention, and when I look over, she gestures with her hands to calm down.

Justine sits back and peers hard at me, which is so uncomfortable, I look at everything but her. I count eighteen tables, four plate-glass windows, and twelve fluorescent lights in the ceiling.

"You got his cleft chin," she finally says.

"Yes." I must sound too eager, because she backs up again when only a moment ago she had leaned forward to get a better look at me.

"Go ahead," Mary mouths. "Give it to her."

"Not yet," I whisper.

"What was that?" Justine asks, turning an ear to me.

"Nothing." I shoot Mary a look to stop bugging me. I know what I'm doing.

"Would you like a soda?" She points at the machine and starts fishing around in her pockets. "I've got quarters."

"No, thank you."

"Your birthday was two days ago," she says, almost knocking me out of my seat. "At least let me buy you a bag of chips."

"You remembered?"

"I always remember." She taps her head again. "I have a good memory for certain things. You turned . . ." Squinty eyes while she computes. "Eighteen?"

"Uh-huh."

She pulls out a tissue from somewhere and blows her nose with it, then dabs her eyes.

I grin, say, "Don't cry. You didn't miss a big party or anything."

One of her front teeth is chipped. I can see it when she smiles, which doesn't last long. "No, but I missed everything else."

I don't want the visit to go there, down a melancholy road. It won't do either of us any good. A lot of boo-hooing, that's what it will be. It's the perfect time to give her my gift, lighten the mood.

"I brought you something," I say, giving in to Mary's suggestion, even though I had planned on waiting to give it as my parting gift. I reach into my pants pocket and pull it out, eager to see her expression.

Immediately, her eyes spark with recognition and the bracelet is snatched from my hand.

"Who's Leni? I've always been curious."

Justine's eyes glaze over as she traces the faded flowers and embossed letters with a shaky index finger. "Where did you get this?"

"Dad left it for me. With some other things." I pause while she studies it. "Who was she?"

"I'm not supposed to talk about her."

"Oh. I'm sorry." I knew I shouldn't have given it to her yet. We need more time to get comfortable with each other. I cast Mary an angry look, which only makes her shrug.

"She was my best friend," Justine says, then puts the bracelet to her nose, breathes in deeply, like I've done, hoping to catch a whiff of the same memory.

"Is she . . ."

Justine's eyes close. Her face drops, lips part. It's like she's left me, gone somewhere I can't reach. I wait for her to return, my eyes following the second hand on the wall clock. Almost a minute passes before she opens her eyes and says, "She isn't anything now. But once. Once upon a time she was bad. No. Not bad. She was good, but she did a bad thing. A very bad thing." Justine's voice has become almost childlike. It's confusing me. I want to ask a thousand questions, but I'm afraid to interrupt her. I press my lips together to keep my mouth shut.

"It's because of Leni that I'm here."

So it wasn't my father? Now I'm even more confused.

ROSIE GIRL

In an instant, Justine's whole demeanor changes. She sits up straight, drops her shoulders, takes in a deep breath. "You seem like a strong young woman."

It's the cardigan. It conveys maturity.

"Are you?" she asks. "I must know before I continue. That you can handle the truth."

I nod. "Yes."

"Because I have a feeling you didn't come here for chips. You came here for answers."

I nod again.

Her eyes are the same color as mine, as if the deepest part of the ocean was poured into them. But her lashes are light and match a set of thinning eyebrows. Based on my birth certificate, she was twenty-five when she had me. That makes her forty-three, but she looks fifty-three. This place has aged her.

"Our first house wasn't ten miles from here," she begins. "A nice little two-bedroom, two-bath with a winding porch and plenty of yard. But the basement." Justine's face scrunches in on itself. "It was very small. Tiny, even. With a single window I could never manage to keep clean. You had just turned three years old when Leni put you in there." She pauses, says, "Locked you in there," the switch of a single word changing everything.

I'm a little shocked, but I don't have long enough to process it as Justine continues the story. "I can still remember the dark wood-panel walls, the musty smell they gave off. The scratchy blue blanket they found you wrapped up in. Rusty tools littering the ground you could have hurt yourself with."

My mind is spinning, trying to place the familiar pieces of her story into another story. Next to me, Mary's eyes are about to pop out of her head.

"But why . . . I mean, why would Leni doing that be the reason you're here?"

Justine's pink lips start to quiver, creating deep lines around her mouth. The tears come, leaking from her eyes. She pulls out another tissue. I imagine she stocked her pockets full of them when she heard who'd come to visit. I silently beg her to keep it together, hope she doesn't crash and burn before telling me how she ended up here.

I'm not prepared to receive the bracelet when she suddenly sends it sliding across the table. "Take it back." She raises her right hand, makes a little wave. I follow the direction of her gaze to a surveillance camera behind me. Maybe it's a game she plays. I don't know why she's here, so I'm at a severe disadvantage. In a way, it's like flying blind.

"Uh, okay," I say, kicking myself for upsetting her, shoving the bracelet back in my pocket.

She wipes away the last of her tears, then adjusts the red bow in her hair so it sits directly on top of her head. It looks both silly and beautiful.

"I'm sorry if I upset you," I say, hoping I didn't blow it. "But please . . . I don't understand about Leni. Why did she do that to me?"

"Because she was jealous."

"Of me?" I shake my head and let the question spill out. "What kind of friend does that?" There's so much to process, but the one thing I'm grateful for is the lost memory. I can't even imagine being a little girl, locked in some shed . . . I mean, basement. She said it was a basement.

"That's the thing, Rosie." It's the first time she's said my name. "She wasn't exactly a friend. She was an alter."

"A what?"

I don't think she hears me, because she doesn't answer and picks up where she left off.

"At first, Leni was a protector. One of my therapists even called her a savior."

The word makes me flinch, and I glance sideways at Mary who's inspecting her nails.

"But then she turned on me after you were born. That happens sometimes when they feel threatened or no longer needed."

"Who are *they*?" The more Justine explains, the more jumbled things become. And the more I start thinking my mother really is crazy. She belongs here.

"The alters, Rosie. Four years ago, I was finally able to integrate all twelve of them." And just like that, she stops talking and her eyes well up again. "Oh, dear. I shouldn't have tried to explain all this to you. Forgive me."

I don't want to forgive her. I want her to go on. "But what about Leni? What happened to her?" If I were a dog, I'd be frothing at the mouth, desperate for another morsel of information.

"Don't you understand?" Agitated, she twists the tissue between her fingers until it rips in half. "There was no Leni. It's just what I called her."

Justine's eyes pull away from mine and dart anxiously around the room. Then I realize what—who—she was looking for. Al has reemerged through the door at the back wall. He's not with a patient, and heads straight to our table.

"You ready, Justine?" he says, holding out his hand for her to take.

She looks up at him and nods. "Yes, Al. Thank you."

"What do you mean? Where are you going?" Panic seizes me when I realize she had been signaling him to come get her. Instinctively, I reach out for Mary, trying to calm myself, trying to squelch the anger I'm feeling at Justine for cutting our visit short.

"You all right?" Al asks. He has a nice, caring smile, one that works with a pair of soft brown eyes. He helps my mother and now he wants to help me.

"I'm fine."

"'Cause you almost fell over, reaching for that chair." Al's got Justine by the elbow, ready to guide her. The familiar way he does it, coupled with the way she allows him to do it, leads me to believe they've walked the halls of Oakridge for many years together.

"Please don't go. There's still so much I don't understand." Like everything. Not a single piece of information fits into any sort of puzzle that makes sense. "I've come a long way. We both have." I gesture to Mary, who's got the strangest look on her face—a kid caught with her hand in the cookie jar. Like she's been spotted.

The blood drains from my mother's face. When she looks up at Al, they communicate silently. A nod, a lowering of the eyes. I don't understand what's happening, why they're leaving me out of some secret exchange. But I don't care—I just don't want her to leave. I've waited too long, traveled too far, paid too much.

"Stay." I'm pleading, almost whining. "We still have another half hour. You haven't even met my best friend yet." I leave my chair to stand near Mary, put my hands on her shoulders like she's a child. "I made her sit here because I didn't want to scare you off. Right, Mary? Tell her I didn't want to scare her off."

But Mary remains silent, and my hands seem to float off her shoulders when Justine approaches me. She's left Al's side and now holds my hands in hers. "So you call her Mary."

ACKNOWLEDGMENTS

How can this feel like the hardest part? And yet it does. Because I want to acknowledge every single person who ever said a kind word about my writing or didn't look at me sideways for having what seemed like an impossible dream. But since I can't, I will thank those I can, those who've made that dream possible.

Tremendous gratitude goes to my fierce agent, Leigh Feldman, and her assistant, Ilana Masad, who took a chance on me. Unlike the characters in my book, I have no problem feeling indebted to you both. Many thanks to the incredible team at Putnam—my editor, Stacey Barney, assistant editor, Kate Meltzer, and copy editor, Chandra Wohleber—for helping me carve, whittle, and polish my manuscript into the story you've just read.

Before I had the good fortune to work with these amazing people, I've had some other amazing people who helped me get here:

Momma, who bought me a Smith Corona typewriter when I was a little girl and listened to every terrible story I banged out on it. I know a mother is supposed to love everything her child creates, and you are no exception, yet you still offered constructive criticism that helped redirect me. Because of you, I will always strive to "grasp the subject so the words will follow."

Sam, the son who set me straight many years ago at the dinner table and told me to spice things up. Thanks for kicking me out of my comfort zone and keeping me company there.

Jared, the son who routinely saved me with his vast knowledge of sports history. Thanks for offering words of encouragement when I needed them most, even if I couldn't hear you at the time.

To both of my incredible boys, thank you for indulging my countless text messages that yielded the most accurate representations of young adult minds (and plenty of "uh, people don't say that anymore").

I am beyond grateful to Donna Liberman, the greatest friend, sharpest critique partner, and brightest spot in my universe. *There are friends, and then there are friends like us.*

Much gratitude to all of the professionals who shared their wisdom and expertise: Dr. Marlene Steinberg, Dr. Kenny Herskowitz, Attorney Eric Sulzberger, Private Investigator Wendy Stanford-Perez, Private Investigator Jim Blackburn, Principal Thelma Fornell, Florida Department of Juvenile Justice Inspector Kate Turner, and Licensed Mental Health Counselor (and best friend!) Sofi Haya Matz. To the many friends, near and far, whose answers to even the tiniest questions helped me push through some tricky parts. And thanks to my dear friend Sara Schermer, who read the very first draft and loved me enough to be brutally honest about it.

I'm also grateful to many friends in the South Florida writing community, who over the years have taught me, challenged me, and listened to some of my worst stuff—most notably special members of the SCBWI Aventura critique group: Dr. Stacy Davids, Norma Davids, Angela Padron, Steven Dos Santos, and Marjetta Geerling, my first true mentor.

Extra thanks to writer friends Debbie Reed Fischer, Ricki Schultz, and Karen Kendall, who often advised me about the crazy world of publishing. Shout out to YARWA, my virtual writing family that offers all of its members a constant stream of support, and fellow 2017 Debut Authors who helped me navigate these choppy, yet wonderful waters.

Lastly, without Shep, none of this would mean anything. Thank you for giving me a life I had only dreamed of—one filled with passion, laughter, and adventure. *I've loved you for a thousand years, and I'll love you for a thousand more.*